24 KARAT SCHMOOZE

24 KARAT SCHMOOZE

Marc Blake

FLAME
Hodder & Stoughton

British Library Cataloguing in Publication Data
Blake, Marc
    24 karat schmooze
    I. Title II. Twenty four karat schmooze
823.9′14[F]

ISBN 0 340 76860 6

Typeset by
Avocet Typeset, Brill, Aylesbury, Bucks
Printed and bound in Great Britain by
Clays Ltd, St Ives plc

HODDER AND STOUGHTON
A division of Hodder Headline
338 Euston Road
London NW1 3BH

For Claire

WINTER

CHAPTER ONE

I hate my hair. I hate my hair and I hate my clothes and my heart is broken and I want to stamp on his kidneys. I hate him, I hate him, I hate him. I love him.

On balance, she wasn't taking it well.

Rox Matheson, fingering her unkempt blonde thatch in the dark glass of the train window, frowned at the spider of black roots. She decided not to bother dyeing it again. She'd let it grow out and have a decent head of hair. Eight months since that misogynist bastard stylist in Chorlton had talked her into this bizarre crop (her mates called her 'pineapple-head'). No, she'd let it grow back so it tickled her shoulders and flowed down her back, and then? Then — so long as mouse was the 'in' colour in London, she and her beautiful mane would get the proper attention they deserved. Ha.

She pressed her cheek to the cold glass and tried to remember a time when boyfriends hadn't had the power to reduce her self-esteem to atoms. She gazed at her reflection. A small sharp chin, above which her lips were pressed together to form a tiny central dot. Her upper lip was full and bowed outwards, lending her a slight overbite. Growing up, she'd always wanted one of those wide, full-lipped smiles, *American* smiles. Her nose was tilted upwards — but not so it was piggy — and her eyes, behind their oval wire-rimmed glasses, were grey. Her eyebrows were way too bushy and her pale forehead met the hairline square on. Rox liked to think she had the look of someone in a costume drama, but knew that if it came to it she'd not get the part of the dutiful fiancée, but the consumptive maid. That or *lawks-a-mercy* barmaid. Scale model of course. She was five-two in bare feet, five-seven today in her Buffalo trainers. She stretched out her legs, propping the big black rubber bricks of the soles up on the lip of the empty seat opposite. The right upper was peeling away and, when she waggled her toes, the leather formed an open scar.

There was a shudder as the 4.40 p.m. Manchester Piccadilly to Euston carved through a cutting and rocketed out across the sad sodden countryside. The sky, earlier clotted with slate-grey cumulus, had become a uniform inky blue-black. They barrelled on at a hundred and twenty-five miles an hour until the train approached Watford where it slowed to and maintained a stately speed of three. Rox peered out and saw a gritty suburb limp past. Was this London? What a dump. She stuck a hand in her coat pocket and pulled out a shower of calcified flakes.

Oh yeah. The Pringles.

These had been an essential component of a three-week misery marathon that comprehensively redefined the word 'wallow'. Locked in her bedroom, she sat rocking back and forth on her duvet playing the most heartbreaking songs in her CD collection and crying along until her throat and eyes were red raw. The gin and vodka didn't help, and neither did reading books that suggested that men were merely *different* and all you had to do was to develop *effective coping strategies*. They got thrown across the room. She surrendered to Jerry, Trisha and Oprah or stared into space, mainlined chips or cereal when she could manage solid foods and had her best mate and lodger Ally trawl ASDA for double Belgian chocolate ice-cream. Rox did not wash, slept for nearly sixteen hours a day and perceived the world as a corrupt and tyrannical parent. It was like being a student.

Or what she'd seen of student life from the sidelines.

A couple of nights ago she had raised herself from her pit in response to a firm rapping on the bedroom door.

'Rox. You coming out of there?'

Now Ally *had* been a student. At the uni over in Hulme doing English and Drama where she had ponced about for two years until she ran out of decent blokes and had to sleep with southerners.

'Go 'way.'

Sensing the waves of a silent sulk, she clambered out of bed and pressed her ear up against the door. 'Al. What's up?'

'I'm not saying.'

'You want to tell or you wouldn't be out there.'

There was a pause. Rox stood on a chair and peered through the frosted panel of glass above, her fingertips leaving a perfect set of prints in the thick layer of dust. Ally was sat on the floor with her arms wrapped around her knees in the emotional crash position. Rox clambered down and came out onto the landing. The boards were chilly underfoot and studded with the cold metal eyes of hammered-in nail heads. She'd not yet got around to getting carpet as the general idea was to leave it all bare or get it sanded like on the telly shows, but this was Chorlton, in Manchester, in the pigging winter.

Turning to pull her bedroom door shut, she glimpsed back inside. It was a disaster, a holocaust, a crime scene. It wanted ringing with yellow tape, with an official looking board: 'Serious Incident. A heart was broken into and stabbed in this vicinity between the hours of 7 and 8 p.m. on the second of February. Did you see the bastard? Name of Mark.'

'What's up, Ally?' she asked. 'And don't give me man trouble 'cos I'm the one who got dumped and that gives me first dibs on pain for *ever*.'

'It's not blokes.'

'What then?'

Ally looked up. 'Remember that money you lent us?'

'The three hundred and fifty quid. Yeah.'

'Don't fancy going out for a drink, do you?'

The 125 limped through Stanmore and Edgware and came to the back end of Highgate where the driver announced 'Euston' in terse Tannoy. The passengers came alive, rustling and pirouetting for their bags, writhing as they burrowed like maggots beneath the steel skin of the carriage. Rox, among them, felt her insides liquefy as a mixture of fear and anticipation surged through her. She had never been to London before and reckoned it was time they got acquainted before she reached her quarter century.

That night, she and Ally had gone to a different bar than normal so as there'd be no chance of Mark seeing her all scriked up. They hid in the snug and Rox regressed to drinking snakebite. Later, at home, they had carryouts (six bottles of Pils) and a curry in the kitchen. Rox spooned out flame-coloured portions of massala and brick-yellow korma from the foil containers. It looked like a doomed science project.

'Have you not got any way of finding out who it was?' she asked.

'Naw. The student rep at Uni was the only one to speak to him. The guy said he'd been running these weekend courses down south for years. It was gonna be tops. Casting directors, workshops in voice and movement. Acting masterclass. And the star attraction was Michael Caine.'

'*The* Michael Caine?'

'The same.'

'I lent you three hundred and fifty quid for the star of the chuffing *Swarm*?'

'You were upset and malleable.'

'Al, he was in *Jaws IV* and . . . and *Bullseye*, the worst film ever made.'

'Not heard of that one.'

Rox started chewing. 'Michael Winner,' she said, which explained it.

Ally furrowed her brow. She was younger than Rox by two years but a lot taller, which for some reason meant that she assumed she knew better. 'Hang on. Don't forget *Alfie*, or *The Italian job*. Or *The Ipcress File*.'

'All made before we were born.'

'*Little Voice*. He were good in that – for an old geezer.' Rox waved her fork dismissively.

Ally pulled her hair back so it wouldn't fall in her curry. 'I'm dead sorry, Rox. I'd of said what it was for when I asked you for the lend, but you've been a goner these past weeks.'

'Still am.'

'Maybe. But look at the weight you've lost, you cow.'

Rox tilted her gaze to her tummy, which was peppered with neon grains of Pilau rice. She forced a grin. 'S'pose getting dumped has some advantages.' With the thought of him, her face collapsed again. Ally held out her arms and they hugged each other.

'Is there no way you can get the money back?' Rox asked, breaking away to rustle up some Kleenex.

'I don't reckon so. There were about a hundred of us there on the Saturday. Mostly students, actors, some of the Drama department staff. By half ten when nothing was happening, they went and got the Uni bloke. Turns out he's new. He'd taken the deposit on the hall and sent on the cheques to a Post Office box number.'

'What a wally.'

'He went to phone and comes back with a face like a wet kipper. The contact number wasn't working. Terry Asher – he's this actor, all method and no brains – gets up and decks him. Big cheer goes up. Then this Hippie bint makes a speech about capitalism. Anyhow, the upshot of it all is thirty anorexics in paisley leggings occupied the Students' Union building.'

'Not much of a protest. Sort them out by tossing in a packed lunch.'

Ally smiled. 'Last I heard is they hadn't the energy to make any demands.'

'So what did you do?'

'Got it out of my system.'

'Arndale?'

'Tube top and a pair of combats on the card.'

'Not a total loss then.'

Ally stared at the volcano on her plate. 'I'm sorry, Rox. I thought this was gonna be worth it; you know, help me on my way.'

'What about my money?'

'Bank says it's been cashed.'

Rox drained her bottle of Pils. She hated rip-offs.

The commuter current had risen to a broiling series of rapids. Using her shoulder-bag as ballast, Rox paddled across the concourse to a pillar and stared at the labyrinthine map. The black line, Graham had said. He was Ally's computer geek brother who lived down here in Camberwell. When Al told him Rox was coming down, he had offered – well, been pressured into offering – to let her stay for a few nights. She stared at the network of lines. Euston was missing, worn to a silver bullet crease. Black line south. Couldn't be that hard.

'One pound seventy. For this!'

Sensing sport, those passengers who could move craned their necks in her direction. They were trapped a hundred feet underground between Waterloo and Kennington on the worst Tube line in the western world: business as usual for everyone but Rox.

'How long are we stuck here for?' she demanded.

They tried to bury her in blushes but Rox was too hot and fractious to be embarrassed. She glared at a prematurely balding suit, his head strangled by a tie that suggested he had a personality at weekends.

'Well?'

He muttered it to her breasts. 'It's never usually more than twenty minutes.'

'And then we get a refund, right?'

That got what passed for a laugh in the tube. Creased faces on the turning away.

'And you put up with this?'

She stared them down. Rox was good at staring people down. It came in useful at the Garage, the bar and restaurant in Beech Road where up until recently she had been manageress. That and knowing how to deal with trouble. They called her 'Toxic Rox' at school and it had stuck. It was something she was privately proud of. She had a fierce tongue and needed it in her dealings with drunks, obstreperous customers and local residents. And she *hated* being called Roxanne. It was Roxy by birth, Rox or Tox by adoption, no argument.

She and Mark had run the business smoothly for the last couple of years. First off she'd seen nothing wrong in his suggestion that she not bother coming in until eight for the evening shifts. He said it'd give her time to rest up in the afternoons but neglected to mention he was using it to shaft the new waitress in the flat above the bar.

Until she found out.

'It was *me* that gave her the job in the first place,' Rox howled. 'Yeah. Thanks for that.'

She wiped the grin from his face by lobbing a houseplant at it.

The evening of the big bust-up, Rox had arrived early and gone upstairs to find Corinne serving up a different menu than the one on offer in the restaurant. During her brief tenure she had charmed the customers with her hair-flicking displays (long, dark, split-ends) and had alienated the staff with her pathological passive-aggressiveness.

Rox didn't go ballistic at first, but she did pinch Corinne hard enough so she let out a yelp and clamped her mouth tight shut. Mark wasn't best pleased as his cock was in there at the time.

Once it was verified that the damage was more to his pride, Mark sent Corinne away and Rox started in, blaming him, blaming herself, bursting into tears and begging him to talk about it. Turned out not to have been the best course of action.

'Things've been a bit stale between us for a while now, Tox. We don't seem to have any time for each other.'

'Okay. I'm running the place six nights out of seven while you get pissed up with your mates. Does that give you a clue why?'

'You know what I mean.'

She was searching for the old Mark, but he'd sunk beneath his skin.

'What *was* this – a stupid bloody fling?'

'It was. Yeah.'

'So it's over, right?'

'Uh, actually, I, er, no . . . I think I'm in love with her.'

She felt like he'd punched the air out of her. 'Why? Is it the big tits? Does she swallow?'

'I can't talk to you when you're like this.'

'Have you even *thought* about what we'd do about the Garage if we split up?' Once he'd explained about how he'd spoken to the accountant about getting the place valued to estimate her share, Rox gathered her pride and glared at him like the scorned woman she was. Holding her counsel, she slammed the door and strode off home to make a start on the uncontrollable weeping.

'This is Camberwell, yeah?'

Pitch black outside and needles of rain slicing diagonally onto the amber apron of the bus garage.

'Catford Garage, love.'

'But I asked you for Camberwell.'

'Didn't hear ya – wiv your accent and that.'

'Where is it then?'

'About five miles back.' The driver pushed open the Plexiglas shield of his cabin, forcing her down onto wet tarmac. He pointed off into the rain. 'You wanna take the next 185 heading back to Kennington. That or you go up New Cross and change.' He reached up and pressed the emergency door button. The doors snapped shut. Rudely, she thought.

'But this is a 185.' There was pleading in her voice as her breath clouded and the cold began gnawing at the backs of her hands.

'End of me shift.' Stuffing the cash box under his arm, the driver sauntered off, dreaming of beans and chips and the *Standard* in the lemon light of the canteen.

Rox studied her watch. Nine o'clock. She sloped across to the big route map and got her bearings. Lewisham, Eltham, Blackheath? That's not *London*. And this bit was easily as crappy as Levenshulme or Gorton.

She had done a lot of standing at freezing bus stops in the night in her teenage years and had given up on it as a bad job. The only way to make them come was to walk. She headed straight back up Rushey Green through Catford, striding past its growling pubs and clenched shops, its bust businesses with their broken promises of unlimited credit and cheap travel. It stank of scratchcard poverty and piss.

She traversed Lewisham's new road layout and trudged up Loampit Vale. Somewhere along the way, her right shoe started coming apart, the scar yawning wide and her sock growing damp. Each footstep was a spongy squeeze followed by a flip-flop slap as the sole snapped back. Outside the South East London College, she spotted a cache of discarded elastic bands (thank God for posties). She used a bunch of them to bind her toes to the thick wedge of rubber.

Two buses passed by in quick succession.

Cursing, she rearranged her bag straps and trudged on.

'Rox, I feel dead bad about the money.'

She and Al were in the front room now. The good telly

was over, not that they'd been watching.

'I'll make it up to you, honest I will.'

'S'okay. I just hate the idea of some poncy git coming up here and making prats out of us all.'

Ally lay on her back, a wineglass on her bare stomach. It toppled over and a burgundy bead darted round to the small of her back. 'Bugger,' she said.

Rox let the liquid in her own glass climb to the rim. They were all out of drink except for a suspicious bottle of Sangria that someone had brought back from Majorca the previous summer.

Ally set to, mopping at herself with a tissue. 'I weren't going to tell you about it actually. Not yet. You know, because you're still so cut up about Mark.'

Hot salt tears coursed down Rox's cheeks. 'Al – when am I ever going to feel any better?'

Ally gave her her best sympathetic look, all sorrow with the eyes, and hope with the mouth. 'Maybe you should think about getting away for a bit?'

'Boring you, am I?' she snapped, regretting it instantly. Her best friend had gotten the brunt of all the bitterness lately. 'Ally, I didn't mean it. You've been brilliant.'

Which had both of them sobbing like Smash Hits award winners.

They decided on a brew.

In the kitchen, Rox had the arms of her sweater pulled over her hands, the hot liquid warming them through the wool.

'You know, you're right. I'm as useful here as a condom in a nunnery. I've lost my job and my boyfriend and I'm OD-ing on Trisha and Kilroy . . . Christ, Is it that bad? Have I been watch-ing Kilroy?'

'That *is* poor.' Ally pronounced it *pew-er*.

'And I can't even go out and see anyone 'cos they're all at the Garage. Mark's got custody of all my friends.'

'I'm right then, aren't I?'

'We can't afford to go abroad.'

'I didn't mean us. I'm working in the shop anyway.'

Ally's latest day job was demonstrating mobile phones in MegaPhones, a retail unit in Stretford.

'I'm not staying with me mam. No one can drink that much tea and live.'

'How about you going down south? My brother lives in London.'

'Graham?'

'He's grown up now. Honest.'

Rox thought about it. Be good to get some distance, clear her head. Okay, so this was partly Ally's way of assuaging her guilt over losing the money, but she quite fancied doing a bit of detective work. See if she couldn't find this bloke. And when it came down to it, he had ripped her off, not Ally.

'What have we got to go on?'

'The poster. And the name on the cheque was CR Enterprises.'

'If I go, will you look after the house? I mean better than normal. Pay the bills and wash up and that?'

'Sure.'

It was becoming real. 'It'd only be for a few days.'

'Course.'

'And if Mark calls – tell him I've gone to be a crack whore in King's Cross.'

The directions given to her by a drunk in the Goldsmith's Tavern were more like notes for a pub crawl. She caught another bus, which deposited her outside the Walmer Castle mid-way between Peckham and Camberwell. It was the last on a slurred list, one that the leering hominoid had recommended as being 'full of strippers what flick juice out their minges'.

She didn't go in.

The wind pummelled against her back, pushing her forward up Southampton Way. Built as a breakwater against poverty, a row of new ochre Lego houses lined the first hundred metres, but gave way to a domino row of tomblike estates and blighted buildings. Cars grew rust, their windows downgraded from glass to taped-on carrier bags. Litter clung to scrubby triangles of grass and the isolated pub was a stiff knot of testosterone with a radial reek of stale ale.

Rox longed to see a friendly face – or even Graham's, she thought with a smile. She'd met him only the once when he'd helped Ally move her stuff into her place. A lanky sullen lad, he was steeped in acne, incoherent, capable only of lugging or loafing. Boyfriend material only for the dim or desperate.

The house, through a curtain of rain, was redbrick Edwardian and contained within a tight terraced row of brick cages. There were no names on the bells. She pressed the middle one. Eventually, a thundering rattled the frame and the door flew open.

'Aya, Rox.'

'Aya, Graham.'

He was older, his hair longer, his face filling out, eyes darting anxiously behind big glasses. He wore a long, loud shirt, trakky bottoms and slippers with the fluff gone grey. She ducked under his arm, stomped up the stairs and headed for the warmth of the telly in the lounge. It was all Festival of Britain furniture. Lara Croft posters. Woodchip. The crippled sofa sat slumped in a corner with knotted warts and sprigs of horsehair emerging from its coarse hide. Picking his feet in the other chair was a lithe youth. He was naked except for the neon stripes on his nose and the swimming goggles.

'How's it going darlin'? Looks like me luck's *changed*.' The rising inflection. Bastard Aussie.

'Aya,' she said, mutely.

He stood up, his body a slender sausage of muscle. He thrust out a hand. 'Pete. Gray's flat*mate*?'

He snapped off the goggles and ran his fingers through his blonde shoulder-length hair. 'He said you were coming.

Didn't say you were a bit of all right. Can I get you anything?'

Rox gazed through him towards the tiny kitchenette. 'I'm starving actually. Any chance of some scran?'

'Scran?'

'Grub. Food.'

'Sure. I'll toss something in a pan. What d'you want?'

'Anything that involves you standing near hot, spitting fat?'

Graham sidled crab-like into the room and threw his arms wide. 'What d'you reckon to it, Rox?'

She dropped her bag and threw herself on the sofa. 'It's a palace, this.'

He pushed his glasses into the ditch between his eyes.

'Anyway. Welcome to London.'

CHAPTER TWO

Reece stood at the International Arrivals area in Terminal Two at Heathrow in his dark Hugo Boss suit. It was a good cut and looser around the waist with the training he'd put in of late. Underneath, he wore a crisp white shirt and a black tie and his chin was freshly shaven. The call had come in at three and after he'd showered he laid out his clothes on the bed and went through to the bright living room in his towelling robe. There, he made coffee, sat at the glass table and set to with his black marker pen. As carefully as a child, he inscribed the words 'Herr Schmidt' in capitals on the rectangular white placard.

It was the usual bunch at the rim of the funnel, some of them company reps, the rest friends and family. Reece didn't fit the latter category: not for him the eager radar eyes or quickening pulse of those longing for a loved one. He was among the chauffeurs and drivers, those cologned, disinterested sentinels who perennially roamed these hollow halls. He held his sign in large-knuckled hands. The pads of his palms had hard calluses from the daily pummelling he gave the wheel of his car. A different motor today. On hire. Beamer 323 series — power-steering, midnight black, tinted windows. Class job.

The jaws of the sliding doors jerked arhythmically and disgorged the contents of the 4.20 from Koln. It occurred to Reece that this routine was a bit like that programme where ordinary members of the public transformed themselves into has-been singers: 'Tonight, Matthew, I shall be . . . a sweaty tired businessman.' A clump of suits came first, ready to take on the capital and, later, adultery on expenses. A lone businessman emerged and veered to one side cradling his mobile to his ear like a long-lost child. Next, an anxious woman looking for love: that or her first smoke in three hours. Reece liked people-watching, imagining the highs and lows and awful mundanities of their lives. He had a lot of time for this hobby.

He remained a boulder in a flow that increased then subsided around him, impervious to the imploring eyes seeking out exits, or lame trolleys. His client, when he came, was a straggler as fat as his luggage. A pink billiard ball head with a mist of light brown hair, eyes drilled into his putty-like face and an expression of distaste pasted onto thin, downturned lips. Reece tilted the sign in his direction. The man wrestled the trolley to within a yard of him.

'Schmidt. IBS Koln. *Wir gehen nach dem* Kensington Hilton, *ya?*'

Reece nodded, folded up the sign and held out a hand. Schmidt didn't take it, so he swept it round to indicate the exit. The German abandoned his trolley and promptly strode off in that direction. Reece eyed the luggage. Two large suitcases and a yellow carrier straining with bottles and gifts.

In the car, he left the glass partition down in case his passenger wanted to talk. They peeled out of the terminal, through the long orange tunnel under the runway and out towards the M4. The traffic was sluggish.

'Staying long?' Reece's voice was low, a rumble over the larynx, a growl if and when required.

Schmidt looked up. He was working out on his laptop and his fat fingers twitched over the keys. 'Four days.'

'Been to London before?'

'Once, when I was younger.' He lowered his head and muttered curtly: 'If that is all?'

Reece didn't mind either way. Talk. Don't talk. In London

there was too much of it on the radio and in the papers and in the back of his regular cab. Sometimes he listened, sometimes he didn't: usually picked out what was relevant. Besides, the German had told him enough.

' 'S the point of that?'

'Give the boy an interest. Get him away from Star Wars.'

'Yeah, but a stick insect? That ain't a pet.'

Archie Peacock rubbed a hand over his bristly number one cut. 'Easy to look after. And if it dies all I've got to do is put another stick in the cage.'

'None too bright your Darren, is he?'

Archie glared at him. 'Joke – prat.'

Steve Lamb went on, chiding 'You didn't pay money for it, didcha? I mean, when you're down that end of the pet market, you might as well shell out on a wasp.' He laughed; emitting a long cancerous wheeze that sounded like a pair of bellows collapsing.

Archie tossed his empty can of drink high in the air and whacked it hard with the baseball bat. It flew into the back of the hangar and the echo bounced and spat around them. He tapped the ground a few times, enjoying the deep, wooden, hollow sound. Archie was a short, stocky man in his early forties, with pinched eyes in a broad face and lips that were always on the verge of a quip or a query. By contrast, Steve Lamb was gaunt and lanky in his greasy denims. He had a face like a chisel, with deep smoker's lines etched down his cheeks. He thought he resembled Keith Richards, but that was true in a fifth-generation Xerox, seen-through-muslin kind of a way. His only real connection with any kind of superannuated rocker was his insistence on skinny ties, a thick forelock and bushy sideburns. He sat perched on a packing crate at the lip of the huge hangar and blew on his hands as he started on another roll-up. Steve wasn't bothered about being seen as this section of the trading estate was deserted, pending another go at a business centre.

'He's overdue, ain't he?'

'He's on his way. Don't get your knickers up your arse.'

Steve torched tobacco. 'Speaking of arses. This bird the other night. World-class jacksie, like a couple of melons. You could build a shelf on it. She had this sort of thong thing went right up her crack. Gorgeous she was. Tell you what – I'd use her shit for toothpaste.'

Steve began to cackle, but Archie was walking away, well-used to hearing about this other night, that other bird.

Coming off the motorway at Heston Services, Reece glimpsed his passenger's face in the rear-view mirror and began a mental countdown. The car slunk past the Granary and approached the tall green turrets of the petrol station.

'We are not stopping. You are not paid to stop for fuel.'

Fourteen seconds. And they call the Germans efficient? He continued on past the filling station, went up the service road and turned left onto North Hyde Lane. Schmidt was alert, leaning forward, jowls wobbling.

'*Die autobahn* goes straight into town. I know it from the map.'

'Quick route.'

'No quick routes. Take me back, *so fort!*'

Reece had hoped his passenger wouldn't be tiresome, but he was prepared for it.

They wove through service industry hinterlands boxed in by crumbling brick walls. Above them a network of broad curved girders cradled a half-empty gas tank. Schmidt babbled on as they snuck over the Grand Union Canal and doglegged through the back streets. They came to a pair of tall metal gates crowned with curls of razor wire. As arranged, one of the gates had been left open and the BMW slid through, sloped across the patch-work tarmac and came to a halt. Reece noted that the handbrake

emitted no groan, unlike his regular, older vehicle. He turned to
the German, whose face was now daubed in the brighter shades
of the anger palette.

'Right then . . .'

'You will lose your job. I will not have this.'

Reece gripped the man's forehead in one large hand and
pushed him back in the soft leather seat.

'Your English is good, so let's not make this any harder than
it needs to be. Take out your wallet, your mobile and any jewellery you got and put them on the seat next to you. If the suitcases have a combination then we're going to need to know that
as well. Understand?'

The pouches of Schmidt's face gathered into a pout. 'This is
. . . a robbery?'

'It's not the guided tour.'

The German folded his arms. 'I give you nothing. How dare
you abscond me here?'

Reece faced front and eyed his passenger in the mirror. Last
chance, he thought. The German remained resolute, a child
refusing supper. With a long exhalation Reece released the auto-
matic locks and Steve and Archie poured into the rear seat. As
the German was dragged away, he picked up the *Standard* and
began to read.

'All right, Reece?'

Archie, tapping on the window. His big friendly face was
grinning and there was hardly a trace of blood on him.

He buzzed down the window. 'How's it going, Arch?'

'Sweet as. Rolex, Laptop, Deutschmarks, even some of them
pissy new Euro things. Some nice gear in the cases.'

'Cards?'

'Plenty. Steve's getting the PIN numbers now.'

In response there was a howl like an animal in its death
throes. Reece peered through the darkness and saw Steve

methodically clubbing at the slumped figure. He was not a nice man.

Archie held up a wad of notes and thumbed through them, moving his lips as he sifted through the fifties and twenties.

'Four ton do you?'

Reece shook his head. 'Give it the bosses. Tell them to knock it off the slate.'

Archie looked offended and proffered the money once more. 'No, ta.'

Archie sighed and pocketed it. 'Schmidt. Good choice. There's always gonna be a Schmidt.'

'That's what I reckoned.'

'How many runs we doing today?'

Reece lifted his paper up off the passenger seat. Underneath were several hand-written cards.

Archie stuck a paw inside and fanned them out. 'Better be sharpish with the next one. It's brass monkeys out here.'

Reece gave a lazy salute and fired up the engine.

Forty minutes later he was back in the Arrivals lounge. Terminal Three this time. Far East. Air China and Japanese Airlines. His board read: 'Dr Chan.' The stream of passengers from Tokyo had a much lower tide level and Reece, at six feet, stood out above them. Many of the other drivers were also oriental, which upped the risk potential considerably. He hoped he'd be able to spot his mark and be out of there by seven. If so he could be back at work by what – half ten?

The scam was used sparingly by his employers lest it attract the attention of the Airport Police and Customs: beauty of it being that none of its perpetrators was easily linked to one another. The cars were borrowed, the locations and staff changed frequently, the cards, money and mobiles soon devoured by London's fraudulent fraternity. The real risk was to Reece as the front man. He knew that if shit hit fan he'd be the one eating his meals off a tray in a place where the reading material was other men's tattoos.

Nicotine-hued faces and print black hair flashed past, the procession ordered, unhurried. He held the sign further forward over the chrome barrier, anxious to speed things up, pull in the next mark.

Sure enough, a gleam of recognition beamed in his direction and a trolley twisted round and trundled towards him.

'Sorry? Dr Chan. Is me. Thank you.'

He gazed down at her. A sparrow, late thirties, oval face, professorial. She was unruffled in her beige business suit despite having only just disembarked from the long-haul flight. He studied the deep chocolate brown of her pupils. She began to fidget, displacing the weight of her heavy shoulder-bag. Reece gave a half smile, bit of warmth.

'Sorry, love. I think I've made a mistake.'

Without further explanation, he crushed the sign in his hand and strode off.

CHAPTER THREE

Rox squeezed her eyes shut and pulled the blanket over her head. Overnight, the detritus bedded deep within the sofa had undergone some kind of genetic change and seemed to be moving about beneath her. She tried not to think about it.

Last night, the boys had eventually offered her the use of their beds. Pete had said that of course he'd be in there *with* her, heh, heh, but seriously, he wouldn't do anything unless she wanted something long and hot for the cold night.

She told him she'd rather suck on the element of the one-bar heater.

She had gotten his measure fairly quickly. Unbelievable that this twenty-five-year-old from Melbourne (whose knowledge of feminism consisted of the opinion that Germaine Greer had once been a babe) was actually a teacher. A substitute teacher in physical education. She gave his academic career a month, figuring the odds to be an even split between a paternity suit from one of his pupils or a sexual harassment case from one of the other teachers. His bedroom was pristine in the ancient and primitive sense of the word and every surface was draped with unwashed clothes. A tall black sound system stood like a monolith in a corner. Conversely, Graham's bedroom resembled the storeroom at PC World.

She settled for the deadly sofa.

Despite the fact that she was dying for a pee, Rox couldn't face them at this hour. From the muffled conversation, it sounded like Graham was in the loo and Pete eating cereal and taking a shower at the same time. She hunkered down, a patch of matted horsehair reddening the skin on her forearms. The toilet flushed. A kettle boiled. Badly concealed whispers, steps approaching. '. . . cup of tea for when she wakes . . . aarghh, sod.'

The doggy smell of wet carpet filled her nostrils. The elderly plumbing rattled its bones. Doors banged. Finally, an avalanche of feet tumbling down the stairs. Only when the front door shook in its frame did she fold back the flap of the sleeping-bag and reach for her glasses. Someone had toppled over her trainers and the left one was soaked inside and out. Great start to the day.

An hour later she had grabbed some cereal and was dressed and ready to go, nervousness nagging at her as she brushed out her hair and stared at the *London A–Z* left for her use. The page covering the local area was a solid maze of streets, the knotted ganglion of the Elephant and Castle at its centre. Why had she heard of that place? That and the Walworth Road? Got it! The old Labour Headquarters. A bunch of her friends had come down in May '97 for the celebrations. She'd been hosting a parallel event in the Garage and hadn't been able to make it. She felt a wave of nausea and the turgid ocean of Mark was there again, broiling and churning in her guts. He'd been on great form that night, both showman and host and, later on, attentive lover.

Bastard.

She threw up her breakfast in the brown toilet pan. Afterwards, as she cleaned her teeth again, she took the optimistic route. Hey, she'd been awake for nearly half an hour before thinking about him. Progress.

Before leaving Manchester, she and Ally had gone to the police station nearest the uni, where a detective constable told them that the issue was a matter for the Fraud Squad. They were given a number to call, but each time they rang it was either unattended or busy. Rox, by then impatient to get moving, told Al she'd contact them down in London. After all, that's where this con merchant came from. It all seemed a bit daft, but what the hell. She was here now.

Pocketing the spare key, she stepped out. The cold air stung her face and the sky behind the burnt-out tower blocks was grey as zinc. It felt like Russia.

'Yes, love?'

Why did everybody in London persist in calling her love? 'Can I see someone about reporting a fraud?'

'You want the Crime Business group.'

'Do I?'

'The Fraud Squad's a part of it. Which section?'

It came to her from off the telly. 'Serious Fraud. Well, not that serious. Certainly not trivial or owt.'

He looked at her as if she were another species. 'Where you from then?'

'Manchester.'

A smile jogged round the sergeant's lips. 'Don't they have cop shops up there?'

She gave him a sixty-watt smile. 'Tell you what. Can you direct me to the offices of the Police Complaints Committee?'

That seemed to do the trick and she was hustled through into another bland waiting room

Rox was proud of herself for having found New Scotland Yard without too much trouble. All she'd had to do was to catch a bus to Victoria. Okay, it was the wrong bus and she hadn't had the money for the right one and had discovered that London's homeless don't like being asked to give change. In the end she broke a tenner in the local newsagent's.

She got off a stop too early, not wanting a repeat of the previous evening's peregrinations. The big road was stuffed with pac-a-mac wearing tourists and she didn't feel out of place with her *A–Z*. The walk down Rochester Row and Victoria Street was further than it looked and she was disappointed to find that the famous revolving sign was dead teeny.

Opposite her, a detective in shirtsleeves was working out on a notepad. He had steely grey hair, a matching moustache, and the pouches of skin under his eyes were like wrung-out teabags. The staccato tapping of his Biro ceased as the chewed end popped into his mouth.

' . . .Certainly sounds like fraudulent trading and misrepresentation, but right now there's not a lot we can do. I'll take the details, but unless he tries it on down here, there's not a lot to go on.'

'What about the money? I lost three hundred and fifty pound.'

'Better off going through the small claims court.'

'Is there nothing you can do?'

'Do you have a solicitor?'

'No.'

'If you're on benefits you'll be entitled to free legal aid.'

'Do I look like I'm on benefits?'

He forced a groan out of the chair. 'I'm only making the position clear.'

'That you're not bothered.'

'I didn't say that. It's that with nothing to go on . . .'

She produced the poster advertising the weekend course and flattened out its creases.

'He was good in *Zulu*.'

Rox exhaled wearily. 'Michael Caine never showed up.'

The detective raised a finger and lowered his voice to a flat Cockney tone. 'Not a lot of people know that.' A beat. 'What d'you reckon?'

'To what?'

'To the impression? The lads say I do him well.'

She folded her arms. 'Look, I've no way of finding out who or where this bloke is, much less of suing him, so what good's a solicitor? I thought you people had records, some sort of data-base?'

'That's right. The NCI. And there's a top-notch forensic lab down in Camberwell (she arched an eyebrow at that). But what are you going to do when the invisible man's done a bunk?'

Rox tugged at the poster, but the detective held it steady with the heel of his hand. He swivelled it round, pointing to the lower edge.

'Might want to try getting in touch with chummy here.'

In tiny nine-point typeface it read: typeset and printed by J. Lovell & Co.

She unleashed her first real smile in a long time.

Rox wasn't getting any more used to the tubes. Each journey was a muttered mantra of place-names and directions as she meandered through the tunnels in search of Charing Cross. She emerged, surprised and a little delighted in Trafalgar Square. There was Nelson's Column, the lions, the pigeons and Whitehall stretching off into a Monet mist. It was like one of those old Sixties films shot in London, except for the traffic clogging every inch of road space. She went and stood by one of the fountains, taking in South Africa and Canada Houses, Admiralty Arch, the National Gallery. She then noticed the grime in the corners, the stolid, vengeful faces of the drivers, the deformed beaks and stumpy legs of the pigeons. A pack of jabbering Japanese shivered past. She felt small and alone.

She crossed over to the main line station, took the Greenwich line to Charlton and walked down Hope and Anchor Lane to the Meridian Trading Estate. On advice from the DS at Scotland Yard, she'd looked up the printer's address in the *Business Yellow Pages*, called up, got an answerphone and decided on a visit. Couldn't do any harm.

The gates opened onto a series of low-rise units, each one

tagged with plastic letters and all of them clad in bruised, corrugated metal.

'I was after talking to someone about a print job?'

She had to shout to be heard above the noise of the machines. The print shop reeked pungently of inks and solvents and a team of Asian lads were screen-printing T-shirts on a spider-like rotating device. *Mission Impossible II* knock-offs. One of them pointed her to the office, which was partitioned off and stacked high with reams and rolls of paper.

She rang for service. It brought a fat man clattering down a set of iron steps, fag in hand. Five days of stubble did not detract from his baldness, and his huge hairy stomach spilled out from between his waistband and T-shirt. He looked like Deputy Dawg minus the canine charm.

'Yeah? What the fuck d'you want?'

'You'll not get that job like that, will you?' she said, sweetly.

'What job?'

'Greeting people at the Disney Store.'

He stared at her. His lips were brick red and horribly moist.

'Look, I wanted to talk about a print job your firm did. It was a poster for an acting thing. I was after the bloke that ordered it.'

The printer hoisted a porcine thigh up on the desk. 'And you are?'

'Rox Matheson. Are you Mr Lovell?'

'I'm his brother.'

Rox doubted there was room for more than one of them in the world. She brought out and unfolded the poster. 'Can you take a look at this?'

Lovell scrutinised it blank-faced, then poked at the glossy paper.

'Him, Michael Caine. He was good in *Get Carter*. "You're a big man – but you're out of shape!"' he yelped dementedly.

She wondered if the mention of the actor's name down here set off some kind of Tourette's syndrome.

'Your' – she hesitated in what she hoped was a meaningful way – '*brother's* got his name on this.'

Lovell batted it from her hands.

'That toe-rag never paid me.'

'So you *are* Lovell then?'

His face changed colour, the lips losing it. 'He was a right cowson. Had the Pakkies on a double shift for that job.'

'Who?'

'Kayman or summink, he calls himself. Take a gander at this.'

He loped out of the office and led her under the stairs through to the back of the long metal shed. There were stacks of paper, old print jobs, dusty boxes of cards. Many of the images featured near-naked girls with tanned breasts, stiletto heels. Long phone numbers were predominant. Lovell delved into a pile and tugged out a ream of slippery posters. They were identical to the one in her hand, a space left blank for the venue.

'He comes in here, orders up a print run of two thou, promises us a load more work. Took a couple hundred off us on spec and does me a dodgy kite.'

'Kite?'

'Cheque.'

She frowned behind her glasses. 'He had you thinking you were quids in and then he took what he wanted in the first place. Clever bugger.'

Lovell glared at her.

'What's he look like, this Kayman guy?'

'Young geezer, lanky. Jew boy, probably.'

She winced at the anti-Semitism, imagining that it hadn't been a problem when the order was put in. 'So when was he here?'

'Back in November.' Lovell tossed the posters to the back and kicked the pile with a brown slip-on shoe. 'What you after anyway?'

'I want to find this guy. He owes me money.'

'You ain't VAT or nothing are you?'

'No.

He held up his palms. ' 'Cos all the books are square.'

'I'm sure they are, but I'm not with them.'

He took a step forwards. 'How do I know?'

'Hey – we've *both* been ripped off. I thought we could get together and track him down.'

'Do I look like Batman?'

'You want an honest answer to that?'

'Are you taking the piss?'

Lovell's approach forced her to back off. With his massive girth he wanted a verbal warning announcement, like 'Fat bloke reversing . . . Fat bloke reversing . . .' She refrained from mentioning this notion, as opening her mouth had so far only led to trouble. She took the poster and tracked backwards through the shop, trying to reason with him, but finding herself outside.

'I wanted to find this bloke, that's all.'

'Off my property. Now.'

She looked around. 'I am off your property. This is communal, this.'

Wrong answer. Lovell moved fast for a whale, charging after her bellowing curses. She dashed past a tyre rebalancing centre, out of the gates, and down to the river. Reaching a jetty, she ran behind one of the thick wooden pilings and crouched out of view. Below her, the oily water was a brown broth, slapping and spitting at the supports. In the distance the Millennium Dome mushroomed against a granite sky, too clean, too white, a part of a colouring puzzle that hadn't yet been filled in. Her breathing returned to near normal and she risked a glimpse. Lovell had stopped at the river's edge, winded by the flaccid putty of his enormous gut. He looked around, spat in the water, then limped away.

Touched a nerve there, she thought.

*

'Ally? Aya.'

'Hey – how's the big city?'

'Filthy, overcrowded and too bloody big.'

'Brilliant.'

Ally had always wanted to come down south but her mam was ill and couldn't be left, or so she said. Rox doubted it. There was bedridden and there was bone-idle and Ally's trips to see her in Altrincham were mostly guilt-induced. The truth of it was Ally was as scared of the capital as she was. And of course it was far easier to slag it off from afar.

She was dying to hear of Rox's adventures though.

'The transport's a bind, but I spoke to a policeman in Scotland Yard and was chased by a printer in Greenwich.'

'Ooh. Did you go to Dome?'

'Bit busy running away.'

Rox sipped her tea. After a day of Mcfood and traffic fumes she sensed unfriendly swellings under her skin. She wanted a bath, but there was only the shower, which went from drizzle to scalding hot in a nanosecond. Nowhere to put her makeup bag or hairbrush either, so she'd had to stack her stuff by her bag in the corner of the lounge. And nowhere to hang her clothes (one dress for best, top and trousers for a night out, the interview skirt she'd worn today). Maybe Graham would give her some wardrobe space.

'Did you see sights?' Ally asked. 'Madame Tussaud's. Planet Hollywood?'

'*Ally*. I was in mortal danger.'

'How about the Trocadero?'

'I managed to get a name. Kayman. Can you give that guy at uni a call? Ask him where he sent the cheques?'

'Will do.'

Ally then launched into a series of suggestions about where she should visit next. As she chirruped on, Rox dreamed of home and felt a hollow sag as her organs turned to mulch. Three weeks and counting since it had all evaporated. No more being with Mark, going for walks in the cemi, sitting around watching telly or having sex. She'd have to become one of those people who believed that no sex was better than bad sex when what she actually wanted was *any* sex.

Four years it was — a whole sixth of her life. There'd be no more having a right good laugh with their mates, taking the mick out of City fans, hanging around waiting for Mark outside the Vinyl Exchange in Oxford Road. I'm even missing that, she thought, incredulously.

She knew Al passed the Garage on her way home from work and that there was a chance she'd seen him — but what did she want to hear? That Mark was weeping in the gutter? That the massed villagers of Chorlton had torched the place and put him to the sword? That they had tarred and feathered Corinne and force-fed her chips until she was dead fat?

Yes, okay, any of them.

For the next ten minutes, she yessed and noed and all-righted until Ally rang off. Then she stared at the wall and failed not to cry.

CHAPTER FOUR

Grinding in low gear, the grubby tow truck struggled through the evening traffic towards Nunhead. As Steve and Archie's presence was not required at the airport today, they had returned to their day job. Sub-contracted out by the council's parking/fines department, their clamping operation involved the immobilisation and removal of vehicles in the Croydon area. It was a step down from beating the crap out of people.

Technically their patch covered only certain parking bays and business premises, but they took a more entrepreneurial stance to these demarcations. Anything over the yellow lines was considered fair game. Or on the yellow line. Or cars they liked the look of. Plus Archie wasn't one to brook argument, especially when he was busy trying to strip an entire forecourt of motors. He did the muscle work, dragging out the old yellow clamps, working the pipe wrench on the snap ratchet and slapping on the stickers, while Steve did the drive over to the pound in Addiscombe.

It was often borderline as to whether any of the vehicles were illegally parked or not. Anyway, those punters who wanted to get home before midnight usually paid up front. Steve and Arch did not welcome any of the major credit cards; cash spoke eloquently and anyone who wanted to create real trouble had Steve Lamb's temper to contend with.

Their clamping compound had once been part of an NCP

car park and was little more than a big square of cinder ringed by a knitted wire fence. Any information notices pertaining to their business were placed out of sight on the back of the hut. Stuck in the window on the front was a scribbled note saying 'Back in 5' – a permanent feature: point being to make it as difficult as possible for the mug to get his motor back. Especially the punter with the top of the range vehicle, since they had other plans for them. Their daily rates were astronomical and it might be argued that they were in effect stealing cars and ransoming them back to their owners.

That was the legal part of the operation.

'Nice Jag you brung in today.' Steve grinned lopsidedly in the red tail-light glow of the car in front. He ran a hand up the scarp of his forehead, through his lank hair and patted the back of his scrawny mullet, which flopped over the scuffed collar of his anorak.

'Should be useful up Finsbury.' Archie blew on his hands. The heater wasn't working and Steve couldn't be arsed to get it fixed.

'Heard from the Petersons about our cut?'

'Not as yet.'

'That Kraut was loaded.'

'Don't get torn up about it,' Archie said.

Steve wrenched the wheel and the truck lurched through Brockley Cross and barged across the low carapace of the mini roundabout. The gears let out a shrill screech as they clambered up Telegraph Hill.

'Boozer tonight?'

'Later on, yeah,' murmured Archie, making calculations about his itinerary. The Merc outside his place would have to be returned to the lot and swapped for the newer Jag. Take that up Golden Lane and get one of the drivers to bring him back. What with present conditions – freezing fog and the traffic being chocker – he reckoned he wouldn't see the Railway until last orders. Plus, he'd need to put in an appearance with Shirl and the kids.

Finsbury Cabs was sandwiched between a bar and a derelict office supplies showroom. Like all minicab offices, it didn't need much front, only the revolving amber light and the controller behind his hatch. The illegal part of Steve and Archie's operation was in providing them with chauffeured cars on a short-term lease: an activity that the cab firm owner pretended not to know about. This is where they took the vehicles from the pound, their locks having been picked and duplicate keys made up sharpish. They had a rotation system, adding to or taking away from their stock as and when required. It usually took their owners a good week to ten days before they managed to locate the lot down in Addiscombe and, what with all the aggro of getting their motors back, they weren't going to spot the increased mileage.

'Comin' in for a cuppa?' Archie asked, as they pulled up outside his home.

Steve hadn't been in Arch's place in a while. He couldn't stand small children and if truth were told he wasn't up to the job of being Darren and Ronan's godfather. His gifts of forty JPS hadn't gone down too well that Christmas.

'Yeah, All white.' He clambered down from the cab and slammed the door. Rain spat at his face.

'Wipe your feet on the way in.'

Once he had the frosted glass door open, the kids rushed at him, almost toppling his chubby frame over in the hall. Shirley called through with her daily report from the kitchen. Apparently, the stick insect had been a casualty when Darren used it as a pretend light sabre in a fight with Ronan's hamster. There were other ructions, but Archie had gone off, doing the Frankenstein walk with the boys wrapped round his legs. Steve leaned on the kitchen doorframe and gave Shirl a big grin.

'All white, love?'

'All right, stranger. Long time.'

The kitchen was lemon in the light, ochre units, flowery tiles, steam billowing from a pan on the cooker. Shirl heaved it off the flame and doled out piles of spaghetti hoops onto heavy beige plates. She was late thirties, but looked older, her hair swept back off a lined forehead, face swollen with the trials of motherhood. Her body had given up the struggle with calories and clothes sizes. She spooned out two measures and set the pan aside.

'I'm doing the kids' tea. You want anything?'

'Couldn't hurt.'

'Pizza do you?'

'Yeah. Why not?'

Twinkle in his eye. Steve had gone after her once, until she'd put a stop to it. Shirley bent to the oven, checked the pizza hadn't gone nuclear and straightened up, tucking a wisp of hair behind her ear.

'How's work then, Stevie?'

'Fair to middling.'

He hung there, a lemur with a leer. He'd been handsome in his prime but now he was coming up on seedy at top whack. No one to iron or mend for him. Sad. Still, he got about a bit. Always on about it. He'd find someone, no bother. Neither of them knew what to say next. She smiled and lowered her voice for the first time that afternoon.

'Get Arch to call the boys through, will you?'

Archie came through with his sons clamped to his thighs. They greeted Steve with the same disinterest as he did them and settled down to decorate their faces with spaghetti juice. Shirley carved the pizza and slid hot triangles onto each plate. Steve sat next to Darren, feeling like a giant. Reasoning that he couldn't very well ask a seven-year-old boy if he'd had any gash lately, he ignored him.

'I was wondering sunnink?' he asked of Archie. 'You got any news on that painting we had away back in November?'

Archie, sipping his tea, coloured a little. 'The one from Dulwich?'

Steve bit into a burnt bit of crust. 'Unless we took some others I don't know about.'

A look went from man to wife. Shirley's expression said, 'You tell him.'

'What?'

'Nothing,' Archie sliced at his pizza.

On a moonless night the previous autumn, the pair of them had stolen a small Rembrandt self-portrait from the Dulwich Picture Gallery. In keeping with the primitive security measures, the pair had used old-fashioned methods themselves. Tape was stuck over window panes before they were broken, security guards were bribed to shut down the system for fifteen minutes and chewing gum was placed over the sensors on the back of the painting. Easy job: Dulwich, like Kenwood House and the Ashmolean in Oxford, were known as easy marks. Candy from.

'I thought you was going to sell it on?'

'Buyer fell through,' said Archie; his reddening face focused on his plate. 'I had a call. Bloke's got cash problems.'

'Who ain't?'

Archie crammed a forkful of food in his mouth. 'Says he'll bell me when he's solvent.'

'How solvent? You said it was worth ten mill.'

'Not to us, more like half that.'

'So where is it?'

'Go on, tell him,' said Shirley.

He glared fiercely at her, then turned to Steve. 'We don't talk business while we're eating,' he said, sniffily.

Shirl chuckled. 'Course, he's Mafia now. Nunhead branch.'

Steve said, 'What's going on?'

The children studied their father, mouths gaping open, spaghetti hoops churning about inside like worms.

'You haven't lost it, have you?'

'No, he ain't lost it,' said Shirley.

'Well then?'

Archie pursed his lips.

Ronan said, 'Daft Mall.'

'What's that?' asked Arch, taking a sudden interest in his younger son.

Ronan whispered in his brother's ear. Darren translated for him. 'Ronan says Dad looks like Darth Maul.'

Archie lost it.

'Right. Come on.' He strode through to the lounge and they all trooped in after him, with Shirley worrying a drying-up cloth in their wake.

'There it is.'

There was the gas fire, the wooden mantel with the darts trophies, the puckered crescents where old cups and glasses had stood too long. On the wallpaper above were streaks of carbon and above that hung the Rembrandt self-portrait. Steve folded his arms.

'Why din't you tell me?'

'No reason.'

'What's that on it?'

Archie turned round. A crayon line grazed across the lower third of the canvas, sauntered over the frame and shrank to a whisper on the wall.

'Ronan!' he bellowed.

The kids turned tail and scampered upstairs, aware that smacks were imminent, food and telly privileges to be revoked; later, promises squeezed out of them like toothpaste. Shirley rolled her eyes and turned helplessly to her husband.

'I can't keep me eyes on them every moment of the day.'

'But it's the poxy *Rembrandt.*'

'Will it be all right?' she asked, like an anxious relative.

Arch plucked it from the wall, grunting at the weight of the gilt frame. He carried it over to the table and laid it down. He brought the light close in on its cord and blew on the surface, hoping to dislodge a few of the waxy flakes.

'Dunno,' he mumbled.

Shirl went off to put the kids' dinners in the bin. The boys would get chips later on, but for now she had to make a show of solidarity.

Steve sat on a chrome chair and lit up.

'Not near the picture.'

He went back through to the kitchen and crimped the end off it. On his return, Archie was still bent over the surface.

'Turps should clean that right off if I use a cotton bud. Shouldn't affect it too much 'cos of the layers of varnish.' He propped the portrait up against the wall and squinted at it like an expert.

'Why you got it up there? That's money in the bank for us, that is.'

Archie Peacock thought for a long moment, finally tearing his eyes away from the image.

'Tell the truth, Steve, I've taken a fancy to it.'

CHAPTER FIVE

A drab grey sky had leeched the colour from the buildings and the faces of the commuters. This suited Rox fine as she emerged from Chancery Lane tube and began walking up the Gray's Inn Road. The loss had got to her hard today and she was feeling lonely on top of miserable. It was a bit like having no skin, she thought. All raw and bleeding. And what was worse was that all the Londoners around her seemed so busy and purposeful and so utterly smug. She bet that none of them had ever had their hearts broken, or knew what it was like to wilt inside or to want to burst into tears all the time. How did they do life? She quite fancied screaming, if only to get a reaction. Wasn't going to though: she'd seen how they ostracised the poor, the helpless, the different. And was she the only one to give money to those Asian, Bosnian or Irish women cowering with their kids in the filthy tube corridors? Seemed like it. On the other hand, she'd drawn the line at buskers with tin flutes. After all, there were limits.

Ally had given her the address where the cheques were sent — a Post Office box number at the Mount Pleasant Sorting Office in Farringdon. Rox had concocted a plan whereby she would masquerade as a friend of the box owner who had been sent to pick up the mail. If it worked, great: if not, she'd try pleading for information. That or crying, which she was good at. She studied her *A–Z* and a shiver of fear ran through her as she turned into Rosebery Avenue. Nearly there.

The previous night was an improvement on her first. Once she came off the phone to Ally, Pete bounded in straight from the school sports field reeking of stale sweat and mud. He'd flopped down and demanded that Rox make him some tea and toast. Feeling like shit anyway, she did as asked. After that, he took a shower and paraded naked around the flat with his lumpy manhood swinging about like a New York cop's night-stick. She asked him if he fancied a toss and Pete's eyes lit up. She told him to sod off and do it somewhere else then.

Stupid, stupid, stupid. He took this as encouragement and bullied her into going to their local. The Brewers was a testament to the corrosive properties of stale beer and nicotine and its clientele looked like they were still in shock from the Second World War.

Pete tried to get her pissed.

'No one gets me pissed,' Rox told him. Point of pride. He took it as a challenge. After the fourth pint she grew bored of his pawing and gurning and crappy jokes and suggested a game of darts. She scored 301 in twelve and three shots went wide, two of them into Pete's leg. He came home leaking claret from his calf. She then went to see Graham in his room, noting that his skin was the same eggshell colour as his monitor casing.

'Aya, Rox. How's it going?'

'Gave Pete acupuncture with pub darts. What you doing?'

'Internet chat room. I've been on with this seventeen-year-old babe and . . . hold up. 'He made a few strokes, his hand hovering above the keys.

'What is it you do all day?' Rox asked, miffed that her three dimensionality could be so easily usurped by two.

'IT manager . . . software systems place down in Bromley.'

Meant nothing to her. She peered at the screen. 'Hey, how d'you know she's seventeen?'

Twin rhombuses of light shone in his glasses as they sat in

an awkward silence. After a moment he closed down the computer and offered her a can of drink.

They talked about her getting the money back and she confided in him that she was here as a kind of retreat, so she could stop thinking about Mark, which of course had the opposite effect. She told Graham what he'd said as she walked out of his life.

'It were great though, weren't it, Rox?'

After four years. Like it was a good match or film.

She had yelled, 'It has not been great. Great was the first eighteen months when you swore you'd love me until the day you died, and devoured me with your eyes and your body.'

Trouble was she said it three hours later to her pillow as she pummelled the life out of it.

Graham was propped up on his bed. She told him she so wanted to hate Mark, but every time she tried to focus her rage, the despair and the love and the pain came all in together. 'With your broken heart,' she announced in a calm medical manner, 'you get free depression, hollowness, loss of appetite and mouth ulcers.' She had two, one welling behind her lower lip, another nestling under a molar. Plus, she'd pulled her fringe into a blonde curtain over her glasses and looked a sight and didn't care.

'Still, maybe one day I won't feel so bad. One day, eh, Graham. Gray?'

His body was limp with sleep.

She headed for the tall escarpment of the building. There were several entrances and eager red postal vans buzzed around it, protecting their queen. It took three goes before she found the correct department. It was back on Rosebery Avenue, a lifeless waiting room done out in grey and navy. The bell summoned a surly postal worker, keener on his overdue fag break than on servicing the public.

'It's Box 1401,' she said.

He grunted, went off and delved in a series of pigeonholes, returning with a bundle of envelopes. She had to sign and simply copied the next signature up on the list.

She left the office, her heart hammering her ribs and mouth dry with excitement. She decided that if the Royal Mail ever wanted anyone to endorse the poor quality of their security procedures, then she was their girl. She clung to the envelopes, noting that some but not all were addressed to 'CR Enterprises'. Her head swam with success and she had to stop and lean up against some railings. The letters came in buff, beige and white and the postmarks were from back home, several from Leeds. Bastard's trying it on again, she reckoned, feeling none of her usual antipathy to those across the Pennine Ridge. She was just starting to tear one open when a silver-ringed hand gripped hold of her arm.

'Oy. Give us those.'

A girl, about her age, scrawny, ghostly white face, hair in long filthy Rasta dreads. Her black-painted fingernails nearly punctured Rox's skin.

'Get off.' She tried to shake free but the bony grip held firm. She passed the bundle to her other hand, holding it away like sweets at school.

'Give us them now or you got trouble.' She spat the final word like *trabaw*.

The girl had a rude wide mouth and vacant eyes with blown pupils. She was either a junkie or putting in the training. Rox made to speak but the girl slapped her powerfully with her other hand. Rox's jaw snapped shut, sending a nauseous metallic sensation through her. Before she could react, the girl had spun her round and was pulling her to the ground by her collar. She fell and the girl kicked at her with high, laced DM boots. Rox threw a punch, connecting with nothing, then the girl was on her, trying to grab the package. She held on for as long as she could, but the hard fingers pecked and jabbed until they secured their prey.

Now the girl was up and moving off.

Rox bounded to her feet and followed her assailant, outraged more than anything that no one had come to her aid. The girl moved with a paranoid canter she'd seen a lot of in Moss Side. She wore a ratty bobbled black coat and below her waist were cut-off denims over black leggings. It was part Goth, part Tank Girl, very King's Cross. Rox checked her glasses and wiped a hand across her mouth. Blood on her chin from where a silver snake ring had caught her. Bitch. Fuming, she increased her pace as the girl sank into the entrance of Farringdon Road tube.

Shoreditch resembled the backs in Manchester town centre. A huge Meccano-like railway bridge clambered over broken-down old Victorian shops owned by textile wholesalers. Most were boarded up and the wind whipped rubbish into tiny tornadoes, giving the place a ghost town feel.

Rox had had time to build up a head of steam. This bitch wasn't going to get one up on her, she decided. She knew the type from back up North; they were the first ones to smoke at school and graduated to hanging around the clubs trying to talk their way in free. When they showed up in the Garage they were never the ones paying. They traded on their looks, which were not spectacular but the kind a lot of men liked. Dirty, was how a couple of male friends had put it. Tarty was what women called it, although this girl wasn't that blatant. This was harder and more provocative, a London look.

Thoughts buzzed as they zigzagged about in the tubes. They changed lines three times. Rox at first thought she was trying to lose her, but when they came up at Old Street, she realised you had to change this often to get here. The girl didn't seem bothered by Rox's amateurish stalking. She'd not been hard to spot, peering through the window of the next carriage or stood a few steps below on the escalator.

Cold air chilled her face and hands as she slipstreamed her

foe. Rox wondered what she'd do if she reached her home, or even met up with the mysterious Mister Kayman. And how to confront her? She'd not planned anything more after getting hold of the letters.

They came to a big junction and thousands of tons of traffic thundered past. The lights were against her, so the girl turned to Rox.

'Why don't you piss off, you little cow?'

She spat at her and it landed on her coat. Rox balled up her anger and as soon as she'd turned away, she jumped the girl from behind and slung her arms tight round her neck.

'I'll put you in the traffic unless you tell me about them letters.'

She writhed, but couldn't reach behind her. Rox kept up the pressure, even when a nail dug into her hand. Although the girl was taller, she couldn't have weighed more than eight stone. Rox had lifted a lot of crates in her time and reckoned on it being a fair fight so long as she stayed away from those rings.

'Who are you?' she blurted out.

'Piss off.'

Rox thrust the girl's head forwards. It narrowly missed the wing mirror of a motorbike. The despatch rider swerved maniacally.

'Try again. What's your name?'

'Jesus. Charlie. All right?'

'Charlie what?'

'Charlie Ribbons.'

'CR? So it's you these cheques are going to?'

'Get off me.'

The voice was nascent Cockney, but Rox realised her instinct had been wrong. This girl wasn't as tough as all that. Under the sallow skin, fine bones in her face came out of breeding. Put that with the dreads and she got a Trustafarian vibe. It was a type she had met through Ally, slumming it up North on the Arts and Media courses, always the most vociferous about slagging off the South. She tightened her grip.

'I've heard it were a bloke doing these rip-offs. Your boyfriend, is it?'

'I ain't telling you nothing.'

The lights changed and the crossing beeped to announce the next round. This one was in Charlie's favour. She dropped low and kicked her heel back into Rox's pubic bone. Rox yelped and fell away. Charlie loped across the junction, rammed the 'walk' button on the other side and started out into the traffic. Rox whipped off her glasses, stuffed them in her pocket and ran off in pursuit.

Charlie ducked under the arches of a row of old works buildings and disappeared into Cotton's Gardens, a cul-de-sac lined with warehouses. A deafening roar drowned out the traffic as a goods train rumbled over the bridge. Charlie went to a pair of metal gates set in the wall and slipped through. Rox kicked the door running and it flew back on heavy hinges. She entered a dim courtyard, and took a punch from a hand gripping keys. Tumbling onto cobblestones, she lashed out with her foot, hammering into Charlie's calf and bringing her down. Rox managed to slip behind her and grabbed two handfuls of hair. Playground stuff, but it worked.

'Ow, me fuckin' hair.'

'Stop your mithering. It's not yours.'

'You're pulling me extensions out.'

'Then give me some answers. Who's this bloke who's ripping everyone off?'

'Dunno what you're on about.'

Rox paused. 'Hold still, this might hurt a bit.'

It did. A coiled rope of woven hair landed in Charlie's lap. She screamed.

'Who is he and where is he?'

'Davey's cashing his giro,' she burbled. 'He'll be back later.'

'That's his name? Davey. Davey Kayman?'

'Yeah, Kayman.'

'And he's your boyfriend? Partner in crime? Pimp, what?'

Charlie lashed out with her elbow, catching her in the face. She then scrabbled to her feet, kicked at Rox, and went through a pair of red-rusted doors at the entrance to an adjacent building.

Rox lay under the brick archway of the gates and tested her injuries. Her cheekbone was tender, but not broken. Her back ached, not to mention the pain in her pelvic region, which made her want to pee. She limped out into the street and leaned up against a wall to get her breath and bearings. She'd not been in a scrap like that in ages, not since a year ago when a bunch of secretaries made up like Coco the Clown caused trouble during a hen night. Here I am, she thought, not two days in London, and street fighting like an urchin.

Still something to put on the postcard home.

She shivered with shock and cold. Inside the gates was a courtyard boundaried by brick workshops. She studied the intercom and the bank of buzzers. There were a variety of businesses: photographers, cutters and finishers, a design agency. Davey might work in any one of them. Wait, scratch that. Charlie said he was collecting his dole money. She peered through the milky reinforced glass panels. Inside was a flight of concrete stairs wrapped around an old wire-framed lift. Clunking machinery sounds sank down from above. She back-pedalled to the street and looked up. The top floor was gabled and a disused winch peered out from above like a gargoyle.

She made a snap decision. Assuming either one of them lived or worked here, then obtaining the actual address would give her something concrete for the police. With that in mind, she started pressing buzzers. She buzzed and listened, pressed and waited. No replies from some, squawking denials from others. Eventually, when she said she was with Charlie, somebody buzzed her up.

Unable to figure out how to summon the lift, she clattered up three flights, sliding her hand up the smooth wooden banister on the wall. There were solid iron doors on each floor, all riveted and painted duck egg blue, and set into thick brick walls tiled up to shoulder height. A door on the top floor opened out into a reception area. There were framed glossy prints on the walls, low green sofas, *Vogue* and *Harper's* on a chrome table. A prim little madam in a Barbie power-suit sat at a curved beechwood desk.

'Aya,' said Rox.

'You the go-see from Elite?' Barbie answered her own question. 'No, I don't think so, not dressed like that.'

Rox saw nothing wrong in her combat trouser, greatcoat and bruises ensemble.

Barbie flashed the falsest smile she'd seen since she was last in the perfume department at Kendall's. 'Unless you're from *Uglies* and they're doing midgets now.'

'Stuck up little twat,' said Rox. 'Sorry. Did I say that aloud?'

'Get out of here.'

'I'm a friend of Charlie's,' Rox said.

A smile blossomed. 'Why didn't you say so?'

Night in the Grove in Camberwell, a large, semicircular pub stuffed with Rox's favourite people in the whole wide world: art students. Worse still, Pete was wearing a shirt loud enough to match his ego. He was eager with his rounds, all oops and spills and winks to the women. Graham was sitting on a stool supping his pint, unable to connect with the world, mouse hand twitching with the early onset of RSI. It was Friday night and the plan was to drink here then go clubbing, either down in Coldharbour Lane or over in New Cross. Rox was telling them how her day had panned out.

'Barbie takes me through to this studio, where this photographer's got this girl—'

'Naked was she?' interrupted Aussie Pete.

'No, she were smothered in baby oil,' shot back Rox, knowing the image would occupy his thoughts while she concluded her story. 'He asks me how much Charlie I've brought. That's when I realised I'm going to have to stop meeting people with the same name as a major drug.'

'What happened then?' Graham asked.

'He threw a wobbly and they turfed me out.'

'So you didn't find out where the girl lived?'

'No.'

After being removed from the building, she had taken up a vantage point in the street, hoping to see Charlie re-emerge or to catch a glimpse of her elusive boyfriend. A slate sky turned black and produced hard, slanting rain. She scampered under the railway bridge in Shoreditch High Street and watched as the walls streamed water, runnels of it making the mould glisten and the posters flow with particles of soot. She grew numb with cold and returned to Camberwell.

After showering comprehensively (scalding was fine when you were frozen), doing her hair and changing into fresh clothes, she felt a lot better. The bruise on her cheek was turning purple so she covered it with foundation. The other scratches, she didn't mind about. They were the battle scars from her second foray into sleuthing. Perhaps she'd get a chance to show them off sometime?

'It's dead impressive,' Graham said. 'Next You'll get caught in gunfire and car chases.'

Rox tapped lightly on the table. 'Hello. Reality check. Not computer game.'

'Least you're getting to know your way around.'

She sipped her pint. 'Know what I was thinking? It's dead unfair they call the worst Tube line the *Northern*. And why are there not any Tubes down here in South London?'

He shrugged.

'And it's expensive. And filthy.'

'They took the bins 'cos of the IRA.'

'Litter bins are a major terrorist target, are they?'

Pete dragged himself away from eyeing up the talent. 'Taken

to the capital, then, have you?'

'It's bobbins.'

'Mary Poppins? What are you on about?'

'I mean it's shite.'

This had Pete confused, but so did most things, what with him being a gym teacher.

'You're not staying then?'

Mark flashed into her head, at the bar at the Garage. Corinne's head on his shoulder, gazing at him all doe-eyed and wet knickered like he was God Almighty.

'Dunno,' she said. 'See how it goes.'

CHAPTER SIX

'I said let's have a bop. I did not ask you to grab my arse with the manual skills of a Kwik-fit fitter.'

'Same difference.'

'Pete. Which part of "piss off" did you not understand?'

They were shouting at one another upstairs at the packed nightclub in New Cross. The decibel level was a shade lower than that under Concorde during take -off.

'No worries, Roxanne. I like a challenge.'

'It's not Roxanne, it's Rox. And you're not my type.'

'Hey,' he went, grinning down at her, 'bit of a spark between us though, eh?'

'Only if I had a cattle prod.'

His beer goggles were on and he leered at her with antipodean confidence, a look that implied that the world and its inhabitants were only there for his personal use. The hall smelled sweetly of draw, strobe lights threw shards of light and the walls perspired freely. It was fuggy and close and Rox wanted another drink: a soft one this time.

'Get us a coke, will you, Pete?'

As he shouldered through the crowd, she turned to find Graham taking a breather. His glasses were misted up and his hair pasted to his head.

'What do you reckon to the club?' he shouted.

'Nothing special.'

He looked hurt.

'Actually, Gray. I've not been clubbing in a while. I think I've gone off it.' She wasn't particularly enjoying being deaf and slithery with sweat and in continual fear of falling off her shoes. Her main difficulty was in trying to stay afloat in the wash of bodies. The thought occurred that she'd rather be working behind the bar where she'd have some control. Depressing, that.

'I was only trying to make you feel at home. I really like you, Rox.'

He bent down and hugged her, almost squeezing the stuffing out. When he pulled away, she studied his gurning grin and realised he was E'd up. Bugger. Now she'd have to spend the rest of the night avoiding them both – and even if she went back to the flat, there'd be no telling what time they'd come barging in or what kind of state they'd be in.

Pete returned with floppy plastic glasses and handed them round. A different bass-line shook the floor and the wash of cymbals flowed in and out of their ears like a sea on fast forward.

Pete threw back his lager. 'So, Roxanne. I was wondering if you were so balshy 'cos you've lost your fella, or if it's 'cos you've got a height complex?'

'What do you think?'

He winked at her. 'Personally, I reckon you're a bit of a Lezza.'

The coke covered his face and chest, turning his shirt a deep blood brown.

As Rox headed down the stairs, Pete bellowed into Graham's ear. 'That's a tenner you owe me, mate.'

She collapsed out of the club. A side road slid away off into pitch blackness. Up the other way was New Cross Road, the skirts of its tall Victorian pubs ribboned in silver and ruby red from the after-images of speeding traffic. A clump of tragic taxis hugged the kerb. Sensing custom, the drivers squeezed heat from their cigarettes and hailed her from their South London souk. Rox, feeling chill and alone, pulled her coat up around her ears to blinker herself from the clamour. She made for the busy road.

'You all right?'

A honey voice, deep and reassuring like a doctor's. A youngish man silhouetted against the streetlight. His hand hovered by her elbow, cupping but not touching.

'You need a cab?' he urged.

She found herself nodding like a frightened child. 'To Camberwell. But I've not got a lot of money on me.'

'Three quid sound all right?'

'I've got that.'

In moments, she was sunk in the rear seat, warm air flowing around her as the car moved away.

'You're not local,' the driver said.

'How'd you guess?'

'North of the river?'

'A bit further than that.'

'Tottenham?'

'Manchester, you pillock.'

'We've got most of their fans down here.'

'I know,' she said, a smile in her voice and a thaw on the way.

'First time here?'

'That's right.'

She sat up. His hair was short and dark, cropped close around the temples where it shaded to grey. A strong jaw, stubble; a neck girded by the rim of his leather jacket. She approved.

'You at the college?'

'What college?'

'Goldsmith's — we're passing by it now.'

'No.' The burr of his voice was so calming. She wanted to hear more of it and was relieved when he spoke up again.

'Why are you down?'

'That's a long story.'

'Get a lot of long stories in this job.'

She wondered if this was an invitation for her to talk or a coded way of telling her he didn't want to know. She formed words but they wouldn't come. He wove lanes and they headed for Peckham. She glimpsed his eyes in the rear-view mirror. They were studying her face. He looked away, but without shame.

'You left the club on your tod?'

'That's right.'

Okay, now she wasn't so sure. Was he checking out that she was alone so he could mug, rape and kill her? Or was he surprised that she'd left on her own without a man because her trapping off shouldn't be a problem? Rox shook sobriety back into her fuzzy head. This is daft, she thought. From what she'd heard of London, the first option was much more likely. Was she reading too much into what was a friendly enquiry? Either way, she felt a chill as they drove on through the dead dark streets.

'What do you reckon to it then – London?'

'Where do I start?' she replied in the falsely cheery tone she reserved for cab drivers. 'It's dear and dirty and the people are dead unfriendly.'

'Seen much of it, have you?'

'Not a lot – no.'

He took a sudden right, veering off up a side street bordered by the elephantine trunks of plane trees. Their speed increased as they hit the sodium-drenched Old Kent Road.

'Maybe I'll show you round?'

'Now hang on.'

'No charge, obviously.'

Looked as though the mug, rape and kill option was firming up nicely. Rox gripped her bag in one hand and the door handle in the other and tried to keep her tone even, controlled.

'Will you stop here, please?' she squeaked.

'This isn't Camberwell.'

'Look – stop here. I want to get out.'

He pulled up. A group of lads swaggered past, one of them

bleating incoherently as he drummed his hands on the roof. They stared in at Rox, their faces aglow, polished by drink. She felt like some malformed exhibit in a Victorian sideshow. When she didn't respond, their potential ardour evaporated and they started cursing her, one of them baring his behind, another lobbing his lager bottle into the road.

'Off you go then,' said the driver.

She bloody would and all, only then he turned round to face her and smiled. It was a great smile, lighting up his face and eyes, the teeth white and even, his lips made paler and more sensuous by his stubble.

'Look, I didn't mean to frighten you. I've had a bad week that's all. And I can't have you thinking us Londoners are unfriendly.'

She dragged her eyes to the Neanderthals, staggering off up the road. 'What about them?'

'That's not a London thing. Drunken arseholes are everywhere. It's a franchise.'

'What you on about? Show me round?' She hoped her bruise was still covered up and that her slap was still in place. Didn't want him thinking he had the Phantom of the Opera in the back.

'Give you the tour. Best time to do it, middle of the night.'

'Traffic's also on my list of why London's so shitty.'

He scratched his head. 'Give you that. We'll pick up a coffee on the way.'

He faced front and gunned the engine. She melted as they took off and it wasn't until they had stopped again and he'd gone into the Old Kent Road McDonald's for the drinks that she realised she hadn't actually accepted his offer. However, she still used the time to check her face, respray selected bodily interstices with perfume and wonder what the hell she was doing here at 2.30 a.m. on a Saturday morning with a fluttering inside her chest.

'What's your name?' she asked, taking the hot cup from him.

'Reece.'

'That your first or your second name?'

'Just Reece. Yours?'

'Rox. Rox Matheson.'

'Interesting.'

'I know what you're thinking.'

He pre-empted her. 'That with a name like that everyone's going to think you're on the game?'

She smiled. 'My mam and dad were big fans of Bryan Ferry in the Seventies.'

'So it's Rox as in Roxy Music not Roxanne as in Sting?'

That put him as older than her by a decade, so he was what – thirty-four?

'My mates call me Tox, for short. I used to be called Toxic Roxy at school.'

'Nice of them.'

'Watch it, you!'

They drove off, heading up towards Borough.

'If your folks had been fans of Ron and Russell Mael, you could've been called Sparks . . . or sparky.'

'Let it go, Reece.' She liked saying the name.

'Fair enough.'

They drove up over Tower Bridge, circled the City and came down Fleet Street for the Victoria Embankment run. Reece was going on about gryphons and no roads and Londinium and the feudal system but she wasn't hearing any of it, merely listening to the sound of his words and relaxing in his company in the warm car. End of a long day.

They came up to Big Ben and turned left over Westminster Bridge.

'If I'm not out of order – where d'you get them bruises?'

'A fight with a girl. I came down to London because I lent a friend some money. She's had it ripped off by some Cockney prat. It was supposed to be an acting weekend. Michael Caine was meant to talk at the end.' She paused.

'Yeah . . .?'

'I was waiting for you to do your impression. Everyone else has.'

'Oh, not me,' Reece said blithely, then muttered through the side of his mouth, 'You're only supposed to blow the . . .'

She slapped his shoulder playfully. 'Anyway, cut a long story short, I've got the bloke's name and where he lives. Shoreditch it's called.'

'Who was the girl?'

'His bitch of a girlfriend.'

'And you beat her up?'

'Yeah.' She grinned. Why not take the credit?

'You're hard as nails, then?'

Was he laughing at her? Patronising her because it was obvious how titchy she was? They went back over Lambeth Bridge, so he could take her past the Tate and then on down the Embankment.

Reece asked, 'What about the bloke?'

'He's called Davey Kayman. Turns out he'd no intention of doing the course. All he did was have the posters printed up and get the money sent to a Post Office box. The cheques go to a business account in his girlfriend's name.'

'Sounds like he's a long firm merchant.'

'What's that?'

'Con man. There's a million tricks. One of the most popular is you take out a short-term let on a warehouse.'

'He lives in a warehouse.'

Reece paused, teacher-like, to see if she was going to keep on interrupting. When she didn't, he continued. 'You get hold of a few fake references and moody letterheads and set up as a distributor, say, in white goods. You order up a ton of stuff in bulk and pay upfront. That gives you confidence with the suppliers and on paper the business is totally legitimate. Then next time you double the orders so the suppliers think they've got a right result. Only this time it's on the knock. On credit. Course what you're doing is selling off the stuff on the QT. It takes the creditors a couple of months to latch on – but by then you've upped sticks. All there's left is an empty warehouse and a pile of bills.'

'Right.

'What this Davey's done is found an easy mooch.'

'Mooch?'

'Mark, punter, sucker.'

'He did it through the bloke at the Students' Union.'

'There you go then.'

'What can I do?'

'He's a fly-by-night, so he'll be a bastard to catch. And you've played your hand. He knows you're looking for him, so you can be sure he'll forget about using that PO box as the drop.'

'I still want me money back.'

'Good luck to you,' he replied, meaning, wise up, no chance.

She threw him a mean little frown, which he missed in the rear-view mirror, so she said, sarkily, 'Thanks for your support.'

'Any time.'

They crossed the river at Chelsea Bridge and parked at the gates to Battersea Park. He stepped out and came round to her door.

'Fancy a walk?'

She shrugged and followed him as they strolled towards the Peace Pagoda. Reece walked with easy strides, taking care not to outpace her. He had his jacket zipped up, hands in pockets, breath clouding in the freezing air. He was slender but muscly with it. Rox had noticed his large hands on the wheel. And that there were no rings on his fingers. Just checking.

'What about you, Reece? You from here?'

'Born and bred.'

'Whereabouts in London?'

'All over.'

Blood out of a stone. 'Come on – give.'

'Southwark. Near Southwark Park.'

'And is this your proper job?'

He seemed surprised. 'Do what?'

'Most minicab drivers are something else – like failed doctors or divorced blokes trying to dig up alimony. Y'know, your average rocket scientist.'

He shrugged. 'Not me. I work out of two offices – do nights out of the Elephant, which is why I was down your way tonight. Some days I do chauffeur work for a firm up the City. Directors, bankers, airport runs, that sort of thing.' He paused, considering his words. 'Mostly I do the nights. Easier to get around.'

She came closer. The moon peered out from between the high pillars of the Pagoda.

'So you admit the traffic's crap?'

'London wasn't built for it,' he said.

'You must get nothing but piss-heads in the cab?'

He put one foot up on the bottom step. She trotted up a couple more so as she could look at him face to face.

'It's mostly drunks, smack heads and nutters – especially weekends. There's fights, runners, puking up, blow-jobs, people trying to have a bunk-up. Not all at the same time, obviously.'

'Obviously.'

'Still – the money's good.'

'And you think I'm going to get back in that seat?'

He gave a thin smile. 'Oh, they don't get far with me. Anyone tries it on and they're out. Hard, if needs be.'

Despite the glibness, there was an edge of cruelty to his tone. Rox believed he was capable of backing up any threats he might care to make.

'Don't like talking much, do you?' she said.

'Come take a look at the bridge.'

They crossed the Pagoda steps and went to the towpath to look at the Albert Bridge. It was a hammock of light, the reflected water swaying and glistening underneath. On the opposite bank, a lazy necklace of headlights paraded past. Behind them, in the park, the shredded fingers of the trees stretched towards purple clouds pasted to an indigo sky. A breeze shook the branches. They applauded woodenly.

'Okay, it's not so bad at night, I'll give you that.'

Reece cupped his hands over his mouth and blew into them. 'Trick is to catch London unawares. If everyone's driving, then I walk. If they're hurrying then I hang about. Watch people and You'll see them looking at the pavement when the good stuff is above street level. Have a look sometime.'

'I will.'

'You got anyone?' he asked.

'Er, no, well, I did. I just broke up with my boyfriend. Four years.' Damn — why had she told him that? She tried to salvage the statement by tossing more words in after it. 'Of course it'll be the long drought now. Men scattering away like I'd clapped my hands in the middle of a flock of pigeons . . . Is it a "flock" — or is it a murder, like with crows?'

'You must be feeling shitty.'

'Yeah.'

'Like someone tore the heart out your body and tossed it in the river?'

'You been married, then?' she asked, guessing there was some resonance here.

'I had someone — a while ago.'

'What about now?'

He shook his head. 'Were you in love with him?'

'Lots. Never find anyone else like . . .' She realised how whiney she sounded. 'I'm sorry — I know I sound pathetic. Don't say anything.'

He said it anyway. 'Sure you will. Beautiful girl like you.'

She glowed inside. 'Midget girl like me.'

'I like short girls. And you got a lovely face. Why is it glasses make beautiful girls look even more beautiful?'

She didn't know what to say.

He looked embarrassed. 'Perhaps it's because they look vulnerable? Something about flawed beauty or . . . something clever like that?'

It came to her. Reece was shy. He was talking to cover it up, as she'd done moments ago. It was irresistible. Without another thought, she tilted up on tiptoes and kissed him. His lips were warm and his stubble cold and he responded quickly, throwing his arms around her and pulling her to him. Tingles shot through her as their mouths and bodies meshed. She darted her tongue into his mouth. He held her, clamped to his body, alternating deep, thrusting kisses with softer pecks as her lips opened and closed involuntarily. He pulled away and kissed her all the way down her white, naked neck. She let out a low moan and her breath plumed in the air. He returned with renewed vigour, kissing her hard until she felt it in her marrow. She reached up, holding his face, immersing herself in him.

Slowly, he subsided. She opened her eyes and when she failed to focus, realised that she must have taken off her glasses. There they were in her coat pocket. Reece held onto her, swaying, oblivious of the cold and the biting breeze. He plunged one more time, a deep roving kiss that sent fresh shudders through her. Then they were apart.

'You've not eaten tonight then?' she offered.

He grinned. Around them it was as silent as London gets, only the sound of a breeze and a low rumble, like a purr. Somewhere a car alarm was shattering sleep.

Reece said, 'Time I got you home.'

He took her mittened hand and led her back to the car, opening the passenger door as they reached the Mondeo.

'I'm to ride in front? I am honoured.'

'I want you where I can see you.'

After he'd moved his clipboard and the box he used for the night's takings, she slid inside and he fired up the heater and engine.

'Camberwell, wasn't it?'

They headed up Nine Elms Lane and he reached out a hand

and took one of hers in it. She played with it, feeling the calluses, the big knuckles.

They had to swerve to go under Vauxhall Cross and he took his hand back, but as they came round the Oval it strayed across and this time slunk over her thigh. She sat back as he stroked her, breathing through her nostrils, closing her eyes. When she next opened them his hand was gone.

'Whereabouts in Camberwell?'

'Oh, umm. Southampton Way. Halfway down.'

His voice was seasoned by the night. 'By the way. It's a "kit" of pigeons – when they're in flight.'

'Thanks. I wanted to know that.'

'Good.'

She remembered about Graham and Pete. 'Shit, I can't ask you in. I've not got a room.'

'Some other time.'

They came to her row of terraces and pulled up. Reece reached inside the glove compartment and held out his firm's card. 'Here you go. Get me anytime after nine on this.'

She took it. 'I ask for you, do I?'

He nodded.

'When do I call?'

'Whenever you like.'

'You want my number?'

He peered at the house through the windscreen. 'I know where you live.'

She reached for the handle. 'Well . . .'

'Hold up.'

He took her face in his hands, holding it as delicately as if it were bone china. He kissed her once, languidly; pulling away at around the time her blood reached boiling point. Rox determined not to skip when she got out.

'That'll be three quid.'

'Wha . . .?'

'New Cross – Camberwell.'

She looked for a smirk but there wasn't one forthcoming. 'All right. Fair do's.' She paid and clambered out.

'Well, er, see you then?'

'Ta daa.' Reece said.

The car drew off, tail-lights shrinking. Rox worried the key in the lock and crept up the sagging stairs, an idiot grin stapled to her face.

CHAPTER SEVEN

A Limo slid along Park Lane. In Hyde Park, sheets of silky mist hung above the grass, the trees rustled like paper and the late-night-traffic heartbeat had all but petered out. In the car, the driver was mute. Behind him, settled into marshmallow-soft creamy leather, were two passengers. The excitable one was on his mobile, jaws cranking out commands.

'It don't matter what the Sinatras are fetching, silly bollocks, you can't do more than a couple each time or the price'll come right down. That's standard economics.' Davey's face remained a solid sneer. 'No. And I *know* where you've gone and bollocksed it up because I *saw them!*' His voice became loud, the pitch teetering on rage. 'I did. I *seen* them.' Lips tightened on his teeth. 'Where d'you think? The one's you left round mine. You are giving me the right hump. Right, what you're gonna do first thing tomorrow is get some solvent and rub all them signatures off. I paid three notes apiece for them eight by tens and I'm bollocksed if I'm gonna toss them out . . . wasn't *me* who put "Diana, nineteen-fucking-ninety-*eight*" on 'em, was it?'

Shaking the mobile dead, he prodded the aerial into his companion's gut. 'You believe that prat?'

Latimer winced. 'Who?'

'Jonno. He was supposed to be hoiking these autographs round the trade fairs and now he says he can't even shift them. I had assumed he knew when Di died.' He slapped his palms on his thighs. 'But of course I'm the mug 'cause I never checked his handiwork. You know what? He can't even fucking spell. We've got Kennedy with one "n", John Wayne, W-A-I-N, and his attempt at David Duchovny is a JOKE!'

'You want to look out for a dyslexic autograph collector.'

Davey's obsidian eyes glowed. He pinched his nostrils with his fingertips, produced a hand mirror and bent to the task of frosting his nasal passages. Beside him, Simon Latimer, twenty-eight and going on forty, sat marinating in sweat after their marathon Mayfair meal. He wiped a hand over his thinning crown, swiping it round to liberate his junior jowls from his collar. He shuffled in his seat, looking to release a gust trapped deep in his bowels.

The Edgware Road jogged past. The Techno Gods of Panasonic and Sony stayed safe behind their metal veils. There was the strange graffiti of Arabic scrawled in neon or on glass. Poultry in the late-night chicken outlet crowed dubious Southern States provenance. Inevitably, there was the drunks' pharmacy, kebab and dagger on grimy yellow, the midnight cure-all.

'Davey? This would be a good time to talk about the loan?'

He came up clawing air, neck muscles straining, eyes ablaze. 'What loan?' He sneezed vociferously, spittle spraying.

'*Gesundheit*. You know what loan.'

Davey turned lazily. There was no real reason to come the innocent. 'I'm disappointed in you Si. You keep on at me about this any longer and it's no. No I won't square it with you.'

'But . . .'

'I've always seen you right, haven't I? Even back in school. Especially back in school.'

'I've got running costs at the Cab Company. The partners are screaming.'

Davey warmed this over. 'What you talking about, running

costs? You make a fortune out of that firm. Chauffeur end's gold dust.'

The driver moved imperceptibly. It was down to Latimer to speak up for his workforce.

'The City's cutting back . . . and when the big orders do come in it's chaos. When there's some do at the Guildhall, we have to scramble drivers and the result is we lose all our regular work. There are cowboys everywhere. And' – a helpless shrug – 'the recession's coming, I'm telling you.'

'Bollocks. The drivers are creaming you, taking on private jobs or under-declaring the work. You want to bung up the weekly rental. No, tell you what – get in a couple of mates to pose as punters. Ask the drivers if they'll work for cash? Non-account work. Soon flush 'em out.'

The Limo swerved, narrowly missing a traffic island.

Davey got that all right. He stared hard at the back of the driver's neck.

'Yeah – like I give a toss about what you think?'

Simon made calming motions with his fat little hands, then said wearily. 'So, about the money?'

Before the evening got stale, Latimer had tried out the scratched record technique he'd seen on the consumer pro-grammes. Problem was, they weren't up against Davey Kayman: a lizard in a suit who'd turned the winkling of funds out of people into a master craft. Folding lent to him stayed lent and once those hands had a grip on your nest egg they closed up on it like talons. He'd won, you'd lost. Mug. Poodle. Sucker. That was you, boy. Furthermore, when he wasn't talking up a blizzard, Davey had the knack of making his creditors feel guilty, grubby, beholden to him. He had a fine line in feigned surprise and outrage, like everyone was holding this fiscal *grudge* against him. And all this tallying it up, spelling it out like it was the Riot Act? Bollocks to that. I mean, if there still *is* a debt, then whose job is it to remember the amount? Not mine, old son. Don't give me the hump. As a matter of course Davey disputed any and all amounts with such vehemence that the lender would begin to question in his own mind the sum involved.

Interest?

Penalty payments?

Not on the cards.

The car coursed along the furred artery of the Finchley Road and hunched into the back-street capillaries, the driver looking for speed humps in the hope of braining the mouthy git in the back.

'What do you reckon to this?'

Davey delved into the deep canvas bag at his feet. There was a chink and an aged wine bottle appeared in his hands. The liquid was black through the emerald glass of the bottle.

Simon's lips formed a perfect oval. 'Where did you . . .? You didn't lift that from the restaurant?'

'Nah.'

'Well that's . . .'

'From the cellar – when he was showing me around.'

'B-but, we spent the evening discussing partnership with these people. You said you'd be in touch with his lawyers.'

That grin, the lips stretched over the teeth. 'I did tell him that, didn't I?'

'What you want to go pinch a bottle of his wine for?'

Davey snapped his fingers like a pair of castanets. 'Keep up, will you?'

Simon thought about it. 'You've . . . no intention of going into business with him? You only wanted the claret.'

'Burgundy,' answered Davey, displaying the bottle as if it were his first-born. He read out the label in a French accent that was a car crash of aspirated vowels and glottal stops. 'Société civile du Domaine de la Romanee-Conti – that's the most valuable piece of dirt in Europe, that is. The vineyard's a

Grand Cru and it's got its own Appellation Controlée. Guess how much?'

'No idea.'

'This is worth nine large.'

Simon let out a low whistle. 'When did you learn all about wine?'

'You know me. I'll mug up anything in a week.'

And forget it the week after, thought Simon.

'While you was gassing on about overheads, I was sussing out the cellar. Locked tighter than a virgin's fanny that place – except we was given the grand tour.'

'But they'll notice it's missing?'

'Eventually. So? Can't pin it on me.'

The car slowed to a halt. Davey hadn't told his friend any more about his plans for the wine, but somehow Simon didn't think it would involve its consumption.

Clambering out with all the ease of a manacled suspect, Latimer told the driver to stick a tenner for himself on the docket and hauled his bloated frame off towards his apartment in the Mansion block.

'Shoreditch,' said Davey, without glancing back.

After a silent, albeit bumpy ride, Davey dismissed the driver and let himself into the warehouse complex. Shouldering his bag, he rammed the lift doors shut and watched the cables unfurl like snakes as he sank to the basement. The light down here was the colour of tallow and the tiled space had the tang of chemical solvents and aged school corridors. The lift shuddered to a halt. He tore open the gates and, spinning his keys gunslinger style, fitted them into the solid door. Once inside, his hand crept around for the switch.

'Daveeyyy.'

And she was on him, tearing at his clothes, pulling his suit jacket off his shoulders.

'Charlie. Mind the bag.'

'You got it?'

'Mnnn.'

Her mouth clamped on his and sucked greedily. Her lips, under smeared crimson, were chapped and cracked. 'Fuck now.'

'Bit late—' was all he managed to say as she slid down his chest and unzipped him. She gobbled ferociously, salivating and sucking and pulling him backwards, her nails pressed into his buttocks. Davey slid to the hard wood floor.

'Can't you wait?'

'Been waiting all night.'

She threw herself astride him, her long braided hair chopping up her face. She wore flannel trousers and nothing on top but a pair of men's braces. Under them, on the small hillocks of her breasts, her nipples were erect; one pierced, both raw from chafing against the straps. Her skinny arms were flecked with blood, a game of lacerating noughts and crosses with no winner.

'What you done to yourself now?'

'I was bored.'

'You ain't a bleeding pin cushion.'

She glowered at him. 'Some northern tart was here today, looking for you.'

There was a spasm in his cheek, a kind of tic beneath the skin. 'Oh yeah? Looker?'

'Short-arse.'

'I'll have the both of you then.'

'Piss off.'

'What'd she want?'

Charlie pouted. She smelled of tobacco and draw and the alcohol bite of cheap knocked-off perfume. 'You gonna screw me or what?'

'Dunno.'

Her bloodshot eyes were a maelstrom. She clamped her haunches to him, grinding her bony hips, writhing, full of drugs and fury. The dreadlocks fell across his face, covering his head like a photographer's shawl. She squeaked breathlessly in his ear.

'Fu-uck me hard. Ffff me to the bone. Hurt me, babe.'

He rolled his eyes. 'Fuck's sake, Charlie. I come home from work to this?'

He threw her off with a grunt and she rolled noisily against the wainscoting, hitting it face on. Davey clambered to his feet, brushing off as he strode over to the kitchen area.

Charlie touched her lip. It was bleeding. She bit down hard so the blood gelled and beaded and dribbled down her chin. She grazed a hand across her neck, down over the nub-like promontories of her clavicles.

Davey was hunting about in the kitchen drawers, tossing things into the mess on the floor.

'What you after?'

He turned. She stood smiling dreamily, blood on her lips and face and dabbed about her breasts and neck.

'Yeah, yeah. Mrs Dracula.' He said impatiently. 'Come on, Charlie – where's the drugs?'

She released a deep scattergun chortle. 'Said I was bored. I've had 'em all.'

He slapped her properly this time.

'You're dysfunctional, you are. You wanna talk to someone.'

Charlie lay where she fell, letting the tears mix with the dust and the dirt.

'Reece been in?'

Half twelve and a leaden sky was pressing down over the City. Archie Peacock rolled into the bullpen of the Finsbury Cab office and stuck his head through the hatch. The controller's lair was panelled in wood-grain Formica gone the colour of tea-stain. The bin overflowed with cans and burger bags: on the rear wall, the veined map of London was jabbed with pinpricks, finger-smeared from myriad searches for that holiest of holies, the quick route. The driver's dockets were fanned out like a hand of poker.

'He's getting coffee.' The controller was rheumy-eyed, his tongue roiling in his mouth as he massaged his lower gums. The radio begged his attention.

Archie looked out at the rectangle of pavement, reflexively checking for wardens.

'You got anything for us, Archie?'

'Picking up as it goes.' Slithering out a notepad, Archie flipped through the tiny pencilled pages. 'Hyundai. Lantra. Four-door. T reg.'

The controller tapped a biro on the desk. 'Who's got that? Tango Three? Ishmael? Could be Ajay. Yeah. Golf Two Five. Want me to give him a shout?'

'Yeah. Go on.'

He radioed.

'Someone actually wants that piece of shit back,' continued Arch. 'Come down the lot asking for it. Got the right hump when we said we couldn't find it. Steve had to promise it back by the end of the day, steam-cleaned. Punter gave us two hundred notes upfront. Sweet as.'

A voice came from over his shoulder. 'That's law-abiding citizens for you.' Reece was wearing his black leather jacket with a fresh shirt, his stubble salt and pepper. He was mothering a take-away coffee.

Archie cracked a grin. 'All right, Reece?'

'Arch.'

Archie lead him outside with his eyes. Reece levered open the drink carton and blew on the froth. Archie leaned against the wall.

'Message from Tel Peterson. We're all clear on the airport run for now.'

Reece nodded.

'You want the rest of your cut?'

'Put it towards my favourite charity.'

'Do what?'

'Bill and Tel do a lot of work for kids, don't they?'

Archie shrugged. 'That Kraut you brought in was flush.'

Reece looked away at the traffic. 'You ever hear of a bloke called Kayman? Con merchant round Shoreditch way?'

'Goblin?'

'By the sounds of it. Small-time.'

Archie's face remained as solid as the brick behind him. 'Nah.'

Reece said, 'Let us know if you do.'

'He stitch you up?'

'No, it's a favour.'

Reece chugged caffeine. He was dog-tired, having gotten only two hours' sleep with the kids in the flat below OD-ing on Saturday morning TV. He had gone down to the gym for a while in the hope he could tire himself out enough to sleep, but it hadn't worked. Never mind, Sunday tomorrow. He'd kip in all day.

The wind ruffled Archie's turn-ups. He could never get jeans that were short enough on the leg. 'S'pose you're off down the match?' he asked.

Odd in the way he asked it, like the weak kid at school who tried to drum up mates by trying to convince you you were as pathetic as he was.

Reece said. 'Too knackered, mate.'

Archie measured his next question. 'Don't s'pose you fancy coming down the Nash?'

'Whose ground's that?'

'National Gallery. I got to go down there.'

'Oh yeah?'

'Only, I . . . ain't never been in there before.'

Reece said, 'You know there's a dress code.'

'What? Like in pubs? No work-clothes or trainers?'

'That's it. You gotta wear a cravat. Or a beret – like Frank Spencer.'

Archie tumbled it. 'Toe-rag.'

'What you going there for?'

'It ain't nothing noncy. I got to check out this Rembrandt geezer.'

'What for?'

Archie balanced the books with a testosterone stare. 'Business.'

Coming up to last orders in the Railway Tavern. Archie sat in the collapsed lung of a velvet banquette avoiding his family, who were at home on a triple video binge: *Dirty Dancing* (for Shirley, later), *Armageddon* and *Godzilla*. Shirl had put up a fight over the ratings on the last two but Arch jumped to Darren's defence when he claimed that a 12 meant a 15. She'd pointed out that Darren was seven and Ronan only three, but Arch argued that the boys would both be asleep by the end. Darren said it didn't matter anyway because CGI monsters weren't scary (he'd gone off The Phantom Menace). The argument had been curtailed by the scrabble for the last decent films in the Peckham branch of Blockbuster.

Archie was reading, lips moving, finger tracing the words, pint of John Smith's in front of him.

'All white?'

Steve was in his Saturday best; white cotton shirt and denim waistcoat (JPS snug in the left-hand pocket), belt with a big buckle, jeans worn over black Cuban-heeled cowboy boots. His aftershave could have stunned a horse. His hair was gelled back; his arm adornment a drunken woman in a sparkling top she'd outgrown by five years and two breast sizes.

Archie grunted acknowledgement.

'Listen, boy. Me and . . .' a pause as Steve realised he had no idea of the woman's name, '. . . her, are off in a bit.'

Archie stared in disbelief at the woman, who lurched forwards and grabbed hold of the back of a chair so tightly that her knuckles went bone white. Her eyes were rolled up in a doll's face — an elderly doll's face at that.

'Looks like she's a bit off now.'

Steve's cheek creased. He wasn't good with the comebacks. Grabbing Archie's book off him, he held it high above his head. 'Whatsis you're reading anyway?'

Archie reached for it. 'Give us it here.'

Steve stepped away, turning his back on him, scrutinising the cover. 'The Ff . . . The fff . . . fido guide to . . .?'

Archie was behind him, short arms clawing the air, commencing the pub-fight tango. '*Phaidon Guide to the Life and Works of Rembrandt Van Rijn.*'

'Any pictures?'

'Gi's it here.' This time Archie barked it with enough menace to squeeze a grumble out of the older regulars.

Steve handed it over. Archie settled back into his seat and smoothed the cover. The blurb claimed it was illustrated with sixty-four colour plates. Of this, he was glad. It made the reading chore easier.

The woman fell against Steve's hip. He ignored her and sparked up a JPS so he could think.

'That's the bloke you got up in the lounge, innit?'

Archie took a deep chug of his beer. 'Yers.'

'You fancy borrowing it me for a while? The painting?'

'What for? You don't know fuck-all about Art.'

'Impress the birds.'

His latest girlfriend negated this point by promptly slumping to the floor. After she'd been picked up and poured onto a chair, Steve budged Archie up along the seat. The landlord bleated on about Last Orders having come and gone and homes to go to and that the doors were closing. Archie spoke quietly, respectful of the funereal procession of passing punters.

'You sticking around for stay-backs?'

Steve jabbed his cigarette in the woman's general direction. 'Nah. Taking her back to mine.'

'Better off with a coma patient from Guy's, intcha?'

Steve's laugh sounded like rattlesnakes were loose in his chest. 'Path of least resistance, old son. I'll have her up the Gary. So you gonna lend us that painting?'

'Nah.'

'Why not?'

'Just not.'

'Ain't got other plans for it, have you?'

'No.'

'Only I'm due two and a half mill once you flog it.'

Archie stared at the gleaming prow of the bar. 'I ain't giving it you. You'll only take it down the Roman Road like it was the usual hooky gear.'

Steve, teeth bared and mouth grimacing, flung his arm around Archie's neck and squeezed until his face changed colour and his nostrils chugged out the last of the air in his lungs. Archie's hands flailed for his glass, but his fingers knocked it to the floor.

'Listen, you're my best mate all white, but I want to see my cut. Time you got another buyer lined up.'

Archie rasped thinly and Steve Lamb released him. He funnelled air into his lungs, rubbed his hands around his neck, signalled for a fresh pint.

'Made your point,' he said, glowering.

Steve plucked his fag from the ashtray and sucked down the smoke as if nothing had happened. 'So how long's it gonna take – to find a new buyer?'

Arch remained deadpan. 'No idea, mate.'

CHAPTER EIGHT

'. . . Al, it was brilliant. Totally sexy.'

'What? A snog in the middle of the night from a chuffing *minicab* driver?'

'But he's normal, well, a bit weird, bit quiet – but dead good-looking.'

'And you trapped off just like that?'

She elongated the vowel. 'No-oh. He drove me all over London first.'

'Oh, fine. And what d'you go make the first move for? Breaking the rules, that is.'

Rox was delighted to share in her success. 'I don't know. S'pose I felt reckless. It was scary at first, but after I was with him for a bit I sort of felt *comfortable*, like he'd not do anything to hurt me.'

'Where've I heard *that* one before?'

She nibbled at her lower lip. 'Mark's not exactly grieving over me, is he?'

Ally let the pause hang. She'd given in to peer group pressure and had gone to the Garage on Saturday night. Mark was there with Corinne and, yes, they were pretending that Rox had never existed. Ally said nothing to them, but bitched loudly all night behind their backs. She was still stinging from this minor betrayal and hoped Rox wouldn't ask about them this time. She kept it cheery.

'Nothing like the next one for getting you over the last, that's what I say.'

'Or in your case, the last and the next one at the same time.'

'Watch it, you.'

'Kidding, Al.'

'Did he take your number? Are you seeing him again?'

Her turn to hold back. It was Sunday morning and lambent light was bleeding through the threadbare curtains. Rox was burrowed down by the skirting, phone cupped to her ear, finger in the other trying to block out Fatboy Slim, which Pete was blasting out at top volume. She'd been unable to reach Ally on Saturday as she wasn't allowed to take calls at MegaPhones, despite it being a mobile phone franchise (minimum wage didn't mean maximum privileges). Still elated, and with her flatmates dead to the world, Rox had celebrated by going up to Oxford Circus and buying herself a new top.

Rox said, 'I've got his number, so it's up to me when I call him.'

'Ooh, how terribly modern and very *London* of you.'

'Thought I'd wait a bit. Especially since he's on nights. Or I could call and have him delivered here.'

'What?'

'He gave me his work number.'

'He gave you the number of the cab company?'

She hesitated. 'Is that not normal?

'Rox – what do you actually *know* about this bloke?'

She blustered and evaded the question, saying that everybody was a closed book at first, but in her heart she knew her dossier on him was empty. All she knew was he came from Southwark Park, which sounded nice. Perhaps she'd go there sometime, or Reece might even take her? The edifice of their night together began to crumble and fragment. She knew what would happen when she called him up. Some leery controller would take the message and when Reece came in, they'd give him all the oi-oi shout, and Reece would laugh and tell them about this bird he

82

kissed — no shagged, screwed, shafted, nailed to the ground. Where? Only the Peace Pagoda, gor blimey, guvnor. She raked a hand through her hair. She was losing it again.

'So what's to do about the detective work?'

She snapped back into focus.

'I'm going back. Thought I'd try and get the exact address.'

It was raining again when she left and she had reached East Street market by the time a bus came. It wasn't worth catching, so she carried on, cursing her big broken shoes. She sank down in the tiled walkway at the Elephant, holding her breath against the reek of pulped newspaper, stale burgers and urine: always that stench in these dank concrete furrows.

She entered the station and waited for the lift. Stupid cow, she thought, letting herself think Reece was interested . . . and what sort of a name is Reece, anyway? I'm not getting hurt again. Sod him. I'll deal with this Davey bloke myself. Don't need anyone.

In the Tube, the dark window distorted her features and Rox decided she must be having a bad-hair life. After a wash it had come out as that wispy thatch again, neither short nor long enough to be manageable, and the roots showing through. Horrible — like an evacuee from a third-rate teen girl band. She peered at her small face lost in her big coat and thought of the mangy tube mice that scuttled about under the rails.

At City Road, she joined the queue of penitents at the hole in the wall. She begged a hundred and set off walking for Shoreditch. She took up the same position at the corner of Cotton's Gardens. The rain had ceased but it was freezing and a swollen belly of cloud were grazing the skyscrapers over in Bishopsgate. She waited ten minutes before a profusely sweating, middle-aged man in a tracksuit jogged past her and loped inside the building.

Why not? she thought.

He left one of the red doors ajar so she followed him in. He'd jogged up the stairs, but the lift cage was rising. Inside was Charlie Ribbons, looking bruised and sleepy even though it was past midday. Behind her, scythed by shadows and the metal grid of the wire cage, was a tall man. He wore black trousers, a V-neck sweater, and a blazer-cut leather jacket. As he worked the lift doors open, her heart began to hammer. He was olive-skinned and had black curly hair. His mouth was harsh, the lips brutish, the nose long and proud. His eyes were the thing, deep set and glittering darkly, they appeared inert as if light did not affect them. Releasing a rattle from the gates, he turned sideways: Rox thought of a Roman bust, of a taller, broader Caesar at the Games. Judging by his sneer, the Emperor would be in thumb's-down mode. His arms were powerful, his chest broad, the legs slim.

'Hello again,' Rox said cheerfully to Charlie.

'Piss off.'

'Fine. And you?'

'That's the bitch who was snooping about,' said Charlie.

The man gazed down and gave her a 24-karat grin. 'We're going for breakfast. You wanna come?'

Without giving her time to answer, he went outside. Charlie pushed past her and Rox followed, struggling to keep up as they turned the corner and charged up Kingsland Road. She kept alongside, not knowing what to say or where to start. Charlie clung to him, still in her bobbled string coat, but now in a patterned mini-dress with black tights and scuffed boots, their heels eroded to the bone.

'You are Davey Kayman, aren't you?' Rox offered.

'Who wants to know?' he laughed. His accent was broad Cockney.

'I do.'

'And who're you then?'

'Rox Matheson. A friend of mine lost her money on that Acting weekend you never put on in Manchester. Actually it was my money. I'd lent it to her.'

84

'And?'

'I want it back. All three hundred and fifty quid.'

He and Charlie exchanged an amused glance.

They came to a café, whose plate glass window was blurred by a teary fug of condensation. From the outside it looked like a typical greasy spoon, but when Rox followed them in she saw it had undergone radical surgery. The tables were bleached wood and the chairs like ones she remembered from school. The floor was checkerboard linoleum but blemish-free, not a cigarette scar nor age-spotted blob of blackened gum on the mopped surface. In plastic tubs in the chiller display unit, the standard sandwich fillers of cheese, ham and egg had been supplanted by gua-camole, bacon bits, the livid yellow of coronation chicken.

The man ignored the elaborate hand-written menu on the blackboard and ordered full English breakfasts for himself and Charlie. Rox asked for a tea and joined them at their table. He drew a line in the fogged-up window. It made a wet gash and the condensation tears chased one another towards the lower sill.

'I know you must be him, otherwise you'd have denied it,' said Rox.

Charlie looked like she wanted to hit her.

'You've got no idea who I am,' he said, coldly.

'I'll sit here till you tell me. Now, I've seen the Fraud Squad and they know all about you, so why not cough up the money you owe me and we'll say no more about it – right?'

A smile played on the man's lips as he studied her. 'You got balls, I'll give you that.' A muscle in his cheek flickered and went away. 'But you don't come here making accusations on people until you know what you're talking about. You got no evidence and no back-up far as I can see.'

Rox turned to Charlie. 'She had the letters . . .'

He overrode her. 'That's mistake number two. I don't see any filth here – you ain't produced a summons or nothing. Now, I know the law in these situations. Studied it, right? Criminal and civil. This is slander and I can have you for this.'

Rox was about to defend herself when the breakfasts arrived. There was silence as the pair attacked their food. Charlie in particular shovelled it down, her dreadlocks forming a curtain around the plate.

Rox said, 'I should've guessed you were a recovering bulimic.'

'Piss off.'

'Try and help and they throw it back in your face.'

Charlie sneered at her, a pantomime Rock God kind of snarl that wouldn't fool anyone beyond the fourth year.

Rox turned her attention back to the man. He was what her mam would've called 'roguishly handsome' – but then she rarely left Oldham, read *New Woman* and thought the same of the milkman. He stared back, scrutinising her. Rox wasn't bothered. She was used to serving behind a bar and had developed the knack of ignoring the male gaze when it suited her.

'You *are* Davey Kayman, aren't you?'

He wiped a hunk of bread around his plate, gathering egg yolk. He stuffed it into his mouth and held out his other hand to her. Rox shook it awkwardly.

'So, you got a problem?' Davey asked.

'I told you.'

'Down here for long?'

'Until I get my money back.'

'Where you staying?'

'None of your business.'

'Not a hotel, then?'

'With friends, if you *must* know. Look, I want the money.'

'You working?'

'Not at the moment. Look—'

'What do you do?'

'Work in a bar/restaurant. Now, are you going to pay me?'

His eyes came alive. 'Yeah, all right. Fair do's. I don't carry that much folding on me, so You'll have to come back later.'

She furrowed her brow behind her glasses. This was both good and bad. 'When later? – and how do I know You'll let me in?'

He rolled his eyes.

'Which flat's yours then?'

'Basement.'

Charlie looked over in surprise.

'And you come alone, or you don't get in,' Davey added.

'W-when?'

'Couple of hours, give us time to get some dosh. Say four o'clock?'

Rox nodded. This was so unexpected that all she could do was go along with it. And if he didn't let her in she'd . . . well she'd call Reece and ask him what to do next. If he did? Was it worth the risk? It was, after all, why she was here. She had the urge to get away, to be back out on the street where she could pace and think. She pushed her cup aside and got to her feet.

'All right.'

'I'm not paying for your tea and all,' he said, sarcastically.

Rox went to the counter. Davey came with her and paid for the breakfasts with a new scarlet fifty-pound note. Rox felt embarrassed about the small bundle of notes curled up in her tiny purse.

'Later then?' Davey said, hoovering up his change.

The lift sank to the basement and Rox had an attack of the jitters. She had been walking the streets for close on two hours, fretting and thinking about what she'd do when and if he gave her the money. In terms of her personal safety, she reasoned that there were plenty of people in the warehouses, so if anything happened she'd scream the place down. She tugged the lift doors apart and saw a short corridor. There was only one solid blue door, with a spy-hole at the centre. She was about to knock when it flew open and Davey ushered her inside.

'Take your coat?'

No sign of Charlie Ribbons. Davey's sweater sleeves were rolled up, displaying hairy forearms. The place had a new smell, all fresh paint, putty and mastic. He led her though into the living area, which was combined with the kitchen. It was hard to tell the original function of this space but it had probably been a workshop. Running along the length of the outer wall were a series of small square paned windows; each frame attached to a heavy iron ratchet. Through the glass she made out the cobbled courtyard at eye level. Behind her, white partition walls divided up the space. The floor was shiny hardwood, the ceiling dotted with twinkling halogen lights. Off to her left, the kitchen area had a hob, fridge and twin sinks (expensive by the looks of them) and the finger-shaped breakfast bar jutted out like a jetty. Its surface was covered in takeaway containers, dirty crockery, overflowing ashtrays.

The rest of the room was also a tip. Piled-up pizza boxes, old newspapers, electronic equipment, flyers, rolled-up posters: *the* posters. Also, a computer nestling in blocks of polystyrene, keypads in bubble-wrap, bundled-up boxes of perfume and a free standing clothes frame on which hung twenty or so jackets in gossamer film. Dotted about like silver molehills were several chrome kettles, their umbilical electrical cords drooping loose and plugless. The bedroom door was open: inside was a mattress, the epicentre of a jetsam of discarded clothes, shoes, books and encrusted cereal bowls, their spoons covered in skeins of stale milk.

'Does Fagin know you've got all his stuff, then?'

'Funny,' Davey remarked, impassively.

'No one could live in this.'

He went to the sink and pulled out two cups, examining the buttons of hard black coffee welded to the bottom. 'Coffee?'

'If you clean out them cups.'

He made a half-hearted attempt to rinse them, filled a kettle, then opened the fridge.

'Where's my money?'

Davey shot her a pained glance, but she realised this was because he'd just smelled the carton of milk in his hand.

'Have to be black. The milk's off.'

'Whatever. About the money . . .'

'Gawd, you're as bad as Simon Latimer, you are.'

She looked at him blankly.

'Said you're in the catering trade?'

'I was a manageress in a bar restaurant.'

'Know much about wine?'

'I know the good stuff's not called *maison*.'

Rox thought of her and Mark in the Garage, smiling and kissing about a hundred years ago. She erased the memory like wiping an Etch-a-Sketch.

Davey grinned at her and the points of his canines grazed his lower lip. 'You might be able to help me out, as it goes. And make a bit of dosh for yourself.'

'I'll settle for what I'm owed.'

The kettle shuddered on its plastic plinth. Rox folded her arms, then straightened her glasses and attempted to wipe her hair away from her face. Davey stopped the near-epileptic kettle with a flick of his finger. Ignoring it, he reached under the counter of the breakfast bar and pulled out two aged bottles of wine. He revolved them so that the labels faced her, and caressed their stubby glass necks.

'You'd know a good one if you tried it though, wouldn't you?'

'Probably.'

Davey dug out a half-pint and a pint glass from the filthy sink and found a metal corkscrew, which he rattled in his hand. 'I've got a bottle of 1990 Domaine de la Romanee-Conti. A Grand Cru from one of the finest vineyards in the world,' he said, by rote. 'But I've also got another bottle.'

'Of?'

'Plonk. I've had the label faked up. Look the same these two, don't they? See the code and the number on it? They do that 'cos the output of the vineyard is so small. Fancy having a guess as to which one's the business?'

True, the bottles were old, the labels posh. 'No, I don't.'

'Fifty says you can't tell the difference.'

'Look, give me what you owe me and I'll go.'

Ignoring her, Davey went to a coffee table. From a mess of papers, he pulled out a glossy brochure. He flipped it open, showing her the double-page spread. 'This is Corney & Barrow's catalogue. They're big-time City of London vintners. You probably heard of them.'

She said she had, although she hadn't.

'This mob are the only UK agents for this stuff. The wine is worth nine thousand quid a bottle.'

Rox studied the picture, then glanced up. The bottles appeared to be identical in every detail.

'Like I said, one of them is as dodgy as a three-pound coin. My problem is I know which is the hooky one. So does Charlie. I need an independent adjudicator. Someone who knows their booze.'

'Get a wino off the street.'

He raised his eyebrows. They were thin with a noticeable dent where they curved to the temples. 'See here, Rox, you've done a good job tracking me down. I don't usually leave a trail, so I'm impressed. Now, you can have your money any time you want, but why not give it a go? I'll give you an extra pony if you're right.'

'What?'

'Fifty notes. Hang on.' Davey reached into his jeans pocket and extracted a wad. He peeled off twenties and fifties until he came to three hundred and forty. 'Got a tenner on you?'

She brought out her purse and unfurled the tight-packed notes. Four twenties, a ten and change. She handed over the ten and he gave her a twenty in return. He put the stack of notes on the counter, then topped it with another fifty-pound note.

'That's yours if you can guess the pikey one.'

She reached out for the money. 'No, I'd . . .'

Davey slapped his hand flat over the money. 'Go on. No harm done.'

She sighed and pointed at the left-hand bottle. 'I think it's that one.'

He plunged the corkscrew into the aged cork, puncturing it and bringing it out with a proficient pop. Gripping the bottle, he poured a sloppy measure into each of the grimy glasses.

'Go on, taste it.'

Pure confidence, she thought. And to risk that kind of money? She took the glass. Inside it, the wine was the colour of molasses, its bouquet a blend of fruit and musk. She raised it slowly, but when the wine kissed her mouth she took a defiant draught. Her lips puckered like the skin on a three-day-old balloon.

'Piss-poor plonk,' she said.

Davey held out the small bundle to her. As she was about to take it, he drifted away, the money still in his hand.

'Hold up—' He dipped below the counter once more and added two more bottles to the originals, shuffling them as if playing find the lady on a street corner. 'Right. You're fifty notes up. Double or quits. It's one in three now. I'll lay four hundred against yours you can't spot the real one.'

Nervously, Rox took a sip of the wine. Despite the taste, it warmed her throat and crawled into her stomach. 'No, look. Just give us the money.'

Davey began counting out another four hundred pounds on top. 'See, I have to know my copy's convincing and I'll risk losing a few centuries to prove it. Odds are in your favour.'

A minute later, Rox was knocking back the drink with eight hundred pounds fanned in front of her. Davey's smile had gone, replaced by a scowl. He topped up her glass, mixing the cheap wines together.

'How did you know which one it was?' he asked.

'I'm a good guesser.'

'Ain't gonna risk the last one.'

'What last one?'

'You'll have to look away.'

She did so. There was a clinking of bottles. Now there were five in all, including the two opened ones. One was a dustier specimen. A tingle went through her.

'I'll guess the real one,' she said. Not the dusty bottle, which looked as fake as spray-on snow, but the one Davey had put behind it. It was somehow right. She couldn't tell why, but it seemed like quality.

'Eff off. You've taken me for nearly a monkey already.'

She brought out her eighty pounds and the twenty Davey had given her. 'That's nine hundred. You going to match it?'

He seemed astounded. 'I was right about you. You get this and I'm down nine big ones on the wine and all. No, I can't do it.'

'Chicken.'

'No can do.'

'Bock bock.'

He waved a hand. 'Aww, go on then.'

She pointed to the bottle, glowing with pride.

This time Davey took an age in opening it, struggling with the cork, which seemed to be crumbling. He poured out two fresh ones and this time Rox tasted nectar in the dirty pint glass.

She beamed. 'There you go. Another nine hundred pound, please.'

Davey levered open the second of the three remaining bottles. 'Try this.'

A shiver went through her as she sipped the contents of the second bottle. 'It's the same. So . . . so you've opened up eighteen grand's worth of wine to prove . . . what?'

He turned shark. 'You got it wrong, *Roxy*,' he spat. 'None of them are real. I got that stashed away as it's got to be kept at the right temperature. All you've been drinking is cheap Burgundies. What we're doing here is comparing my forger's last three goes at the label. That's it. You lose.'

'Then the bet's off. If there was no real one in the first place, then—'

'Bollocks. You was happy enough to piss around with *my* money.' With that, he whisked back the pile and clamped his hand tight round her neck, his strong fingers crawling up and digging into her jaw and cheeks. She was unable to cry out and the pain was excruciating.

'You think I'd waste that kind of folding on you, you silly little cunt? You come here to *my home* demanding I give you some kind of *refund. Caveat emptor*, love. Let the buyer beware.'

He propelled her towards the door and thrust his face up close to hers, his fingers kneading her skin, tightening their grip. His scorpion pinch was so hard that she welled up with tears. His teeth were clenched, nostrils flared. 'You fucking *amateur.*'

He punched her then, hard, in the stomach and the air was sucked out of her. Before she knew it the door was slammed shut and she was in a heap on the cold concrete floor. She failed to keep her face together. Her lip went and hot tears drowned her eyes. But what if he came out? Did her more damage? Adrenaline got her to her feet then helped her to belt up the stairs and burst out of the building.

The sky was black as ink. She found a dark place deep in the cul-de-sac. Cradling her face in her hands, she slid down on her haunches. What a naïve, stupid fool! she thought. He'd strung her along like a sucker. Not only had she not got her money, but she'd lost another ninety pounds. It was a perfect and terrible humiliation. She was hurting and alone and . . . and how could she possibly tell anyone about how daft she'd been? She wasn't surprised that everyone kept hitting her: in fact she fancied joining in. She crouched there for a long time, scriked up and sad, miserable as a Monday, feeling as crap as Christmas.

CHAPTER NINE

Reece was suited and booted and driving a roller he had collected off Archie in EC1. The job had come out of the Finsbury cab office, extra work, driving his boss around for the day. It wasn't strenuous. The traffic was manageable and all the hanging about had racked up a decent wedge of waiting time. They had begun at Latimer's place, then visited his bank in Finchley. Afterwards, it was over to Stoke Newington and a wait in WC2 before swinging south of the river. Latimer went to the cab office under the arches at the Elephant, then Reece brought him back up over Southwark Bridge. Latimer wasn't up for small talk. His cellular kept mewling and demanding he pet it to silence. Reece had no use for a mobile, believing they only brought you grief and that the radiation fried your brains – which was why you kept forgetting where you were and had to announce it in the street. Also, he didn't know enough people to make owning one worthwhile.

Latimer's phone went off again outside the Islington Business Centre and he asked Reece to head down the Essex road. It was twilight and teeming with rain, pavements and puddles shimmering like fish-scales in the neon. The traffic had become bogged down, soot-sodden, nightmare, murder. On the corner of New North Road, a wet man in a black coat hailed them and clambered in.

'I wanted you here ten minutes ago,' he growled.

'You think accounts take care of themselves?' replied Latimer, as he made space among the files and spreadsheets scattered over the seat.

'What's all this?'

'Income predictions. I've got cash problems. I told you.'

His companion sighed and reached for his wallet. 'Then it's your lucky day.' Producing five twenty-pound notes, he tucked them into Simon's breast pocket. Latimer sniffed the money, as if it were a fragrant buttonhole.

'It's a start.'

'If you don't want it . . .?'

He clapped his hand over his heart.

'Want to know where I got that?'

'Not really.'

'This northern bint shows up at my place. She was after me for dosh – whiner she was, like you.'

Reece tuned in, learning of how Davey had swindled Rox out of her money. He measured the man in the mirror. The dark eyes, protruding nose, touch of the pikey about him. His best guess was bog standard East End boy, raised on dipping and drumming, probably a spell in remand or borstal. Then it would be thieving out of lorries late at night and shifting it sharpish round Brick Lane and Roman Markets. Nothing he hadn't seen before. Davey's fancy whistle spoke flash and gab and he matched it with the flannel he was giving the boss. Latimer lapped it up. Reece put him at twenty-eight years old and a comer. Hard?

That remained to be seen.

'You take me to the nicest places.'

'You mean this *isn't* the Dorchester?' said Reece, feigning surprise.

It was eight thirty in the evening and they were sat on the slidy red plastic seats in the Old Kent Road McDonalds.

It was bright and brash and the muzak was an insult even to lifts.

'Thought I'd better come dig you out.'

'I was going to phone you,' lied Rox. She was feeling far too insignificant for that.

He shrugged minutely.

She had been delighted when Reece appeared in the lousy living room: partly at seeing him again, partly as his presence raised her from the pit of her depression. On her return to Camberwell, she'd been too ashamed to tell anyone about what had happened with Davey, so she crawled into her sleeping-bag and hibernated for the evening. This morning, she had gone walking, making a triangle as she strolled down Southampton Way, along past the church and the Art College to Camberwell Green and back up the Walworth. The area was polluted, grim and grotty: worse even than Oldham market on a wet Wednesday. It suited her mood fine. Walking was what she did when she needed to figure things out; especially as a teenager, getting the bus to Saddleworth or Diggle for the moors and sticking Portishead on her personal stereo, which never helped any.

Her major problem now was she was short of funds. When and if Mark decided to pay her last month's salary, it would still have to go through the bank and she was well over her overdraft limit. She had her Apex return but couldn't face going home, not when it would be piling failure on failure.

Reece had waited politely in the corridor while she put on some slap. He was clean-shaven and wearing that look she liked; black jeans, a plaid shirt, a musky scent around his leather jacket. It made a change from the prats in sportswear and cheap trainers she and Mark used to sling out of the Garage at weekends. She frowned, annoyed at herself for thinking of home and of Mark again. She focused on Reece, wondering whether he would try to kiss her or whether she'd have to instigate matters again.

'I've clocked this Davey character and it looks as though you've fallen for one of the old ones.'

She scoffed her chips, her glasses hard white pebbles in the fluorescent light. 'Tell me something I don't know.'

'In London it takes seven seconds to start a traffic jam.'

'I didn't mean that.'

'Okay.'

He bit into his burger.

'It's the short con,' continued Reece, setting aside his neon roundel of gherkin. 'He played nice, promised you your money back, made you a bet you thought you couldn't lose. Once he had you believing you had one over on him, he changed the game.'

She murmured agreement, swallowing hard at the memory of those cold hard fingers, those reptilian eyes. 'How much did he take you for?'

'All I had in my purse – and I never got my money back.'

'So that's?'

'In all. Four-fifty odd now. D'you think I should take legal action? We know where he lives and . . .' The words petered out at the first showing of his smile. Reece wiped his mouth with a deck of tissues, reached into his jacket and slid a wad of notes across the table.

She slurped her shake, eyeing it with curiosity.

'Here. I know you're short.'

She glared at him.

'Of money,' he added, flushing a little.

Cute, thought Rox. 'I can't take that.' She said.

'Course you can.'

'I can't pay you back. Not for a while at least.'

'Don't matter.'

She fingered the cash, wrinkled up her nose, pushed it back at him.

'It stays here then,' Reece said, making no move. The notes curled gently, like butterfly wings.

'I can't. It's kind of you but—'

'I'll leave it here then. It'll be the first time McDonald's staff ever got a tip.'

Reluctantly, she clasped it in her hand and tucked it away in her pocket.

'That's better.'

He rose and stacked their cartons.

'This was short and sweet,' she said.

'Got to go to work.'

'Don't you fancy a quick drink?'

He shucked on his jacket. 'Not really.'

She pouted and peered up through the straw curtain of her fringe. 'Go on. Swift half?'

He went and dumped their trays in the brown bin, then came back. 'All right then.'

She travelled in the front again, this time checking out Reece's car. It was a recent model Ford with all mod cons and features, comfortable, but not in a dad's car kind of way. He kept it immaculate and she was pleased to note there was no hanging air freshener or jewelled tissue box on the parcel shelf (What were those for anyway? she wondered. Something masturbatory?). His radio aerial was fixed to the roof, its base wrapped in a neat sack of chamois leather. He handled the vehicle expertly; the radio tuned to Jazz FM. She hadn't dared look at the money he'd given her, but it felt like a lot, at least enough for another ten days – more, if she used the spends wisely.

'Where are we going?' she asked, as they made for SE1.

'Little boozer I know. Used to be a nice place.'

'So you're from round here?'

'Yeah. Where you from in Manchester?'

'Oldham originally, but I moved around a lot and lost the accent.'

'You *lost* your accent?'

'Aye, I have that,' she said, laying it on thick.

'What's it like – up North?'

'You've never been?'

'Can't see the point.'

Her jaw fell in disbelief. Was he that metro-centric? The

clichéd Londoner who never ventured beyond the M25?'

'You what?'

'I can get everything I want in London. The rest I've seen on telly.'

'You *are* joking.'

'If I want pissy rain, we get that here — only not every day. Crap bands? We've got them and all. Wide-open spaces — Greenwich Park's good or you could take a drive out to Kent. Food? North's not exactly known for it.'

Rox felt her ire rising. 'What about the heart of the Industrial Revolution?'

'That's over.'

'What about cheap, good food and beer? Clean air and no traffic? Proper friendly people — unlike *some* I could mention.'

Reece shrugged.

'I knew it. You Londoners think you're the be-all and end-all, with your stinky crappy capital. It's a mess. No one gives a shit about the crowded tubes or the homeless. And it's too bloody big. And it's all greed down here, is what it is. Everyone out for themselves — never giving a thought to others.'

'What do you really think?'

The smile crinkled her lips. 'That *is* what I think.'

'I'll have the money back then. If we're that unfriendly.'

'No,' she said, folding her arms over her breasts.

The tall Victorian buildings dwarfed them as they came up Baylis Road.

Reece said. We're not going to agree about anything, are we?'

They drew into Lower Marsh, almost directly beneath Waterloo Station. Reece parked up, emerged from the car and gazed in awe at a painted, slender three-storey pub. Overshadowing it were the massive iron girders of the main line railway.

'They've tarted it up,' he announced.

It looked all right to her. 'When were you last here?'

'Couple of years ago.'

'Duh. Things change.' She was being deliberately obtuse, trying to get a reaction out of him.

He walked towards the pub. 'Yeah, they changed the name and all.'

He bought her a pint and he had a coke and led her upstairs. It was laid out almost like a gentleman's club, with comfortable old leather-backed sofas, low lighting, an open fire and free newspapers hanging off dowelling rods.

'It'll do, I s'pose,' he said, disappointment in his voice.

'It's fine. God it's only a pub.'

They sat down. He sipped his coke.

'Are you not drinking then?' she asked, then realised. 'Oh yeah — you're driving.'

'I don't drink.'

She had started to ask him why when her words were deafened by the arthritic grumbling and heart-stopping metal shrieks of Network Southeast's antediluvian rolling stock. As their hearing returned, Rox felt a clamouring in her chest and knew she had to say something.

'What did you mean back there? Not agree on anything?'

'We're very different.'

Evasive. 'Reece, you said there was someone once — is that part of it?'

'Of what?'

She knotted her brow, took another pull of her pint. 'Look, I'm okay if the other night meant nothing to you. Really, it's cool — and don't bother letting me down slow. I'm getting that used to being dumped I'm thinking of applying to the council to become a waste contractor.'

He smiled a little at that, then leant in and kissed her. She felt her nerve-endings go and her insides turn to marsh-mallow. This time, it was softer, passionate but not urgent, caring, if anything. Finally, once the world had receded, he pulled away.

The 9.37 to Reading drowned his first attempt at explaining.

'I want to go slow, that's all,' he said, to her eyes.

'So you've not got anyone?'

'Not that I know of.'

She took off her glasses. Leant forward to give him a nice sloppy one. He was a bit fuzzy, so she put them back on.

'How's it going with your ex then?' he asked.

'We've no contact.'

'Best way.'

'Unless you know any hit-men?'

'Might do.'

That was the thing about him. With anyone else it would've been a jokey aside, but with Reece you never knew. 'I hope he gets disfigured by a burning schooner of Sambuca. Or his girl-friend gets whiplash in a hair-flicking incident.'

'Could happen.'

'Or they could reintroduce witch-burning.'

'Didn't know they'd stopped it up there.'

'Think you're funny, don't you, Mister Cabdriver.'

'Not really.'

'And why are you not drinking? Not much of a man, are you?'

He lowered his eyelids. 'This the northern humour, is it? Insults?'

'Piss off, if you can't take it.'

'The friendly Northerner.'

They were grinning at one another like drugged fools. He took her hand, warmed it in his.

'Listen – I've got to shoot in a minute, but I've been having a think about Davey Kayman. You serious about getting your money back?'

'Course I am.'

'How serious?'

She gave him a baby frown. 'What have you got in mind?'

'You'd have to turn him over, same way as he did you. First thing we've got to do is find out what matters to him.'

The dull heartbeat of a diesel engine throbbed past, then another shrill silver shriek as wheels bit wet rails.

'How do we find that out?'

'Think about it.'

'There's his girlfriend.'

'Possibly.'

She raised her eyebrows, imploring.

'Okay, put it this way – it's time we invested in some Class A drugs.'

CHAPTER TEN

'It certainly *looks* right.'

It was a bright fine day and a flotilla of cloud was floating past the City of London. Inside the private room deep in the heart of Corney & Barrow, natural light was not permitted to enter. The air smelled of varnished oak and the steel table in the centre of the room was polished so it shone like mercury. There were three men gathered around it and the eldest was scrutinising the label on a bottle of wine.

'I should hope so,' said the client, a youngish man with dark curly hair. He wore an Armani suit with a navy shirt, a club tie (although the vintners would have been hard put to name the actual club) and a Freemasonry pin. His accent was estuary English, although he was doing his best to cover it up. 'The reason I'm bringing it to you is that my employer – whom I can't name for security reasons – is looking into selling off his cellar of some particularly fine Grand Crus.'

'Yah, kay. He's come to the right place,' said the younger vintner, who was tall and gauche and had a floppy fringe of sandy hair.

The client went on. 'He'd put it all up for auction at Sotheby's but he doesn't want the publicity.' He lowered his voice. 'To be frank, there's an adverse *political* climate back home that requires him to relocate. So what he's doing is liquidating certain assets. With me?'

They were.

'Now, the Burgundy I have with me today is a sampler of what's to come. Dipping our toes in the market, if you like.'

They liked.

'What I'm suggesting is you do your checks on the provenance and we'll come to some sort of arrangement.' He drew his lips back over his teeth and smiled.

The sandy-haired vintner picked up the cooler bag from the floor. 'You say it's been kept at an, mm, even temperature?'

'Since it left his cellars in France.'

The elder vintner placed the bottle down, removed his reading glasses and gazed at the client with rheumy eyes. 'Domaine de la Romanee-Conti, 1990. An excellent year.'

'Good as the '95,' agreed the man, who had the brochure at home.

'What kind of arrangement are we talking about?' posed the elder vintner.

'For now, these at an agreed price. In sterling.'

'God. Cash? Fnnh. Don't think so,' snorted the young vintner.

The client reached for the bottle. 'That's the way King – my employer – wants to do business.' He revolved it in his hands. 'You know he's got ten of these at home. Drank two in one night with Colonel Gaddafi.' He winked at them. 'D'you fancy opening one up, get a little taster?'

A silver corkscrew lay on the table. He took it, rattled its wings in the air and swung the screw at the red foil seal.

'Don't,' gasped the two men, flailing their hands to avert disaster.

The client cradled the bottle to his stomach and ran his thumb around the foil wrapping, denting it. He sighed.

'If you don't want the business, it makes no odds to me. I'll pop round to Christies.'

The elder vintner regained his composure, although his eyes

remained fixed on the corkscrew. 'What kind of figure had you in mind?'

The client studied him levelly. 'That's down to you.'

'The price on a burgundy of this stature is astronomical.'

'No, it isn't. About eleven thousand pounds at restaurant prices. We checked when my employer was dining out. In the end he settled for half a bottle of Cheval Blanc. That's not bus fare either.'

'And what did he do with the other half of the bottle?' gulped the younger vintner.

'Gave it the dog, I think.'

Jaws masticated the rarefied air.

'Now,' continued the client, 'let's not drag this out. You can sell these on for nine apiece, but in the circumstances, we're prepared to take a loss. Say, seven point seven-five each?'

'God,' spluttered the younger vintner. 'For the three? That comes to over twenty-three thousand pounds.'

The client bowed his head.

The elder vintner was also doing his sums. 'I'd have to talk to the finance people upstairs.'

'Course you will.'

The vintner looked as though he was having teeth pulled. 'They might be keener if your employer were to accept a round twenty?'

'I'd have to come back to you on that.'

'And we'll need time to prove the provenance. Ten days.'

'You can do it in three.'

'Yes, that's true.'

'Then I'll come in on Friday morning. Let's agree in principle and I'll let you know what he says.'

Receiving a nod from the elder vintner, the client shook the hand of each man in turn. Minutes later, he was collapsed in the back of a black cab, as it scurried over to the Dorchester. There he would call them back from the phone in the lobby, confirming the revised offer of twenty thousand pounds. Not bad, thought Davey, for three bottles of what, one day in the distant future, would turn out to be plonk.

Down at the tangled, tawdry Tottenham Court Road end of Oxford Street, Charlie Ribbons was dipping in and out of the shops. She favoured the cut-price outlets, Asian-owned, brimming with goods: chunky watches, Goth rings, high shoes perched on pegboards, racks of jeans and combats, carousels of lame gag T-shirts. She had selected a place where the starting price on the leather jackets was a hundred and seventy. A rack of them were attached to a rail by a long metal chain. Tinsel, she thought, beckoning over the eager young assistant.

She had him remove the chain and help her into one of the pricier leathers. Tugging her dreads out over the collar, she inspected herself in a mirrored pillar and asked about one in brown with a fleece lining. Mentally calculating his commission, the boy went off to the stockroom to check.

Charlie glared at the CCTV in open defiance. She knew no one would be covering it, unlike in the bigger stores where they had guys paid to do that and some of them could *run*. Worst of all were the cameras on top of the buildings up and down Oxford Street. The filth was on watch all day, making dipping a right pain so you had to have a whizz-mob of at least five – or so Davey had told her.

Merging with a blur of Belgians, Charlie tore off the plastic security tag and dropped it in one of their bags. Minutes later she resurfaced up near the Plaza as plain-clothes swooped on the hapless teenagers.

Rox, who had been following her, slipped behind a column. She'd tailed her from Shoreditch to Tottenham Court Road where, after discarding the ubiquitous flyer (Speak Englis Good!), Charlie had begun her one-woman crime wave. Despite the bored black guys by the security cattle-grids and the visibly high police presence, she had gathered an impressive haul: Rox knew that her pockets and plastic carriers contained a couple of PC Games (minus shrink wrap and security tags), several tops, bras, knickers and CD's. And now the expensive jacket. She half expected her to make off with the sign saying GOLF SALE. Charlie crossed over and used a shop window to admire her skinny frame in the new jacket. Rox moved behind a phone-box and kept her in view.

She was scared – not about confronting Charlie—but of the small wrap of paper in a compartment in her purse. When Reece had driven her home from the pub, he'd made a detour into the darker stretches of Peckham, leaving her in the car for ten minutes while he disappeared into a derelict block of flats. She kept the doors locked and was relieved when he returned – but not when he gave her the cocaine. They argued about the plan but she still ended up back home with the drug. It seemed like they were going to argue about everything and she wondered when or if this relationship would get going? On the plus side, she supposed it wasn't all bad, a bloke giving you drugs and money and nice kisses . . .

There was a gap between the buildings where a flight of steps led down to a back street. Rox hadn't noticed it before, what with the tall shops and the crowds of French students in bluejeans and cagoules (what was it Reece said – look up?). As Charlie crossed the gap, Rox moved swiftly, barging into her and sending her flying down the stairs. She regained her footing and grabbed hold of the handrail.

'The fuck did you do that for?' she bleated.

'And how are those elocution lessons going?'

'Piss off.'

Rox trotted down, approaching her. Charlie flared her nostrils and tensed her scrawny body, ready to fight.

'Hold on,' Rox said. 'I want to chat, that's all.'

Charlie attached a sneer to her face. 'What do we have to talk about?'

'Your shoplifting career?'

Rox enumerated every article Charlie had lifted that morning and described exactly where she'd pinched it from.

'So what?' she said, defensively. 'Can't prove none of it.'

Rox kept coming. 'No, but there's millions of bobby's round here and if I scream out there's a chance one'll get you.'

Charlie stepped down onto the lower pavement. It was bronzed in grime and the back alley reeked of urine and stale wheelie bins. Strewn about were the sleeping-bags and flattened boxes of the homeless. Ramillies Street hadn't half the gaudy appeal of the famous shopping street above them.

'What do you want then?'

'Look – I'm not here to fight. Okay, so Davey's had me over, but it's only a few hundred and I'm sure he means to give it back. I thought you might have a word with him.'

'Why'd I want to do that?'

'Ever heard of sisterhood?'

'I hate my sister.'

Figures, she thought.

Charlie fished out a piece of fresh gum and stuck it in that wide mouth. She didn't offer any to Rox, who was studying her parched lips, the ghostly skin, the outcrop of acne on her temple.

'So – you calling the filth?' Charlie demanded.

Rox shook her head.

She seemed to relax, although her jaws kept moving.

'What's wrong with your sister, then?'

'Stuck-up cow.'

'You been with Davey long?'

Charlie rearranged her bags with overt impatience. 'You won't get nothing out of Davey.'

'Why not?'

She rolled her eyes. 'He don't give anything away. He does what he likes.'

'You mean he does nothing for you either?'

She forced a superior smile. 'He does plenty for me.'

Rox threw in a prepared question. 'Does he get you good stuff?'

'Do what?'

'You're named after it – unless your name's Charlotte and it's an affectation.'

That struck home, producing reinforced effort on the chewing. 'What *about* Chas?'

'You want some?'

Charlie shrugged. Rox made great play of looking around. There were people passing at the top of the stairs. The other way was Marlborough Street where the black taxi's chugged past, the Bikes buzzed and the Sohoites mobiled. Bisecting the alley was Ramillies Place, a canyon of soot-encrusted buildings leading down to the stage door of the Palladium,

'Come on.'

It was deserted, a gang of construction workers having left for their liquid lunch. Above them, the cold sky was a thin strip of pewter. Rox produced the wrap.

'You want a toot or not?'

'You first.'

This wasn't part of it. She'd not had coke in ages, the last time being New Year's Eve under sufferance when Mark had laid out a couple of grams on the bar. She'd been fine, but Ally – who was dead sensitive to chemicals – had had to be talked down from the top of the Victorian Lamppost in Chorlton Green. Rox hadn't even sampled the goods Reece had given her and had deliberated about tipping them down the toilet.

Huddled against a wall, Rox reluctantly folded back the paper leaves. Charlie reached over, dabbed a finger in the powder, stuck it in her mouth and rubbed it round her gums. Now she showed interest.

'What you giving me this for then?'

'Peace offering.'

'Still won't get nothing out of Davey.'

Rox came in with the second part they had prepared. 'I want

you to know I'm around and I can get good gear. If there's one thing we do do up in Manchester it's drugs.'

'That where you're from?'

Rox nodded as Charlie rolled up a tenner. She produced a small mirror and sprinkled a mound of powder on it.

Charlie urged, 'Go on, more than that.'

Generous with other people's drugs, thought Rox, as she created a hillock. Charlie provided a razor blade and after loosely chopping it into two lines, Rox shut her eyes and inhaled. Before the chemical tinge had a chance to hit the back of her throat, Charlie was sucking up the other line faster than an Electrolux. Rox refolded the wrap and pressed it into her dry bloodless hand. 'Go on. You have that.'

As her fingers closed in on it, Rox noted the eczema-scarred knuckles.

They stood there, snorting back the powder, giving their nostrils a good workout, waiting for the rush.

It came at once.

'Hold on,' Charlie said, 'this is a bit speedy for coke.'

'It is, isn't it?'

'Fucking is whizz and all.'

'You have a point,' remarked Rox. 'I'll mention this to my dealer.'

She wrung out the rag, draped it on the draining board and as the last of the suds gurgled away, she placed the new blue plastic washing bowl in the tidemark-free sink. Every last dish, pan, cup, knife and fork had been cleaned and put away and the rubbish taken out. This, itemised for Graham and Pete's information, included forty-seven beer bottles. Numerous squashed cans. Several silver takeaway punnets. Rotten fruit (an aged relative must have dropped by, otherwise, why *pears?*). A leaning tower of pizza boxes. The spare remote control from the telly. Scraped toast and carbon residue. Three empty packets of Coco

Pops and a dead mouse. The floor was vacuumed, despite her first having had to spend an hour de-gunking the ancient Hoover. The shower had been cleaned and the black bits scrubbed out from between the tiles (a retchworthy task). Also, the furniture had been polished so the tea-stains came up like new. The dead houseplants were in the bin and the telly screen was so clean that when it was turned on the static crackled like kindling.

It was definitely speed.

The News was on, but she wasn't watching it. Rox dug into her bag for the thick notebook she'd earlier purchased in a stationery shop on the way home: the one she'd made a load of lists in – and the one she had decided to use as her London Diary. She began – after smoothing down that beautifully crisp first page (a feeling as pleasurable as folding down hotel sheets) – by writing about the day she arrived. After an hour she had written up as far as the meeting with Lovell, but then lost interest. It became *impossible* not to do something about the filthy flat.

She would get back to it now, she decided. In a bit, once she'd sorted out her clothes. And she should do a wash. There was a Launderette in the parade of shops on the corner. But it was past five thirty – would it still be open? If it was, she could write as easily in there. Kill two birds. Huh, kill Reece, more like. It was hours since she'd taken the sulphate, with no signs of the effects abating. She'd have to do a lot of drinking if she wanted to sleep tonight.

Yeah, she'd best pop down the offy.

Down in the hall the door flew back, its latch elbowing the wall as Pete and Graham came thundering up the stairs. Rox said nothing as they stumbled into the lounge. They looked bewildered, like disgruntled cats in unfamiliar territory. She half expected them to turn tail and bolt for the comfort of the filthy Kebab house on the Green.

'Tricorder reading, Mr Spock?' queried Graham.

Pete's voice rose in antipodean panic. 'Where's my bastard beer bottles?'

'I threw 'em out.'

'B-but, the labels. I was collecting them. They're all different.'

'Pete, stop your mithering. Have you not heard of tough love?'

CHAPTER ELEVEN

Three days later, Christmas came late in Shoreditch. The provenance of the Domaine de Romaine-Conti had been verified and Davey had come out flush. He went shopping for expensive shiny things, returning home in a taxi stuffed with parcels. He purchased – in cash – a digital camera, a Sony S7700 DVD player, a state of the art wraparound headset, a pair of ray-bans, a gold sovereign ring, a silver wristband for his watch, a Play-Station, some CD's, DVD's and an inflatable dinosaur. The spirits and cigars were due to be delivered by Oddbins later. Admittedly some were impulse buys, explainable by his ingestion of enough pharmaceuticals to stun a roadie. His saliva was a thick paste, his eyeballs dry in their sockets and his jaw muscles ached from hours of involuntary mastication: a great day out.

He was spread-eagled on the floor, trying to connect up the new widescreen digital TV. The plasticky scent of new wiring teased his nostrils as he wondered idly what would happen if he snorted silica gel.

'Davey?'

Charlie was at the breakfast bar concentrating on a joint. She wore a pair of Davey's leather trousers (turned up at the ankles) and a tight grubby T-shirt with 'Power Babe' printed on it.

'Hmm?'

'Can we shift some of the money you made today back into my account?'

'What for?'

'I'm overdrawn and the old man's being a sod about giving us any more.'

There was a pause as he fiddled with the wiring. 'Get us a beer, will you?'

'Get it yourself.'

Davey jumped up and went over to the fridge. 'Told you not to worry about him, didn't I? You know I look after you. No, don't answer that, you know I do. I mean *look* at all this gear, you ungrateful cow. And now you won't even get us a lager . . .?'

Charlie stuck a hand up inside her T-shirt, pinching her left nipple as hard as she could. She twisted harder and her face took on a pained expression. Davey grabbed his bottled beer and, ignoring her, used the counter as leverage to get the top off. He struck it with the palm of his hand and a melamine chip flew across the room as the beer hissed open. He knocked off the cap and drank deep. Charlie moaned and lifted up the T-shirt to expose her bare breasts; one nipple was raw from her efforts, the other punctured by a nipple ring.

'Daveey baby. Want sex now.'

'Not now.'

She pulled off the T-shirt and tugged at her teats until they reached the furthest point of their elasticity. She released them, spat on her palms and massaged her nipples until they stood erect.

'Charlie – I've had that much sulph and sherbet I might as well be a junior doctor.'

'So?'

'So I got the Paul Daniel's.'

She grunted irritably, then began clawing at her breasts with her nails, leaving striations on the swell, her aureoles going from rust brown to rose madder.

'Come on. You wanna fuck, don't you? Or . . . or I could suck you off?'

She dropped to her knees and reached for his trousers, but he swatted her away. She stared up at him.

'Aww. Let me wank you off . . . In my mouth . . . and all over . . . all over my face.' Her hands went to the zip of the leather trousers. She undid the top button and unzipped herself, then wet a finger in her mouth and thrust it deep inside her crotch.

'Baby, want you. Want your spunk in my mouth.'

She crawled towards him, gazing up, her gash of a mouth opening and closing like a fish.

'Gawd. All right then,' Davey said, slamming the beer on the side and releasing his half-tumescent cock.

She squealed in delight as she took it in her pale hands.

'And you'll transfer some money into my account?'

He wasn't listening.

'Shut . . . Shut it! Darren, leave him alone. Hold up, hold up.' Archie Peacock muffled the receiver with his palm and, placing his foot on his smaller son's back, slid him away across the floor. Ronan thought it was a great game and released a yelp of glee. Darren, imprisoned between the wall and his father's bulky thighs, tried to claw a way out so as he could thump his sibling.

'Pack it in,' warned his dad, giving him a hefty flick on the ear.

Archie hauled the phone out into the hall. The extension cord unravelled and disappeared under the door as if someone were sucking it up like spaghetti.

'Right – who's the buyer? Do what? A Jap? I expect he'll prob'ly want to go stick it in the bank and that'll be that, eh . . .? Well he can't exactly put it on display, can he?'

He listened, a finger tracing the outline of one of the roses on the wallpaper. It came to him.

'Hold up, mate. Which self-portrait was he after? No, this one's 1634. Geezer's wearing a beret. A black one with a scarf and all . . . No, we're wasting our time. I know what it's worth. You can't fool these people — they got the catalogues. Your bloke's after the one painted the year before — same hat but a different expression. Yers, well I 'ppreciate your efforts, mate, course I do, but it's no go on this.'

Archie made a few more conciliatory sighs and intakes of breath and then severed the connection. He reeled in the line as he re-entered the lounge. '. . . The bleeding hell's going on?'

Even though Darren knew that getting his brother to swallow the figurine of Jar Jar Binks was wrong, his expression still tried for innocence. Archie plucked it from Ronan's mouth, tapped his elder son on the shoulder and stamped upstairs to the bedroom.

Opposite the bed was the dresser, on which the small telly had stood up until a week ago, when Archie had given it to his mum in the home. The portrait hung there now with the twenty-six-year-old artist staring out at him. Golden light caressed his right cheek and the protuberant nose. The rest of the face was in shadow, including the eyes. There was a playful look about them, as there was in the mouth, which was slightly open. There was an indication of a moustache that would later become more flamboyant. It was a joyful painting, done on the year of the artist's marriage to Saskia, when he had recently been appointed a citizen of Amsterdam and made a member of that city's guild of painters. The new confidence showed in the paint-ing, in the strong composition, the daring use of light and shade and in the portrait's directness. It seemed to Archie—who lay on the bed, hands knitted together behind his head—as if it were suffused with an inner light.

Locating the gents was a complex procedure in the maze-like pas-sages of the Soho nightclub. Effort was rewarded, as the decom-pression was pleasant in a room of cool marble, china sinks, gold taps, free cologne and flattering mirrors. It was savvy of the management to have focused on the décor (towels instead of warm-air distributors, spotless, spirit-level-flat lavatory cisterns) as this was where most business was done. It was joked that anyone using the cubicles for their proper function might forfeit their membership. On that score, you had to be nominated to join, but some guested it until they knew the staff who were easily bribeable, as most of them were fledgling thespians.

Davey Kayman stood at the urinal, releasing a golden stream and admiring the green glass riser that prevented splashback on to his Patrick Cox loafers. He went to wash his hands. Another man, older, wearing a Paul Smith suit past its best, joined him at the basins. They nodded fraternally as they caressed their hands in water. They separated, tugging down towels with a clinical clunk. Then as one, they made for the same cubicle. The man gave a polite chuckle and leaned up against the doorjamb.

'What's the etiquette? First come first snorted?'

Davey studied the face. Jowls, cheeks silting up with fat, tired tan crescents under the eyes, broken capillaries.

'You a journalist?'

'Of a sort.'

Davey went in and began unfolding his stash. 'The papers?'

'Telly production. Investigative docs.'

'You do that "Police Camera Action"?'

'Bit cheap and cheerful. I'm the other side. Do a lot of work for the Beeb.'

Davey laid out lines, manoeuvring the blade with the speed of a croupier.

'Actually,' continued the older man, 'we've had a major commission from the Head of Factual. The team's out celebrating.'

Davey inhaled first and stood to attention. The man bent down after him, revealing a pale pink circle of skin on his crown.

Davey said, 'Know what? I'd always fancied getting into that telly lark, I mean how hard can it be?' His cheek shook in spasm. Chemicals always affected his tic and because of it he tried to stay straight when on the rob. 'A lot of what they put on is, let's be honest, *shite*. I mean, I dunno what them tossers in charge are up to, 'cause I could make better programmes myself.'

'I'm sure you could,' came the muffled voice.

'Plus, looking at things in Perspex, where I am now is lucrative, but it ain't what you'd call long-term.'

The producer surfaced and gave back the fifty-pound note. 'What do you do?'

'Events.' Without waiting for the man to question him further, Davey asked, 'Much money in your game?'

'I make a living.'

'Surprise me.' Davey was thinking; middle-class prick. You could crush his balls with a brick or kill his children and he still won't tell you his salary.

The man brought up a thumb and finger and caressed a pockmarked chin. 'I suppose if you want a ballpark figure, then the production fees for our last series would've come to about . . . eighty?'

'Eighty grand?'

'Around that.'

'Clear?'

He nodded as he reached for the door handle.

'Davey Keller,' said Davey, trying on the new variant of his name for size. He thrust out a hand, the other rising to grip the man by the shoulder.

'Tom Ashby,' announced the producer, warily.

'I'd like to hear more about your work.'

The main room was stuffed with dancers, but the sounds had changed from retro seventies and northern soul to standard chill-out stuff: the easy listening of Faithless and Saint Etienne, never-ending Beloved and Orb mixes that accompanied the realisation you had run out of drugs.

'No, you see I work for an *independent* production company. We're commissioned by the broadcaster to make programmes.'

Davey had isolated Tom from his friends, steered him to a booth and was plying him with scotch. Charlie sat close by, creating beer label confetti and praying that they might cab it home soon. Davey's only instructions had been to tell her to keep her skirt rucked up around her thighs. He liked her to tease other men, even when he wasn't watching.

'They pay *us*, the company. That fee is based on what it cost us to make the series, usually somewhere between 150 and 300 grand per programme hour. Our production fee comes on top of that.'

'The mark-up.'

'If you like.'

'Eighty large isn't bad for the cream. And for that you need a decent idea you can punt out to these telly people?'

Tom sipped his scotch. 'David. No one's going to commission you unless you're an established programme-maker.'

Davey's eyes flared angrily. He hated being patronised.

'Your best bet, if you have an idea for a series, is to come to us or one of the other Indy Prod companies. If we like it, we'll offer it up to the network.'

Davey had been in overdrive for the last hour sweet-talking Tom. He'd found that he loved telling stories – probably had an estranged son somewhere he reckoned. All the time he was thinking ahead, concocting the mother of all exposé's, weighing the elements, looking for a way in, keen to leech every bit of juice, gen, info out of the guy before dawn. This was new. Something *fresh*. He liked fresh. It kept his blade sharp.

'That's all fine and kosher, Tom, but I don't share my ideas.'

'That's understandable.'

'Wouldn't want them getting ripped off, no offence.'

'None taken.'

'It's not that I don't trust you, 'cause I don't trust any fucker.'

'You'll do well in telly.' Tom toasted a cigarette, the glow deepening the ravines on either side of his nose.

Davey asked, 'So what do I need if I want to do this properly?'

'If you don't go by the Indy route or take it in-house, then you might try getting a name attached. A programme-maker. You'll need a director or a producer, but it has to be someone *known* in the business. With me?'

Tom Ashby took a deep drag and wondered if the message was getting through. There was always a price to pay for accepting freebie pharmaceuticals – usually kow-towing to some media whore. At least this time, *he'd* been allowed to shoot off his mouth. To mentor this young man who seemed genuinely interested in his work. It was rare to find true fans of the genre these days. Everyone was so bloody soaked in the daily excursions of traffic wardens or Welsh gargoyles that it devalued any serious journalistic credibility whatsoever. He was about to make this very point to his protége when he noticed that Keller and his companion had disappeared.

On his way out, he found the drinks had been put on his tab.

As the newly purloined gunmetal Alpha Romeo Sportivo rose up on to Blackfriars Bridge, the biting crosswind failed to make an impression on its sturdy bodywork. The river tussled beneath, oxtail brown, lapping at the blackened slime on the bridge supports. In the distance, the water was shining silver under a gap in the clouds, milky sunlight giving it the appearance of a sheet of undulating chain mail.

'Smashing motor,' said Steve Lamb.

Archie replied, 'Traffic's a nightmare.'

'Murder.'

Pedestrians buckled in the wind; brollies blown, owners bent out of shape as if they were suffering from cramps. Steve stop-started through the lights, then came down onto New Bridge Street, ending up jammed between a glazier's van and a bus.

'Turn that crap off, wiwya?' said Arch. He was tiring of Tarrant's drool – all right in the van but here it felt wrong, like they ought to be listening to Radio Four or something posh like that. He rifled through the glove compartment for cassettes: nothing inside but the spec brochure.

Steve rammed the horn. 'Eyes right!'

A secretary. Knee-length grey skirt, pretty face, blonde corkscrew hair.

'T and A on THAT.' Steve fumbled for the switch, but by the time he had the window down they had gone past her. He smacked a palm on the wheel.

'I tell you about this bird?'

'Name?'

'Shelley . . . no . . . Annette. I dunno.'

They crossed Fleet Street and went up under Ludgate Circus.

'Posh tart, right? Offers me back to her place out in the sticks. Up Oxford way . . .'

With more than a trace of weariness, Archie asked, 'Is this the one where you come in her mouth and she spits it out and then the dog eats it?'

Steve went quiet for a bit.

Then, as they took Cowcross Street for Smithfield and the serrated concrete obelisks of the Barbican, he asked, 'So what's happening with the painting, then?'

'Nothing doing.'

There was a pause.

'Arch?'

He employed his Parker-out-of-*Thunderbirds* voice, 'Yerrs?'

'You'll tell me when you get another offer, wontcha?'

'Course I will, Stevie boy.'

In the Beech Street tunnel, marmalade light made the body-work khaki. In Golden Lane they passed Simon Latimer who was out front, jawing with a couple of the drivers, Rawpinder and Kilo three-seven. They threw a left and tucked the motor away in Baltic Street.

Archie opened his door. 'All set?'

'All white.'

He trotted round the corner and beckoned to Latimer, who was not best pleased.

'You took your time. I've got a wait-and-return to the airport and drivers going spare.'

'Sorry, chief. Anyways, You'll like this one.'

Archie waited for Latimer to catch up. Simon moved with a duck's waddle, as if his shoes were too tight. They turned into the smaller street. A pile of leaden clouds was forming, darkening the grimy façades of the buildings.

'We can't chauffeur people in that. A sports car, that is.'

'It'll do the job. Top speed a hundred and fifty. Let Steve show it you.'

'What for? I can't use this.'

Steve Lamb had the door held open like a salesman preparing to give a client a test run. He even had on a pair of thick driving gloves, although the leather was scuffed and nicked in places. As Latimer approached with his arms raised in complain-mode, Steve grabbed him by his tie and smashed his face into the driver's window. Blood spouted from his mouth as two of his crowns shattered. As he fell, Steve tugged his tie around so he had him by the throat and began repeatedly ramming the car door in Latimer's face. The metal buckled, as did Simon, moaning as his nose broke open and gouts of blood spattered the front of his shirt.

Somehow he forced the door away, only to fall back on the pavement. A bad move as the two men started kicked with all their strength, smashing ribs, bruising his back, creating internal damage. Steve's face was flushed a deep crimson, spittle flying from his twisted lips as the oaths and grunts spewed out of him. Archie was more restrained. He'd kicked Latimer in the thighs and was hoofing at the arms clasped tight over the cab owner's bruised, bleeding head. Latimer, whimpering pitifully, tried in vain to crawl away from the volley of blows.

Archie held up a hand. Steve paused in mid-kick, then bent to the car and pulled the baseball bat from the floor behind the driver's seat.

'No, hang about. He's had enough.'

Steve glared challengingly at Archie, breathing hard through his nostrils.

'You reckon?' He spat on the ground.

Arch ignored him and bent to the supine form. Latimer was crumpled on the kerb like an over-stuffed refuse sack.

'Listen, arsehole. The Petersons ain't happy. There ain't enough coming out of this place, so get it sorted before we get told to have another word. Right?'

Latimer groaned incoherently as Archie used the heel of his trainer to tilt him into the gutter. When Arch turned back to the car, Steve was already gunning the engine.

CHAPTER TWELVE

Davey snapped the mobile shut. 'The *work* you've got to put in to sort out this schpiel.'

Charlie was lacquering her toenails black, going for that run-over-by-a-car look. 'You mean the three hours on the blower?'

'And the rest.'

He'd been busy, as was the case whenever he had a new idea. Davey liked to look at the big picture, to get a feel for the scam and how it would come across, and this was going to be bigger than anything he'd yet attempted. Serious money. Firstly — knowing he'd need a kosher company title — he'd scoured the documentaries on the satellite, focusing on the high number/low quality channels. He video'd the credits and took down the details of the producers and the production companies. What he would need was an obscure — even foreign-based — outfit, whose title he could lift. It was, he reflected, essentially the same as the old trick of using a dead child's details to obtain a snide passport.

CrossTalk was a Quebec-based operation which, judging by their lack of recent output, was on the verge of bankruptcy. They had only produced one series of note — a co-production with the Canadian Film Board about endangered wildlife in the waterways of British Columbia. In what was presumably a bid for the late-night viewing market it had been broadcast as 'Beaver Fever'. Pretending to be from BBC Worldwide, Davey called up and asked about buying up the rights. He spoke directly to a man named Sommers, who was both a director of the company and their financier, thus confirming they were in trouble. According to him they were moving away from documentaries towards a broader-based appeal, which he took to mean porn. His partner, Donald Hayes, was away for the next four months. Nervous breakdown? Davey wondered. More likely he was touting his showreel around in a bid to keep them afloat. He thanked Sommers and had him fax through their brochure, promising that the BBC would be in touch, as they had been impressed by their beaver.

Done. Donald became David Hayes on this one. Davey always kept his first name: that was rule number one. Too complicated to keep remembering to answer to another and easier for associates to remember when verification was required.

Problem now was to find a tame director. He contacted PACT and deceitfully obtained a copy of their *Producers and Directors Directory*, discovering that there was a plethora of piss-ant little operations around Soho and the West End. He decided to start with W1.

The major hurdle was the PA's, an army of over-educated, prematurely embittered young women who took out their feelings of worthlessness on anyone who fitted neither their business nor their social circle. As he rang round, Davey soon modified his speech by dropping his customary bluster for insouciance and retaining enough estuarine English to render him fashionable. It took several aborted calls before he grew bored and started in on the directors' home numbers. For this he got Charlie to use an old one.

'Hello. I've got David Hayes for Toby Lomax . . . In a meeting?'

Yeah, right, thought Davey. Staring into space more like.

'Could you tell him this is Eagle Life and it's regarding an insurance repayment?'

There was a muffled pause.

'Yes, I'll hold.'

Davey winked at her then took the receiver.

'Hello. Mr Lomax?'

Charlie padded off; blowing on her freshly painted tangerine fingertips.

'Toby, David Hayes from CrossTalk. No, don't know anything about insurance' – he grinned cheesily at Charlie. 'Listen, I loved your exposé on cowboy builders and I think you're the bloke I'm looking for. What are you up to at the moment? Right, right, sounds great.' Thinking, then why are you sat at home, silly bollocks? 'Look, this interesting project has come my way and I think you'd be perfect for it. Sure . . . I can only make Tuesday. We'll do lunch. Meet you there? Fine.'

Charlie used her knuckles to push her dreadlocks over her shoulders. 'You do realise you sound like a complete wanker!'

His canines showed. 'Yeah, I do, don't I?'

The phone rang. Davey snatched it from its cradle and went nuclear in seconds.

'What? That is bollocks. No . . . all right. I'll be up there later. LATER.'

'That's better,' she said.

Ribbons of pink cloud striated a flat indigo evening sky. A freezing Siberian wind made the litter skip along Leytonstone High Road, and random gusts rattled the stork necks of the streetlights. Glowing tail-lights illuminated Reece's face as he headed out along Eastern Avenue for Gant's Hill. In the back he had his first fare of the night. Davey Kayman.

'Go round onto Cranbrook Road. Take the first right and you can park up.'

First words he'd spoken since Reece picked him up. He wasn't holding out for a tip.

Around the large roundabout were a cluster of post-war

buildings and shops, which, down all of the five radial roads, gave out to neat suburban housing. As instructed, he took a right and found room on an asphalted space ringed by a low white fence. Davey got out and Reece settled down for the wait. Except that his passenger bent to the window.

'You might as well come in.'

Reece followed him back up the main road past a row of frosted portholes by the club entrance. Two bullets of muscle stood aside to admit them. Inside, the interior was empty save for the staff. A long bar was girdled by high stools and off in the recesses were sunken booths with corduroy seating. There was a central dance floor being washed by revolving coloured spots. Usual crap, thought Reece. A Nineties idea of the Fifties. Vegas lounge meets Essex on a duff night. Why did they keep on redesigning these places? Wasn't it bad enough all the old pubs had gone without turning everywhere into a psychotic child's playroom? He ordered a coke, without ice, from a boy with a dyed blonde Tintin cut and a voluminous white shirt made lilac in the phosphorescent light.

Davey was being talked at by the under manager, a pallid pot-bellied Scot with a jabbing finger and an axe to grind. Reece was near enough to get the gist. He'd not been paid and neither had the staff. A chef in grubby whites and a weasel-faced kid came out of the kitchen to back him up. Davey held up his arms in capitulation. What could he do? *He* hadn't been paid either. Yes, he knew they'd been waiting three weeks for their wages. Most people had theirs monthly, through the books, know what I mean?

Reece watched impassively as the atmosphere began to sour. Davey had an impressive patter, from hurt to insolent in seconds, then back to wounded innocence and finally full on losing his rag.

'Piss off then,' shouted Davey. 'If you don't wanna work for me then no one says you have to. I've been flyering and poster-ing the bollocks out of this shit-house for a month and still we ain't getting the punters in. You wanna hang around Barking freezing your arse off then you're welcome to it. No punters, no takings, no wages – got it?'

The Scot and his cohorts didn't get a chance to argue as Davey was already making for the door. Reece jumped down and followed, feeling a hard knot of muscle forming across his back. They were outside and had reached the car park when the chef and the Scot charged at them from the rear door.

Reece dealt with the Scot by ducking below his first punch, bringing a fist up under his chin and stamping down hard on his knee. Bone snapped like kindling and the man went down, howling. The chef had wrestled Davey to the ground and was delivering blows with his feet. Reece rounded on him with two jabs to the kidneys. Hot pain seared Reece's shoulder. He spun and saw the rat-faced kitchen porter sporting a metal bar. He took it off him and tossed it aside. It rolled away with an even, drilling tone. Reece laid into the porter with a series of regular punches to the stomach and jaw until he crumpled. Another blow to the throat immobilised him.

The Scot lay clutching at his shattered knee, alternately whimpering and cursing. Davey was gamely trying to take on the chef, dodging away, then kicking at him like a child in a play-ground fight. Reece locked eyes with the chef, came in hard and fast and promptly headbutted him. The man's tunic blazed burgundy. Reece stepped back and gave the nod to Davey, who went in with fists and feet.

Adrenaline reactions. Check for witnesses or the law. Only silence in the sodium light. Also, no one at the kitchen entrance. Reece scanned 180, made out two hulking shadows on the street and knew instantly that the bouncers weren't going to get involved. The bosses getting friendly with one another? Forget it. Sweep back. The Scot sobbing, his words inaudible. The porter slumped against the wheelie bin, spark out. Davey doing his best with the inert body of the chef. Reece got in the car and fired up the engine. Davey looked over.

'You coming? Or is this the staff disciplinary hearing?'

He came. They headed for Ilford.

Davey said, 'You're a bit handy with your fists.'

'Boxing. Where to now?' Reece said, deadpan.

'Town. I mean shit; you've done me a right favour back there. We *killed* 'em.' Davey looked at his hands, which lay trembling in his lap. 'We fucking *murdered* 'em.'

As Reece came out onto the Romford Road, he revolved his left shoulder in his jacket. No real damage done.

'I owe you one, mate,' said Davey, tugging out a fat black leather wallet and exposing its innards.

Reece noted that with what he had in there, he could easily have paid off the nightclub staff in triplicate – plus given them a bonus. As he fanned notes, Reece waved them away. Davey looked at him with curiosity, like a new specimen.

'What's your name?'

'Reece.'

'Davey Kemmler.' He reached his hand through.

Reece took and shook the proffered paw, thinking to himself, that's a new one. Kayman wasn't it, last time?

'What's the game? You didn't have to look after me back there.'

'I wasn't looking after you.'

'Oh yeah?'

'They started it, I finished it. If you'd started on them, then you would've got the same.'

Davey nodded, impressed. 'So what you doing driving a cab?'

'It's a living.'

'Poxy money.'

Reece chuckled. 'Got any idea of what I can earn in a week doing nights? Plus airport runs and wait-and-returns?'

A shrug.

'Two, two-and-a-half round Christmas.'

Davey filed this away for reference. 'How long you been driving?'

'How long have you been withholding people's wages?'

Davey smiled. 'Since they built the Ark.' He leaned forward. 'I could use you.'

Reece said, 'Sure you could.'

They rose up over the Blackwall Tunnel northern approach and began the descent into Bow and the East End proper. The sky was the colour of aubergine, the road frost-hardened, lime and orange in the light. In the distance the tower blocks were riddled with light. They had the look of old computer punch cards.

'Where you from then?' Davey prompted.

'Around.'

'Talkative, ain't you?'

'So I'm told.'

'Suppose you're signing on?'

'No.'

'Then you're one of them drivers that's screwing Latimer?'

He was tiring of Davey's accusations. 'I saved you a hiding. Don't mean we're blood brothers all of a sudden.'

Davey went quiet for a moment, then, 'You ought to come and work for me.'

'Not for sale.'

'Start making real money.'

'And that promise would be how empty?'

'Oh, you're good,' said Davey, sliding back down in the seat.

Reece felt a glow of satisfaction. 'You ever hear of the Petersons?' That got a grunt. 'They part-own this firm and I work for them.'

'Nice boys,' snarled Davey.

'I'm working off a small debt at the moment.'

'Gambling?'

Reece nodded. 'So You'll have to get your own muscle, or driver, or whatever it was you were after.'

'How much you into them for?'

Reece thought about it. 'Put it this way. If you were to tip me thirty-odd grand that ought to cover it.'

CHAPTER THIRTEEN

Following her amphetamine-fuelled blitz on the Camberwell flat (and the subsequent grinding ratty comedown), Rox determined on a truce with the guys. The agreement, thrashed out between the three of them in the Brewers, was that she'd help out her hosts (cleaning, shopping, cooking – for money) so long as they treated her with a bit more dignity. She'd had enough of the squalid conditions, of having no privacy and of Pete's lame attempts to bed her. She knew they weren't going to change – only maturity or a love affair would do that, and she wasn't sticking around long enough for either of those to happen.

So she established a routine. She rose at eight with Graham and Pete, went shopping or cleaned for them in the morning, then spent the afternoon at the cinema or walking. Her perambulations sensibly excluded the North Peckham estate, but she'd been up Denmark Hill and had taken the bus to Nunhead Cemetery. She hauled her *A–Z* about with her wherever she went, relying on it and the bus map to improve her navigation skills. She was gaining a real sense of the geography of South East London. Without much money (nothing from Mark yet and she was damned if she'd beg for it) she eschewed the West End. The wealth there was too conspicuous, the trinkets too alluring: It made her feel excluded and unwanted.

The last two evenings she had cooked (comfort food so far,

but she planned on widening the boys' culinary horizons with sauces and poultry), then settled down to telly. The domesticity was soothing and — although not her natural inclination — she could see the safety in it. For one it helped her stop thinking about her busted heart. Two, it helped her barrier thoughts of that bastard Davey Kayman. Three, Reece had not returned her calls.

It was morning. She folded away her sleeping-bag behind the sofa, said 'tarra' to Graham as he left for work and went to the kitchen to get her breakfast. Pete was headed for the shower and grunted a grudging hello as he passed her. After some sharp words he'd agreed to cover his nudity on pain of her coming at him with a clawhammer. She brought her cereal through and sat at the table. Rox had a notepad beside her on which she was drawing up a shopping list. A pale trapezium of sun sliced the table in two as she spooned cereal into her mouth. Pete emerged from the cubicle swathed in threadbare towels, his feet stuffed into gungy flip-flops.

'Rox? If I leave some dollars, can you get us some shampoo?'

'Sure.'

'Looks like you forgot to be upset today, huh?' he added. He went to his bedroom and the buzzing monotone of a hairdrier started up.

Rox reached for her specs and looked at herself in the square of mirror she had propped on the mantelpiece. He was right. Her perennial scowl seemed to have drifted away. She let her face fall. What was he on about — *forgot* to be upset? As if she had any choice in the matter? But hold on . . . She seized her emotional tiller and tacked for calmer waters. What if I was staying upset on purpose? If it were up to me to decide whether I spent the day happy or not? In addition to her walk, she had, the previous afternoon, gone to the local library where the surly assistant told her to go find the self-help section herself.

She had. *Men are from Mars* led to some heavy 'yeah, rights'. A glance through a dog-eared copy of *What Color is Your Parachute?*

bored her. Finally, she alighted upon an American tome called *Paint that Man Out of Your Hair*. It was ironic, as thoughts had occurred to her of going home, redecorating, even putting the house in Chorlton on the market. She read the book from cover to cover and despite the gung-ho exhortations of *personal growth* (she thought of warts), she admired the theme of *controlling yar feelings.*

Rox attempted a small smile at the mirror. It didn't feel genuine, so she pulled a face. A moment's inspection led to tugging at the twin tendrils on her fringe and trying to get them to stay behind her ears. Still way too short. The doorbell rang. She went down.

'Hi, kid.'

'Aya, Reece,' she said nonchalantly, given that her arms had folded crossly of their own volition. 'Bit early for you – or should I say three or four days late?'

His breath steamed in the cold air. He seemed immune to the animosity. 'Just finished my shift.'

'Suppose you wanna come in?'

'If that's okay.'

She led him upstairs, hoping he wasn't staring at her bum in her trakky bottoms. Pete was on the landing searching for his keys, ready for the off.

'One out, one in, eh?' he said, winking.

'Did you *want* your CD player smashed while you're out?'

Once Pete left, Reece took off his jacket to reveal a thick dark sweater. He moved jerkily, as if there were a rod fastened to his spine. 'Do you want him sorting?' He asked.

'There's enough testosterone in here without you starting.'

She went to stick the kettle on. 'So what's to do?'

'Do what?'

She said it much louder than she'd intended. 'Why've you not answered my calls?'

'What calls?'

'I rang you and the controller said he'd pass the message on.'

Reece winced. 'Shit — I've been working out of the other office all week.'

'And I'm supposed to believe that?'

'Do you want a lie instead?'

The directness of the rebuke brought her anger down by several degrees.

'And what d'you mean by giving me speed? It was supposed to be coke.'

A quizzical look.

'I shared it with Charlie like you said — only it were speed. She bloody *laughed* at me, Reece.'

His face clouded over and he half-rose from his seat. 'S'cuse me. I gotta go have words.'

'You're going nowhere. Sit down.'

He shook his head. 'I don't believe he did that. Bloody Ten Benson.'

'Who?'

'Ten Benson. That's his name. Or nickname. He's been called that long as anyone can remember. Smokes ten Bennie Hedgehogs a day, no more, no less. He's a gofer, get-you-any-thing sort of bloke. Don't believe he tried shafting us like that.'

'Don't you know anyone with any *real* names?'

He half smiled, but she knew he was still thinking about the rip-off, taking it as a personal affront.

The kettle boiled.

She sighed theatrically. 'You want a brew then?'

'Tea? Yeah, please.'

He called through as she poured boiling water into the cups. 'The girlfriend didn't take it too well then?'

'Didn't think I was Mizz Best-pal-big-time-drug-dealer, no.'

'We'll have to cook up something else.'

She made the drink, put his in front of him and sat down. 'So why've you come by?'

'Guess who I had in the back of my cab last night?'

'Karl Marx?'

'No.'

'Alexander Pushkin? Emily Brontë?'

'Davey. There was a ruck.'

'No tip?'

'He part-owns a nightclub out in Essex. Cut a long story short, I helped him out and I reckon he'll want to use me again. Thought I'd let you know.' As he lifted his cup, she noticed the stiffness in his shoulder.

'You've been hurt.'

'Don't matter.'

'Yes, it does.'

She tried to touch his shoulder, but he shrugged her away. Rox refused to be put off and began tugging at his sweater, pulling it up to his shoulder blades. There was a dark coloration, the shores of a large area of bruising.

'Jesus, Reece – this was the other night? Let me see.'

He grunted loudly, but allowed her to pull the jumper over his head. The whole area from his clavicle down was swollen with a livid purple bruise.

'You've not even got anything on it.'

'Too busy working.'

'You might have a broken shoulder. What did you get into?' She saw the red striations where he had skinned his knuckles. 'And your hands!'

'Don't matter,' he said irritably.

'Let me find something to—'

'Don't give me the Florence Nightingale shit!' he snapped.

She sat down sharply. '*Control yar feelings*,' she thought.

He covered his injuries with the sweater, sipped at his tea, ran a hand through the bristly mat of his hair.

'Sorry,' he said.

'I don't know the first thing about you, do I?'

'What's there to know?'

'Where you live, for starters?'

'On the river.'

'Can you be more specific?'

'No.'

'You live alone?'

'Yes.'

'Can you speak in words of more than one syllable?'

'Yes.'

'Are you sure about that?'

He stretched it out. 'De-fin-ite-ly.'

She smiled a little. 'Why don't you want to tell me?'

He looked at his tea mug, the veins around his salt-and-pepper temples throbbing. 'Because I'm involved with people who the less you know about the better.'

'Isn't that for me to decide?'

Reece pierced her with his eyes. 'No, because you can't hide it if you know. And if you do, then someone can get it out of you, use it against you, all sorts.'

'Don't be so fucking melodramatic.'

He showed surprise, but there wasn't the backup anger she had expected from the comment.

'Reece. Since we're talking – why are you backing off from me?'

'I'm not. I'm just not ready yet. Nor are you.'

A short pause as she considered it. Hated him for being right. What was he – a friend? She straightened her glasses. 'You had someone, didn't you?'

'Kelley. We were going to get spliced, only there was a problem.'

Rox's voice went tiny. 'Sort of problem?'

'Let's say I mislaid the money for the wedding, for the do and for the honeymoon.'

'When was this? Where is she now?'

'Far as I know, she moved to Australia. End of. My fault.'

Her mouth had dried out. She wetted her lips with her tongue. 'And now?'

'Paying for it.' He stared at the patch of light on the table.

Scudding clouds above made it alternately shrink and grow.

This much out of him was a revelation and she guessed she dared not risk prodding him further. He was so matter-of-fact, living in a world encapsulated by boundaries he'd clearly set himself. She ached to know more but sensed that if it was going to happen then it would come all in his own sweet time. She would say nothing more.

'I suppose a snog's out of the question.'

Except for that.

The grin played around his lips. He leaned over and planted one on her cheek. 'You seem a lot better.'

'Wow. A whole compliment,' she said, glowing like she'd swallowed a lightbulb.

He tried and failed to stifle a yawn. 'I'd best be off. Get some kip.'

'Will I see you?'

'You around tonight?'

'Might be. I'll keep in touch.'

'You're a sight. What happened? Take on the wife and lose?'

Simon Latimer sat uncomfortably on the revolving chair in his office above Finsbury Cabs. His right arm was in a sling, his face puffed and raw like a landed fish. His left eye was a florid crimson, the lid swollen and closed. His ribs were bandaged under a bulky grey tracksuit, the first time he'd worn it aside from car-washing duties. It was too much pain and effort to clamber into a suit and tie.

'A message – from my partners.'

'They never heard of e-mail?' Davey was sharply dressed today, Armani, decent pair of shoes, crisp new shirt. He stood between the desks, prodding at the greasy grey keyboards.

'Davey. This kind of grief I don't need.'

He perched up on the desk. 'I thought you was coining it in?'

'I was.'

'So?'

'They started bringing in their own drivers to run the chauffeur end. Now the dockets don't square with the workload and I'm bearing the loss. Over three months that's a lot.'

'But this place can work?'

'It does work. Did work, before those bastards moved in.'

'Petersons?'

Latimer nodded. 'My fault in accepting their offer. Fifty-fifty, and they bring in extra account and chauffeur work. Also, we're tied in with their firm in the Walworth Road. Idea is we share the work between sites. Trouble is my drivers end up giving free rides to all their friends and relatives. And they are one *big* family.'

Davey indicated Latimer's sling. 'Who done this?'

He raised the cotton triangle. 'The *mensches* who do the chauffeur cars.'

'You want to get insured. That's industrial injury, that is.'

'More like occupational hazard.'

'You thought of torching the place?'

Latimer tried to laugh. 'They'd bust my other arm.'

Davey went to the wall map, raked his eyes over it. 'What's it worth, your end of the business?'

'All told? Thirty, thirty-five grand?'

Davey stared at the wall.

'You're not thinking of buying in? Save my life, that would.'

'I can only go to twenty-five.'

Simon looked at his lap. 'I can't do anything with that.'

'Fine. Stay here then. Rot in it.'

'It's too low, and there's five and a half grand you owe me anyway.'

He threw up his arms. 'Si, I offer you a chance to get out of this and all you do is insult me, you silly bastard.' He went behind Latimer and pressed his hands on his shoulders, leaning in close. 'Tell you what. You go home, have a think about it, and when you've decided this is for the best, then we'll go have a talk with these Peterson people.'

'They're not great talkers.'

'They'll talk.'

'You know what you're letting yourself in for.'

'Bunch of South East London slags. Hardly the Yardies is it?'

'No, but . . .'

He was at the door. 'Oh, and what's the SP on this Reece bloke?'

'Reece?'

'He's one of your drivers.'

Simon sat in concentration. 'He's just a driver . . . isn't he?'

'He's into them and all. See, I already know more about your business than you do and I ain't even started yet. Now, once you've sorted out a meet with them, bell me and have Reece drive us down there.'

By the time it dawned on Simon that the deal had effectively been done, Davey was being driven away in one of his cabs.

Reece took her hand and slipped a plastic bank bag into her palm. They were sitting in the Brewers as he had a few minutes before he was due to start his shift up at the Elephant & Castle. A thin rain flew against the windows, beads of it adhering to the dark panes. Outside, a night wind rustled chip wrappers and clattered cans of Fanta along the broken pavements.

'What's in the Lucky Bag this time? PCP? Smack? Elephant tranquilliser?'

'Guaranteed grade A Chas.'

'You sampled it?'

'Let's say I have it on good authority.'

She felt fear course around her body. 'Reece — I know it's a bit late to ask, but you're not an undercover cop, are you?'

His response was immediate. 'No.'

'How do I know?'

'You'll have to trust me.'

All this talk of dangerous people, and of using her to get to Davey. For all she knew she was a pawn in some hidden agenda. She didn't like, and had never liked, holding drugs. Hated the associations they brought with them of desperation and oblivion. Sure, she enjoyed getting off her face once in a while, but in a controlled way. She'd had her days of waking up in strangers' beds, flats, gardens. She stuck her hand under the table and passed it back to him.

Reece took it, crumpling it in his fist. 'You haven't heard the idea yet.'

She rolled her eyes.

Reece said, 'We'll do one back on him. You can tell he's on the marching powder, drug snob too by the looks of it. The product is straight from customs, very pure.'

'Customs?'

'Friend of a friend.'

She cast him a dubious look. 'What friend? And what happened to Ten Benson?'

'He obliged me with a refund.'

'You beat the crap out of him?'

'Not all of it.'

She glared at him. 'That doesn't impress me, Reece.'

He turned his mouth down in an aw-diddums kind of way that she didn't particularly like. 'Say Davey's out on the town some night. You come over all pally – they know you, so that's OK. It's even better now that they think of you as a bit of a joke.'

'Thanks,' she snarled.

'When you tell him you've got this great stuff, he'll go, *Yeah, yeah, sure* – until you give him the sampler. This, he will like. He will ask for more. Then you and I sell him a bag so cut with flour he'll be shitting scones for a month.'

'Nice image.'

'I'll stick close by, make sure it doesn't go arse over tip.'

'When?'

'When the time's right.'

'He'll know, you know.'

'He won't. We'll make sure he's out of it at the time. Also, I know he's got the bunce to pay you back. I've seen it.'

He took her hand in his, stroked her knuckles and entwined their fingers. 'I want you happy, that's all. If Davey's what you want, we'll get him, don't you worry.'

'I do — least I think I do.'

He smiled. 'Let's *start* with him, shall we?'

As he rose, she realised he'd slipped the bag back into her hand.

CHAPTER FOURTEEN

Steve backed the breakdown lorry into the pound and he and
Arch set about unhooking the Mercedes. Steve lowered the ramp
and unfastened the heavy leather straps on the wheels, while
Arch pulled off the scuffed yellow Denver boot. In minutes they
had the motor down on cinder. Owing to the rain they had the
damp cowls of their tracksuits up over their heads, lending them
the look of dissolute monks. The real order of the day – busting
into the car – would begin shortly, but first they sprinted
through the oily spitting puddles and made for the Starburger in
the parade.

The windows were clouded over, the air rich with fag fog and
the cloying odour of hot fat. It had been chucking it down since
dawn and a line of flattened boxes had been laid from the door
to counter to absorb the worst of the wet. Muddy scars and
bootprints were trodden into their cardboard corrugations.

'All white, love. Do us a couple coffees,' said Steve to the
matronly waitress at the till. As she turned to froth up the milk,
Steve tossed Arch a disapproving glance, muttering, 'State of
that, eh?'

They took their seats, Archie pressing his bulging gut under
the chipped plastic rim of the table. Steve pulled out a folded
copy of the *Sport* and studied the form. A PVC'd, spike-heeled
girl on the cover.

'Reminds me of Katrina, that one. Gawd, things I used to do to her.'

Archie propped the laminated menu between them and rapped the triangular stand down hard. 'You wanna eat summink now or after we do the drop?'

Steve scrutinised it through his habitual hangover haze: door-mats of meat, Belisha beacon bright scampi, a token lurid lettuce. 'Later,' he said.

The waitress brought their coffees and they set to with the sugar.

'I had another thought about that painting,' Steve said.

Archie held his cup an inch from his mouth. 'Give it a rest.'

'No, listen, right. You ain't found a buyer yet so I got this brilliant idea. What we do is ransom it back to the gallery.'

This was new. Steve thinking. Specially at nine forty-two of a morning.

'What for?'

Steve folded his brow and pushed aside his cup. 'What for? Five million quid. I can't *believe* you ain't bothered one way or the other.'

'So what's the plan, Stan?'

'First thought I had was we send some snaps of the painting along with a note. Like sending a Polaroid of a kid you've kid-napped. But then I had another think' – his tone dropped to a bronchial wheeze – 'what we do is send 'em part of it. Of the actual painting. Cut a square off the bottom corner, tell them if they don't pay up, then we send another. And so on.'

Archie had to admit he was impressed.

'It's perfect. They can do all them tests on the first square so it'll prove it's pukka. I got the idea off the telly. John Paul Getty junior, I think it was. They cut his ear off, did the old Van Gogh job on him. Paid up after that.'

Archie notched up another few points of admiration. Not

only had Steve arrived at a plan that was potentially do-able (not that he wanted to, of course) but he'd made a stab at pronouncing Van Gogh without getting gob all over the table.

'If they don't pay up right away, we send another square. Put the pressure on, like sending another finger or a toe.' He sparked up a JPS. 'So what d'you reckon? Magic, innit?' He sat back and chugged a celebratory smoke ring, the proud father of his invention.

Archie drained his cup and wiped the froth from his lips with the back of his fat fist. 'Stevie, boy, you do have a good 'un there, only there is a slight catch.'

'Do what?'

'We're all right for sending them the first couple of squares, but what happens if they don't pay up?'

'Keep going until they do.'

The veins in Archie's temples began to crawl like worms. 'Yeah but there's a point at which you have five million quid's worth of Rembrandt, right? And then – bang – you got a bastard JIGSAW PUZZLE.'

The waitress frowned at them from behind the carton of Chupa-Chups that they used for the tips. It wasn't full.

Archie continued. 'And what we end up with is a buggered painting, plus the risk of us getting kippered.'

Steve narrowed his eyes. 'Only 'cos you like the bleeding thing. You don't want it spoilt.'

'That ain't the point.'

'What is the point?'

'The plan's flawed.'

'I ain't Professor Stephen *fucking* Hawking, am I? You come up with something.'

'It stays round mine till we find the right buyer.'

'Let me send 'em a square. See how it goes?'

Archie was on his feet, thumbing coinage out of his pockets. 'No. Now let's get back to work.'

*

Davey Kayman aka David Hayes, producer, strolled into the Groucho Club with the insouciance of a builder padding out a job. He nodded at the brunette at Reception and easily spotted Toby Lomax on one of the sofas adjacent to the bar. He was middle aged and hiding it badly. He wore cords, a ski anorak and a heavy frosting of white stubble. The Bloody Mary in front of him didn't look like his first. He was everything Davey expected of a television director who'd lost it big-time. Public school, pissed, pliable.

'David Hayes,' he said thrusting out a hand.

Lomax half-stood to greet him. As he mumbled his hello, Davey turned to the bar and ordered a rum and coke on Lomax's tab. Settling with his back to the wall, Davey could almost hear the instrumental lead-in before the sales dance began. Naturally, he would lead.

'First off, I gotta say how much I like your work. "Essex Cowboys" was "appointment to view" television.'

He had read the *Guardian* 'Media' section and *Broadcast* for the jargon.

Lomax said, 'We were up for an award.'

Probably not directorial, thought Davey. 'Great hand-held stuff, and the on-camera confessions – brilliant. We were very impressed with the tapes.'

'We' – always invent a 'we'.

'You didn't catch it when it went out then?'

'I was abroad. Now, what I have in mind is right up your street. Usual hidden cameras, big exposé. I've the inside track on this one and it'll piss on the DocuSoaps from a great height.'

Lomax sat up like a child hearing a fresh story. His eyes were bright and his hands, resting lightly on his knees, hardly shook at all.

'It's real Tobes.'

Lomax frowned. He'd never been called Tobes before. 'Is it for Channel Four?'

'You got contacts at Four?' His hesitation was enough. 'No,

I was thinking Carlton. Who's there now?'

'Terry Binding of course.'

'Right.'

The director lent him a dubious glance.

'I've been away for a while. Canada and LA.'

That went across.

Lomax slugged back the sludge in his glass. 'Look, I don't mean to be sort of rude, but can you tell a bit about where you're . . . coming from?'

Davey raised an imperious hand. 'No problem. I've produced several award-winning docs out in Canada [hard to prove or disprove]. I started in Nature but now it's Human Interest [vague enough]. CrossTalk are doing so well that I'm over here to set up the production offices in London [so no definite address]. This is a project I've been developing for a long time and' – he paused for a moment – 'did you get the tapes we sent?'

'I don't think—'

'I had a box of them biked over to you pronto after we spoke.'

Toby sealed the lie for him. 'Must be the despatch company. Who'd you use?'

'Finsbury. I'll get onto them.'

'A nightmare these people.'

'Can't get anyone to *do* anything these days. It's not hard to drive some VT's across town. Could've done it quicker myself.'

Lomax domed his eyebrows in sympathy. 'Too right,' he said.

'It's that sort of incompetence that caused me to leave Britain in the first place,' snorted Davey, employing the wounded arrogance of the ex-pat.

Common ground having been discovered, they promptly colonised it and set to, tilling and turning over England and its psyche, of which neither was particularly enamoured. Lomax hated the critics and anyone with the power to scythe him down before his proper talents had had a chance to bloom. Davey disliked the apathy, the obstructive judicial system and threw in the traffic, oh the traffic. Bonded, Toby shone with vodka and the radiance of a small man listened to. Davey made ready to land his catch.

'Here's the title. London — *London's Underworld Uncovered.*'

Toby repeated the phrase silently, rolling it around in his mouth.

'The criminal fraternity. The bosses, the sharks and the con men. The real ones — at it. We'll be using hidden cameras, taped confessions, grasses, swindlers, ropers, outside men — exposing every scam in the capital. And none of these "former burglars": it's gonna be right on the nose. Catch them nicking gear, black-mail and extortion, short and long cons, the works.'

'Sources?'

He showed his teeth. 'Excellent and reliable.'

'Sounds very good,' beamed Lomax, thinking already of unearthing his old BAFTA acceptance speech.

'Better be. I'm telling you, it's eight half-hours that'll grab the viewers by the bollocks.'

'Presenter?'

'Nah — voice-over. No point in pissing away money on talent. Plus, those investigative journo's are up their own arses. Egotistical fuckwads.' He spat.

'Fair point.'

'So, you up for this? Think you could handle it?'

He replied in the affirmative. Davey had correctly guessed that Lomax would film the sex-life of a tortoise if there was money in it. He'd be dumped as soon as they got started anyway. There was, however, one more thing — the only real reason for this meeting. 'Can you sort out a meet with Terry Binding at Carlton? Tomorrow or the next day?'

He blew air. 'Not a chance.'

'I need the favour, Tobes. Act of faith and all that. The guys at CrossTalk, Vancouver, are going to want something concrete from a broadcaster before they start throwing money at us. I'm flying back in a couple of days, so I want this nailed.' He placed a friendly hand on Toby's shoulder. 'Do what you can, then bell me. Anyway, got to go. I've a shitload more meetings this after-noon.'

'On this project?' asked Lomax, nervously.

'Yeah.'

'You're seeing other directors?'

Davey gave a shark grin. 'Yes, but only for sex.'

'Where can I reach you?'

The M4 overhead section was solid with traffic. Under its damp, supports, a Rover ploughed along the Great West Road. It broke free of Brentford and the fat tyres made wet furrows in the rain-slicked road.

'Funny. We had a Rover s'mornin'.' Steve said.

'Yeah. Sweet.'

Steve beamed and thumped his hand on the wheel to the beat of the radio.

Despite the appalling weather, Archie and Steve had made a success of the day. The lot was heaving with newly clamped motors, their owners too wet or tired to argue the toss on the soaking streets. The sky was lowering and the streetlights blinking on when they made their last delivery to the city. There, the con-troller told Archie he had an airport run going with a drop in the Croydon area. Did they fancy taking it since it was on their way?

Magic, said Arch, without consulting Steve. He was well miffed about his suggestion that they chop up the Rembrandt, and was keen on getting home for another eyeball of it.

They took a Rover, which the firm had been using for ten days – the maximum safe period before the owner showed up at the lot with the required 'documentation'. Still, this was two birds, one stone. Pick up the punter, drop him, and get home early. They'd split the take. A score each.

'Your best bet is M25 to Junction Seven, come in via Coulsdon on the A23.'

'Piss off,' retorted Steve. 'Come back this way, drop down by the Bath Road, through Hounslow. Cut through Teddington, over to Kingston and you're home free.'

'What about the by-pass? It's chocker.'

'Like you ain't bollocksed on the M25? That's been solid round the Gatwick turnoff ever since they built the bastard.'

Archie wasn't having any. 'Your way, you come up against the traffic heading out on the A3, A4.'

'Against the *grain*, Arch. I am not going round the poxy M25.'

Archie couldn't be arsed to take it any further. Once Steve's mind was set, it was hard to dissuade him. Still, least they'd be doing the drive in silence once they were POB.

Negotiating around Heathrow was surprisingly swift and they soon pulled up outside Terminal Two. Archie went in, returning ten minutes later with a jet-lagged businessman. Archie told him he'd have to have his luggage in the back seat with him as they had a problem with the boot. Reluctantly, the man folded his long limbs into the back seat. He had an intelligent face with a brow creased with worry lines.

Steve pulled away from the kerb.

'Everything all right, sir?' asked Archie from the passenger seat.

The client's face seemed puzzled, strained. Archie wondered if he was going to have a coronary.

The man clutched at Steve's shoulder.

'Stop the car,' he barked. Steve did so, pulling up only fifty yards from the Terminal building.

'S'matter?' asked Archie, alarmed.

The passenger scrabbled at the door.

Archie was mystified. 'Steve,' he warned.

Steve released the central locks with a thock and the man flew out.

'Wait here,' he called breathlessly, and ran off.

Steve looked at Archie. 'Prob'ly forgotten something.'

A couple of minutes later, the businessman came cantering

back with an armed Heathrow policeman, who was talking urgently into his radio. As the adrenaline kicked in, Steve put on his best gormless face and buzzed down the window.

'All white? What's occurring officer?'

Their passenger pushed his face into his. 'I'll tell you what's happening. You're being arrested. This is *my* car. I've been abroad for a week and I hadn't had the chance to report it stolen.'

'It was clamped, mate,' offered Steve, limply.

Archie said nothing, just closed his eyes and leaned back in the smooth leather. It wouldn't wash. Not this time.

CHAPTER FIFTEEN

Ally sounded like she was cresting on a chocolate rush. 'Aya, Rox. How's it going?'

'I'm close to getting Cyber-boy and Drongo house-trained.'

'Any luck with the money? You coming home?'

'Why, have you burnt my house down?'

'No-oh,' she drawled.

Rox put on her glasses. 'It's a long story with the money and that, but me and the cab driver are gonna hopefully pull a fast one on this Davey Kayman bloke. But before you ask about Reece, it's all gone weird. We had that snog, then he backed off, says he's getting over someone.'

'So?'

'He's not ready yet, he says.'

'What is he – gay?'

Rox took a deep breath. 'Just because he doesn't want to shag the arse off me straightaway doesn't mean he's gay.' Why was she defending him all of a sudden? she wondered.

'Not one of these bloody arty-farty sensitive types is he?'

She laughed; thinking of his muscled, bruised shoulders and knuckles.

'How's Chorlton?'

'Guess what?'

'You got the sack again?'

'Yeah, but apart from that – ooh, I've got to tell you. Mark's split up with Corinne. He wants you back.'

'Does he now?' Power coursed through her like a switch had been thrown. A thousand volts of self-esteem, vindication and revenge surged round her system until she felt giddy.

'He's been phoning me non-stop. Actually, that's why I lost the job at *MegaPhones*. He kept pestering me there.'

'Really?'

'That, and I were selling off the stock out the back. Anyway, he says he can't live without you.'

'Good. I want him dead.'

'And he'll do anything to get you back.'

She gave it world-weary. 'Not true, Al. I know Mark. He'll buy me some stuff, tell me he's dead sorry and as soon as I'd given in to the sympathy sex, we'll be back to where we were.'

'So you're with this cabbie now?'

Rox ran a hand through her hair, tugging at the roots. 'Come on – I want the gory details about Mark. Tell me Corinne stood in the middle of the bar and took the piss about how lazy he was when it came to muff diving.'

'Not quite. Turns out she had another boyfriend – Karl – over in Rusholme. She'd told him she was a nurse working nights at Withington. So on Saturday evening, a friend of his busts his arm in a fight and him and Karl go to Casualty . . . expecting to see Little Miss Nursey.'

Rox thought of Reece and of how he'd reacted when she'd tried to soothe his injuries. 'And?'

'No one had heard of her. He wakes up her flatmate and gets her to give him the address of the Garage. Karl put a dustbin through window.'

'I like Karl.'

'Good. She went back to him.'

'Even though she lied about being a nurse?'

Ally giggled. 'Apparently, she had the uniform and everything. She's known for making up stories. Living in a right fantasy world.'

'Yeah, but one with two *real* boyfriends in it . . . so Mark's gutted then?'

'Oh, yeah.'

'Did Karl do him any damage?'

'He was behind the window when the dustbin came through.'

Smiling, Rox tried to untangle the phone cord. 'Look, Ally, whatever you do, don't give him this number. I need time to think about it. Okay?'

'Right-o.'

Rox hung up and did some skipping around the room.

A vicious wind scythed around Portman Square. It shook the brown boughs of the trees, lashed the buildings and whipped the faces of the commuters. Davey and Toby bundled out of a cab in front of the offices of Carlton Television. Toby paid. He had procured a 'ten-o'-clock' with Terry Binding by pulling in a favour and swearing that their pitch would not exceed twenty minutes. They signed in, were given their plastic ID cards and took the lift. Davey noted that Lomax looked more bilious this morning.

'Been out celebrating?'

'Something like that,' answered Toby Lomax, eyes fixed on the illuminated floor numbers.

Terry Binding looked to be a man in a hurry as his desk was cluttered with videotapes and his computer screen blazed with unread e-mails. Davey liked people who were short of time: it gave him a chance to present the big picture quickly, work fast, set up a blizzard of facts and figures. Binding was in his late forties, whippet-thin and aquiline with a skull that looked as though vultures had stripped the meat from it. His remaining hair was left long to de-emphasise a pair of overlarge ears. He adopted the cowering yet alert posture of a greyhound as he perched on the corner of his black ash desk. He was frosty with Lomax, tolerating rather than respecting him, and their opening salvo was brief. Davey was introduced and given the floor. He skimmed through a CV he'd lifted from a number of Canadian documentaries, and set to talking up the project.

Late the previous afternoon, he had dropped in unannounced on Lomax and winkled out of him some of the many technical and financial details he'd need for the proposal. Davey then worked through the night, breaking down the series into bite-sized pieces and printing it out on sheets of A4. It was a smorgasbord of criminal activities, most of which he'd been involved in himself at one time or another. He decided that if McLean, Mad Frank and McVicar could do it, then so could he. He appended the submission document with a budget of £100,000 per show.

Binding listened, making the odd jotting on the cover of a report beside him. Davey concluded his pitch by offering up a blank tape. It was one he had doctored by damaging the plastic capstans in the spool mechanism. It was supposedly a promo of all his work to date.

'Shit, must be you've got a different system over here,' he fumed.

'No matter. Now, you're seeding Toby here to direct, that correct?'

Davey fanned an arm at Lomax as if he were Moses with the tablets. 'Well . . . "Essex Cowboys?" I mean.'

Lomax grinned like a toddler who had wet himself. Then he coughed hard, paled and, clutching his stomach, rose from his seat.

'You all right . . .?' Binding asked.

'Stomach cramp. Bad pint.'

Of vodka, thought Davey.

'Look, would you mind if I sort of, used the little boy's room?'

Binding ushered him out and they heard the anxious squawk of the PA followed by Lomax bumbling off down the corridor. Binding took his time in closing the door.

'Who was it you said you worked with in Vancouver?'

'CrossTalk. We're not as well-known over here.'

'Say you did the cutting edge on sanitary conditions in world-class hotels?'

'Name any Michelin four star and I'll guarantee not to get us a table.'

'And you were in Montreal.'

Davey nodded.

'You must know John Cassidy?'

He gave an indistinct nod. 'So how about it? See, the thing is with the nature of this material, we'll need to go into pre-production very soon.' Good that, he thought. The 'we' and this 'pre-production'.

Binding tapped his pen on the report. 'The figures are rather high.'

'It's the night-time filming,' bluffed Davey. He'd heard that camera crews were notoriously expensive anytime after tea.

'I'm still not convinced about these contacts of yours. I mean, how did you get an in with these crime families if you've been in Canada for the best part of a decade?'

Off the top of his head. 'My sister's married into them.' Thinking, Charlie, you might be needed here.

'But if they're as dangerous as you say, then aren't you risking her life?'

Davey gulped down a breath. This wasn't turning out as planned. What was this prat doing, questioning every little thing?

'And surely if you have this knowledge of crimes past and present, isn't it going to be a nightmare on the legal side? And how's your liaison with the Met and the Crime Business Group? And your sister's connection isn't – frankly – helpful to us.'

'She's divorced now.' Time to nip *this* one in the bud thought Davey. He leaned forward and hissed, 'Terry, I'll be straight with you. I'd love to answer these questions but you know as well as me that the creases get ironed out later. We're looking at the whole sheet. Has it been done? No. Will it pull in the punters? Yes.' He raised his eyes to a framed photo on the wall. 'Will it stick another gong up there?'

Binding eyed him levelly.

Two, three seconds he gave it. 'Terry. I've got the Beeb all over me like a rash. And it doesn't need to be said that Channel Four are snapping at my heels and all.'

'Frank Goreham is it?'

'Yeah.'

'Frank Goreham works here. He's a line editor.'

His cheek shuddered. 'Who'm I thinking of then?'

Binding wasn't going to offer up anything.

'Well?' Davey pushed.

'I don't know. Neil?'

'Yeah. Neil.'

'Which Neil do you mean?'

Davey wiped a finger over his cheek, smoothing out the muscle, then held his hand level in mid-air. 'Middle-aged. So high. Bit of a gut on him. Likes, er, trains.'

Binding launched a finger at him. 'Yes.'

Davey's cheek stopped juddering.

'Neil likes trains, because Neil is my four-year-old son.'

Fuck a duck, thought Davey.

Binding pivoted off the desk and thrust out a hand.

'Mr Hayes, it's been nice to meet you.'

Never, ever, back down. Front it out. 'I've been producing for ten years, mate, and got the campaign medals to prove it. If that tape had worked you'd have seen my showreel. Blown your socks off, it would. As for this, well it's so new you can't see it. And so what if I'm not pally with all your mates?'

'You're quite at liberty to take the idea elsewhere.'

'Too right I am.'

Binding buttoned his jacket, a supercilious smile creeping across his slender face. 'And if you come up with something more, do get in touch.'

'I will.'

'We must do lunch.'

Kiss of death thought Davey. Rumbled.

In the corridor, a pallid Toby Lomax was sipping from a paper cone of water. He sloped alongside.

'How'd it go?'

David Hayes clapped him on the back, guiding him back to the lift. 'He's up for it but he wants us to work on the idea a bit more. What we'll do is put some rough footage together, convince the bastard.'

'Okay. And CrossTalk will cover the costs of filming?'

Davey's reply was lost in the hum of the lift doors.

Steve Lamb liked a pint and loved pubs. His view was that a decent boozer provided everything a man needed out of life. First off there was your drink. Be it beer, whisky or gin, your friendly barmen (evil bastards if you'd had one too many) were *legally bound* to serve you up the poison of your choice.

He liked his bitter, always had, London Pride his nightly tipple and woe betide anyone who didn't stand his round. 'Get the beers in' was the family motto, or it would have been if he'd had a family. Beer was the best of British, and then there was your chasers, your winter warmer, your one for the road, your No-I'm-driving-oh-alright-then, your nightcap, the Go-on-love-try-it-you-might-like-it and his proper drinks, Jack and coke, rum and black, vodka and orange. The local pub relied on him to deplete their stock, so much so that he frequented two of them, the Gregorian on the Jamaica Road where he was sitting now and the Old Justice. He spent time in others of course, as he liked to get about. There was the Red Cow, the King's Arms, The Bell, the Two Brewers and the Prince of Wales. He was an equal opportunities drinker. Then there was The Railway over Nunhead where he sank a few every now and again with Archie Pea.

Great thing about pubs was they were like birds; they never ran out. You finished with one, you moved on to the next. After a bit, you came back to the first, spruced yourself up a bit, behaved, and she'd have you back. You smelled that sweet perfume of hers like it was the first time. Old Oak, fags and hops. Then there was the gleam of brass; the beer towels laid out all neat along the polished wood at opening time. Optics winking at you.

Course, that was the other big reason for pubs. The birds, the crumpet, the gash, the muff, the minge. God in his infinite had placed all manner of big titted girls in there solely for your inspection. And he was naturally both accommodating and scrupulous in his attentions, oiling them with compliments, greasing with a wink and slap, spunking his wad at them. And they better come through. All right, so the numbers were down, but still, three nights a week; well. all white — two — he was on a dead cert for someone else's Doris, some foreign bird, some barmaid or her mate. And once he had them in the car park, in the motor, up the alley, he'd show them a good time. Give 'em a bit of whooah. Wallop.

Then get back inside in time for staybacks.

Yip. All kinds of reasons for chucking one down your neck. Christmas, New Year's, high days and holidays. End of the week, hard day, bad week, tough month, mid-week match, match post-mortem, pre-match Saturdays, post-match Saturdays, Friday nights, Saturday nights — sacrosanct they were, no bloody going down the flicks for Stevie-boy — this was valuable drinking time. In fact, now he thought about it, you add in the Sunday morning hair of the dog and there's no reason why you shouldn't actually live in a pub. Except if he did, he'd never leave until they carried him out in a box. His chest wheezed like a bus in traffic as he let out a throaty laugh. Funny that — out in a box — with the job he had on tonight?

Following their arrest at the airport, he and Archie had been taken to the police station at Heathrow and charged. They demanded to be allowed to call their brief. Steve didn't have one but Arch had the number of the Petersons' approved solicitors. This was done and in two hours both men were free. Arch cried off going for a drink. There was something else. On their way back, the brief had passed on a message to Steve to bell Tel Peterson. This he did from a call-box. Steve was offered a one-stop way of covering his legal fees and making a few grand on the side. He accepted, and was drinking now to celebrate both his release and to summon up Dutch courage, the heavy gun nestling uncomfortably in his waistband.

Chauffeur cars were thin on the ground this evening, but Reece had blagged a decent Beamer on seniority. It was freezing out, but the wind had dropped and the traffic thinned out. He'd picked up at seven and now the car slinked down off the overpass and purred along the Old Kent Road. Davey Kayman and Simon Latimer were in the back, on their way to the meeting with Tel and Bill Peterson.

This was one of his old stamping grounds. There was the Gin Palace and the World Turned Upside Down, old boozers tarted up in the Eighties, quiet now, hours until their guts heaved with beered-up bodies and the pavements turned to terraces of turmoil. Not even the most hard-up drivers picked up from there. The Rising Sun passed by, dead and gone, abandoned by the brewery. Trouble was everything had been *firkinised*. Reece remembered when there used to be only the two of them in this patch of London, the one off Newington Causeway and the Fox in Lewisham. So many of the pubs had lost their carpet, darts and wallpaper, turned into airy hangars. And where had the old drinkers gone? The toothless old codgers nursing stout, Capstans sucking the last breath out of them? Probably up north in Heritage Britain.

He smiled and thought of Rox, and when he'd taken the Mick. He didn't reckon much to the North, but it was so easy to get the rise out of her. He'd wanted to kiss (what he privately thought of as) her pixie face again and again, to cuddle her into him, to caress and . . . glad he'd put a stop to it. Get too close and it'd be too easy to start saying things, doing things, moving things on. He wasn't ready, not yet. Too many hassles. Even being in that pub with her had given him the sweats.

They came past the Thomas à Becket, its famous gym clinging on, the pub a husk of its former notoriety. There was a row of shops; many of them abandoned since Tesco carved a new heart into the place. Only the bookies, charities and fast-food places survived – hardy weeds of the high street.

Latimer's mobile went. He pulled it from his sling. He was given curt instructions. He pressed 'off'.

'Reece, do you know a pub called the Walmer Castle?'

He nodded and turned left down Peckham Park Road.

'What's this?' blustered Davey.

Latimer said. 'Change of plan. We're to meet them at a different place.'

'Bollocks we are. Turn us round and take us back.'

'David,' he replied sternly, 'they always do this.'

He sat back and fumed. Davey wasn't in the mood tonight. He had plans. Didn't need anyone playing silly bollocks. 'All right. But Rice, or whatever your name is – you stick to us like shit in case there's trouble.'

Reece said nothing, wondering about the change of venue.

This pub was untouched by refurbishment; it had a horseshoe bar, deep blood-red carpets, fruit machine in the corner, dartboard and hand-written posters advertising strippers and the karaoke. They trotted inside and sank into a buttoned banquette. No sign of the Petersons. It transpired that getting the drinks in was going to be a Mexican stand-off between Reece's employer and Davey Kayman.

'It's me who's getting you out of schtuck,' Davey warned.

Latimer tried to obtain the barman's attention with his undamaged arm. There were a few drinkers in, huddled round the horseshoe, couple of blokes playing darts, their mate on the machine, losing. Couple of middle-aged women getting in the V & T's before their other halves came home. They were locals from the Pelican or Sumner Estates. One old boy at the bar looked familiar. He was deep in conversation with a black bloke. Both of them in big coats, weathered faces and hands, clawing at their drinks. Reece knew the old boy. Tommy McCormack. Knew all about him. He blanked the man and scoped his gaze through the bar to the seats on the other side.

Rox Matheson was looking straight at him.

A bolt of fear shot through her. What the hell was Reece doing in here? She slid down out of sight, glimpsing Davey Kayman as well. If this was the night they were going to do the switch, then this was a pretty dumb way of going about it. Graham was babbling on about websites and e-commerce and how he was going to become a millionaire. She wasn't listening. She'd chosen this pub as she'd wanted to celebrate Mark's newly enforced period of celibacy by going for a curry. It was still early when they reached the bottom of the road and she'd suggested they drop in for a quick one. What were *they* doing here? And what would she say if Davey recognised her? Were they friends? Should she pretend not to know Reece? Sod him. What was going on?

'This is bollocks,' said Davey. 'It's a wind-up.'

Latimer responded quietly. 'Why would they want to wind you up when you're carrying all that money to *give* to them?'

Reece wondered what was going on between Davey and the Petersons? There was something wrong about this. His hackles rose and a familiar shiver ran down his spine. Adrenaline began to pump. His fears were justified when the doors opened and a cold gust of wind ushered in Steve Lamb.

He was wearing a balaclava and his tattered driving gloves, but Reece knew the greasy denim coat and the cowboy boots of old. More interesting was the gun in his hand.

Everything froze save for the tinned music, which became much more irritating. The gun was big and black in his fist.

Reece thought of leaping across the bar and covering Rox.

Davey thought his time had come early.

Latimer thought his time had come.

Graham had not turned round and didn't know why it'd gone quiet. Rox's horrified face told him. He turned, shut up then.

The barman and the customers stopped breathing.

Two seconds.

Lamb moved forward, arcing the gun around, holding it high enough so that any vigilante might be dissuaded. Its black nozzle scoured the faces, passing Graham's, Rox's, pausing at a middle-aged woman, across to the barman, then Latimer.

Davey's hand tightened on his pint glass. He'd throw it in the man's eyes, put him off his shot. This couldn't happen *now*, not when things were beginning to go so right! The glass was too heavy to lift. His heart jackhammered in his chest.

Latimer fainted.

Five seconds.

The gun paused on Reece. He stared into the eyeholes of Steve Lamb's mask.

Six.

The gun moved towards the back of the man crouched over the bar.

'Message for you, Paddy,' said Steve in the worst approximation of an Irish accent Reece had ever heard.

The gun fired three times in rapid succession. The noise was deafening. The bullets blew apart Tommy McCormack's head, spattering his brains and face all over the bar and barman. Blood and viscera spewed and spouted everywhere, streams of it flooding over wood, on glass, on the floor. A fourth bullet tore into the man's back, smashing his spine irreparably, blasting out his organs into his lap. He fell, dead in the seventh second, no more a man, a body blasted full of holes, an instant corpse.

Eight, nine, ten seconds. Lamb lowered the gun, took a step backwards, turned and was gone.

Smoke and the smell of cordite filled the air. Stiff silence.

The first scream went off five seconds later.

Reece said, 'Take Latimer to the car.'

No words came out of Davey. His face was ashen, eyes welded open in shock. Reece added. 'Hit-man. Long gone. Move.'

Davey tugged at Simon. Reece pulled him to his feet and hustled them out, then stepped over McCormack's corpse, avoiding the blood pooling around him. Three paces and he was at Rox's side. She was contributing to the howling, as was Graham.

'The bloke was a grass,' he hissed. 'None of our business. Come on, out of here you two. Now.'

She didn't respond, so Reece lifted her up and carried her outside. He made sure that Davey had gone up the side-street to the car.

'Can't stop, but this might be the night. I'll call later. What's your number?'

Graham, stumbling out after, told him. Reece memorised it, then hugged her briefly, gave a few reassuring words and disappeared.

It was several minutes before she was able to speak: by then a terrified Graham had pulled her halfway up Southampton Way.

'Least he finally asked for my number,' she said, with a weak shivery smile.

CHAPTER SIXTEEN

In his attempt to snort a line, Davey had tipped most of his coke on the floor of the BMW. Latimer was recovering slowly, but there were beads of sweat on his bruised brow. The car idled, vapour puffing from the exhaust. Reece hoped Rox was handling it – never a pretty sight a murder, and best if you kept your mind and mouth shut.

Latimer's mobile rang. He dropped it between his knees and Davey had to fish it from the floor. Fresh instructions were given, which Simon passed on to Reece. A trattoria in New Cross Gate.

Davey's face was set, his eyes returning to their obsidian hardness. He made like a porker with the remains of his stash, then began giving it large.

'Well, that's *it*, isn't it, Si? They've shot their bolt. If that's supposed to put the frighteners on us, well shit a brick. I've seen worse.'

'You have?' Latimer asked.

'Remember the old North London families. Make this bunch look like amateurs. Anyone can walk into a pub and start blasting. Go to any boozer round Plaistow and there's a slaughter hour: two for one and a free cocktail umbrella. These silly bollocks haven't got any reason to start in on us, so you can keep schtum.'

Reece listened unimpressed at the stream of braggadocio as he carved through the villainous playgrounds of South East London.

He pulled up in the bus lane in Kender Street. As the trio stepped out, he asked whether they'd need him later. Davey demanded to know why. Reece told him he'd other work on. Regular customers. Davey shot him an odd look and told him to stick close by. They'd be going on to a club in Hoxton if all went well.

The trat was cheapo Italian with red check tablecloths, clumpy wooden chairs and stained stucco walls. The front window was clouded over. Reece led them in. The owner, who was avuncular and balding, greeted him effusively even though he'd not seen him in many months. Latimer and Davey stood behind him, timid like children. There were ten or so diners; three sets of couples and a table of four. Sitting with the best view of any comings and goings were the Peterson brothers, in front of them were goblets of wine, the remains of a meal, an overflowing ashtray, and three gold B & H bricks. Neither were matinée idols.

Both were middle-aged, had broad foreheads, thick noses and cliff-like faces that spoke of forty years of drink and Deptford. Tel was the thinner of the two with a full set of Tom on his fingers, a chunky bracelet and a solid black mullet hairstyle that looked like it'd been done with car-spray paint. Bill was heavy-set, filling his shirt to capacity, face and hands vellum-hued from the remains of a winter tan, silver slicked-back hair, tufts of it curling up over earlobes the size of boulders. Introductions were made and Reece obtained the nod from his true employers. Without a word, he backed out, leaving Davey and Latimer to it.

Fifteen minutes later, Reece was in the kitchen in Graham's flat. They were in shock on the sofa. The TV was on, partly to claw back some normalcy and partly as Rox and Graham expected that the channels would soon collapse into each other for an immediate Newsflash – Man Gunned Down in Cold Blood in Peckham Pub. Reece hunted around in the cupboard.

'Rox, best we do it tonight. Davey's out of gear, I know, I saw it. He'll want to score after this and that's where you come in.

He's carrying a lot of dosh.' He took out the sugar and flour and tossed them onto the table. Then from his inside pocket, he produced seven grammes of coke wrapped in a clear bag.

'There's a way of mixing this properly, so we can get the good stuff on the outside where we want it. I've only got a few minutes, so you'll have to do it after I'm gone. I'll show you how to wrap it up and all. Then you're to go to the Firefly club in Fanshaw Street. I'll see you get in. But before you do, walk down Hoxton Street to Curtain Road. Keep going until you get to Bateman's Row. Stick the bag up a drainpipe and take only the sample in with you. When you bring him out I'll be nearby.'

He looked at her then. Rox was staring up at him, glassy eyed, her cheeks streaked with tears.

'Reece, a man was murdered.'

He crouched down in front of her. 'He was a grass. It was a score settled, been coming a long time. Done as a warning and to scare Davey.'

'It was *horrible*.'

'I know.' He fixed her coldly. 'But you've got to keep it together for tonight. Davey's just as freaked by it. That's our advantage.'

Rox could not fathom why Reece wasn't affected. It was the single most shocking thing she had ever seen in her life. The man's head blasting apart, the smell of gunpowder and blood and him slumping to the floor like that. He lay so still, like a dead animal.

'Rox. You listening? Am I getting through?'

She nodded dumbly.

'Will you do it?'

Davey kicked off breezily. 'If you wanted to show us what you can do, a short film would have been better, sort of an induction-day thing. And you could have had a brochure, fancy logo, shield or a coat of arms — or how's about a bulletproof vest?

And then you'd have one of them taglines everything's got now, like: McDonald's — Fifteen Billion Slaughtered, or whatever it is.'

The Petersons looked blankly at one another.

Tel said, 'What he's on about?'

Bill shrugged his huge shoulders. Bill rarely said much: didn't need to. He shuffled the gold B & H bricks, releasing a fag from the top one and toasting it with a gold Dunhill lighter. He had one of those signs in his office down in Catford. It read: 'Don't let the bastards grind you down.' He was the bastard doing the grinding.

A bottle of claret was brought to the table, but Davey refused it. Simon didn't and took a deep draught. A single rivulet streamed down his chin and stained the collar of his shirt.

Davey glared at them. 'Well?'

'Well what?' said Tel.

'Are we going to talk? 'Cos frankly' — Davey surveyed the room. The table of four had left and the others were making ready to pay — 'I'm getting fed up with all this sub-Godfather crap.'

Okay, thought Simon Latimer. He's done it now. The guns are coming out.

The Petersons exchanged another glance.

Tel said. 'We'll stick with the Godfather crap if it's all right by you.'

'You know,' rasped Bill, '*Godfather III* wasn't all that bad as it happens. You gotta watch it in context.'

Latimer, who could bear it no longer, broke the fragile ice of convention and thumped his uninjured palm on the wooden table. 'I want *out* of this arrangement. I can't run a cab company paying out what I am at the moment. I can't *possibly* keep finding what you ask — it's unreasonable. And those guys who' — he wanted to say, beat me up, *violated me* — 'do the chauffeur end, I can't deal with them, not anymore.'

He stopped talking. Davey had found a fork and was jabbing the tines into his flabby bottom.

Davey said, 'I want to buy you out of Finsbury Cabs. You

leave it alone and I get it clean.' Without pause, he produced two money bricks from the side pockets of his long black coat and deposited them on the table. 'Ten grand,' he said, simply.

'Need more than that,' said Tel.

'Gesture of faith. I need to realise some other projects first.'

'What's your form?' growled Bill. 'I ain't never heard of you.'

Here we go again, thought Davey. Two résumés in one day. He took a swig out of Latimer's glass and pushed back the chair, scraping its heels on the stone floor. He crossed his feet at the ankles and his hands at the wrist. Spoke to them as if they were special children.

'There's Wandsworth and Feltham for starters; there's car-theft and frauds and all that – but I feel I've paid my debt to society.' He grinned, showing all his teeth.

The Petersons were unsure of whether he was the world's biggest liberty-taker or too thick to realise who he was dealing with.

The doorbell went and in walked Steve, grinning sheepishly as he approached. Latimer and Davey recognised him by his coat and the smell of cordite and whisky, which clung wraith-like to him. Bill and Tel acknowledged him minutely with their eyebrows.

'Terrible thing just happened over Peckham way,' announced Steve, archly.

'Oh yes?' Offered Bill.

'Some grass just got hit in the Walmer.'

Tel looked at Bill. He spoke equally falsely. 'Lucky we was in here having our meal here in public, away from such things.'

Bill nodded sagely, then scooped up one of Davey's bundles. His beady gaze rose to Steve's lined face. 'You must be traumatised having witnessed such a thing. Here, this'll help.'

Steve took the money.

Davey's mouth fell open. His five large passed straight on to a killer – product of hard graft that was. 'I'm not paying his wages,' he hissed.

The Petersons studied him.

Bill said, 'That's compensation that is. And you don't want to talk about it in front of him, You'll give him a syndrome.'

Davey didn't know what to say to that. He felt like he was having a bit of a syndrome himself.

Steve clicked his fingers for the waiter, then took a table on the other side of the room.

'Where was we?' asked Tel, politely.

'Uh, we need to hammer out' – Davey screwed his eyes shut for a second – 'work out the finer points.'

'Like the price is thirty-five large?'

Latimer looked at him anxiously. Did Davey have that kind of money? Mind you, he never knew he had the ten until it appeared.

Davey reached out his hand. Tel and Bill shook it in turn, not crushing it too much. Bill pocketed the other money brick.

'Anything else you want doing?'

Davey was ready for this. 'As it goes, there is.'

As Reece entered the restaurant, eight pairs of eyes swivelled towards him.

It was gone two and her fried nerves and the trance beat had given Rox one major headache. She took a deep breath as she emerged from the cubicle, crossed the floor and laid out her pharmaceutical store by the basin.

'Fuck me, it's the dodgy dealer. Got any more coke – or is it Proplus tablets now?' Charlie wore kitten heels and a pedal pusher/crop top ensemble, her belly exposed like a consumptive.

'Modelling for Egon Schiele are you?'

Right over her head. Rox wasn't surprised. An ex-boyfriend had introduced her to the work of the waif-like Austrian artist. No one else had heard of him.

'What you got there then? Daz?'

'Proper Chas this time. Top grade.'

And Charlie, no matter what degree of unsisterliness she felt towards Rox, was never going to refuse free drugs. She explained, as she snorted, that the thing is right, they're like totally *egalitarian*. I mean *anyone* can have a blast or a snort or a sniff. There's no class divide, no north and south, not even young or old no more now the old biddies were toking to clear their back pain and glaucoma and MS. And did she know that Queen Victoria used to take cannabis for period pains? And coke and all?

Yes, Rox did. And had heard so from many other drug bores over the years.

'That's the greatest thing about it. Classless. Doesn't matter who the fuck you are or where you come from.'

'Shouldn't that be *whom* the fuck you are?'

That got a look.

She did chirpy. 'So, does Davey need anything?'

Charlie trotted through to the metal gantry. In the broiling mash beneath, Davey was caning it. He reeled and listed about the floor, mouth open in feigned amazement, brimming with laughter, a bottle of bubbly in his hands which he sprayed racing-driver style over a gaggle of shrieking bottle blondes.

'Complex set of social signals,' observed Rox.

'I'll take you down.'

They found a corner, bare brick, a field of miniature water bottles underfoot.

'She's got some top sherbet,' shouted Charlie.

'Ey-oop. It's toot northerner.'

She resisted the urge to hoof him in the genitals.

'Gi's a taster, then.' Davey's eyes were wild and black and his shirt was soaked in sweat under the arms and all the way round the back.

Rox did as instructed.

'Where d'you get this then?'

'Fell in with a bad crowd.'

'Got any more?'

'A lot. Fifty a gram.'

'Discount for a bulk buy obviously.'

She was following Reece's script. Davey wasn't interested in why she was dealing or whether she'd want to pressure him again for her money, merely in the deal or chance of it. Charlie, in her nagging, give-me-drugs stupid bitchy girlfriend way, was a bonus in that she distracted him all the more.

Rox said it would have to be later and not here. And that she'd better see his money. Davey brought out a wad from his trouser pocket. Waved it in her face. Latimer, delighted to be off the hook, had lent it him earlier.

'See you outside then,' Rox called out, after giving directions. He raised a thumb.

The sky had paled to indigo. It was below zero and Rox had to keep blowing on her mittens and stamping around in her black chunky trainers (still not mended) to keep her circulation going. The Shoreditch streets were deserted, and it was like London had gone post-nuclear. First time she had seen it like this: the city without its scarf of pollution or the omnipresent gunmetal clouds. In the stillness the buildings seemed less ashamed of their age and dilapidated state, the asphalt yet to be scarred by the daily tonnage of traffic. It was vulnerable, charming in its way. She felt as though she were privy to one of London's little secrets.

Except she was so cold. So bloody cold. *Cawwldd.*

Rox Matheson, what the fuck are you doing?

W-what the fu-f-fuv-fuv-fuv-fuv-fuvv-v-v-v. Fuv.

You witness a murder. Then some dodgy bloody minicab driver (with whom you may or may not be having a relationship) comes along and tells you to go be a drug-dealer for a night. That's all right then. You and Graham down a half bottle of Lemon Vodka (Pete's — ha-*haaa*) for courage, and you load up with drugs and take the last tube to Old Street.

As planned, stash the stash. Walk to the club. Your name's on the list. As Roxanne. Funny joke, Mr Reece.

You spend a charming evening chatting sociably with low-lives, offering them Class A substances and later repair to the streets for high jinks.

Only it's been bloody *ages* now.

She jumped.

Nothing, only the wind bending that broken piece of corrugated iron.

Fuv-fuv-fuv-fuv-fuv.

Fourth or fifth time something had scared her like that. A cat, a motorbike, a plastic bag for God's sake.

What the hell am I doing down here? I've had a shitty time, conned out of my money, taken drugs and seen someone killed. Could have stayed home for that. Fuv-fuv-fuv. And was Davey going to show? Turn up mob-handed? Maybe he knew those people in that pub? Even arranged that killing?

What was that?

Straining to hear, huddled against the wall.

Everything glinting with the frost. She was glad she was wrapped up. Couldn't feel her toes though. Nose raw.

A piece of torn newspaper tumbled past.

Fuv-fuv-fuv.

One thing she knew. She was going straight home after this. Not to Mark, but to Manchester. She'd had enough. Once the vodka kicked in she made her decision. She'd told Graham, who just went off and turned on his computer. Going to look up murder websites, he said. She'd packed her things, stuffed them all in her heavy bag: the one that stung her shoulders. Had it beside her now.

First train out of Euston whether Davey came or not. Cup of tea and one of those scalding hot rubbery egg and bacon butties in the buffet. She felt warm just thinking about it. And the relief of getting home to her own bed. No more smelly bags or crappy, itchy sofas.

She let the air come out of her nostrils in hot puffs. Nh-nh-nh-nh-nh.

Sod it. I'll go to the station now. She went to the corner and peered up Shoreditch High Street. A lonely florist's Renault van puttered past on its way to Nine Elms. She turned back and nearly rocketed out of her body. Under the black iron railway bridge stood a man.

'Reece! Christ you . . .' She hugged him hard. 'Scared me.'

His tone was unemotional. 'You want the bad news or the bad news?'

She sagged. 'What?'

'Davey's bought out the cab-company.'

'What's that got to do with—?'

He cut her short. 'I owed them a lot of money. The game's changed. Davey's took on the debt. He owns me.'

'He *owns* you?'

'He sent me here as his rep, to make sure you weren't trying to scam him.'

'What do you mean, owns you?'

'I'll be working for him until I can clear my slate. He's my boss now.'

'How much do you owe?'

'A lot.'

'Why don't you do a runner?'

He gave a defeated smile and hugged her to him. 'Doesn't work that way.' In the embrace, she felt his warmth, his smell and more, a connection between them. She held tight, tighter. Her voice, when it came, was tiny.

'Come to Manchester with me?'

He said nothing, acted as if he'd not heard, kept holding onto her.

'All this for nothing. You must be frozen.'

He rubbed her mitten, which led to a shared glance and rapidly towards a kiss. His mouth was hot. He moved it close to her ear, so close that the proximity sent a tremor down the small of her back.

'Better get you warmed up. Where d'you wanna go, Rox?'

'Euston Station,' she said, feeling the prickle of tears on her face.

He pulled up at the cab rank. Above, the sun had risen and its rays danced on metal, chrome and glass. Bright red buses hauled, hacked and coughed along the Euston road.

'You got everything?'

'What about the money I owe you, Reece?'

'Post it me.'

'If I knew where you lived.'

'What about your Sherpas, your rations, your ticket?'

She waved it in his face.

He scratched his stubble. 'I thought you might make a go of it down here.'

'Bosnia would be safer.'

'Granted, you're not seeing London at its best.'

'Scratched record, Reece.'

She faced him and didn't know what to say. So much maybe, or so little, but was it worth it? Worth explaining again how tired and freaked out she was about the murder and by London in general and by Davey bloody Kayman. He'd have to remain one of those life lessons. And in the future when she spoke of him, and even laughed about it in a shallow brittle kind of way, she would have to *cantral har feelings*.

And Reece?

Reece was so backward in coming forward. Still an unknown quantity. She'd have liked him to physically stop her from getting the train and take her somewhere where everything was going to be all right.

But that wasn't going to happen. Was it?

He had her bag out on the chilly pavement. She stood on tiptoes and pecked his cheek. It was awkward and her glasses went askew.

'What time's the train?' he asked.

'Twenty past.'

'You better get moving.' He indicated her bag. 'Want me to lug this over to the platform?'

She shook her head.

'You going to be all right?'

'Me? Course.' Big lie. 'I suppose I'll see you then.'

'Good luck.'

'Ta-ra then,' she said, crinkling her face in that happy-sad way.

'Bye.'

'Bye.'

Why weren't there better words for it? She shouldered the bag and punched him on the arm and walked to the glass entrance doors. There, she stopped, turned and waved. Reece, leaning against the car, raised a hand. She couldn't tell his expression.

Reece watched her go in, cross the main concourse and gaze up at the clattering indicator board. The early morning commuter throng blotted her out. He focused hard, but she wasn't there anymore. He climbed into the Mondeo and sat staring through the windscreen at the spindly arms of the barren trees. After a bit, he lowered his face and leafed through his dockets.

It was all different now. His stomach felt bad.

Something made him turn for another glimpse at the station entrance. Rox was right there, pressed up against the glass. Reece threw open the door and began to walk, trot, run towards her. She raised her hand for him to stop. He held out his palms.

What? he mouthed.

She waved again, a small and sorrowful one, and this time she was gone for real.

SPRING

CHAPTER SEVENTEEN

Winter had dissipated, the ground had softened up and green nodules dotted the ends of every twig. A bitter February had segued to a wet March, and April brought erratic gusts that flew in all directions, twirling the litter, rattling the poster frames at bus stops and chasing across the open spaces like panting puppies.

London liked spring. The buildings dried out, the parks flourished, people stopped scurrying into pubs or taxis and filled the streets. Scarves were lowered to reveal not raw dripping noses but bright faces. Brollies were still mislaid, but colds, flu and visits to the gym had all but petered out. The buses wore thick mud skirts, as did the cars, the idea of cleaning them still several weekends away. And for the thousands of commuters, the aged Underground network became tolerable again, but only in the way that a tramp grows accustomed to wallowing in his own stink and filth.

Cones grew, a proliferation of them, a herald of spring more certain than the first cuckoo or early daffodil. With it, the roads were torn up and the streets mined, potholed and patched. Intestinal cables slithered and spewed forth from flooded craters. Ungainly vehicles rumbled back and forth with tar and grit and sand and gravel and earth. Teams of swarthy, all-weather men in grubby fluorescent tunics looked at the holes, crawled on the machines, erected temporary traffic lights and stanched the traffic flow.

With cone and contraflow, these brave road surgeons hustled the shocked motorist aside, this operation not for their eyes. How could a road user understand the importance, the technicality of the work being done here? This was *essential* maintenance. Then, when the surgery was complete and the surface scabbed with tar, they sutured the next, for these were men of purpose, men armed with lucrative contracts and an urgent mission statement – to piss away millions of pounds paid in council tax before the end of the financial year.

Rox Matheson reached the centre of the Heath and turned round in a full circle. First she took in the jagged procession of traffic on Shooters Hill, then the pyramid tip of Canary Wharf peeking above the entrance to Greenwich Park. From there, a bowed elderly brick wall limped to the bandstand and the overgrown triangle of land, which had formerly been a plague pit. Then there was the wide sweep of the Heath, which, after recent rains, blazed a luminous acid green. In the distance, the spires of St John's and All Saints stood like rockets awaiting take-off. Her gaze moved on to Blackheath's Royal Parade, from here a Lilliputian row of shops set among the Victorian buildings. Halfway along was Giuseppe's, the restaurant in which she now worked. She checked the time. Coming up to six-thirty. She was due to start her shift. A fresh howl of wind brought colour to her cheeks and she set off, hands thrust in pockets, legs aching from the long afternoon walk.

It was spring and she had turned her life around.

Rox had a job.

Rox had a flat.

And she was back in London to make a go of it.

The morning she left, the 125 delivered her to Manchester

Piccadilly at around ten. She thought of getting a bus home but was so tired that she splashed out on a cab. Ally was delighted to see her. Rox was delighted to be back, although not so pleased at the mess. It looked as though Al's bedroom had escaped and swallowed the house. Everything looked smaller too, even when the sun came out. She slept in for most of the day and was dragged out by Ally at nine in the evening.

In the pub, her version of events didn't come out as she'd planned it on the train home. She'd thought to make herself more heroic or at least a tragic victim, but neither role befitted her. Later, back home, she refused more drink and made a start at clearing up.

The next day she pre-empted Mark's hearing of her return by going straight round to the Garage and knocking him up. She was pleased to note he looked thin and drawn, although she would've preferred emaciated.

'Will you come back, Rox?' he asked.

'What if Corinne hadn't dumped you? You wouldn't be saying that then.'

He hesitated too long.

'Mark' – she was managing to get his name out without the withering sarcasm – 'you were right to stop it. The trust's broken so there's no point in going on. I'm here 'cause I want what's mine. Half the bar.'

He looked terrified. 'But we'd have to *sell* it.'

'That's what you wanted a couple of months back.'

'Not now. Things have changed.'

'You mean now your trainee whore's upped and left?'

'B-but we built this place up?'

'Not as a concubine's palace.' Proud of that one.

'I told you, it's all over with Corinne.'

'And with us.'

'But Rox – I love you. You know I do. Always have . . .'

She was surprised at the ferocity with which she thrust out her hand. She held it, wavering, in front of his face. 'Stop it,

Mark. Grovelling isn't going to make us feel any better and you don't mean it anyway.'

'I do. I want you back,' he whined.

She lowered her arm. 'All you're after is forgiveness, for *you*. It's not about *us* or me, it's about you getting what *you* want, which is for me to give in, give up, and let you win. What's done is done. You've dumped me and now I can live without you, so let's think on.'

Bless him, he'd started to cry. Rox felt like a complete bitch, but when she thought of Corinne's lipsticky mouth clamped around his dick, she felt justified. And she still hated girls with flicky-flicky hair.

'And I've a month's wages owing,' she added, once he'd stopped grizzling.

She bullied him inside (strange being back in here, in lots of ways this was still more like her real home) and forced him to open up the till.

'What happened to you in London?' he asked.

'That'd be telling.'

An image of Reece popped into her head, leaning on his car, smiling down at her, his hands on her waist.

She stayed a week, during which time she saw all her mates, then contacted the bank and mortgage company and engaged a solicitor. Valerie Hutchison was an old school friend whom she bumped into by chance in a firm in the town centre. Val was a trainee and Rox, deciding it was serendipity, demanded that she handle her case. Val explained that if Mark refused to buy her out of the business then she had the right to force a sale. This might become protracted but it looked as though he'd not got a legal leg to stand on. She told Rox not to worry and that she'd get onto it. Was there anything else?

There was. She wanted to sell her house in Chorlton. She'd be sad to see it go but the time had come to move on.

She'd been up to see her mam in her flat to discuss it. Despite

Mam claiming to have the 'gift' and being able to read a palm quicker than Teletext, she was still surprised when her daughter showed up at her door. Rox omitted all but the touristy details of the capital, and once she was awash with tea and had been force-fed her bodyweight in carbohydrate, she brought up the subject.

Mam was fine about it. She'd not wanted to live there after Dad died anyway, which was why she'd moved. She said the house wasn't important and what was were her memories of Iain. Oh, and by the way, she had a message from him. Mam waved her hands dramatically in front of her face and announced that her late father was proud of her, but wanted her to feed up a bit and to take care in the big shoes lest she break an ankle.

Rox asked if she might leave some of the furniture at hers once the house was sold. She wasn't too happy about that, pointing out that the place was already like a bric-à-brac shop. Rox said she was sure Dad would love to have all his old stuff around him. Mam said she'd ask, but he'd probably only want small things, like the portable telly. Rox refrained from asking what dead people watched these days but imagined it'd be the 'Last of the Summer Wine'. She then broke the big news and told her mother she was moving to London.

Mam looked drained, and gazed disconsolately at the last inch of tea in her cup. Then she raised her head. It confirmed her prediction, she said, that Roxy was soon to go on a long journey. After that there were tears and hugs and Rox made promises to keep in touch.

She still felt guilty when she left.

She spruced up the house, had it surveyed and put it on the market. Ally had squeezed other friends for possible accommodation and had won a stopgap over in Whalley Range, starting in a fortnight. They said tearful goodbye's at the station, promised their undying friendship and Rox returned to South London.

*

Arriving at work, she tied a white linen apron around her waist and checked that the special's menu had been updated from the lunchtime session. As assistant manager she ran the place when her boss was absent, a frequent occurrence of late as he was away developing other business interests. Apart from serving she organised the rotas, checked deliveries, ordered stock and sorted out the takings at the end of each shift. It was in essence the same as her old job at the Garage and most nights she didn't get home until past one.

Giuseppe's was usually busy, especially in the evenings when the bulk of the customers preferred pizza to their genuine Italian fare. Although the food was excellent and the staff pleasant, the location was the main reason why they survived the competition. It overlooked the Heath, ensnaring passers-by like a puddle attracts a child. Rox got her post on two counts. First, capability; second, height, being she was the only applicant shorter than the owner, Giuseppe Salvatori. Mr S, as he liked to be called, was a diminutive tyrant from Genoa who ploughed through staff like a hungry dog gets through Chum. In his mid-forties, he sported a bouffant of ebony hair that kept the hairspray industry alive and the ozone depleted. With his profits, he was looking into starting up a sister restaurant in the West End. Rox was only too pleased too have found her feet.

On her return, she scoured the *Standard* and found a bedsit in Lewisham. There were many flat-shares on offer, but she'd had enough of shared bathrooms and fancied some time in a mess of her own making. The deposit on the room was extortionate and the communal areas frozen and neglected. She was forced to make a complete change of bedding and scroll up newspapers to fit the gaps in the sash windows.

She got a stopgap job out of *Loot*. By exaggerating her knowledge of London's topography, Rox became a Tour Guide on an open-topped doubledecker. On the first day, she gripped her microphone tight and confused Buckingham Palace with the Tate Gallery; mixed up the Albert Hall with St Paul's and jumbled the parks. By midweek she had corrected her errors, but boredom set in. Her clients, it turned out, were predominately non-English speaking and by the end of the week she was deviating wildly from the script. It was a rush to lie so brazenly. However, the Tour Company management operated spot checks and she was caught out telling porkies to a cluster of videocam-wielding Japanese. Taken aside, she was informed that this was Monument, not Trafalgar Square and that Nelson had not been 'taken away for his annual birdshit removal'. They put her off the bus, but she kept the jacket. Might be fun at parties, she thought. If she ever got invited to one, that is.

She did some nude modelling at Goldsmith's College in New Cross. It wasn't for the students, who'd never stoop so low as to work from the human form, but for Adult Education classes. The pervert-level seemed low enough and she got twenty quid in cash, a drink off the tutor and filthy feet. For this she had to sit stock still – one side of her roasting from the heater, the other raw, making her feel like a kebab. Nonetheless she enjoyed the sensuousness of being minutely studied, although she covered her tummy when she could. She wasn't happy with the results, except for the work of one elderly gent with myopia who always made her tall and thin and sexy-looking. The term soon ended and on asking the tutor about other work, she was advised to put her details on the notice board. Putting 'Life Model' on a five-by-seven card felt strange and she was glad there hadn't been any replies.

The position at Giuseppe's was advertised in the South London Press and she accepted with relief. News came that a buyer had been found for her old home. There was no chain and the sale proceeded rapidly, so much so that she went out flat-hunting, nearly dying of shock at the prices. It took the best part of a month but she'd found a one-bedroom place in Hither Green. A step up from the congested lung of Lewisham.

The multiple owner-occupied Victorian semi was a short bus journey from work and stood on the low slope of Burnt Ash Hill. Rox didn't care that the mortgage was enough to cripple a Third World country: she had her own front door, a tiny bathroom and a doll's house kitchen tucked away in the eaves. The bedroom would fit her pine double bed, once she had it sent down, and the lounge was roomy and bright when it was bright, and that was getting to be more often these days.

The evening shift was uneventful, some twenty-odd diners, most of whom arrived between half eight and nine, all locals as the tourist season hadn't yet kicked in. The last pair was dithering over coffees. She told Chef to turn off the oven and close up. Jane, the other waitress, wanted to get away to see her boyfriend so Rox released her. It had been a double shift and she was aching to get home and have a shower.

The couple settled up and left. Rox took the catch off the door and went to the back to start doing the credit card slips. A shadow paused outside, studied the menu and moved on. She thought nothing of it but a few minutes later the presence was out there again. Couldn't be a late diner as she'd turned the sign around and blown out the candles. An inner vestibule and velvet curtains halfway up the windows obscured her view. The door rattled. She looked up, expecting Jane.

In a moment, she had it unlocked and open.

'Hello, stranger.'

'Aya, Reece.' She struggled to keep emotion out of her voice, even though she was overjoyed to see him again. He looked tired and his stubble was as thick as iron filings. The jacket was different, lighter, and he wore khakis instead of jeans. Otherwise, the same hands, same handsome face, same touch of grey about the temples.

Reece said, 'Finally tracked you down then.'

'You win the prize.'

'Weekend for two in Barbados?'

'Blackpool. But I'd take the cash equivalent, if I were you.'

'Which is?'

'Fiver.'

He chose a table at the back and they sat facing one another. She suddenly felt self-conscious in her tight T-shirt (translated as 30 per cent extra in tips). The honey growl was still there in his voice.

'You look different.'

'Better or worse?'

He gazed at her as if appraising an artefact: eyebrows forced together, lips screwed up tight. She'd had a major rethink with her hair and had dyed it chestnut brown to get rid of the rest of the blonde. It was closer to her natural colour and had grown long enough to tie back with a Kirby grip. No more crappy fringe problems.

He gave an appreciative nod. 'Better, I'd say.'

'Ta. Want something to eat?'

'Uh, yeah, sure.'

She gave him a menu and hustled through to the kitchen. Chef was out smoking by the bins and agreed to make one more meal. On her return, Reece pointed at *Petto di pollo alla Luisetta*. She didn't try to get him to say it, but called it through the hatch.

'Drink?'

'Coffee'd be great.'

She poured one from the jug by the bar. She brought it over along with her glass of white wine, her regular end of shift treat.

'How did you find me?'

'Dumb luck. You walk on the heath a lot?'

'Yeah. It's dead nice round here.'

'Saw you this afternoon on my way back from Eltham. You came in here and it was too early to eat, so I figured you must work here. So what's up?'

She told him. His food arrived and he attacked it voraciously. She almost made a comment about it not being fast food, but remembered he always ate like it was his last meal. Reece expressed fascination with her struggles and admiration for her ditching Mark. She omitted to mention the nude modelling. Didn't feel right.

'So why've you come back?'

'Oh, I don't know.'

He tilted his eyes up at her.

Rox said, 'Oh, all right. I thought I'd slip into being back home in Manchester and that'd be the end of it. But when I saw all my mates going to the same places, doing the same things, I just thought, I don't want to do this any more. Guess I fancied the change.'

She wondered whether he would ask her what she'd meant by that last wave at the station? Or tell her why he ran towards her? Perhaps it was all forgotten now, spark gone, chance missed. They were friends playing catch-up, that was all.

'What about you? Still driving the cab?'

He nodded. 'Latimer's managing the firm but Davey's the guvnor.'

'Thought someone would have caught up with him by now.'

'His kind always slips away.'

She felt hot bile; an anger she thought she'd cremated. 'Reece – how can you carry on working for him when you know what he's like?'

'He took on my debt.'

'What *is* this debt?'

He sighed and lowered his fork. 'I used to fancy a tickle. Gambled on anything – nags, dogs – you name it. I should have been called William Hill.'

'What and have *two* names? Two *proper* ones?'

Reece grinned briefly. 'I had a slate. It's the way they operate: let you build it up until there's no way you're going to clear it. I'd always thought I was a bit clever. Thought I'd get out before it got too much to handle.' He paused, shrugged his shoulders in defeat. 'I had an unlucky run . . . for about five years. Surprise,

surprise, it turns out I was just another mug punter.'

She fingered the neck of her wineglass.

'Anyway, so I'm in the hole for twenty grand and Kelley and I are due to get spliced. Muggins here decides that *this* weekend, not only is he going to clear the lot, but also he's going to come home with enough dosh for the wedding, the honeymoon and the dress she's bought on tick.'

'You won — obviously,' said Rox.

He rubbed a hand through his hair. 'An accumulator. Never forget those nags — Three-legs, Mister Ed and Dog Meat.'

'And that finished your relationship?'

A nod. 'I've kept away from bookies and arcades ever since. I was down on the coast a while back. Nightmare. Slots every-where, even on the pier.'

'How much did you owe?'

'Forty-two grand, but I've got it down to around twenty-seven now.'

'In how long?'

He gazed upwards, doing his arithmetic. 'Year and a half all told. Trouble is the interest. Davey's as bad as the Petersons. At the moment he's docking me five hundred a week.'

'You can't let him do that.'

'Way it goes. One day I'll clear it, then I can do what I like.'

'Like what?'

'I heard there's openings in genetic science.'

She didn't feel like smiling. 'But Davey's nothing to do with your debt. And you've not gambled for ages. Why d'you let him do this?'

He said nothing.

Rox sipped her wine and studied him. His eyelashes were long and his irises sky blue, the eyes of a much older man. She felt pity that his life was beholden to someone else and annoy-ance that it was these low-lives. But underneath the irritation there was a kind of understanding. He was a man who would keep his obligations, carry things through. And that — in a world where no one gave a damn for loyalty, morality or ethics — was to be valued. She also wondered if he wanted to snog her again, as she'd quite like that.

Rox put down her glass. The wine was chilled and the condensation had run down the flute and made a crescent on the polished table. She stuck a finger in it, broke the meniscus and dabbled a shape. As soon as she realised what it was, she hurriedly scrubbed it out.

'Well . . . good to see you again,' he said.

'You too.'

He put his hands flat on the table; ready to lever himself to vertical.

'What do I owe you?'

'On the house.'

'No, go on.'

'Forget it. And any time you want to drop in there's a meal if you want it.'

Reece considered it. 'And pudding?'

She smiled. 'Yeah — and by the way I owe *you* a couple of hundred pound.'

He stood, laid his jacket over his arm. 'Give it me next time.'

Rox knew then that they had established a bond. With him it would always be next time. She would tender the money and he'd refuse it, keeping the push and the pull, the pitch and the yaw of their pact. Perhaps that was why he'd lent it her in the first place on that freezing night in New Cross? To make a connection, as he was afraid he hadn't the strength of character to enchant her? And now, in the fresh knowledge of his old gambling problem, it occurred to her that he felt he had to use money as an emotional link: his refusal to take it back was the only way he could be sure of keeping her close.

Reece was at the door, waiting for her to release him.

'By the way,' she said. 'I've not forgotten about Davey Kayman.'

'You ought to.'

'Exactly why I'm not going to.' She shuddered at the thought of him, his coldness and indifference.

Reece leaned forward and she thought he might make contact, maybe even . . .? Instead he applied a gentle pressure to her arm.

'If you want to get him, it's gonna be a waiting game, Rox.'

'I can wait. Don't you worry.'

He released his grip, raised his eyebrows. 'All right then. See you soon.'

'Yeah, you too.'

I hope.

CHAPTER EIGHTEEN

They were parked in Whitecross Street and the car stank of
petrol. It was a cloudless night and a nearby church had chimed
out two sonorous tones. Archie Peacock and Steve Lamb were
back in business.

'Gi's it here. Steve, give us it here.'

'No, you'll only spill it.'

Arch said, 'You can't drive the motor *and* lob bottles at the
same time.'

'But I'm on the right side for it. You'd have to toss 'em over
the roof.'

'Well, we'll come in from the other direction.'

Steve sat sullen in the driving seat and released a shiny packet
of JPS from his breast pocket.

Archie added, 'You can do the fireworks next time.'

Steve waited a moment, then keened. 'Why don't *you* drive
and I'll lob 'em?'

'Cos I said so. And I made them up, so I get to throw them.'

In a cardboard box between Archie's feet were four Lucozade
bottles filled with petrol and stuffed with rags from an old pair
of jeans he had shredded earlier. The energy drink, it said on the
bottles.

'Uh — Steve?'

'What now?' he spat, fag jerking in mouth.

'Best you don't light up until we're done.'

He rolled his eyes heavenwards, but lowered the Zippo. Archie prised it from his hand and tucked it into his palm.

Steve revved the engine.

The Petersons' brief had beavered away on their case and their court appearances were now scheduled for May. Neither was worried. True, they both had form – particularly Steve, who been up before the beak on a variety of charges from malicious wounding to rape and assault – but they reckoned they were going to walk away from this little jolly. Theft and TDA? Slap on the wrist. Where the brief had been clever was to point out that their being nicked at Heathrow meant they came under the jurisdiction of the airport police rather than the local Met. The Heathrow cozzers were far keener on high-profile pulls like terrorists, drug dealers and International criminals to bother with two blokes who'd nicked a car: It was paperwork, three cups of instant and a couple of Neurofen.

The business was gone and the lot in Addiscombe impounded along with the low loader. Croydon Council was looking into their contract and the CID had had them in for several interviews. Steve and Arch hadn't a lot to say.

Steve sailed past the cab office and did a U-ey, taking a slow run in from the other way. Archie lit one rag from the other and scored two direct hits, one in the doorway, the other through the controller's booth. On impact, the window shattered, the petrol dispersed and anxious liquid tongues of flame licked the woodwork. The top layer of linoleum on the floor bucked and began to blister. In seconds the outer door was sheathed in orange and dockets were propelled skywards by the heat, hanging momentarily in the air like fiery paper birds. Steam poured from the laminated map and the phones began to pool in the heat. There were shouts of surprise as two drivers leapt out, over the flames.

On their next run, Archie lobbed the remaining bottles. One hit the revolving light, snuffing it out; the other smashed on the pavement, spreading a puddle of flame, which rolled out towards the gutter. The lino floor had risen, hissing, its back arched, the grimy pattern melting. Underneath, the next layer was preparing itself for combustion. Smoke poured from the bust window.

'Missed one,' sneered Steve.

'Yeah, yeah. And the rest.'

Archie looked over his shoulder as they drew away and was pleased to see the controller leap through the doorway and scamper off to the nearest call-box. The first of the fire engines passed, siren blaring, as they sped off down the Clerkenwell Road. The message had been delivered.

Steve dropped Archie, then headed back to Bermondsey for some kip. He lived in a wharf on the river with a view of London Pool. It had been converted back in the late Eighties. Lot of building work going on round then, what with the townhouses going up, new roads and Thames walks and things with *phases* – which made Steve think of Star Trek. Back then he was living at his mum's on the Peabody and saw the yuppies move in. He became an active member of the welcoming committee, helping to decorate their Golf GTI's with paint and key scratches, burgling their homes and spraying cheery messages on the new climb-free brick walls, asking of the Yuppie wankers that could they fuck off, please? Eventually, wailing that the area had no tubes or supermarkets, the urban professionals crawled off back to their spawning grounds in Fulham.

He picked up the place for an aria after the crash of eighty-seven. Flush as the result of a recent tickle (don't ask) he found that a deposit of a third of the asking price in notes was acceptable to the cash-poor housing conglomerate. It was the ultimate shagpad, he reckoned. Up on the second floor with a big lounge with glass sliding doors opening out onto a little wooden balcony right over the water. Lapping of the waves? The birds loved that. The kitchen was at one end in sort of a nook, but it never saw a lot of use. He had a big telly, top of the range CD unit with Bozeman speakers, and a black leather couch you could sink right into. The bedroom was opposite the bathroom and shower. Good size it was, with the built-in wardrobes, which were handy for stashing all sorts of gear.

Steve tossed down his keys and gazed at the king-size bed with longing. It was his oldest and truest companion. Seen more action than a tart's bra, he always joked. He flopped onto the satin sheets, thinking it was true what they said about black never showing up anything – except the KY and cum stains, of course. Sometimes it looked like a family of snails was squatting it. He gazed up at the remaining ceiling mirrors. Two of the bastards had fallen on him when he was on the job once. Now there were just blobs of glue and a patch where a bit of ceiling plaster had come down.

He awoke past noon and went for his customary breakfast in the Gregorian pub on the Jamaica Road. Since the tug at Heathrow and the subsequent events of that day, neither he nor Archie had had any work to speak of and money was getting tight. He sank his first pint and wondered what to do with himself. There was the bookies of course, or he could rent a porn vid? Or pop round Archie's – see how he was getting on.

He leaned hard on the bell. There was thundering as Archie's powerful legs motored downstairs.

'Took your time, you cu——?' Steve's cigarette drooped. The filter adhered momentarily to his lower lip, then it tumbled to the ground.

Archie wore a paint-spattered T-shirt and a pair of jeans – but it was the face that concerned Steve. He had grown to accept the wispy 'tache and tuft of hair under his lower lip, but this? I mean – a beret?

'You turning into a ponce?'

'It's a funny 'at. Rembrandt always wore funny 'ats.'

'Looks like a ginger to me. Oy-oy. Backs against the wall!'

'You coming in or what?'

Steve went in. 'Where's Shirl?'

'Down the shops.'

'She know you've turned into a Michael?'

Arch beckoned to him with a paint-encrusted finger. The cloying tang of oil and turpentine filled the air. He led Steve upstairs into what had once been his elder son's room. It had been stripped of furniture, the carpet rolled back and the nursery themed coloured walls painted over with white emulsion. An anglepoise was rigged up to shine down on the Rembrandt. In the centre was a large wooden easel, beside it a paint-smeared bedside table, on which were a palette and several jam-jars full of turps and brushes. On the easel was a stretched canvas. Steve padded round and regarded the image on it.

'You're copying it.' His mouth hung open and his tongue roiled around his gums. 'What you copying it for? You faking it? Gonna pass it off as the proper one?'

'Nah. I'm only doing it to learn his technique. Like one of his pupils. He had all these other artists copying his *tronies*.'

'Do what?'

'Tronies. Means a head. They were like models.'

With a leer. 'Models?'

'Not that sort. For characters. In the history paintings.'

Steve stared at the picture. 'You got the eyes wrong for a start. And the mouth's too big. Don't look like him at all.'

Archie fought the urge to poke him with his maulstick. 'It's my first go, ain't it? Can't expect to get the hang of it straight out. There's underpainting, drawing, getting the brush strokes right.'

Steve turned to face him. 'You look like him and all. That the point?'

Colour came to Archie's cheeks. He waggled a brush in the milky green-grey jar of turps. 'Anyway, what was it you was after?'

'You been sorted for last night?'

'Not yet.'

'Soon as you do.'

Arch scraped at a patch of colour with his palette knife. Steve lit up, leaned against the wall.

'I still say we flog it.'

'When we find a buyer.'

'Come off it. It's been – what? – seven bleedin' months now.'

'I said it'd be . . .'

Steve cut him off. 'Archie. Don't be an arsehole. That's five mill sitting right there. You said so yourself. And I reckon you're getting way too happy with it. You don't *want* to sell it, do you?'

Archie selected a small flat brush.

'What if I was to take it off you? Do that ransom thing I talked about?'

'You wouldn't be that stupid though, wouldya?'

Steve stood fuming, trying to come up with a suitable rejoinder.

Archie then redrew the lip-line for the eleventh time that day.

Reece drove up through Woodford Green and on towards Buckhurst Hill. A procession of cumulus clouds filled the sky, growing dense over Chigwell and greyer out over the M11. He was trying to listen to GLR, but Davey's outbursts kept hammering through his concentration. He and Charlie were suited up; him in funereal black with a waistcoat; her forced into a plain jacket and knee-length skirt, but combined with her menacing boots. She had recently put studs in her nose, tongue and eyebrows and Davey had permitted her to retain these as he reckoned his old man would like it.

Davey was on the mobile. Sounded like Latimer bleating at him.

'Nah, it's got to be the Petersons playing silly bollocks. Sod 'em. SOD THEM, SIMON . . . Don't worry about it. What's the damage? Window boarded up yet? Yeah, well you can tell 'em that when they say *twenty-four* hours then it don't mean *they* get to pick the hours . . . Get the insurance round. No, I haven't got time for that. I've got a meet with some investors . . . course I paid up. Think I'm stupid? You are giving me the right hump.' Davey killed the cellular, then held the machine out in front of him and pulled a face at it.

Charlie smiled. 'Your old man's an investor, is he?'

'Will be.'

Reece sat up front. Remained silent. He had a good idea that Davey hadn't paid the Petersons a cent since their meeting a month back and torching the office would have been their version of a second invoice.

He had been to Finsbury Cabs earlier in the day and seen the scorched woodwork and the controller's cabin with its guts leaking out. The place reeked of charred cinder and blackened shrivelled plastic. There was no structural damage as taller buildings braced it on either side. Sadly, the driver's bullpen was unharmed save for water damage, which had bowed the linoleum floor.

He hated the driver's area. It was full of mismatched chairs, each with the Dalmatian pockmarks of innumerable cigarette burns. There was an old Fablon covered table, scarred by a succession of bored card-playing drivers. A telly hung from the ceiling, its racing commentaries a siren call to his attention. All damaged now. Good. Trouble was, he knew what Davey would do. Patch it up, get the radio working and off they'd go, business as usual. Maybe he'd go back to the Walworth firm and do nights there for a bit?

Reece pulled into a long brick-cobbled drive. The house was less than a decade old, single storey at the front but connected to a series of pavilions that stretched back among grounds as large as a golf course. New money built this: Essex money out of the old East End. The front porch was colonnaded and gabled, the door gleaming. Bow windows at the side were dead-bolted and ruche-curtained with porcelain horses arranged on the sill. In the ruddy brick, there was a jagged settlement crack; in the driveway, a black Porsche, the dealer's sticker still affixed to the rear window.

'Wait here,' commanded Davey as he and Charlie clambered out.

Reece watched them go inside and put the radio back on. Davey could have told him how long they were going to be. Still, part of the game.

'Drink?'

'Rum and coke. Large one.'

'And for you, Charlotte?'

'She'll have the same.' Davey's tone was as frosty as the greeting he received from his father who had been swimming at the time of their arrival and hadn't been best pleased at having to pad wetly across all that marble to answer the door. The maid was off cleaning elsewhere and Debbi – his third wife – had gone riding. Sam King, née Samuel Kimmelmann, strolled to the row of decanters at the bar. He was tall; a good six five with a skeletal frame, long lean limbs and thin tapering fingers. He had changed into slacks and a patterned sweater with an outcrop of greying hairs gathered at the V. He was shaved and cologned. He had a generous mouth and the tile-work of his teeth was neatly pointed, grouted and polished. His nose was too small for his face, like the snub of the Sphinx. Clearly, major excavation had occurred on the site. He dug ice from a bucket and filled three crystal glasses, anointing each with a generous measure of rum. He flipped the catch of a small fridge beneath the bar and brought out bottles of coke. Proper glass ones.

'What brings you here then?'

'Just passing,' Davey said.

'That'd be a first,' replied his father, with a stage wink to Charlie. 'Does your driver want to come in for one?'

Davey looked at him blankly.

'Or perhaps a beer?'

'He don't drink,' Davey said.

Sam chugged coke into the glasses; expertly tilting them so that the brown froth did not breach the rim. Distributing them, he sat opposite in a white armchair and placed his drink on a bamboo and glass table. Father and son held one another's gaze, waiting to see who would open the bidding.

'I like the studs, Charlotte,' Sam said, finally.

'It's Charlie.'

'You know, something I don't get these days is why the girls are all using the boys' names? It's all Joe and Alex and Sam and Nick and George. Whatever happened to nice old names like Sarah or Rebecca?'

'They divorced you,' shot back Davey.

Everybody sipped their drinks.

'What are they for?' Sam asked, aiming a finger at the rings on Charlie's face.

'Decoration.'

'You don't think you're pretty enough?'

She stuck out her tongue. 'An' thith oneth for oral sexth.'

'Right.'

'When I suck cock, I like to work the stud up from the bottom of the shaft to that sensitive bit under his helmet.'

'The glans,' Davey said, bored.

Charlie cast him a sidelong glance. 'I like the control. I can make him come when I want. I usually like it deep down in my throat, but sometimes I like to pull out and get that nice hot spunk all over my face.'

'Nuts?' enquired Sam, leaning forward and placing a bowl of cashews between them.

Davey took a handful, chomped on them and scoped the room. Above the fireplace — marble surround, gas tap in the hearth, redundant brass bucket and tongs — was a garish oil painting that reached to the ceiling. It was a nude on a horse, her

207

bleached blonde hair tumbling, breasts thrust forward. Shoes on, of course.

'Debbi, is it?' he asked.

His father nodded. 'So how's business?'

'Good, yeah. Very good. Got a little minicab place running in the city now, plus we're doing a lot of chauffeur work. Club in Gant's Hill is chocker every weekend. Thinking of putting strippers in weeknights, that or themeing it. Sold some wine earlier on, brought in a lot of bunce, but that's nothing to what I got planned. See, I'm gonna become a pro-ducer. On telly.'

'You are?'

' 'Kin' straight. I got a director and everything. I'll be getting it on the BBC or the ITV soon as.'

'What is it – a comedy show?'

Davey's angry tic flashed on his cheek. 'Documentary. I'm gonna present the series.'

'We have an Attenborough in the family?'

'None of that poncy animal lark. It's more your exposé. True crime. Might even do one on your game.'

Kimmelmann senior stroked the side of his tiny nose. 'Like that fat Australian fellow? Crock?'

'Yeah, but don't worry. No one's gonna get stitched up. It's a fast one. The TV people got no idea. Plus they don't give a toss anyway as they get kippered all the time. I'm looking to clear a hundred grand on it.'

'We had him round, you know,' said Sam to Charlie.

'Who?'

'That TV journalist. The fat one. Pleasant fellow. Got a couple of girls in. Black on white. Turned out he had a thing for coprophilia.'

'That's playing with shit, ain't it?'

Sam gazed upwards. 'That ceiling fan's never been the same.'

The blades revolved unevenly, stirring the dry, centrally heated air.

'How's the porn game?' Charlie asked.

'Never better.'

'We didn't come here to talk about you,' fumed Davey.

His father said, 'No, I presume you came here to borrow money. Am I right? You never change, David. And how many more times do I have to tell you you shouldn't diverse until you have one business in the bag. Wines, cabs, you're all over the place. Make a success of one of them first.'

'Anyone can sell wank mags, can't they?'

Sam's confidence remained intact. 'Maybe now, but when I started it wasn't so easy. Only a few outlets in Soho and all of them under the counter. Now you put them in every tobacconist's, every petrol station . . .' He raised his hands, spread the fingers out, peacocks fanning their tails. 'David, I always said you could come in with me on the production end. Editorial if you want?'

'Ten large is what I need to get this off the ground. You can afford it.'

'I can afford it.'

'Well?'

The long tapering finger began to wag. 'I was a millionaire . . .'

'. . . By the time you was thirty,' chimed in Davey.

'I did it through graft, with you and your mother to feed and clothe. No one lent me ten grand. I could have made it in half the time with ten grand.'

Davey was on his feet. 'Yeah, yeah. Change the record. Come on, don't give me this. You can afford it but you'd rather give me the old fanny about making it on my own. You're a mean old sod.'

'Maybe . . .'

'Maybe nothing. You give me the same old bollocks every time. How many houses and wives are you gonna buy on what you make? When's it enough, eh?'

Sam stood straight up. 'From me you get *gornisht!*' He

continued to chastise, falling into Yiddish as his son dragged his girlfriend to the door. It slammed, releasing a cold chatter from the brass knocker.

'Where to?' Reece asked as Davey pushed Charlie into the car.

'Away,' spat Davey. 'Get me away from here.'

CHAPTER NINETEEN

Reece sat at the breakfast bar in the Shoreditch basement poring over the listing pages of *Time Out*. He rarely watched television and had lost contact with its schedules and stars. With a panoply of programmes to choose from he had no idea whether to go for comedy or drama or to flip randomly until something caught his eye. Clutching Davey's remote, he aimed it and replaced the dead black screen with a frenzy of colour.

For a moment he couldn't make out what was going on. A head loomed close to the screen, then there were two of them, but some feet away. The image kept fragmenting in this way and Reece was unable to concentrate on the narrative. It made him dizzy. Now he was looking down at a street from an impossible angle. He had time to make out a man hunkering down in his car before the vehicle zoomed away and a new image filled the screen. Was that an office? He scrambled for the off-button. It occurred to him that he ought to stay in more.

'What d'you think?'

Charlie emerged from the bedroom. She was heavily made up and wearing a pair of tight shiny red rubber trousers and a PVC top with white lacing. It exposed acres of stomach and the faint Y of her cleavage. Her long braids fell down her bare back. She padded up to him, getting up close so he could hear her thighs squeak together and smell the tang of rubber. Dangling from her fingers were a pair of transparent platform stiletto-heeled shoes. She dropped them, placed one hand on Reece's shoulder and tipped first one bony foot down the plastic slope and then the other. She rose up by seven inches.

'Well?'

Reece gave a noncommittal grunt and hauled his eyes back to the magazine. Charlie reached for the joint in the ashtray and purposefully dropped it. She bent all the way down to get it. She came up slowly, eyeing him, then took a lighter off the counter and sparked up.

'Whassamatter with you then?'

'Nothing, Reece said.

He was babysitting. Davey had gone out on business and after Charlie's earlier behaviour with his dad, he'd confined her to quarters with two grams of coke and an eighth. Looked as though she'd had a fair bit of it. Reece had been ordered to ensure she stayed put and was glad Davey had not added 'and keep her entertained' as she clearly had a low boredom threshold. So far she had offered him drink and drugs and had come onto him with all the subtlety of a teenager on cider.

Charlie scrutinised him through a plume of blue smoke, then flew back to the bedroom.

He rifled through and read about an upcoming movie. The journalist seemed to believe his insights were of more import than the actor's musings on character and had peppered his article with snide comments. Reece was finding it hard to concentrate. It was gone eleven and he was thinking of the night. Takeaway outlets festooned with epileptic neon. Pregnant night-clubs spewing out sweating punters. Night buses plummeting back to leafy suburbs as if on elastic. Gangs of flyposters gluing and bandaging the scabbed walls of deserted buildings. Fares going to other drivers.

Charlie emerged again. This time she was wearing a leather micro skirt, a skinny ribbed top and the heels. Anne Summers at King's Cross.

'Well?'

'Well what?'

'Do you *like* it? Are you dumb as well as stupid?'

He held up his palms. 'Not for me to say.'

'Course it's for you to say. I'm asking you.'

He rolled his eyes theatrically. 'Oh – you're trying to get a *reaction*.'

She seemed confused for an instant, then tried out coy. 'You like it. You *do* like it.' She bit her lip, bit down on her lip.

'Not the point.'

'Oh, right, cos I'm Davey's bird that means no one else can look at me?'

He rustled the magazine. 'Perhaps you've seen this movie? Moll tries it on with henchman, boss finds out, boss kills henchman.'

'Davey can't kill you. You're the muscle.'

'He can have it arranged.'

'Davey wouldn't know.'

Before he had a chance to answer, she strode coltishly back to the bedroom, pausing only to give him a wide red smile from the door.

Reece put aside the magazine, placed his elbows on the table, cupped his jaw in his palms and massaged his eyebrows. When he looked up, he thought he heard a noise out in the stairwell. He swung his gaze to the door. Locked and deadbolted. He strolled over and peered through the spyhole. The silent corridor was empty, the dark grille of the lift-shaft inert.

From behind him there was an explosion of sound. Reece spun round. Charlie had inserted a CD into the player and the speakers pulsed with the beat. She had changed once more, this time into an old-fashioned cotton nightdress. At least this merely suggested, rather than revealed, her breasts and figure. She had wiped off all the makeup except for the garish lipstick. Her bare arms, he noticed, were latticed with the faint white ridges of old scars. The nightdress splayed out at waist level, swirling around her as she swayed to the music. Climbing to her knees were a pair of enormous black buckled leather boots.

He came over, turned down the volume and appraised her.

'Bride of Frankenstein, is it?'

He'd expected an outburst, but instead she trotted a little closer.

'You do want me. I know you do.'

They were almost face to face. The sweet wraith of dope hung about her. She'd tied back her dreads and they flopped behind her like a clutch of electrical coils and cables. Her bony shoulders were exposed, small as her breasts, mirroring them.

'You want me so much I can smell it.'

Reece said, 'You really only operate on one level, don't you?'

And then she was sliding down, fingers butterflying over his shirt buttons until they reached the denim rim of his black jeans. She kneeled with difficulty in her huge platforms and her fingers snaked between his fly buttons. He took her wrists and pulled them away.

'All right. None of that.'

'I swallow, babe,' she purred.

He stepped back, leaving her there. 'Don't you care that he might come back any time?'

She shook her head. Some of her dreads fell back over her breasts.

Reece gazed down on her bony body. 'You're fucked up, you know that?'

She hauled herself to her feet. Her hand grazed against his crotch. 'Fucked is what I want. Makes me whole.'

Headlights swung round the courtyard and danced across the windows. A car stopped. Reece stepped away, ears straining as he heard one, two, three pairs of feet hit cobbles. Not Davey. He took her arm.

'Are you gonna pack it in?'

Wrong thing to say.

'Make me.'

'Forget it.'

Charlie clambered up onto the sofa, raised the nightshirt and spread her artificially extended leather limbs like the sleek black mandibles of some giant insect. She wore nothing underneath and the tuft of her pubic triangle was exposed. Reece was transfixed for a moment.

'Come on. Fill me up, babe.'

Reece realised that it was porno desire, hooker's talk. He took a step nearer, wondering how to put an end to it. She began moistening herself with her index and second finger.

'Pack it in,' he warned, immediately aware of how limp it sounded. A teacher losing control.

Then she was up, beside him, grabbing his hand and pressing it to her, getting the scent of her on him. He pulled away, backing off.

A car drew up and a key entered the lock in the red door.

She clamped her haunches to him, moaning urgently. He tried to prise her away but she clung there, the high dangerous heels barking his shins, making it hard to move.

The lift mechanism coughed, whined and shook itself awake.

He heard that all right, and dragged her to the sink, where he dug about and found a crinkled bar of old soap. Tried to get the tap running. She had her hands on his face, raking her chewed up fingernails on him and whispering sweet obscenities.

The lift doors rattled.

He tore her off him and threw her onto the sofa. She landed akimbo and he hated himself for letting it get this far. This *trouble*, which was no doubt what she'd wanted all along. He plunged his hands into the water, soaped them then elbowed off the tap. Charlie lay there grinning, her fingers inching the nightshirt back up over her thighs.

Machinery hummed and the lift shrieked to a halt.

Charlie, groaning in a parody of pleasure, lay there *as if she had already been with him*. She even teased his name out of those blood-red lips. Thoughts surged of how Davey might handle this. The quiet word and a few grand and his card would be marked. One night he'd be in the cab and a passenger would climb in, ask for somewhere remote, out of town. He'd have forgotten about it by then, only realising when he'd be asked to pull over. And then he would feel the chill of the metal on the back of his head.

Lift rattle. Echo. Steps outside.

No, Davey knew the score. He might be a bit of a toe-rag, a chancer and that, but he was *of his kind*. The same breed.

Keys in the door. Charlie faking it good now.

Reece ran to the sofa, jammed his foot underneath it and upended the whole thing. It tipped over backwards and Charlie disappeared, buried underneath.

Davey came in wearing a long black overcoat and carrying a Digital video camera. He scanned the proceedings with the practised eye of a police officer at the scene of a crime. His eyes were hard and dark.

'What's going on?'

'She been pissing about,' said Reece.

He flicked his gaze to the pair of boots attempting to scramble out from under the cushions. 'What d'you mean?'

'Playing dollies, dressing up. Girl's stuff.'

Davey waited while Charlie emerged and stood up, tottering, smoothing down the nightdress. If he'd seen any fingermarks on Reece's face, he didn't mention it.

'Charlie? What you playing at?'

She looked at Reece who *dared* her to squeal with his eyes. Her superior expression passed quickly. 'Like he said.'

Davey said, 'Not screwing the help, I hope.'

'No.'

Davey's cheek twitched, then he gave a vulpine grin and curved his arm in the air as if to gather Reece in under his wing.

'Come on then,' he announced. 'Let's go. Work to be done.'

Reece felt as though he had passed some kind of a test.

*

216

The mud-smeared Ford Transit bumped up onto the pavement near the entrance to Homerton Hospital in Kenworthy Road. The rear doors swung outwards and five youths jumped out. As they huddled together in the cold, Davey shouldered his video camera and shot some footage of them from the passenger seat. Reece sat at the wheel. Having overheard the boisterous bragging on the journey over from King's Cross, he'd made them out as Doleys: callow undernourished youth who subsisted on begging, carding the phoneboxes and muscling crack. The three U's. Unemployed, unemployable and unwanted. Expendable. Doubtless they had been promised cash in hand for tonight. NQA.

Davey put down the camera, slid his door open and went and had a word. Reece watched in the wing mirror as a foreman was elected. Davey picked the tallest kid, about nineteen with a bum-fluff goatee and a big puffa jacket. Davey spoke to the lads, his breath pluming in the air. When he checked his watch, Reece mimicked him inside the cab.

Four forty-one a.m.

A sharp breeze gusted in as Davey slid the door along on its runner. 'You wait here right?'

Reece mumbled acknowledgement.

Davey positioned the camera inside a sports bag wadded full of old clothes. He pressed play, zipped up the bag and went round to the front of the van with it held protectively in his arms. He gave a silent signal and the newly appointed foreman led the dishevelled troupe up to the hospital entrance.

Reece waited.

Twenty minutes later the crew re-emerged laden with the bulky cubes of computer equipment. There were base units, monitors, laser printers and clutches of keyboards lashed together with their power leads. The boys struggled with the weight and a couple had had to resort to balancing their burdens on their heads like old colonial porters. The foreman opened the rear doors and they began loading up. Davey stood by in the shadows as they completed the task, holding his bag low and steady. As the Doleys celebrated ten minutes of graft by toasting roll-ups, their foreman turned to Davey.

'We goin' back in again?'

He nodded.

'Same place. Records department?'

Reece adjusted the wing mirror, noting the distance that Davey kept from them. He might, at a moment's notice, easily assume the identity of a passer-by. Sod that, he thought.

Stepping out, Reece allowed the Doleys to pass and swagger off in again. They were confident, awash with the success of their venture, combating the surge in their systems by chattering and goading one another on. Davey was surprised when Reece put a hand on his shoulder.

'No.'

'No what?'

'You know.'

'What you on about?'

'This wasn't in the job description.'

Davey threw him a sneer. 'What job description?'

Reece increased the pressure. Steel fingers gouged into Davey's deltoid muscle. He winced.

'I own you, remember?'

'You paid up yet?'

'Perhaps I ought to let the Petersons have you back?'

Reece sprung open his hand.

Davey said, 'What is your problem?'

Reece gazed at the colonnaded entrance. Above, the wards were dark save for the cupped glow of the duty nurses at their stations.

'I don't do this.'

'Too late now, mate,' Davey said.

'This carries a three or a five for me.'

'Yeah, and . . .?'

Reece wasn't about to brook further argument. He turned away, zipping up his jacket. 'Let's call it evens – for tonight.'

'You get back in the van.'

'Ever hear of demarcation?'

'Piss off.'

Reece grinned. 'All right then.' With that he strode off to the corner, turned into Homerton High Street and disappeared.

Davey stood impotently, eyes gleaming in the pale orange streetlight. From above there came a throaty chirping. Bastard birds singing. Gripping the camera, he strode to the hospital entrance, following his boys inside.

CHAPTER TWENTY

Steve and Archie dissolved into laughter in the Bulldog coffee-house off the Liedseplein in Amsterdam. They heaved, bucked and howled until, unable to take it, they caromed off one another and flopped about like floundering fish. 'I do not *bel-lieve* it,' cried Archie, whose eyelids were hooded cowls, his eyeballs pink from myriad burst blood vessels.

Steve, trying to snatch back his breath in helpless gasps, pointed a wavering nicotine-stained finger. 'It's . . . it's a fu . . .' was all he managed before the next round of giggles.

It had been a mammoth skunk-sampling session. Archie went again, hooting, whimpering, wiping tears from his eyes and clawing at his ribcage in desperation. He glanced at Steve and they screamed in unison at the sight, then drummed their fists on the thick table. Eventually, they swallowed the laughter, reducing it to reedy mewls. The object of their derision stood in the entrance with his hands on hips and his cheeks ablaze with rage.

Slowly, jaws aching, temples throbbing, they attempted self-resuscitation, sniffing and hawking up in a nugatory attempt to claw back some semblance of normality. But, as their eyes fell upon him, they erupted once more.

'What's so fucking funny?' demanded the dwarf.

✳

Steve and Arch were on an errand for the Petersons in Holland. Earlier in the day, they had met up with a supplier in the Oude Zijde, waiting for him in the Red Light district – a boon for Steve, who intended on frequenting the area later on. They were taken to a house in the Kloveniersburgwal to assay a variety of brands of hash. Once the price was agreed it was to be shipped in bulk to England. Archie had another agenda. The brothers suspected a leak in the operation (several kilos had been lost when a lorry was busted in transit to Lowestoft) and wanted him to ask certain questions of their supplier. Happily, the responses he received were satisfactory and there had been no need for Steve to mash the guy to a pulp.

After that they split up. Archie went to the Museum Het Rembrandt in Jodenbreestraat and Steve to purchase some obscene videos and bizarre sex aids. They knew the Bulldog of old and after negotiating shoppers, trams and pancake house munchie stops, they met back there after lunch.

It was almost four. Archie made a visor with his hand as if Steve's gaze would sear right through him. After much throat clearing and piggy little gasps, he spoke up.

'Sorry mate, but the last thing you want to see when you're caning it on Maui Wowee is a dwarf.'

'No offence, Mister Midget,' giggled Steve.

The dwarf eyed them. He wore a charcoal grey suit and carried a tiny briefcase and umbrella. He had a long pony tail stretching down his back.

'I *am* offended,' he said. His English was excellent.

Archie blushed, although it was hard to tell in his current state. 'Right, right. We're out of order.'

Steve cut in with, 'You escape from the circus then?'

The dwarf leaned on his umbrella. His tone took on a peevish quality. 'No. Nor do I chase women around the streets in a red cowl or leap through time . . .' He stopped, seeing amusement ripple across their faces.

Steve said, 'What you doing here, little man?'

'My wife works here.'

Archie and Steve ducked their heads down and pretended to search about on the floor.

'Very funny.'

'What's her name?' called out Steve.

'Brigitte.'

He came back up, guffawing. 'Bridget the Midget?'

'It is pronounced Brigi-*tuh*, said the dwarf, losing patience. 'And she is not a person of restricted growth.'

'Yeah, she's a giant,' simpered Archie, failing in his attempt at politeness.

'You are a pair of cunts,' said the dwarf.

Steve's expression changed. 'What d'you say?'

'You heard me, I think.'

Steve stood, pitching and yawing as his eustachian tubes got the better of him. He gripped the bench for support, then made himself stop thinking about how he could feel the colour of the wood *through his hands*. The midget had half-turned away when he stepped into the aisle and scooped him up, gripping him by his lapels.

'Don't you call me a cunt, you cunt.'

The tiny man hung in mid-air. 'I apologise. I meant to say your syphilitic mother sucks sailor's cocks.'

Steve pulled back his fist but Archie was there, giggling, holding his arm. 'Steve, you can't. It'd be like hitting a kid.'

That wouldn't have stopped him. What did was the midget kicking Steve hard in the scrotum. He dropped him and clutched at his balls, but before the small man had a chance to get away, Steve clamped a hand on his neck.

'Right you little bastard – Arch, what'm I gonna do with him?'

Archie looked round helplessly. The other smokers were surveying them now, but without the energy or inclination to act. The tableau seemed frozen in time, in space. There was a draught as the door opened and three American teenagers entered. They stopped dead, uncertain of what to make of this bizarre theatre. A grin spread across Archie's face.

'Bowling,' he said.

Steve got the point and, with a grunt, he swung once, twice and, on three, he rolled the dwarf as fast as he could across the floor. The man tumbled over and over and scattered the Yanks. As they fell against one another, Steve pulled a face.

Archie said, 'First attempt.'

'Give it another go, shall I?'

Arch surveyed the tangled bodies. 'Better not.'

A willowy brunette emerged from the toilet.

'Brigitte,' called out the midget.

Their jaws dropped. *This* was the dwarf's spouse? Steve envisaged several pornographic juxtapositions – many of which he'd seen on tape. He thought to make a proposal to view them *in flagrante*, but before he had a chance to suggest it, Brigitte was propelling them to the door. Archie went first, pausing as he struggled with the motor skills needed to manipulate the handle. Memory returned and with much shin kicking from the midget man they stepped outside.

'We ought to give that another go sometime,' said Steve.

'Only when they recognise midget bowling as an Olympic event.'

They burst into hysterical giggles for about three years. Once they had recovered enough to breathe, Archie slid out his Amsterdam guide and began flipping through it.

Steve was mesmerised by the fanning pages. 'What you doing?'

'Seeing what time the Rijksmuseum closes. I want to go see "The Nightwatch". Here we go, last admissions, four forty-five. You wanna come?'

'What is it?'

'Best collection of Dutch art in the world.'

'Give it a miss.'

'What you gonna do? Find some pygmies to juggle?'

'Nah, might pop back up the Red Light district.'

'See you later in the hotel then?'

Steve saluted, missing his temple and poking himself in the eye.

'All white then,' he said, blinking furiously.

It was a shock for Steve to be out among people, balance askew, eyes as big as Belisha beacons, mouth slewed to a moronic grin. Watching Archie waddle off, the corners of his mouth drooped as the idea began to form.

He began walking, unsteadily at first and listing to the right. He went up as far as the Kiezergracht before catching a bright yellow tram to the Centraal Station. In the plastic bucket seat, Steve fought with his thoughts. They seemed mired in cloudy soup but the idea was there. He rearranged his face into a heavy scowl and tried to marshal his neurones. Go hotel. Pack. Taxi.

Forty minutes later he was in a cab heading for Schipol Airport.

He remembered to strip the minibar before leaving.

'There'll be a lot more. Short cons, long cons, drug-dealing blags, swindles, you name it. Named criminals showing us the tools of their trade.'

It was a bright spring day and Davey – today David Hayes – and director Toby Lomax were crammed into Ian Farrow's hutch in the concrete doughnut – aka BBC Television Centre. Davey had made his pitch for 'London's Underworld Uncovered', ably aided and abetted by Charlie: the drug, not the masochistic girl-friend.

Marley, Farrow's precocious and intense twenty-four-year-old PA, had brought them up to the fifth floor. Farrow's office was different to that of the commercial broadcasters in that it was wedge-shaped and a lot smaller. The desk was bruised, the elbows of the sofa worn, the pot plants parched. Instead of walls emblazoned with awards, there was only a busy bulletin board.

Farrow, the Head of Factual Programming (Independent Commissioning) was a scrawny man whose straw-like hair was bunched at the apex of a lightbulb-shaped head. A nervous individual, his nose was slender, his mouth almost lipless and with eyes that cowered like marbles lost under a sofa. There was a ruddy patch under his weak chin where inept razor work had irritated his eczema. He wore a pale blue shirt, an indigo tie and a suit that matched the dull metal of his filing cabinet.

He knew Toby Lomax of old. They had often shared a few bevvies at the BBC Club, although not so much of late as Toby had been 'getting to grips with some personal issues'. He'd not actually seen Lomax since a session a year ago at the BBC bar off Langham Street when he bought a bottle of Courvoisier and torched his car with it. Toby suspected his wife of infidelity and had stuffed the Volvo with her belongings. Announcing his intentions, the bemused patrons had followed him out into Great Portland Street to watch the marriage go up in flames. A couple of security guards were summoned from Broadcasting House but being trained only to prevent access to BBC buildings, they failed to restrain him and the resultant fire drew the police and fire brigade. His arrest, as Farrow remembered it, was accompanied by the staccato symphony of radio management pummelling mobiles, checking up on spouses, mistresses and other sundry lovers.

Still, water under the bridge now.

'It's gonna be way bigger than all these other DocuSoaps. Guaranteed. Landmark. Appointment to view.'

Davey had hawked his footage from Homerton Hospital over to Toby's editing suite (in his basement at home in Tufnell Park) and Lomax had proven adept at splicing the material. They cobbled together a script and Davey recorded the voice-over with the tape slowed so as he sounded more sonorous.

Farrow was equally impressed.

'It's very real. Real is good,' said Ian.

'We can't identify the hospital yet,' announced Davey conspiratorially. 'Don't want to get my source into schtuck.'

Toby sipped a hot brackish liquid that claimed to be coffee. 'Tell him about that charity scam you uncovered.'

Davey was about to fire up his schpiel when Farrow held up a hand.

'Hang on a mo. Before I hear any more, you do realise you'll have to reveal your sources at some point? We don't want another Channel Four job.'

Davey and Toby laughed, but only Toby knew why. 'Fakes,' he mouthed.

'Fakes, bleeding hell. No problem, Ian. All kosher.'

Farrow said, 'Great. But we'll obviously need written depositions.'

Sure you will, thought Davey, foreseeing an opportunity for his old signature-forging friend to get creative.

'Impressive though, yeah?' Lomax asked.

Farrow rewound the tape. A corpulent figure filled the screen. He was silhouetted against a plain wall being interrogated about arson and insurance fraud. His words came gruffly, gutted by perspicacious editing. Even Simon Latimer's mum would have been hard put to recognise him.

'This chap is good. Where'd you find him?'

'Master criminal, that geezer. Runs half North London.'

'Can you get more footage?'

'Can do.'

'Well,' said Farrow. 'Well, well, well.'

Lomax gave Davey a stage wink. He ignored him.

Ian scratched his chin. 'Off the record, I'd say this stands a good chance in the offers round.'

'When's that?'

'Early summer.'

Davey trampled his desire to toss Farrow out of the window. He wanted it *now*.

'Yes, I think this could happen. The budget's good for Factual next year and this would be front line for Two, possibly even One.'

Lomax beamed, making the mental move from Tufnell Park to Chalk Farm, seeing his reinstatement in London's finer restaurants and fresh plastic in his wallet.

'How's about lunch?' offered Davey.

Lunch was an institution for BBC management: it was said that in the event of fire they congregated not in the forecourt but fled immediately to the nearest restaurant.

'Splendid,' said Farrow.

Davey glared at Lomax.

'Groucho or the House?' offered Toby, dreading the bill.

'Hello, Shirl. All white?' slurred Steve, still suffering joint-lag from the smoke he'd consumed earlier in the day.

'Thought you was in Amsterdam with Arch?'

'Got pulled back. Another job on.'

He stood framed in the doorway. Behind him the evening traffic jerked and bucked over the speed humps, brakes squealing on wet pads.

'Wanna come in?'

'Ta.'

She led him into the kitchen where Darren and Ronan were devouring oven chips. He grunted acknowledgement, hoping they wouldn't ask him about the contents of his plastic carrier bags. He'd have a hard job explaining away the cock-pump.

Shirley flipped on the kettle and used a J-cloth to wipe imaginary crumbs off the counter.

'Looking good, Shirley.'

She primped her hair, turned to face him. Nothing to do until it boiled.

'Smooth talker.'

'Always was, Shirl. Always was.'

There was silence save for the wet mastication of her sons. Ronan gurned at Steve, a wad of chewed chips labouring around in his mouth.

'Eat your tea properly, Ro.'

Steve asked, 'You getting out much these days?'

'With these little buggers?'

'They got dancing down the Rivoli.'

'Crofton Park?'

'You ought to come sometime.'

The water bubbled and boiled. Shirley made a single cup of tea. Steve stirred in three sugars and tentatively kissed the beverage. The boys slid from their chairs and ran through to the lounge. A moment later, the TV grew louder.

Shirley asked, 'So what's the visit for?'

With a grin, 'Told Arch I'd check up on you.'

'Like I'd have time for a fancy-man?'

'Always the quiet ones eh, Shirl?'

'Come on, Stevie. What's the real reason?'

He pretended not to hear her. Took his time in lighting up a fag. 'Know what he did all day out there?'

'Do I want to?'

'Museums and that. He's doolally over that Rembrandt.'

She blew air. 'Don't I know it. You should see the mess he's made in the bedroom.'

She was leading him to it. 'Oh yeah?'

'All his paints and his paintings and the *smell* of that turps. It's like living with a dosser.'

'That's the thing of it, Shirl. He got right paranoid. Doesn't reckon the picture's safe up in the bedroom. He wants me to borrow it away. Stash it until he's back.'

She transferred her weight to her other slippered foot. 'But he's back in the morning?'

Steve rolled his eyes. 'He's gone rental about it. Asked me to fetch it away for him.'

Shirley folded her arms 'Reckons it'll get nicked, does he? More likely I'd sling it in a skip.'

He made his face into a mask of innocence. 'P'raps that's what he's scared of. You want to go up and get it?'

She scrutinised him, studying the deep lines leading from his nostrils down around his mouth, the greasy quiff, now receding to an island, the forehead pitted with the grief-grid of age, eyes heavy, reddened. Finally his fingers as he sucked on his JPS, brown bleeding to yellow at the nails.

'Come on, then.'

He followed her up the steep stairs, keeping up the verbals to confirm the lie. 'Gawd knows what goes on in that nut of his. I mean, what's he think he's going to gain by *painting* of all things. Now, Shirl, what you should have done, and you know it, is to have had me instead.'

'And share you with every other bit of skirt in Bermondsey?'

'Nah, not me.'

'Yes, you.'

She opened the door to the spare room. There were palette knife smears on the walls and the surface of his painting table was drowned in a puddle of muddied pigment. Archie's copy of the self-portrait was almost complete – a good stab, although still undeniably amateur. The original hung on the wall opposite. There were several other canvases.

Steve asked, 'What's all these then?'

Shirley flushed. 'Nothing.'

'What is it, Shirl? You know I'll get it out of you.'

She adopted a matronly tone. 'If you must know, he's had me modelling for him. Flesh tones, he says.'

'In the nuddy? Let's have a butchers?'

She placed herself in front of the stack. Steve tried to get round her but she wasn't budging.

'Nothing I ain't seen before, love.'

'Not mine, you ain't.'

His face was inches from hers, his breath rank. 'Not for want of trying.'

'Drop it, Stevie.'

'You're not bad. You know that?'

'Get away.'

He dropped and stamped out his cigarette then put his hands around her, making contact on the small of her back. One hand moved to her bra strap.

'Stevie,' she warned.

'We got as far as this once. Further.'

'Long time ago. Take it and go, Stevie, eh?'

He swung his eyes at the bedroom wall. 'We could go through. He'd never know. You and me, it's unfinished business, ain't it?'

'He's your best mate.'

He released a cackle. 'Bet you ain't had a good shafting in a long time.'

She slapped him hard, hissed, 'Take it – and piss off out of it.'

He stared her down, assessing whether it would be worth it to . . . but there'd be ructions. And the kids would hear. Not worth the bother. He raised his chin and his mouth turned down at the corners.

'Your loss, love.'

He stepped back, unhooked the Rembrandt and stuck it under his arm.

'You'll be glad to see the back of it,' he said, like things were back to normal.

'Yeah, and you.'

She glared him all the way down the stairs until she'd shut the front door in his face.

CHAPTER TWENTY-ONE

'Hey, guess what?'

Rox took a step sideways and looked through the plate glass window of Giuseppe's Restaurant. 'You're standing, outside – right?'

'How'd you know?'

'First thing anyone does when they get a mobile is pull that one.'

'Oh . . . right.'

Rox opened the door. A gust of night wind came in on his tail.

'Davey gave it me. You can key in all these numbers.'

She feigned delight. 'Wow! You mean I'm one of your pre-sets?'

He didn't get it. 'I put the restaurant in straightaway.'

She was happy and sad. If she was one of his top five pre-sets then he clearly didn't know that many people intimately.

And not even her, came the afterthought.

'How long's it been this time?' she asked.

'Few days?'

'Eight. Not that I'm counting.'

They sat at the same table as before. It had been a heavy shift that evening and Rox had only now had a minute to put her feet up and massage her toes through her stockings. Before they had a chance to speak, the diminutive Mr S appeared from the kitchen.

'I'm sorry. Is too late. We're closed.'

'This is a friend of mine, Mr S.'

His eyes sparkled. 'Ah. Boyfriend.'

'No, not my boyfriend.' Mr S liked to tease her by pairing her up with any reasonable male and then enumerating the many reasons why they were no good for her. 'Reece, this is Mr Salvatori. My boss.'

He stuck out a hand, enveloping the Genovese's mitt. 'Nice place.'

'*Grazie*. What you do?'

'Cabs and chauffeur work.'

Giuseppe's eyes darted between them, searching for the spark. He drilled his gaze into hers.

'Mr Reece would like drink,' he said, meaningfully.

'He doesn't drink, Mr S.'

'Better to be sober to enjoy her company, no?' he replied, winking at Reece.

Reece said nothing.

'I go now. I know you want to talk *alone*.'

Rox felt herself redden.

'He is fine man. Fine. A shave perhaps, and a decent suit?' Giuseppe brushed a hand through his helmet of hair, and let out a long sigh.

Rox said, 'Bye, Mr S.'

'And *cabs*? I don't know. Not always legal.'

'Thanks, Mr S.'

'Always *dirty*, cabs I think.'

'Yes, Mr S.'

'But, your choice.'

'I'm bored now, Mr S.'

He went off to the kitchen.

Rox said, 'Sorry about that. What's the mobile for?'

He toyed with the unfamiliar object, testing the feel of it. 'Guv'nor wants to know he can get me any time.'

'I thought you hated them?'

'Well, it's free.'

She raised an eyebrow, squinted mockingly at him.

'You got a home number?' he asked, looking down at the buttons.

'How about you give me yours?'

He was stern now. 'You know what I said.'

'Yeah, too dangerous. I might start learning about you, getting stuff on you – something terrible like that.'

'I don't do rows,' he replied, bluntly.

She bunched up her mouth in an angry little pout. 'I do.'

She had kind of given up on him in the last few days. Not that there was anyone else on the horizon, but the surprise of his tracking her down again had dissipated and she wasn't about to go through all that longing again. In fact she had denied herself all thoughts of Reece . . . reducing it to once or twice a day . . . ten times a day . . . and palpitations whenever anyone came by after eleven at night. His voice interrupted her train of failed denial.

'One reason I dropped in is you ought to know Davey's up to something. It's nicking computers – and he's filming stuff and all.'

'What sort of stuff?'

'Dunno, but he's had me dropping him off at these telly places. Soho and that. Telly Centre.' He rose. 'Look, I'll give you a bell when I know more.'

'Short and sweet.'

'Yeah, you are a bit,' he grinned.

Bolt out of the blue. She stammered something about having the money she owed him, but he was shucking his jacket back over his broad shoulders and moving for the door. She remembered those shoulders, bruised, back in Camberwell. Reece retreated and was out on the pavement before she even had the door shut. Watching him pull away into Tranquil Vale, she started to think about computers and telly and possible connections.

Davey Kayman had rented out a shop in Cambridge Heath Road, E2. It had a varied history, having been a hire centre and a travel agent's: more recently it had been a mobile phone outlet so it had plenty of power points, which would come in handy.

'Right, see this lot?'

Latimer cast his eyes across a hillock of monitors and base units. A scree of keyboards was silted up against them.

'Ye-es,' he said, with some suspicion.

'Get 'em up and running, check they're working properly.'

'Must be forty, fifty here.'

'And plenty more to come. Then I want you to wipe 'em.'

'Why – what's on them?'

'Old files and that. I got them off the NHS. Picked them up cheap.'

'Is that why they've got "Property of Homerton Hospital – Do Not Remove" stamped on them?'

'Could be.'

Simon's jowls slumped southwards. 'You sure this is kosher?'

'Course. I put an ad in the Office Equipment section of *Loot*. I want you to mock one up for *Computer Weekly*, then get to work making sure these look the business. We want to shift these in bulk. Telling you Si – re-con computers are going to be the next big thing.'

'No one wants second-hand computers.'

'Local authorities do. They have major cost-cutting problems.'

Simon pointed at the casing. 'What about the markings?'

Davey repaid the query with a shark grin. 'Found this firm in Dublin who makes covers for the base units. They're sending over a hundred. You've only got to swap them over.'

'What operating system are they? *Leaded* windows?'

Davey and co had run rampant in the hospital, turning up several old IBM's and Compaq units, even an old Tulip monitor. The keyboards were grime-encrusted and their keys yellowed like old teeth. Furthermore, the rest of the equipment was sun-bleached to pallid beige. The processors were old enough to bring tears of nostalgia to a nerd and prompt an anecdote about the Spectrum ZX80.

'How'd you mean?' Davey asked. His computer knowledge was slim. He thought software was a pair of combat trousers.

Latimer selected a processor, connected up the monitor, keyboard and mouse and booted up. After several minutes of tutting he turned round. Davey was staring out at passing women. Charlie was at home sleeping something off. He'd no time for her whining anyway. Too busy. Getting worse, she was.

'This is crap,' said Simon. 'Runs on Windows 95 and you'll need at least Windows 98. I can patch it up, but you want to replace the processor. Then you'll need to upgrade the memory to four gigabytes so we'll need SIMM cards to stick in the motherboard. It's not worth the bother.'

'You mean I need new stock?'

'They're beyond economical repair.'

Davey felt tension around his jaw. 'The hospitals are full of this old bollocks.'

Simon formed a smile. 'They saw you coming – flogged you the stuff they were gonna throw out. From what I hear, the NHS Trusts have gone mad installing new systems.'

Davey was on his way to the door.

'Right, leave it to me. Forget the Cabs for now. I'm pulling you off that to work full-time in here. I'll put you on a wage.' He surveyed the dusty, empty space. 'For now you go ahead – make these look good. Do your best.'

And he was gone, with no mention of the sum he intended

to pay, nor any ideas as to what to do with fifty PC's that looked as though they wrote documents in copperplate.

'Mazeltov,' said Latimer, with as much dripping sarcasm as he could muster.

It took ten days for Davey to fill the place with 'new stock.' He and his team had been busy, spending their evenings marching into a variety of hospitals in North East London and waltzing out with the latest systems. He was amazed at the lack of security and, armed with a clipboard and his patter – 'Upgrading. Viral Sweeps. Speak to Admin' – he easily placated the overworked staff. His promise? That they had the new computers down in the van. Soon as they'd finished taking out the existing hardware, they'd be back to install it.

Never happened.

When one irate doctor demanded to know why all his files were being spirited away by 'a bunch of ragamuffins' he claimed ignorance and asked the doc if he'd spoken to his boss? He hadn't, so Davey led him through the wards and offices in pursuit of the imaginary head honcho – losing him when the doctor's bleeper went and he had to go and perform an appendectomy. After that, Davey disconnected himself from the replacement end and denied knowledge of any suppliers. He would focus on delivery.

Timing his clearances for the end of the working day, he masterminded a sizeable haul, and the overflow was piled up in the Shoreditch basement. Latimer had no problems with the new apparatus. The operating systems were up to scratch and Internet Service Providers came ready installed. Davey told him to wipe all files (and disable any Intranet systems, once it was explained to him what that was) and clean them up ready for resale.

Some of the casings were stencilled – easily removable with industrial solvent – others had UV markings. The delivery of the base unit casings arrived and Latimer spent long hours with tiny screwdrivers swapping them over. Where they couldn't create a clean unit, he removed the processor and began afresh.

Latimer disliked working in what he termed 'sweatshop conditions', but complaints were futile. Davey did his usual stalling and evading and when pressed claimed prior meetings and buggered off.

The Doleys received a score for each pick-up and anyone asking questions was sacked immediately. Feeling quite the entrepreneur once more, Davey covertly filmed all his operations, ready to put the footage to good use later.

'I'll do the talking, all right?'

How many times had he heard that from Davey? They were crossing the rain-slicked playground of a primary school in Stratford. Latimer felt a wave of apprehension as he carried the PC over the threshold and he got a Proustian rush of floor wax and gym shoes. No shepherd's pie though. They squeaked down the long corridors, giants among waist-high pegs, tiny lockers and awful pasta paintings. They arrived at the office where Davey effusively greeted the secretary. The Deputy Head was summoned and came out to meet them. From school-day memories, Latimer had been expecting some kind of insane homunculus and was surprised when the man was quite amiable.

'Marvellous, marvellous. You must be Mr . . .'

'Keyes,' said Davey. 'This is Latimer, my technical adviser. He'll set up the system and give you a demo.'

This warranted a frosty glare from Simon. It meant *he'd* be going back to the van and lugging the monitor. With a sigh, he placed the unit on a desk piled high with homework books.

By the time he returned, Davey was on his way to concluding the deal. It transpired that the Bursar was not in that day, but that the Dep. Head had been given permission to spend 'up to a certain limit'. Catnip to Davey who took him a good five hundred above this.

'Thing is, it's not about profit margins,' he explained. 'As the authorised supplier for the Local Authority, we look on this as a PR exercise.'

The Deputy Head nodded ferociously. Pretending to know about the real world was a perverse strain in the scholastic community.

'See,' continued Davey, 'the aim is to get the kids familiar with IT, then once they're old enough the hope is that they'll choose our systems.'

Grade A bullshit, thought Simon, never more glad that he had no children.

The Deputy Head confessed to Luddite ignorance, but the secretary was up to speed on IT. Simon sped through Windows and Word and showed her how to create a superior spreadsheet. They purchased fifteen PC's.

'Told you it'd be sweet,' said Davey, waving the cheque in Latimer's face. He had opened a new holding account in the name of 'Complete Computers'.

'Can you do us a sub then?'

He shut the gate against the worn brick wall, pulled a wad from his pocket, separated out a grand and stuffed it in Simon's hand.

'There you go. Don't say I never pay you.'

In the van, Simon had time to do his maths. Davey now only owed him, what, about eighteen grand? He drove appallingly too, throwing the van about, mobile clamped to his ear as he lambasted the controller at Finsbury Cabs. He paused between calls, letting the phone cool off.

'By the way, Si, when we deliver, the rest of them PC's can come out the crap pile.'

'You mean the first lot you brought in?'

A nod.

'But they'll run slow. *Very* slow.'

'Then they can give them to the special kids.'

'You sure that's ethical?'

His canines appeared. 'Ethics – that's where my old man lives, isn't it?'

'We're letting those kids down.'

Davey turned on him. 'Remember the last election? The manifesto? Education, education, education . . .'

CHAPTER TWENTY-TWO

The doorbell drilled through Steve Lamb's hangover. It kept ringing until he could bear it no longer and had to move. The sheet was twisted to a rope between his legs. He attempted to speak but no sound emerged from his parched lips. He raised himself up on his elbows. The pain was so intense that he fell back. He tried and failed to open either one of his eyes. One was glued shut with mucus, the other eyelid swollen to three times its size and filled with pus. His nose was scabbed up and caked in blood. With the tips of his fingers, he gingerly pressed each of the bruises on his chest and stomach. He tried his ribcage and came to realise that he daren't breathe unless he wanted jolts of lightning firing off inside him.

His memory clambered up and collapsed on the parapet of his consciousness. Archie had caught up with him a couple days ago: unawares. Jumped him on his way back from the Gregorian. Arch could be a beast when roused and he was too pissed at the time to fight back. Plus, he hadn't known if the beating was about the painting or because he'd tried it on with Shirl. In the event, he'd thought it best to stay schtum and take it.

It took five minutes to pull on a dressing gown and get to the front door. He poked at the buzzer.

'Who is it?'

'Arch.'

'What you want?'

'Let us in. It's all right. It's not about the painting. It's business.'

Steve buzzed the buzzer, pottered across the lounge and flicked on the kettle. It made a sizzling sound. No water in it and no teabags anyway. He'd have to go down the shop later.

Knock on the door.

Steve opened up and Archie punched him to the ground.

'I lied. Where's my painting, boy?'

Steve tried out a grin but it wasn't going to happen. Arch slammed the door, trod over his supine body and went to the picture window and stared out. The river was grey, the sky like old photocopier paper. Steve crawled to the sofa, emitting a series of grunts.

'First off, it ain't your painting. Second of all, you can piss off. I've got a bird back there.'

'Inflatable?'

Steve didn't say anything.

'Steve, we'll sort this out, all right?'

Archie filled the kettle. He managed to make coffee by pouring boiling water into the remains of a Nescafé jar and swilling it around.

'Come on, Lamb. Where you stashed it?'

'It's doing us no good leaving that Rembrandt round yours.'

'Says who?'

'Says me.'

'Don't give me the hump. Where is it?'

Steve focused his good eye on his old friend. 'I sent the ransom note and the first square to the gallery.'

'You done WHAT?'

'Arch – it's been months! I said I'd do it, didn't I? – back in the winter. It's only a piece off the bottom. All brown paint, not even the signature.'

Archie came at him with fists raised; Steve sat helpless in his dressing gown, too weak to retaliate.

'Hold it,' he barked. 'Archie stop there. You touch me again and I'll fucking burn it, swear to God I will.'

Archie punched his own palm.

'There ain't nothing you can do. I sent it them. It don't mean nothing to me, some painting, but eight mill does.'

'You're asking eight? I told you we'd only see five.'

'Thought I might as well go high.'

'What d'you think it is? Fucking rollover week?'

'That's not a bad idea, as it goes. They don't pay up, then next time I'll double it.'

'Steve, I am not happy about this. Not a happy bunny at all.'

'Sir?'

'What is it, Prakash?'

'What are anal warts?'

When the other children saw Mr Simmons' face cloud over, a hush spread across the classroom.

'And loose stools?'

'Prakash. Put the mouse down, do you hear me?'

'But sir?'

'Now.'

Mr Simmons hurried between the large tables, trying not to bang his hip on their bright sharp corners. It had begun as a normal morning in Year Three at Stratford Primary School. He'd taken the register and the children had done some simple science experiments with leaves and grass. Now it was the turn for reading and writing and Prakash Patel – a clever child with a lazy eye – had been allowed to play on one of the new computers. Mr Simmons dug the mouse out of the boy's hand with enough force to send him wailing into the arms of Amy Spencer, a seven-year-old who ran the Minstrels cartel in the playground.

Simmons scrolled down the screen. It was a long report, documenting a variety of unsavoury bowel and sphincter complaints. He closed the file and found another, broader, folder containing more medical information. He was still sitting there, open-mouthed and bug-eyed, long after the bell had gone.

Latimer had a number of ways to indicate his resentment of the way in which Davey Kayman treated him: one of these was a kind of wilful indolence.

The brush caressed the naked girl, as she lay draped on the chair in an odalisque position. It feathered in her dark brown hair and described a line under her chin. It went around her shoulders and delineated her strong arms. In two quick crescents, it underlined her pert breasts, dotted the nipples then skipped down to tick the small V of her tummy button. It hesitated. It remoistened itself in turps and charged up with paint. It hovered in the air, moving forwards and backwards like an animal riding its haunches before a charge. Now it darted for the canvas, taking on the broad sweep of the outer thigh up as far as the knee, which was hooked over the arm of the chair. It swam round under and deftly coloured in the lower thigh, the crook and swell of the calf. It picked out the pretty painted toes. It repeated its advance to seize the other leg. With confidence, it strode down the big muscle, danced a knotty zigzag of shade on the hump of cartilage and drew in harder, more masculine lines for the calf and ankle. Finally, with almost virgin shyness, it dipped and bobbed in turpentine once more and shaded in the downy triangle.

Archie was enjoying his hobby.

More than a hobby now, it had consumed most of his waking hours since his return from Amsterdam. When he wasn't challenging Steve or running the odd errand for the Petersons, he loved nothing better than to lock himself in his 'studio'. Darren and Ronan were banned from entering and Arch had gone so far as to install a lock, the key for which he wore on a string around his neck. He was getting better too. Ironically, losing the Rembrandt had urged him to break away from imitation and to experiment with finding his own style: that was a messy few days.

For Shirley, the thrill of posing had worn off. She complained of cramp and cold and had privately been terrified about the idea of Steve or anyone else seeing her body on display. Likewise, his offspring couldn't sit still for a moment. Archie thought of carting the video and PlayStation upstairs and sticking them in front of it, but when he touched the equipment, their hair-trigger yelling put paid to the idea. Archie started watching the Open University, even taped arts programmes off the satellite. He took a fancy to Poussin and Vermeer, but Rembrandt was still the bollocks. He gazed at the glossy plates in his catalogues. He studied chiaroscuro, composition and the golden mean and even tried to read some of the poncy articles while eating his tea. He stumbled over 'expressive elements', 'painterly passages' and 'contouring' and decided that the work was enough. Wasn't about words.

He drew his own face over and over again, often falling asleep at the easel. He stopped taking regular meals, content with having a plate of bread and cheese (Wholemeal and ASDA cheddar) delivered to his studio door. He stopped going to the Railway Tavern. Once he was satisfied that he was getting the hang of drawing, he began working in oils again. He tried a still life, mocking up an arrangement of apples with a chequered dishcloth as backdrop. He spiced it up by adding a tyre iron and a double Whopper meal. No good: he wanted to paint flesh and faces and that meant getting a proper live model.

'You all right? Not cramped or nothing?'

'Sorry, what?'

'Are you stiff?'

'Oh, no. Million miles away.'

The girl was good. She sat still, didn't mind what position he asked her to adopt and had no problems about getting her kit off. You expected that of a professional.

'Archie?'

'Yers?' She liked it when he did his Parker voice. Sometimes he even added a little 'milady'. This was her third session. She could only do afternoons, which suited him as everyone was out the house.

'Stop me if this sounds, like, weird, but how can you tell if a bloke fancies you if he's not giving you the signs?'

He blushed. Did she mean him? Had he been giving her the come on? After all, she had a blinding little body. Neat nipped-in waist, good tits and hardly an ounce of fat on her, well, a little on the tum. Hadn't had kids, this one; skin like velvet instead of dough rolled out too many times.

'What signs?' he asked.

'You know, like when he's with you he makes everything a contact sport?'

Archie thought of Steve pawing his slappers. 'Gotcha.'

'Or he's saying horrible things to you, only it's meant to be a compliment because he'd dead interested?'

Not me, realised Arch. He'd not even thought about her sexually – well, it'd crossed his mind the first time, but soon as he started drawing her, she had dissolved into a series of problems of shape, line and form. He popped his bulldog head round the canvas and gave her a wink.

'Come on then? Who is he?'

She arched a superior eyebrow. 'Just some guy.'

'He got a name?'

'You never answered my question.'

He sucked in air over his teeth. 'He'll play his hand one way or the other.'

'We did have a snog once, but it never took. He reckoned we weren't ready.'

Archie cooked up a hot peach, rolled a bristle brush around in it and held it to the canvas. He furrowed his brow, held his breath in and then applied the paint as he slowly let it out.

'Surprised you ain't got a bloke. Nice-looking sort, like you.'

'Did have, but he was a bastard,' said Rox.

'Up north was it?'

'Yeah.'

'They're all wankers up there, aren't they?'

'Easy,' she warned.

Rox had forgotten about leaving her card on the board at Goldsmith's and, on returning home one night, had been surprised to hear a gruff voice on the machine demanding if she was 'still in the modelling game'. She wiped it, thinking it was some pervert, but Archie rang back and caught her on her day off. They agreed to meet in a café in Greenwich. She recognised him by his description. Chubby, cropped hair, Rembrandt 'tache and goatee. He was an oddity, although not by South London standards.

She liked him immediately. They shared pie and mash and he made a few jokes and she thought – why not model for him? Mr S was paying her enough to cover the mortgage, but not a lot else for spends. Like Reece, Archie forced the money on her – seventy-five quid for the session. At the college she'd only been getting twenty-five, less the fiver for National Insurance.

On her way home from his house the first time (embarrassing, stripping off in the bathroom, all those homely gunked up plastic toys.) she felt a pang of guilt. It was too much. Too easy. He'd confessed he was new to this 'art game' and that she was his first proper model. Didn't look like he could afford it either, what with having two kids and not being in regular work. She phoned him back, offering to return the money or to do some free sessions, but Archie was adamant. They had agreed the price. They booked in another date and Rox started thinking about buying new clothes with the spare cash.

'Archie.'

The voice welled up from the bottom of the stairs, followed by a series of creaks as the steps and risers came under pressure. Rox pictured the slippered feet of the maid in the old Tom & Jerry cartoons.

'I suppose you told your wife about this?' she asked.

Silence from behind the canvas.

Oh dear, thought Rox.

A middle-aged woman entered, wearing a Pac-a-mac. Her eyes cascaded over Rox's prone, naked body, then shot to the easel and her husband's face.

'Hullo, love,' said Arch.

'What's going on?'

'Nuffin'.'

'I'm imagining this then, am I?'

Rox saw the man-wife betrayal look zap between them. Archie's mouth formed a gummy 'O', his temples thudded and his eyes flew in a holding pattern, waiting for clearance before the final approach to the runway of her anger. All credit to him, he didn't bother with denial or beseeching endearments: he went straight in with the facts.

'Shirl, she's an artist's model. I hired her from the college.'

'She's stark bollock naked.'

'Yeah. That's what "model" means.'

Rox tried to shrink to the size of a dust-mote.

'I know what model means,' said Shirley, building up steam. 'Why didn't you tell me this was going on?'

Now he'd had it. No answer to that one.

'You never asked.'

The speed with which she grabbed the tube of emerald green was stunning. She squeezed it at him, catching the painting and spattering it in his face.

'Shirl, love. Come on, this is Art. There's nothing going on.'

Rox drew her robe about her and curled up in the corner as more paint flew about, hitting walls and smearing the window-panes. Archie's mistake, she realised, was to go back to denial and therefore guilt.

'In my house, Arch. What about the kids?'

'I always lock the door, you know that.'

When could she crawl away and get her clothes? Not yet. Finger-painting was about to become fist painting.

'Couldn't have hired some old witch, could you? Oh no, that's not how it works, is it? How much you paying her?'

'Twenty-five.'

'I see.'

'An hour.'

'Jesus, Arch. That's more than I used to get packing cans . . . she . . . she might as well be on the game.'

Here we go again, mused Rox. Bad enough she'd been given a whore's name, now here she was being damned to it on appearances. She was about to say something when Shirley cornered her husband and started squeezing a tube of sticky blue oil paint up Archie's nostrils.

'Nop that,' he said. Archie's moustache and chin were smeared in blue and green like he was bleeding in negative

Rox slipped out and dressed as fast as she could. Shirley continued her complaints, only they were interspersed with hawking and barking noises, like a blow-whale in season, or a man expelling mucus after a poor dive into a swimming pool. On the landing she glimpsed Shirl, palette and brushes in hand, decorating him with blobs of paint. Not bad, she thought – if a bit abstract for her tastes. She clomped downstairs, but found Archie behind her as she put her hand to the latch.

'Mang om. I am't paid you mor poo-bay.'

'What?' She got it. He was telling her he hadn't paid her. A paint bogey bubbled out of his nostril; Archie's mouth was all green inside, like he'd been necking NightNurse.

'Your momey.'

'My mummy?'

Arch pulled out five twenties and stuffed them in her hand.

'I can't take all that.'

'Mef you can. Mor all the aggro.'

Rox stepped outside. The breeze blew her hair across her face. 'Archie, it was fun while it lasted.' She raised her voice, intending this for his wife. 'The *modelling*. Not that there was *anything* else . . .'

He shook his head furiously. 'Mo, we carry on. Nop here. Moan you. Ofay?'

'Didn't get that?'

He held up his hand, thumb and little finger outstretched to make the sign of the receiver. 'Moan you.'

She shrugged. 'If you say so.'

Archie went back into his war-zone and she caught the bus for work.

Steve spent the day bathing his injuries in alcohol, which he administered internally. In the pub. His eye had opened up enough to scour the *Racing Post* and he managed to write out a betting slip and later tear it to confetti. Afterwards, he took the air in Woolwich, ending up on a bench with a can of Tennant's Extra. He watched the world go by, in particular the younger, female part in school uniform and black stockings.

By early evening he had a raging hangover and had visited several hostelries in the hope of finding a cure. Turning over in his mind was the efficacy of his plan with the Rembrandt. Had he addressed the parcel to the right place? To the right person? Was the ransom note legible? Had he used the correct variety of fonts of torn newspaper? Had he been clear about his demand for used unmarked bills? They're getting it together, he thought. Takes time these days. Better pay up soon though or he'd go and hack out another square with the breadknife. Sod Archie – they'd pay up all right. Mattered to them, Art did. Rich people didn't care about anything except for houses, cars and stuff, which was why a B & E in Kensington got you the same sentence as manslaughter in Eltham.

After a few bevvies, the women in the Old Justice underwent their customary metamorphosis into goddesses of the night: sadly they remained unaware that he too was a living deity. Could have been the bruises and swellings though, thought Steve. While peeing over his shoes in the toilet, he caught the eye of an older man. He leaned against the sweating brick wall and took a closer look. Bloke had strands of lanky hair and sunken pouches under his eyes. Saggy old skin like perished leather. And the state of it! Staring him out and all, with his fists up ready. Steve took a swing at him and punched the mirror, filling the sink with needle shards of light. After that, he zipped up his pants, tucked in his shirt and wandered off home.

He had a porn vid in the slot when the buzzer went. When was he ever going to get through *Nursey nursey ButtFuck*? He answered it and opened the door. A few moments later the clattering on the stairs stopped.

'All right, Steve?' said a subdued Archie at the doorway. 'Shirl's gone and thrown me out.'

'Oh yeah?' Keep it frosty, he thought.

'Can I kip round here while I get it sorted?'

Steve waited as long as he could. 'All white.'

'Thanks, mate.'

Archie struggled inside. Steve noticed the pile of cases behind him.

'What's all that?'

'Painting kit.'

Steve watched as Arch brought in his easel, canvases, toolbox, and other suitcases. Once he'd piled it up into a castle in the centre of the room, he shut the door.

'Arch?'

'Yeah?'

He smacked him one full in the face; rings on, cutting Archie's lip open and almost busting his nose. Archie slammed to the floor.

'That's for the other day – right?'

CHAPTER TWENTY-THREE

'You keep turning up, don't you?'

'I'll go away if you want,' Reece said.

Rox steered him back through the empty restaurant. He didn't object. She sat him down, released her grip.

'Hey. I've not noticed that before.'

A long white scar ran from his wrist and along his forearm, the dark hairs curling over it like fallen trees over a rushing stream. Reece started to ease down the arm of his sweater.

'No, don't. I like scars. They're sexy.'

'Not the way I got this.'

She raised her eyebrows.

'Street fight. Bloke cut me with his blade before I had a chance to grab him.'

'And you were how old?'

'Seventeen, eighteen?'

She chewed on her lip for a moment. 'Wanna see mine?'

'Depends where it is.'

She pulled out her work shirt to reveal a triangle of tummy, then hooked her thumbs in the top of her skirt and tugged it down at the side.

'Appendix,' deadpanned Reece. 'Is that all you've got?'

She plonked herself down, parted her hair above her left temple and ferreted out a gap near the crown. 'Go on, touch it.'

Reece ran a couple of exploratory fingers over the area.

'Got bottled at a party. Five stitches,' she said, proudly.

That did it. Competitive scar competition. He showed her the marks on his knuckles and the stab wound that had narrowly missed his liver. She showed him the tracer lines on her hands (cheffing accidents) and removed her shoe so as to demonstrate where she'd once trodden on a rusty nail. They covered playground and teenage party wounds, resulting in Reece removing his sweater and drawing down the sleeve of his T-shirt. There was a chalky blue tattoo of a lion's head on his right bicep.

'What's this then? Not some kind of BNP Nazi, are you?'

Reece looked at his shoulder. 'Nah. It's a British Lion.'

'And?'

'Name of a pub.'

'What's on the other arm? Dog and Trumpet?'

'The Nosey and Parker.'

She pulled her sarky face and prodded the design. 'So how's that come about when you don't drink, eh, Mister Reece?'

'I was trying to show you this here.' He pulled the neck of his T-shirt over his shoulder to reveal a patch of raised scar tissue across his scapula. 'That's from a milk float.'

'You were run over . . . but very slowly?'

'Nope. Stopped a runaway float in Brockley. Milkman left the handbrake off and I got in front of it. Held onto it long enough for someone to jump up in the cabin and get the brake.'

'That milkman wouldn't have been you, would it?'

He studied her, then broke out an impish grin. 'Can't say it was the longest of my regular jobs.'

'You lived round here as well?'

'Above the old Brockley Jack. Briefly.'

Rox rested her chin on her fists, smiling. 'All this info – soon you'll be telling me all your secrets.'

He started putting his sweater back on.

'Aww, come on. I was only teasing.'

Reece went and poured a coffee.

'I've got more on Davey's latest con. He's having the computers out of hospitals and selling them on to schools. Know what he does then? Only breaks back in the next night and steals them back again.'

'Sod.'

'Clever sod though. He's going back and forth with the same gear. Clinics, hospices, libraries—'

'He can't do all that on his own, surely?'

Reece added spoonfuls of brown crystalline sugar. 'He's got a bunch of kids grafting for him.'

She locked eyes with him. 'I take it you're not involved?'

'No chance. And I'm none too chuffed about him ripping off kids and sick people. Sticks in my craw.'

'What're we going to do about it?'

He smiled helplessly. 'You're the brains.'

'Can't I be the looks?'

He blinked slowly. 'Okay – you're the looks as well.'

She gave him a big cheesy grin, but Reece wasn't playing.

'Apparently, he's cleaning them up, taking off the serial numbers like you'd do with the engine on a dodgy motor. Makes it tough to trace. He's got a laminated card, coming onto these clinics like a pukka supplier. He's got his back covered.'

'But you've seen all this – why not go to the police?'

'We don't know where he's going to do it next. Anyway, that's not my way.'

She sat there trying to figure him out, wondering about this street-code that he adhered to. What internal battles were going on in there, what moral skirmishes? Or had amorality won out? Disinterest? Maybe, it occurred, he's not that bright and I'm projecting this Dark Knight shit onto him. God knows I've done it before; someone came to mind, name of Mark.

'So where's he keeping it all?' she asked, wearily.

'Bethnal Green. My old boss is running things there. But

there's a ton of gear in Davey's crib. What do you reckon?'

'I'll have a think.'

'Aya, Rox!'

It was twelve-fifteen at night and Ally was her usual ebullient self. She was settled into her new place and working at the Palace Theatre as an usher.

'How's it going, Al?'

'Tops. We've had Keith Barron on. And "Spender".

They were down to speaking twice a week now rather than every day, and even this took some negotiating with their respective answer-phones. Ally was sharing with a researcher at Granada and their message was more complex than a cinema booking line. Although Rox and Ally regularly trotted out the respective minutiae of their lives, gaps had entered into the conversation. They still promised undying camaraderie and 'visits – soon!' but time and distance had dug a hollow in their friendship.

'So how's it going with Reece? You shagged him yet?'

'No, but we showed each other us scars tonight.'

'Ooh, the racy life of London Town.'

'Pack it in, you.'

Another thing she had noticed was that her Mancunian drawl became stronger on the phone to Ally. Was it because she was trying to shore up their shared past or – horror of horrors – was London eating into her accent? It was fine talking to Mr S as he was foreign, but the waiters in Giuseppe's mocked her ruthlessly for her use of 'were' for 'was' and for her reverse phrasing (to them) of sentences. 'Your cards want picking up,' she once yelled in exasperation at an obnoxious kitchen porter before sacking him. Nonetheless, she found herself more often substituting 'Hi' for 'Aya' and modifying her manner with the customers by adopting the American approach of being insufferably perky and pestering them throughout their meals.

'He's dead gorgeous.'

'Who is?'

'My new bloke. Have you not been listening, Rox?'

'Bit tired, I guess.'

'Right, I'll start again. His name's Terry and he's a sound engineer at recording studios down the road. He's ever so tall and handsome, sort of Keanu Reeves with acne. Hey, did I tell you we were thinking of going to Ibitha in the summer? He earns tons and if I swap rotas at the Palace I might be able to beg three weeks off.'

'Oh that's brilliant.' Rox swung her feet up onto her thin white sofa and stared up at the peeling woodchip in the eaves. 'We' were thinking . . .? She was covertly jealous that Al had landed a steady boyfriend. Men always surrounded her; hence their in-joke about who was 'Up your Alley this week?' Of course, when she was with Mark it hadn't mattered but now she felt like a hypocrite. Judging by Ally's tone, she was falling in love, which meant they were sailing fast into Three-Into-Two-Won't-Go territory.

Al wittered on for a while until Rox broke through with a feeble, 'Have you told him yet?'

'What – the L word? No way am I losing out this time.'

Rox imitated the rasp of a Mexican in a Spaghetti Western – another shared memory from Sunday afternoon films. 'But I theenk you like heem a lot, no?'

There was a pause.

'Rox. I *did* tell him.'

'What?'

'That I love him.' She gave a squeal of excitement. 'And he told me. And it's the same for both of us and we've been feeling this way for ages and we never told each other.'

She got the full rundown of Terry's attributes and was told how they had done it in his car and in the studios during down-time. There was also their 'meeting story', which had been honed and polished to an event with all the wonder and significance of the birth of Christ.

I'm getting cynical, thought Rox, as she poured out more Chardonnay. And here I am drinking this stuff instead of Boddie's or the usual plonk. Still, no harm in accepting the odd bottle off Mr S at trade: and anyway it tastes all right, does this.

It was a good forty minutes before she was able to unpeel her ear from the receiver. Mark had not come up in the conversation, which was good. She felt only a blunt melancholy about the relationship and their only contact now was through Val, her solicitor. The bar was on its way to being sold but it would still take months. She'd also been meaning to talk with Ally about what to do about Davey. Wanted some support on that. Someone to tell her to let it go . . . forget the plan forming in her head. She cursed herself for being so stubborn, but Kayman was still out there ripping people off and if she didn't act on it, then who would? Not Reece who had left that night with the merest graze of his lips on her cheek. He was still tied into this stupid debt – I mean, why not help her get Davey put in jail and he'd be free of it? Tiredness was taking its toll, the bottle less than a third full. Abandoning it, she staggered to her bedroom, clambered under the duvet and fell asleep.

Camberwell was the same and Graham was the same and the flat was the same in that it had reverted to its previous state before Rox's fruitless attempt at cleaning up. A tide of dirty cups, plates, beer cans, unwashed clothes and general detritus had washed back in. Grime was everywhere too; gunking up the taps, on the toilet pan, fanned around the hobs that had earlier shone from her scouring. Rox found that time had not distilled her experience of the place to an amusing footnote. She felt itchy being there.

'Okay. Up to speed,' Graham said, glasses glinting in the glare of the PC screen. 'There's several ways we can do this. I can download some software, which I'll put on a floppy so when it's used a warning goes off and the whole system crashes.'

She looked at him blankly. 'You might as well be speaking a click language for all I got of that.'

He snuffled a laugh. 'That's good. Click language. Mouse – click. Ha.'

'Yeah, queen of the computer gags, they call me. Now can you explain what I'd have to do in simple terms? Think of me as a telly presenter.'

Graham turned to his backup PC system, which squatted on an old tea trolley at right angles to his desk. There was even less room now in his bedroom, and the combined smell of hot terminals and used socks erred on the side of vile. 'You insert this in here then follow the commands so it goes onto the main hard drive.'

She watched as he mouse clicked and speed-read through several complex inquiries. The machine whirred, then reverse whirred and the floppy poked out of its slot. 'See? Easy as pie.'

'Pi was pretty complex, last I heard.'

'You can operate a PC, can't you?'

'Yeah.'

'You read *Windows for Dummies?*'

'Needed a manual to get through it.'

Graham pressed his glasses to the bridge of his nose. 'Okay, the guy's removed the markings and wiped the files, so what we want to do is to mark them in some way so as when he sells them on, it's clear it's dodgy gear.'

'Spot on.'

He waved the floppy. 'But this is too much hassle?'

'Not if you join the team, Computer Boy.'

'Yes – *that's* going to happen.'

She pulled a face.

Graham went inert as though he was processing information. 'Right. How about taking the memory out?' he said, finally.

'How's that?'

'All you do is slip the casing off the base unit and inside there's this thing called a motherboard. You pull out the memory chips.' He reached for a plastic bag, delved into it and produced a handful of small circuits. 'Like these. Then when you power it up, all you'll get is a BIOS error message. It won't be able to load the operating system. You've wiped its memory.'

'A computer with Alzheimer's?'

'If you like.'

'Sits drooling in a corner like Ronald Reagan?'

'That's about it.'

'Thank God for geeks.'

'We inherited the world.'

'Not bad, Gray. That sense of humour's coming along nicely.'

Gone ten and Reece had been told his services wouldn't be required that evening. He mobiled Rox, who ducked her shift and asked him to pick her up. He swung by the restaurant and they nosed towards town.

'Where to?' he asked.

She was beside him in the passenger seat. 'Davey's computer place. I had a word with Graham, got some ideas.'

'Like?'

'We're going to tag his stolen PC's.'

'He'll suss it.'

'No, he won't.'

'Simon Latimer will. He's a right brainiac.'

'We take the memory out. It's this circuit board in the back. Then I go to the Fraud Squad, tell them anyone reporting buying a system of computers that won't start has gone and bought stolen ones. Give them Davey's address.'

'Sound. But how do we get to them?'

'That's where you come in, Pink Panther.'

'Do what?'

'Technically it's called Breaking and Entering.'

He slipped the wheel through his hands as they rose up

out of the Blackwall tunnel and bore left for the City.

'Reece, I need your help. You did say you hated him ripping off kids . . . and hospitals . . .' She tried for levity. 'And anyway – you're my designated criminal partner. So there.'

He reached out a hand and massaged her shoulder. 'Okay then.'

Cambridge Heath Road was light on traffic and a warm wind skittered litter along in the gutter. Lemon light filtered through the whitewash-smeared plate glass of Complete Computers. Latimer's shape fell on the window as he worked, moving jerkily like a puppet in a Chinese shadow theatre.

'Arses,' said Rox.

Reece said, 'That's it then.'

'What about Davey's place? Is he in tonight?'

Reece admitted that he and Charlie were out. Far as he knew she was with her other druggy friends – Davey, he didn't know. Gant's Hill?

'You want to take a shufti round there?'

'I do.'

Rox had her resolute face on. Now she'd started, she wanted to go through with it. If Graham was right and it was that easy to disable the computers, then returning to Davey's den might be an acceptable risk.

They drove the half-mile to Shoreditch, pulling up in the empty side-street near the warehouse block. There was a party going on in one of the upper floors and a lazy beat hung in the air. They went to the entrance gates.

'This could be even better,' said Rox, excitedly. 'If he's keeping the stuff ready for shipping here then he'll never know we've tampered with it.'

'. . . "We've" tampered?'

'You're not backing down, are you?'

'Me? No.'

She came closer. 'Cos backing out seems to be a way of life with you, Reece. I mean, you know I like you, but when do you get off deciding who's ready for what and when? I give you enough chances to speak your mind, but you always hold back.' She felt that old ferocity swelling in her. 'I still know next to nothing about you – and that doesn't make you much of a mate, does it?'

'I think you mentioned that before.'

'Did I?' she sneered.

'What do you want? My life story?'

'Sometime, yeah.'

He took her face in his hands. 'All right. But first let's get this Bonnie and Clyde shit out the way.'

Before she'd a chance to react he was kissing her passionately, more so even than on that first night, his arms gripping her, the things he couldn't say conveyed in the confluence of their mouths. Afterwards, dazed, she stumbled over to the big sheet metal double doors, which were locked shut.

'Wanna give us a leg up?'

The gap between the top of the doors and the black brick lintel was enough for her to clamber up and slip through. Reece formed a cradle with interlocked hands and she pressed down with the bulky sole of her trainer. She scrabbled up and over, feet drumming hollowly against the metal, then, pivoting, she slid down toes first and jumped away onto the cobbles. Righting herself she came face to face with Reece – who had unlocked an inner door and stepped through.

'Thanks for telling me.'

'Looked like you were having fun.'

She gritted her teeth. 'And how many other keys have you got?'

'All of them.'

'Davey gave you a set?'

'That's right.'

'Come on then.'

They unlocked the external red door and entered the cold tiled stairwell. They went down around the wire-lift cage, mindful of sounds from above. Arriving at Davey's riveted door, Reece released the Yale and mortise locks. The apartment was dark save for a latticework of pale moonlight rhombuses beneath the old windows. Rox's hands tingled and her mouth tasted like she had bitten on a coin.

Reece asked, 'How long's this going to take?'

'Hour or so?'

'I'd better go up top – keep watch.'

'Reece!' she hissed.

'No argument. He walks in and finds us here, then we've had it. If I'm outside and he comes back I can stall him. I'll make a noise so you can have it away. Kick on the pipes.'

She glared at him. 'I'm trusting you, Reece.'

She ushered him out and, as her night vision bloomed, she picked a path through the groundcover of discarded cartons, envelopes and mail. Beside the breakfast bar was a three-foot high pile of pizza boxes; around it a crowd of lager bottles. The floor was a castle of pilfered PC equipment, topped by a battlement of monitors. Power cables sprouted from every crook and gap. Rox back-pedalled to the kitchen area, fiddled under the hood of the Neff oven and located a switch. The low light it gave out was enough to work by. Producing a screwdriver, she breached the hardware moat and set to work, freeing up the processors and unsheathing their metal lids. Simple once you get used to it, she thought – even a Dixon's employee could handle this.

When she next checked, the illuminated hands on her watch read twelve forty-seven. Once or twice she stopped, hearing the crank and whirr of the lift or the regimented tics of boiler controls and radiators cooling. There a heart-stopping moment when a pair of cats chased one another out in the courtyard, their yowls sending perspiration pelting down her back. A good hour of concentrated work passed and by two she had removed the memories. Each PC, she noted joylessly, was stamped with the address of the Maudsley Hospital in South London.

She froze. A waxy line of light appeared under the front door. Someone coming down. Coming in. Reece? No, he wouldn't barge in like . . . no time to think. She scuttled across to the bedroom and hid behind the door, finding to her dismay that her survival response was to squeeze her eyes shut. Useless! She opened them, held her breath. The front door opened; light splashed, roiled and flooded the main room. Heavy footsteps. House keys crashing onto the counter, then . . .

Silence.

She counted, reaching twenty.

The door smashed back in her face.

He came at her, stale sweat, lager reek and the rank stink of cigs. A booze-waxed face looming close, lizard eyed, irises gone, the pupils black, adamantine. Davey's snarl was spittle-flecked, stoked with coke, twisted all out of proportion.

'Fuck you doing here?'

Where the hell was Reece? Davey launched himself at her, his coat enveloping them like a wet sail. She fell half on, half off the mattress, her left arm smacking hard on the wooden floor. He bore down, increasing his weight, forcing his forearm across her throat, increasing the pressure. He drank in her fear, eyes roving about her face, her skin, lips and chestnut hair: a shudder of recognition.

'It's you. The northern slag.'

She made indecipherable Welsh noises.

He lifted his elbow so she had room to breathe. 'Well then?'

Rox had a parade of defiant looks. She gave him her sergeant-at-arms.

Wrong move.

Davey revealed his canines. 'Know where you are, whatsyer-face? Bedroom.'

He clamped a hand around her throat, lifting his torso so he could get to her. Rox tried jerking her knees up, but he wasn't having it. She brought up a fist and tore out a handful of hair. Davey grunted, winced, then smacked her one in the face. By the time she'd recovered he was tearing at her trousers.

Her T-shirt and sweater had ridden up and her stomach was exposed. She tried to yell but he spun her over and thrust her head deep into the covers. She thrashed blindly, shock waves shooting through her as his hand dove into her knickers and invaded her crotch. The fingers roughly penetrated her. She bucked even more, wild now, twisting this way and that, trying to turn, to attack, and get at his face. Then her body jack-knifed and air flowed into her lungs.

Even as she gasped for breath she realised what Davey was doing. He'd positioned her so that he could pull her trousers all the way down. They were already around her knees, making it impossible to kick back at him. He collapsed on her with all his weight. Impossible at this angle to reach behind. She was hoping, praying that he wouldn't. He engulfed her with his body. His breathing became rapid and an intense animal heat came off him. The rattle of metal. His belt buckle. Her eyes tipped out tears, her mouth warped and her throat constricted. She felt it then. His cock, hard and boiling, grinding at her.

'Davey?'

He pulled back. Rox couldn't see: heard though, a female voice. Charlie, speaking in a way she'd not heard before, the amphetamine courage drained out of it and her slacker's swagger pruned back to privately educated roots. Charlie released an inhuman howl, a door slammed shut and the pressure lifted and Davey was off her.

CHAPTER TWENTY-FOUR

Davey beat on the bathroom door with his fists but Charlie had locked it from the inside and had propped a chair up against the handle. He cursed and begged and spun a web of evasions to envelop her when she came out.

In the bedroom across the hall, Rox lay curled in a foetal ball, too terrified to move. Her eyes stared blankly ahead, ears pounding with a blood rush. She had begun to shake uncontrollably. Davey Kayman gave up on beseeching and began to bellow once more.

'Come on. For fucksake – she was trying to do us over . . . Charlie, CHARLIE! Get out here.'

Then his temper went. He kicked open the door, splintering the lock and snapping the spine of the chair behind it. Charlie did not flinch but stood serenely in the tub. She was drenched in her own blood. It was all over her breasts and smeared angrily across her cheeks and mouth in some primitive display of defiance. It was daubed down her arms and on her thighs and on her belly like red woad. Both her wrists were open and gloating red gashes pumped liquid onto her palms. Behind and around her were bloody handprints on the tiled wall, smears and dashes and splashes of it on the rim of the tub and on the shower curtain. Her eyes flickered, her head rolled back and she collapsed into the tub.

'Stupid BITCH!' shouted Davey, as he leapt at her.

There was more bellowing, and then grunting, and dragging, and shouting and a series of doors slamming.

Then, peace.

It was like waking after a doze in the sun.

Rox's mind was befuddled, filled with candyfloss, her limbs leaden. The room was sunk in an underwater haze, suffused in a greenish hue, seemingly out of proportion, all angles and points. Shielding her eyes, she moved gingerly to the doorjamb, clinging to it as she swung out into the corridor. The living room was bright and hot with motes of dust dancing beneath the halogen lights. Charlie and Davey had gone.

She stumbled to the heavy front door, tore it open and dragged herself up the stairs. Outside, cold air nipped at her face, bringing clarity. She hugged herself. The grid of the railway bridge loomed high above like some giant sentient being. She stepped off the kerb and a car shot past, wailing at her for her pedestrian audacity. She made for Old Street, seeking succour, authority, comfort.

In the Accident and Emergency department at the London Hospital, Charlie's wounds were sutured and bandaged. Despite appearances, she had not lost a great deal of blood and there was no need for a transfusion. She regained consciousness fairly quickly, but hadn't the energy or will to speak of the event. Downstairs, Davey waited in the disinfected lobby area and gave terse answers to the Staff Nurse's questions concerning her physical and mental health.

'No, she isn't on any medication . . . All right then, yeah, she might've had some coke, weed, whatever, since you *found* it in her bloodstream . . . What'd you ask me for if you knew that . . . No, no history of suicide attempts.'

That remark was a direct lie as it was plainly obvious from Charlie's old lacerations that she had self-mutilated before. The

Staff Nurse considered whether she should be kept in for psychiatric evaluation, but felt the case to be borderline. 'What happened tonight?' she asked of Davey.

'I dunno. An accident probably, the glass shower cubicle was bust. She must have fell.'

She asked him to fill out a form giving the full details of Charlotte Anne Ribbon's GP, any possible allergies and the address of her next of kin. Davey demanded to know why. Because it all had to be fed into the computer. He asked what system they used. Staff didn't know. Had it been upgraded lately? She believed so. Davey asked when it would be all right to take Charlie home. The Staff Nurse told him she was conscious and that it was up to her. He went through and spoke at her.

'Charlie — you wanna go?'

Some kind of a nod.

Davey, all politeness, 'Nurse, any chance I could borrow a wheelchair? Get her out to the entrance?'

Dawn saw him wheeling a groggy Charlie out into the Whitechapel Road. Her moans were only partly due to the effects of the anaesthetic wearing off, as there was also the weight of the two heavy computer processors crushing her thighs under the blanket.

Rox arrived home by Black Cab and found several messages from Reece, giving his mobile number and asking her to call. She felt far too betrayed and tired to speak to him, so she turned the ringer right down on the phone, ran the hottest bath she could stand and submerged her body in near-scalding water. She washed until she felt clean and stepped pink and raw from the tub. She then cocooned herself in her duvet, rocking back and forth on her tear-stained pillow. She slept for twelve hours straight, emerging at teatime to heat up a Cup-a-Soup and to call work to say that she had the flu and to ask if someone could please cover tonight's session. Then she dozed again, her body creating a natural morphia so her shattered nerves could begin the process of repair.

It was evening when she next awoke. A deepening sky had erased all but the last of the chalky cirrus clouds. She stood at the window wrapped in her tatty towelling robe, sipping tea. Below her the parcels of back garden were divided by fence, trellis and brick, anything to further the illusion of private space. Some had mats of chewed up lawn ringed by concrete, others sheds or bust-up greenhouses plonked on them. There were neglected yards, choked by weeds and knotty vine, others crazy-paved and strewn with children's toys. Tufts of fresh spring colour appeared here and there; yellow clusters of laburnum and forsythia; blotches of red camellia, flowerbeds dotted with white crocuses. In one small plot there was a cascade of pink where a cherry tree had blossomed early. Fanned out against the skyline were slender tips of horse chestnut and ash. Rox pressed her nose to the pane, misting it with her breath.

Hopeless. She was angry and sad and miserable all at the same time: stupid to try it on *and* get caught. The worst thing, she realised, was that if she went to the police then Davey could legitimately assert she had been breaking and entering. He'd tell them he had used – what was it? – 'reasonable force' to eject her. And that to him meant stopping a hair's breadth short of rape. Christ knows what he would have done with her if Charlie hadn't come home. She shuddered at the thought. He'd made her feel worthless and subhuman and like a piece of meat. A scrap from his table.

Davey, as ever, held the trump cards. She stared out of the window and wished she had the ability to flip her soul inside out and display it as evidence.

And where the hell was Reece?

His calls, urgent though they sounded, were no explanation. He should have warned her – *been* there. Typical of him. His ducking out, his evasiveness, the surly silences. Was *that* his idea of being a partner? Face it, girl, she thought, he's a non-starter.

He happened to be the first decent bloke I met up with when I came down here. Forget him.

Thoughts of Mark came back and of other men she had known. Of her father dead early, too early to see her fully grown up. Of teachers too busy to help her at school. A run of disappointing boyfriends, save for the odd fling she had canonised for its brevity. How should she cope with this? She considered on her habitual way of dealing with bad shit – wallowing in the pain, making a mansion of misery, a tower of torment no one could assail save Ally, her co-architect of gloom. But now Al wasn't here and this wasn't Manchester any more.

Opposite, the lights blinked on as South East London prepared its tea. Rox rested her forehead on the window. The pane smelled of ice. She'd get Davey back. He'd done his worst, now it was retribution time. He would not destroy her. Padding across to the switch, she bathed the room in waxy light, then called work to let them know she was coming in after all.

It was half ten when Reece showed up at Giuseppe's. He stood pressed against the glass until Rox came out and ushered him away from the front of the restaurant. She almost shouted it.

'What're you doing out here?'

'Didn't think you wanted me to come in.'

'I don't. Where the pigging hell did you get to last night?'

He wasn't looking at her. 'You get out all right? From Davey's?'

'No.'

'Shit. What happened?'

She opened her mouth to tell him, but noticed that his eyes were wild and unfocused and his shirt-tails flapping loose. There was a can of strong lager in his hand.

'Jesus. You're pissed!' she exclaimed.

'No, I'm not.'

'Yes, you are.'

'Can I come in? Explain?'

'No. Piss off.'

He shrugged disdainfully. 'Tried to phone.'

'I know.'

'Rox — I looked for your flat but I didn't know where it was.'

'Big deal.'

He swayed, uncomprehending of her sudden harsh attitude. Marshalling his strength, he tried to form words, but before anything came out the diminutive Mr S appeared and called over to Rox.

'If you come to work, then you *work*. Okay?'

'Which one of the dwarves are you?' Reece called out.

'*Va fongoul.*'

'Grumpy, then.'

She hissed at Reece, apologised on his behalf, then hustled him to the corner of the parade. 'You can fuck off. I don't want to talk to you.'

She went back in; ignored Giuseppe's pointed comments and set about hardening her heart. For the next hour she busied herself with her customers and on small time-squandering tasks. However, she still couldn't resist the odd anxious glance out at the dark heath. Why was he drunk? He never drank. The stragglers paid up and left; then Jane and the chef. Giuseppe had on an expensive woollen coat and was spinning his keys around his finger.

'You want lift home?'

'That's all right. I'll lock up, get the bus.'

'No, no. Not if drunk is still outside.'

He came close enough for his aftershave to overwhelm her.

'Not safe for you, Rox. You take lift with me. No problem.'

She was surprised at the ferocity of her tone.

'Leave me alone! I've had enough of men pestering me.'

Giuseppe held up his hands in surrender then stood studying her for an uncomfortable moment while he polished his shoes on the backs of his trousers. Then, making up his mind, he gave in and left. Rox felt like staying on. The restaurant, even empty, was still a public place. It grounded her and anyway she didn't feel like being back in her flat right now.

Reece loomed into view. Must have been waiting for her. His loamy face peered in, eyes visored with cupped hands. She stared back, watching him mouth requests and losing what little respect she had left for him. He began rapping on the big glass pane. Before it shattered, she capitulated and threw open the door.

'This better be very, *very* good.'

He stumbled inside and fell into his favourite seat. Despite herself, she went and put the coffee percolator back on. He stared into space, barely focusing. His voice was weary, sounding like its batteries were running out.

'I got this call. I knocked on the pipes to get you to come out, but you never heard me. I had to go to the other side of town. Couldn't wait. Hospice. My Auntie Jean . . . Gone before I got there.' He looked at his large hands, then brought out a small quarter bottle of vodka and unscrewed the cap.

Rox took it off him. He gripped her arm.

'Leave it,' he barked.

'No, you leave it. You've had enough. And get off me, Reece. No one touches me without my say-so.'

He released her and glared at the tabletop as if it contained his fate. 'I'm sorry. Really sorry. I know I should have stayed. What happened?'

Rox took a deep breath and tried to tell the story with as much distance as possible. As she described the assault, Reece's face, behind the clouds of his drunkenness, hardened with fresh purpose. She could tell he was itching to get his hands on Davey Kayman.

'I'll kill him.'

'Very original.'

'No arguments, Rox. He's out of order.'

'You do that and I'll never see you again.'

That brought him up short. He stared at her, insolently. 'Why? He's nearly raped you.'

'Look, I thought this through. He'd easily get off an assault charge — my word against his. I want that guy to go down for everything — and that means we carry on with the plan.'

'Wha' plan?' he asked, gripping the table and screwing up his eyes.

She knew this stage. He'd had too much about three drinks ago. She went to the machine and poured out a cup of neat black Espresso, then followed up by fetching a big tumbler of water.

'Drink them,' she ordered. And to prove her point that his evening's drinking was over, she took his bottle of vodka through to the kitchen and threw it in the metal bin with enough force to shatter the glass.

'I'll fucking have him,' Reece said, on her return.

Finding an ounce of sarcasm left, she said, 'Change the CD, macho man.'

'What then?'

'Davey doesn't know *why* I was there.'

'But he touched you up. You should be angrier about this.'

'Oh, I'm way beyond angry. Believe me.'

'Good.'

She studied him, all dishevelled, helpless and hopeless, the bravado draining out of him. She wanted to know more about what had brought him to this — especially if tonight was to be the end of it.

'Tell me about your Auntie.'

He threw back the bitter coffee.

'My mum and dad ran pubs. The main one was the British Lion, which is why I got this.'

He began removing his jacket, but she stopped him.

'I've seen the tattoo.'

'Oh, right,' he said, disappointed. 'Brewery shunted them round a lot. I was basically a pub kid. Hung about all hours, knew the regulars and the drunks and sussed out when the

Jackpot machines were going to pay out. When I got to ten years old, they had me collecting glasses and bottling for the musicians who did turns. Didn't go to school much. Other kids smelled the beer on me; sussed out where I lived, thought I was a pikey. One afternoon, I was round Auntie Jean's in Wapping. She was a lovely woman, Rox. Short, like you. Not a real auntie, sort of like my mum's best mate.'

Rox nodded for him to continue.

'My parents kicked it in a fire. Burnt the place to the ground. The fire brigade said it was down to a couple of fags left smouldering on the bar. They were having a kip before the evening session. Jean got a call and told me I had to stay the night round hers. Knew something was up. Next morning I snuck out early and went home.' He attempted a half-hearted shrug. 'Nothing there. Pile of cinders. It's all offices now. Insurance.'

She rested her hand on his. 'And Jean raised you after that?'

'Yeah. Had me back in school, studying. I went a bit wild once I was sixteen, played hell on her nerves. I was a right little bastard. Needed my dad to show me the red card. Anyway, all power to Jean because she put up with me. There was this time when I come in pissed — I used to chuck it back in them days. We'd had a row.'

'What about?'

'Aww, something stupid like I'd not cleaned up or gone and got her fags or whatever, but I ended up giving her a slap. And I was boxing back then. Semi-pro. Middleweight. Didn't hurt her. It was open-hand — but you should've seen the look on her face. I felt like shit. That put the kibosh on the drinking.'

'When did she get cancer?'

'Diagnosed a year ago. Too far gone, they said.'

'Don't you have other relatives?'

He shook his head. 'I tried to call you from the hospice, but you weren't answering. I sat with her until they came for her this morning. Funeral's next Thursday. Wanna come?'

'Sure.'

Rox let the silence creep between them. Okay, she'd lost her dad too, but Reece had nobody at all. Suddenly she felt guilty that she still had a mum: and one she'd not called in nearly a month. The fire went out of her and was replaced by a new feeling, not pity or the lip-service of sympathy, but a genuine altruism. She cared now, and could see between the lines enough to read his needs.

'Look – we'd best get you to bed. I'll call a minicab.'

'I am a cab.'

'Yeah, I know, but we need another car.'

'Mine's out there somewhere.'

He must have driven over, drunk. 'I'm getting us a cab. No argument.'

It was a struggle getting him up the four flights of stairs to her flat and the cab driver flatly refused to help. Reece, still a shade off comatose, had not only offered a running commentary on his lack of driving skills throughout the journey, but had also tossed his bejewelled tissue box out of the window. She barked sternly in Reece's ear, ordering him to move as he lurched upwards with a childish lack of co-ordination. On reaching the top, he collapsed on the rough hessian carpet and would not move even when she opened the door and threatened to leave him out there.

She left him out there.

The timer switch wiped light from the stairs. Rox stood on the other side of the door and waited for the pathetic scrabbling. It never came. Only snoring. That wouldn't do. She opened her door and tried to drag him inside. Heavy as a planet. She tried getting behind him and pushing, which only rucked him up like a carpet.

She kicked him between the legs, which seemed to do the trick.

Reece moaned, rose and stumbled forwards, cupping his genitals. A long line of drool unwound itself from his mouth and abseiled down to his sleeve. Rox hustled him into the bedroom where he leapt on the duvet like a starving man at a banquet. He went spark out.

'Great. Bloody great.'

She undressed him, pulling off his jacket, shoes and socks and struggling like hell with his jeans. The shirt fought nobly, but soon he was down to his underpants. She needed to get him under the duvet, so she rabbit-punched him in the side. A moan and he half-turned away. She hauled the cover from underneath him, freed it and threw it back on top. Then she took off all her clothes except her knickers and lay down next to him. She studied his face and his exposed shoulder, then lifted the duvet and examined his tattoo. His back was broad and she traced a finger above his spine down to the deep furrow in the small of his back. He was hairy, but not too hairy, his waist firm, buttocks taut against the cotton of his pants. She wondered if he'd turn in his sleep. He grunted softly, dreaming, then pulled the cover tightly round him, his legs splaying out, commandeering more space.

She lay close, feeling the heat of him. Not daring to move or to touch.

CHAPTER TWENTY-FIVE

Sunk in Steve's sofa, Steve and Arch were watching telly. Neither was feeling too bright. Steve Lamb's right arm was in a sling, which had seriously affected his heavy masturbation rota. There were cuts and bruises on his face and neck, many of them patched over with Winnie the Pooh plasters. Each time he moved to take another JPS, pull on his nuclear-strength lager or to operate the remote, he emitted a pained groan.

Archie was also damaged. The ligaments in his left leg had been put out of whack and he now employed a metal alloy crutch when he walked. It lay beside him on the armrest. He had a black eye, a long livid cut on his cheek and a necklace of scarlet thumbprints about his larynx. There was another scabbed up gash running from his left ear to the back of his head, but this was concealed by one of his 'funny hats' – a velvet beret, which he'd bought at Greenwich market and refused to remove any time day or night.

'Pause it,' barked Archie.

'Piss off. Good bit coming up. They're gonna do DVDA – and I don't mean that new kind of video.'

'Oh, yeah, ruin the ending.'

Steve cackled, his lungs bubbling ferociously.

'Freeze-frame it, will you? And go back a bit?'

He looked over. Archie had a black Daler sketchbook

open on his lap and was scribbling in it. 'Shit, I thought you was having one off the wrist. Didn't know you was *draw-ring*.'

'Yeah, so back it up a bit. Her kneeling like that makes a brilliant curve.'

Steve froze the image as an over-endowed Swede presented his member to the lips of a nubile brunette. 'Admit it, Arch, you're a filthy bastard like the rest of us.'

Archie considered whether or not to enter into the Art vs Pornography debate. He'd done some reading around the subject and had come to the conclusion that the academics were as turned on as they were offended. Admittedly, sketching off a porn flick called *Star Bores – The Pants-off Menace* – weakened the case, but then it was a free life-class. Sort of. A moment later, he swung his metal crutch down hard on Steve's knees. This produced a howl and spilt lager all over Steve's lap. The crutch was dented in several places from earlier bouts.

'I did ask nicely.'

'You are a right cowson.'

'You never do what I ask you.'

'You still on about that painting?'

The cause of their injuries was the ongoing dispute over the missing Rembrandt self-portrait. Steve had refused to divulge its whereabouts and Archie's patience was as thin as an estate agent's promise. When Steve received no reply to his ransom note, Archie had driven them over to the East Dulwich Picture Gallery. Enquiring as to the whereabouts of the painting they were informed it was away 'for repairs', gallery-speak for 'still nicked'. Over a drink in the Maypole in Brockley Cross, Arch suggested there was nothing doing, otherwise they'd have heard by now. Steve said he'd send them another couple of squares – speed things up a bit.

They furthered that discussion with fisticuffs.

Steve limped over to the window, parted the curtains and gazed down at the black, oily river. On the opposite bank, the lights of Wapping twinkled on its surface, some of them coloured pub ones at the back of the Marquis of Granby.

'Wanna go for a pint?' he asked.

Archie had his mobile out. 'Nah. Gonna make some calls.'

'Shirl again?'

'Yeah. And this girl I got modelling for me.'

'Oh yeah?'

'See if she'll do me a session round her place?'

He leered. 'Session?'

'Painting. I ain't mug enough to bring a bird back here.'

'Share out the gash,' pleaded Steve. 'I'll have sloppy seconds.'

That did it. Archie launched himself through the air. They tussled and rolled on the floor. Steve failing to connect with his bad arm and Arch equally lost with his duff leg. He did, though, manage to ram his mobile phone into Steve's mouth. He was about to administer the *coup de grâce* when it rang. Levering it out, he held the sticky object delicately away from his ear.

'Yers? Righto, guv. When d'you want that done then?'

Steve did some choking, lit up a fresh fag and did some more. 'Job on?'

'Soon, yeah. Petersons.'

Reece produced a cup of tea and set it down beside her. She took it, slurped thirstily and tried to focus on the blur in front of her.

'Time is it?' she croaked.

'Half ten. I phoned your work.'

'Shit.'

She had set her alarm for eight, so as to be awake and up ahead of him. She'd slept through it. She gathered the duvet up around her neck. Shit, shit, shit. What had he seen? And what was he thinking after waking up in bed with her?

Reece said, 'Cheers for seeing me right last night.'

'Anytime.'

'You're talking to your coat. I'm over here.'

The blur moved across her vision.

'Put your glasses on for God's sake, Rox.'

She didn't want to, having of late become shy about people seeing her in them. She'd even bought disposable contacts, which were taking some getting used to. She kept her old specs beside the bed for reading. Reluctantly, she hooked the wire frames over her ears and Reece swam into focus. He was dressed but unshaven. Odd, him standing in her bedroom.

'So, was the sex good?' he asked, nonchalantly.

'Fair-to-middling.'

'Haven't you got a spare bed?'

'No. Some arrogant drunken git went straight for mine and no way was I freezing my arse off on the sofa.'

He pulled a pained expression. 'I didn't have a kebab last night, did I? My mouth feels like a dog's toilet.'

'No, you did the usual drunk things – rambling on, kicking traffic cones . . . insulting cab drivers. Busman's holiday for you.'

He ran his hands over his hair. 'Wanna go do a fry-up? I've got a bit of a head.'

She thought of the immense calorie intake that would involve. On the other hand, it was an excuse to get them out of her flat. She wasn't sure of how she should react to him today, whether still to be angry or not.

'Yeah, all right.'

He waited in the living room while she dressed, then they walked to a café in Lee Green. There, they sipped teas from chipped Pyrex cups. Fluttering newspapers stirred the steamy air. A couple of site workers demolished mid-morning sausage sarnies, one of them gripping the bread in both hands like he was holding a harmonica. Rox studied the puddle of grease coagulating around her fried egg. The crispy bacon, slathered in brown sauce, had been wonderfully carcinogenic.

'By the way, I meant what I said about coming to your

Auntie's funeral. If you still want me there?'

He nodded. 'How much did I tell you last night?'

'You steered clear of any particularly obscene sexual fetishes.'

'Dobbin's secret's safe then.'

'. . . Other than that one.'

They both smiled. It was Reece who went serious first.

'Rox, Davey's gonna get it after what he done to you.'

'Yeah, but not your way. I mean, what if you did kill him?'

He looked at his plate. 'Worth it.'

'And you'd get life imprisonment. Forget it. It was me he attacked, not you, so I'll decide how we get him. Right?'

He folded his arms. 'What're you gonna do?'

She leaned closer in. 'Kay. Here's the plan.'

'We heard about you from another education facility,' said Rox in a shrill headmistressy voice.

She and Reece were sat in the Bursar's office at the Secondary School in which Aussie Pete taught. Surprisingly, he had made it to the end of term without courting any sexual harassment cases – although there were a rash of pregnancies at a nearby Sixth Form college. It was lunchtime and he'd sneaked them into the office while the Bursar was out. Rox was speaking with Simon Latimer at Complete Computers.

'You want our rep to come round with a demonstration PC?' he asked.

'No, we want to order ten Dan Xplora models. With Intel Celeron processor, 32 megabytes of RAM, 14-inch Monitor and fax Modem . . .'

Rox was reading off the spec list of one of the models she'd tampered with in Shoreditch.

'I think we've got them in.'

'Do you provide maintenance cover?'

'Guaranteed for a year. On site – and we're setting up a help-line.'

Latimer was overjoyed at the order and at their recent turnover. Although he'd not personally seen more than his sweetener in cash, the sheer volume of product Davey was shifting was enough to convince him things were buoyant.

'Can you deliver Saturday morning?' Rox asked. 'Term ends this week and we'd like to familiarise the teachers with the new equipment over the Easter hols . . . yes . . . who'll be coming? A Mister Kayman. Good.'

She held up a thumb to Reece, who was sat on the window ledge nursing his fearsome hangover. She hung up and beamed at them both.

'Trap's all set then?' asked Pete.

'Not quite.'

Next, she went to the CID at Shooters Hill Police Station. The squad room was open-plan, trilling with phones, busy even at mid-afternoon on a Friday. She was assigned to DS Strudwick, who was most interested in what she had to say. An adipose man in his late thirties, he favoured the official plainclothes style of leather bomber jacket and jeans. He kept offering her refreshments and chewing on a piece of gum gone to putty. She guessed he'd recently tried to give up smoking. He had a bland policeman's face, unremarkable save for his left eye, whose lid drooped slightly lower than his right. If you sat on his left side you got the impression that he was dozing off.

Strudwick explained that a few years back they had dealt with a similar fraud. It involved an Asian man who ran a computer business in South West London whose entire stock was supplied by a network of thieves and receivers. They had turned over innumerable hospitals in the South East, including the Springfield Psychiatric Unit in Tooting, Greenwich District and Guys. As with Davey Kayman, the computer hardware was sold on to local authorities and NHS trusts – and in their case even onto Europe. The operation was a massive headache for the Met, involving trials in Guildford, Wood Green and Snaresbrook Crown Courts. To their chagrin, the ringleaders only received five years each, as computer theft was deemed to be a 'soft' crime.

Rox provided him with all she knew of Davey's other scams, his addresses and aliases. Strudwick had him checked out on the NCR computer system, but the name Kayman turned up blank. At first he was reluctant to agree to stake out the school, wanting instead to obtain permission to have a team study Latimer and Davey over a period of time. Rox countered this by explaining that once Davey started asking himself questions about what she'd been doing in his basement, it wouldn't be long before he cottoned on. Strudwick took it upstairs, returning with the news that he and a small team would be at the school tomorrow morning.

At home she took a long soak and afterwards sat failing to concentrate on the telly. She was so diverted in her thoughts that when Archie phoned and asked if she would pose for him, she agreed without thinking.

'What happened to you?' she asked, surveying his cuts and bruises.

'Artistic differences,' he answered, hobbling up the steep stairs. Added to his wounds was a livid grid on his forehead where Steve had gotten the better of him with the keypad on his remote.

They settled in the living room, Rox stretching out nude on the sofa. Arch had a wooden board over which was stretched a rectangle of watercolour paper. He worked for an hour with sable brushes and a set of gouache paints, experimenting in a different medium, he told her.

'What happened about your wife?' Rox asked.

'Threw me out. Shirl knows I wasn't playing away – she's just making her point. Besides, I reckon she's a bit bothered about the case coming up. And my not being in work.'

'Case?'

His brow frowned in annoyance. 'Nothing. Anyways, I'll still pay you for tonight. Got a job coming up as it goes.'

'I like the beret. Matches the bruise on your forehead.'

'Ta.'

'Who're you staying with – a rogue Gladiator?'

Archie was about to respond when the buzzer went again. Rox slipped on her robe, padded into the corridor and pressed the communicating button. No answer. When she came back, Archie was washing his brushes.

'Mind if I leave the painting here tonight?'

'Sure.'

He balanced it up on the sofa, squinting at it. Rox came over and looked. Archie was getting better. His perspective was out in places and he hadn't quite mastered hands and feet, but the torso and head were well rendered and the tonal values true to life. She nodded encouragement, not wanting to point out any faults in case he became irritated: She hated it when he shredded his work in front of her. A knock at the door.

It was Reece.

'Door was open,' he said, slipping past her. 'Thought I'd drop by, see if you were . . .' his tone fell to a grumble, masking his surprise. 'Hello, Archie.'

'All right, Reece?' Arch offered, uncomfortably.

The men looked at one another, then at her with an equal measure of confusion and suspicion on their faces.

Rox wondered what she'd done wrong, if anything. 'You know each other?'

'No . . . Yes,' they said, simultaneously.

Rox said, 'Great. The monosyllabic twins.'

'What's that?' Reece asked, pointing at Archie's latest work.

Archie, sarkily, 'It's a painting. Ain't you never seen one before?'

Reece studied it. 'You can't do hands. And that's not Rox. That looks more like that actress – the one in all them period films.'

'Thompson?' queried Archie.

'No. The titchy one.'

Rox said, 'I am here, you know.'

'Why'd you let him do this? You're naked!' Reece blurted out.

'Nude,' corrected Archie.

'Not another pissing contest,' Rox said, folding her arms.

Archie said. 'What's it to you anyway?'

'She's a friend,' said Reece.

'So?'

Reece stared at Rox, presumably sending her some kind of psychic message. She glared back. He bent down and turned the painting around so it faced the sofa. Archie made to move, forgetting about his bad leg. He toppled over then picked up his crutch and supported himself with it.

'What's going on between you two anyway?' Reece demanded.

'Nothing,' said Archie and Rox, colour appearing on their cheeks.

Reece said, '*I* haven't even seen you naked yet.'

'You had your chance this morning.'

She realised it was the wrong thing to say as soon as it came out.

Archie raised his eyebrows.

Rox caught the look. 'He was drunk, Archie. He stayed over.'

Archie beamed. 'Reece doesn't drink.'

Reece said, 'My auntie died.'

'The other one's got bells on it. Bell's whisky.'

'Will you both stop this?' The atmosphere was as charged as an electricity substation and Rox had no idea of why she was embarrassed or whom to defend. 'You can both leave. Now, please.'

Problem was who should go first.

Reece graciously waved a hand at the door. 'I only just got here. On your way, Arch.'

Archie looked beseechingly at Rox. 'We haven't done yet.'

'I think we have,' she replied, with a bittersweet smile.

Knowing he'd lost this round, Archie began packing his equipment. 'We'll do another session soon.'

'If you like.'

After making sure Reece couldn't miss seeing the nude again, he whisked his board into a zip-up portfolio then reached into the grubby back pocket of his jeans and pulled out a crumpled wad of notes.

'Bell you soon,' he muttered as he squeezed them into her hand.

Reece asked, 'He pays you for this?'

'Of course. It's modelling,' Rox said.

'Does he normally leave it beside the bed?'

Archie turned, ready to strike. 'Leave it, Reece.'

'I thought you was married, Arch?'

'I am married.'

'Well, this is a bit . . .'

'A bit what?'

Reece struggled for words. 'Previous.'

'All right. Playtime's over,' Rox barked, ushering Archie out. Halfway down the stairs, he looked back. His shoulders were slumped, his brow furrowed. A thin rain pattered on the skylight above the tall staircase. 'I never got into this thinking it'd hurt anyone,' he said.

She sighed. 'Someone always gets hurt, Archie.'

She shut the door and stormed back into the main room. Reece was sat on the sofa, jacket off, massaging his knuckles.

'What was that all about? You've no right to make those kinds of assumptions.'

He shook his head. 'I can't have you starkers in front of Archie. You don't know what he's like.'

'I don't know what *you're* like.'

'What's he pay you?'

'That's between me and him.'

Reece tried to reach inside her dressing gown pocket for the money. She hit him hard on the arm.

'You pigging sod. Leave me alone.'

'Whatever he pays you, I'll pay you double not to do it.'

She hit him again. 'Go 'way. Get off.'

'You don't have to do it, Rox.'

'I like doing it, so you can piss off.'

'Maybe you do fit your name after all.'

That did it. She slapped him one. Reece didn't react.

'Get out.'

He came towards her. She glimpsed down, seeing his huge hands, feeling small and frightened. There was danger about him – like a firework that had been lit but hadn't gone off. He stood, fists clenched, teeth grinding, muscles flexed. In a second he was kissing her hard on the mouth, a real clench as he held her to him. She wasn't sure if she wanted it or not or where it might lead, so she pulled away, pushing at his chest. At first, he ground against her more forcefully, but when she kept on, he disengaged.

Reece said, 'I thought we, you. . . wanted to . . .'

'Wanted to what?'

He wouldn't say it. Say anything.

'What d'you want of me, Reece?'

He dropped his head.

'You'd best go for now.'

He left and Rox shut the door again, deciding that Reece was about as complicated as a dot-to-dot puzzle.

'Gant's Hill for starters,' said Davey Kayman. 'Then you might want to drop Charlie over Euston way, come back and get me around tennish and we'll take it from there. By the way, you got this week's money on you?'

Reece produced his bankroll and peeled off five hundred. They were stood by his Mondeo in the courtyard in Shoreditch.

'Good boy. Here, what's up with you tonight? Gabbing on nineteen to the dozen, you are.'

He said nothing to his employer.

'Come on, son, spit it out.'

Reece continued to glare murderously at him.

'You got a problem, then tell us. Sympathetic management, that's me.'

The stare remained icy.

'Sod you then. Come on. Let's get moving. Things to do, people to screw.'

Reece opened the passenger door and drove him away.

CHAPTER TWENTY-SIX

Blue morning mist hung over the crocuses and lawns in front of Eltham Secondary School, remaining undisturbed until seven forty-five when the first of the Met officers arrived and were granted access by the caretaker. By eight fifteen a cold April sun was warming the playground. DS Strudwick came with the local schools liaison officer and the Bursar. The officers present unilaterally declined the offer of staff room beverages and the most junior was sent out to McDonald's for coffees. They occupied the main corridor and the office adjacent to the entrance to the building, while DS Strudwick took up command in a classroom on the first floor. Two Squad cars were outside, one at the end of the street, the other tucked away in a nearby cul-de-sac. Davey wasn't expected until ten, but they liked to stack up the overtime. There'd been a flurry of volunteers for this morning's operation, not because of any particular dislike of con men, but because it'd all be over in time for the Charlton match.

Rox arrived in a squad car at 9 a.m.

'What's all this?' she asked, as her escort brought her up to meet Strudwick in Classroom Four B.

'You certainly picked your day,' said the harried Detective Sergeant.

The scene was not what she'd been expecting. Fifty or so cars were parked on the concrete apron in front of the school. Their boots yawned open and about them stalls and tables had been erected and were piled high with objects. A hundred or so punters battled over a plethora of junk, delighted to be purchasing bric-à-brac and memories at knock-down prices. There were vinyl records (Howard Jones, Fun Boy Three, David Bowie's The Lodger), chrome magazine racks and hinged bookends. Sunlamps, PIFCO hair curlers and Bullworkers, Chinese 'dragon' paintings and all manner of crap from attics and basements. Anything purchased today would tomorrow be discarded in another loft or resold at the next Car Boot Sale: the very essence of recycling.

'This isn't going to be a problem, is it?' she asked, disingenuously.

'No, he'll think its a burglars' convention. Probably stop and ask for his nametag.'

'I didn't know this was on today.'

'If you'd thought to speak to someone in *authority* . . .' began the Bursar. She was a tweedy woman in her late fifties with jumped-up typist written all over her. 'Then I would have told you that the Car Boot Sale was booked for this morning. But no, you'd rather break into my office.'

'I didn't break in,' Rox said. 'I set this up so as schools like yours wouldn't get ripped off anymore.'

'Nevertheless, Detective Strudwick and I have yet to discuss whether or not the school will press charges against you.'

'Hey, all I did was pretend to be you. I picked up the phone and lowered my IQ by fifty points.'

'That'll do,' said Strudwick.

Rox swallowed her next snide remark. She'd never liked school and was enjoying the fact that its authority over her had waned. Strudwick's radio crackled into life. He bent to it, then peered out of the window. Rox and the Bursar followed his gaze. A bright green VW camper van with two surfboards strapped to its roof had pulled up a few yards from the main gate. Its engine idled, and moments later, a pair of underdressed teenage girls appeared and clambered inside.

'I recognise those two,' said the Bursar. 'Year twelve. GCSE's this summer.'

Strudwick studied the van, which had begun rocking on its suspension. 'Does this come under extra-curricular activity then?' He asked.

Rox caged her face in her hands. Aussie Pete had said he was going windsurfing in Cornwall this weekend, but hadn't thought to mention that he'd be taking homework with him. The jolting in the van showed no signs of abating. The Bursar waddled off and began fiddling with the overhead projector.

It went quiet after that, save for the babble of traffic from the nearby Rochester Relief Road and the punters milling around the junk. Those vendors who had sold off the better items began to pack up and move out. Strudwick told his men to remain where they were. The camper van started bouncing up and down. Someone had changed positions.

It was nine fifty-one. A convoy of cars was trying to leave the school entrance when Davey's white Transit pulled up and blocked their path. The rear doors of the camper van burst open and a tearful teenage girl ran off down the street. Pete's head appeared, a bemused grin stapled to it. The Bursar squinted at him. Down on the forecourt the caretaker tried to get Davey's Transit to reverse back out. Strudwick let off a stream of invective. The Bursar reprimanded him.

Rox tore down the stairs to get a better view of the arrest.

Outside, a woman bought a crocheted toilet roll holder.

Two of the convoy of cars backed up, but a third slipped through, honking its horn gleefully. It drove straight into Pete's VW van.

Losing patience, Davey's Transit over-revved, sped into the school and pulled up by the entrance. A Doley jumped out of the back.

Strudwick bellowed at his radio.

The woman abandoned the crocheted obscenity.

Two Squad cars burnt rubber and screamed to a halt by

the gates. The men surrounded the Transit van.

Aussie Pete punched out the driver of the car.

The police arrested the Doleys in the act of unloading the computers.

Somebody purchased the *Haynes Manual* for a 1994 Volvo.

Simon Latimer stepped from the cabin.

Rox glared at DS Strudwick as he appeared.

'Isn't that the bloke then?'

'No.'

'Don't worry. I called Shepherdess Walk nick. They'll have someone round his place pronto.'

Latimer and the Doleys were arrested and the Transit and its contents impounded. Aussie Pete too was nicked on suspicion of having unlawful sex with minors. He didn't help his case when he commented that he'd be 'amazed if Vanessa was under age: shit, she could suck a tennis ball thorough a garden hose.'

Rox was anxious to know what would happen next. Strudwick informed her that there was no one at the Shoreditch address and that the officers had gone to get a warrant to search the place. Privately, he didn't hold out much hope, as most magistrates spent their Saturdays cluttering up the golf courses.

'What about the shop in Bethnal Green?' she asked.

'That's in motion.'

No one there either, only the stolen computer equipment.

And no sign of Davey.

Or Reece.

Rox hung around for as long as she could, but was needed at Giuseppe's by eleven. Strudwick promised he'd call when they had an update.

There were empty bin liners and boxes scattered all over the floor. The kitchen was a mess, plates of stale curry, old triangles of pizza and unwashed cutlery and crockery. The phone rang shrilly and the black beetle-like answering machine kicked in.

'Davey, it's Simon. I've been *arrested*. I can't get hold of my solicitor so I'm leaving this message with you. Can you contact Shooters Hill Police Station and bail me out. Or call up one of your people? I've told them this is all irregular but they keep saying it's part of some major computer fraud. Get here *soon* as you can, please. We've got to sort this out.'

The machine's red eye blinked as it bleeped plaintively in the hollow room.

It was four in the afternoon when Rox played her messages. Initially, she thought she hadn't received any, but then realised she still had the volume and ringer turned right down from the other night.

'Rox, this is Reece. Davey's onto it. I dunno how. Bastard must be psychic. It's 2 AM. I'm on a breather. He's had me load up all the gear and drop it over to the shop in Bethnal Green. I'll call later if I can . . .'

'. . . Reece again. Don't know if you got the last message. Listen, you've got my number, call on the mobile. I've had to take Charlie and her stuff over West London. Reckon she's done a bunk.'

'Rox. Where are you? Tell the filth not to bother staking out the school. He's sending Latimer on the job. Batteries going . . .'

She sighed, and was about to call him when the phone rang. DS Strudwick, informing her that Davey had stripped the place. They had turned over Complete Computers when they found it was in Latimer's name. Looked as though Kayman had landed his friend right in it.

'All set?'

Despite neurone- crunching hangovers, Archie and Steve had dragged themselves out of bed – in Archie's case off the floor in the lounge. Steve's lifestyle was having a detrimental effect on him. Both men were still battered and bruised from their latest altercation but the thought of hard cash propelled them onwards. Plus when the Petersons said jump, you jumped. They approached Steve's jag, which was parked up in a resident's space near his wharf home.

'We got everything?'

Steve stared at him, JPS drooping from a cut lip, ash dusting his jeans. 'Do what?'

'Told you this needed crowbars.'

'We ain't got one no more. It was in the tow-truck.'

'Baseball bat?'

'Under the seat.'

'We better hoof it round B & Q then. Bill and Tel want this done pronto.'

Steve clambered into the driving seat and swung the keys towards the ignition. Archie smacked his forehead.

'Don't start the motor.'

'Do what?'

'I was in such a two-and-eight with you I done your car. Sugar and piss in the petrol tank.'

Steve glowered and raised his hands to throttle Archie, but the chubby man shot up his forearm. Steve's cigarette fell smouldering onto his lap. After some energetic yelping and screeching, he threw open the door and hopped about on the pavement. Then he reached back inside for the baseball bat.

'Come here, Peacock.'

Archie backed off. 'No chance.'

Steve's eyes glowed with rage. 'Don't you fucking cross the line.'

Archie returned the glare. 'Not now, Stevie.'

'We'll have to get a bleeding cab.'

Archie's eyes went to the bat. 'Not with that we can't.'

'Then how we going to do the job?'

Archie shrugged. 'Improvise. Sort it when we get to Shoreditch.'

Steve tossed the bat back in the car and strode off towards the Jamaica road, with Archie struggling in his wake on his alloy crutches. When they reached the main road, they found it lined with metal barriers.

'*What* is all this?'

Archie, worn out from hopping, said. 'London Marathon, innit? Fuckers run twenty-six miles for a Snickers bar and a blanket. It's tomorrow morning.'

Steve visored his eyes. 'We'll have to go all the way round.'

The traffic was light, the evening cooling off. The pair eased around the barriers, crossed the street and headed towards the new Bermondsey Tube. It was shut, due to *essential maintenance*. They swore effusively and peered at the setting sun. No cabs — they rarely came through this area anyway unless it was drivers on their way home. Bus? No way was either of them getting a bus. An ambulance roared past and Arch had an idea. He unholstered his mobile and pressed digits. Answered the questions as they came. Ambulance. Jamaica Road. Made up an address.

'What was all that about?' Steve asked, torching a fag.

'You'll see.'

And with that, Archie lay down in the gutter.

'Where have you been?'

Reece looked embarrassed. 'At home sleeping off the drink. Not used to it. You get my messages?'

'In the end, yeah. But my ringer was off.'

'Suppose they didn't catch Davey, did they?'

She shook her head. He had come round to see her at home after finding she wasn't in the restaurant.

She explained about the failed sting attempt and how Latimer had been arrested. Reece chipped in by saying that the Fraud Squad had swarmed over Finsbury Cabs, only the controller had managed to get a message out to the drivers. They in turn mobiled the relief and night drivers and only the fully legal ones were going to show up for work. It would be a busy night for both of them.

'So what went on with you and Davey and how'd he catch on?' Rox asked.

He lowered his head. 'When I left here I was going to have him, but when I got there, I saw your point.'

'Man-listens-to-woman shock.'

'He spoke to Latimer yesterday. It was the order you put in, Rox. He wondered how a school in Eltham could afford top quality PC's, as he'd been passing on the crap ones to the other schools.'

'Shit.'

'Last night, I had to help him shift the gear — otherwise he'd guess we're connected. Charlie went off and he had me drop him at some club. Last thing he said was he'd be in touch as he might not be around for a while. Asked for the mobile back. Realised I had your numbers on it, so I bust it accidentally on purpose. He gave me that look of his — got that twitch, hasn't he?'

Her eyes lit up. 'You'd noticed that too?'

'Course.'

'He's done a flit then?'

'Won't see him for a bit.'

'He must have left clues.' She thought for a moment as she chewed on her knuckles. 'Have you still got his keys?'

'Yup.'

'Let's pop round to his place. See what we can dig up?'

'But the filth have been there all day.'

'I haven't.'

The mobile bleated.

'Kayman?'

'Who wants to know?' asked Davey.

'Terry Peterson. Little matter of funds unforthcoming.'

'That's a long word for you.'

The South London growl took nanoseconds to assume a sinister edge. 'There's the matter of debts owing on a Cab Company – one that's suffered an unfortunate toasting of late or so I am told. Plus the marker on Reece.'

'That's interesting.'

'Have you thought of redecorating lately?' enquired the voice.

'No.'

'You ought to. And next time, leniency is not an option. With me?'

'Might be, might not,' said Davey with playground flair.

'You might not be with us for long, son,' replied the voice, losing any pretence at veiling the threat.

'Ta daa then,' said Davey, then rang off.

'Who was that?' asked Charlie, lying on her clothes in their shiny bin liners.

'Some bollocks. Insurance.'

'Follow you everywhere, don't they?'

The ambulance came to a halt and two paramedics in green uniforms jumped out and approached Archie, who lay unconscious in the street. Steve stood over him with apparent concern, although the fag and the quarter bottle of scotch in his hand didn't look the part. As the medics bent to attend to him, Steve cracked their heads together, then rendered them unconscious with a series of blows. Archie threw open the rear doors and bundled them inside. Steve, gazing into the back of the ambulance, was like a child in a Theme Park.

'Hey – I ain't been in one of these for a while. All mod cons, eh?'

'Steve, get driving, will you?'

He was transfixed. Inside, apart from the gurney and the wheelchair, were several interesting-looking medical things worth playing with. The defibrillator for a start.

'Isn't this the one that goes th-gunk when you press it on someone's chest? Big charge, gets your heart started. I could use that in the mornings.'

Archie pressed his brow with his thumb and forefinger. 'Are you gonna drive or what?'

'More fun back here.'

Archie slammed the doors and went round and clambered up into the driver's seat. He did a fast U-turn and headed back for Tower Bridge at full pelt. Judging by the screams, Steve was having a high old time. And he kept bringing things through to show Archie, like the oxygen mask, the tray of painkillers (Steve knew all the names, diamorphine, diazepam), adrenaline and insulin, canisters of nitrous oxide.

The passengers weren't laughing though, especially when he attempted to try out the defibrillator. But as luck would have it, Steve's electrical knowledge stopped short of unplugging the telly and he couldn't get it running. He found the IV fluids and the saline and juggled the plasma replacement bags until one burst and glooped everywhere.

Archie looked for somewhere to stop in Shoreditch. He pulled into Rivington Street where they gagged and bound the ambulancemen and dumped them in a skip.

They gained entrance to the warehouses, but found Davey's door bolted. A few good wallops with the oxygen tank did for the lock and they were in. They had a good time, exacerbated when Steve let off the canister of nitrous oxide and they giggled their way through the destruction. Steve capped it all by reversing the ambulance into the outside wall, then ramming the gurney and wheelchair through the windows. Afterwards they went off for a drink, with the contents of the ambulance's drug cabinet stuffed into Steve's pockets.

Rox and Reece arrived minutes later to find the ambulance jammed into the side of the building and the basement apartment a mess. The contents of the blood replacement IV bags were smeared over the walls and hypodermic needles had been thrown about like darts. Bandages were tossed everywhere and splints broken over the remains of the furniture. The defibrillator had been used (Steve had finally got it up and running) to send currents through the microwave. The windows were shattered, many of the walls kicked through and the gurney and wheelchair twisted and bent among the wreckage.

'Know what?' offered Reece.

'What?'

'I reckon the standard of our emergency services is deteriorating.'

SUMMER

CHAPTER TWENTY-SEVEN

It was a sweltering Friday in late June. Ian Farrow had suggested that he meet Davey at Albertine's, a wine bar at the bottom of Wood Lane, adding that he'd pop down there as soon as he was let out of school at around five thirty. Shepherd's Bush was clogged with afternoon traffic so Davey had Reece drop him opposite the Fringe and Firkin in the Goldhawk Road.

Fancying a proper drink, he staggered across the busy inter-section and into the pub, where he ordered a pint of Dogbolter, bullied it down and slumped in a corner. Davey didn't like sun. His skin freckled and blistered at the mention of it and he pre-ferred to run on Dracula hours when it was dark and cool and he could feed off sodium and neon. Sunlight blazed through the large windows, scorched the chrome posts imprisoning the bar and formed hot rhombuses on the rear wall. The underarms of his shirt were drenched in damp coronas of sweat. Through his shellac black shades, Davey studied the cars and vans at the lights. Their bonnets were veneered in grime and their engine fans whirring ineffectually against the sluggish heat. Too bloody hot, he thought.

It was T-shirt weather. Pavements were crowded with tables: tables outside restaurants stiffly swathed in linen, tables abutting the pubs gnarled, knotted and garlanded with flattened crisp packets. Plane and lime trees had burst into leaf, forming tunnels of foliage throughout Holland Park Avenue, Park Lane and Chiswick. The Bank Holidays bookending the month of May had relaxed Londoners enough to spill out of town on the weekends. It grew hotter. Coltish teenagers released from exam tyranny flirted in new summer fads. Girls wore tiny tops, spaghetti straps, sandals and bared their midriffs. Boys wore combats and sportswear and spat sullenly on bone-hard pavements. All except the elderly donned shades. Suits grew lighter and men wore inadvisable shorts. Women's legs seemed to lengthen with each bright new day.

Davey fancied the look of a bar on the shadier side of the road. The Vesbar was all *Guardian Space*: pewter, bare brick, plain walls and uncomfortably slender furniture. His sort of place, he decided. A *producer's* place. He hoisted his cellular to his ear. You don't want to let them push you around, the BBC, he thought. They suggest somewhere; you change it. Never give a reason. Wrongfoot them, even when you are on the verge of securing one major commission. He rang through to Farrow's office where Marley informed him that Ian was in a meeting and couldn't be reached. She'd let him know of the change of venue.

Farrow showed up half an hour later. Davey was deep into a rum and coke and had clawed the ice into the ashtray to form an ashy puddle.

'Sorry about the delay. The suits are tossing their toys out of the pram.'

Davey said nothing, letting him think he was more annoyed than he appeared. Farrow signalled ineffectually to the waiter. Davey called out, 'Oi, silly bollocks. Over 'ere.'

The waiter's shoes clicked on the polished floor as he approached them. Farrow said. 'Uum, large scotch please and – same again?'

Davey nodded. The waiter evaporated.

'Don't like to get your weekend off to a bad start, but there's been a slight problem.'

'How slight?'

'A big one actually. Scott's been shunted aside.'

Davey wondered who Scott was. 'So?'

'A new controller was announced this morning. It's Virgil Chinnery.'

'Why's he a problem?'

'He was Head of Factual, as you know.'

'Yeah,' Davey lied.

'He hates the ICG and all the Indies. Chances are he'll restructure the whole department and I'll be out on my ear. Rather scuppers our plans.'

Davey couldn't keep it in any longer. 'Hold up, hold up. Back that one out of the depot. Tuesday you said we had this in the bag. Level One, you said.'

The waiter delivered their drinks. Farrow shut his eyes as the whisky burned his throat. 'We're stuffed, all right?'

Davey stared at him. Inconceivable, this was. Not on the cards.

It had been months since he'd impressed Farrow with his documentary series idea, 'London's Underworld Uncovered.' It certainly seemed that the BBC was keener than Carlton, who had almost thrown him out of their offices. He and Farrow had had several meetings since, and it was all looking good for the project to go ahead. Toby Lomax had long ago been sidelined, Davey had explained that CrossTalk (the name he'd lifted off a real production company) wanted him back in Canada so it was all on hold. Lomax was used to 'on hold' and planned on having it inscribed on his tombstone if he could ever afford it. In truth, Farrow had dressed the concept in BBC-speak and given it to his Head of Department, who presented it to the then Controller of BBC1.

Scott (oh, *that* Scott, realised Davey) had expressed an interest but wanted a title change. A one-page pitch went through to the formal offers round in June, joining the other submissions for consideration by the Channel management team. Following their deliberations, there was an awayday at Warren House in Kingston, where the team let down what hair they had left and dressed casually enough to shock the corporate American business-clones staying there. After that, the commissioning minutes were drawn up and had been issued that Tuesday. Davey didn't give a flying fuck for all the gab and in-fighting, and was pleased to discover that his project had been awarded a Level One status, which meant a commission was imminent.

Farrow had given him this news on the mobile as he strolled through Harlesden. He and Charlie had prudently relocated to West London, laying low and severing any links with Complete Computers. Luckily his name wasn't on the lease at Shoreditch either as there was the ten grand's worth of rent owing to the friend who had sub-let it to him while he'd been away in Dubai. The owner was a tad miffed to hear that both the police *and* ambulance services had ransacked his home, as that was more the sort of thing he expected back in the Middle East. Davey's response was to threaten to set the fire brigade on him unless he stopped whinging.

'But you said the project would get through straightaway,' barked Davey as he charged through the shoppers and dossers.

'But this couldn't be better,' replied Farrow. 'He wants us to think about shape.'

'What sort of shape? Round shape? Square shape? How about docufucking-mentary shape?'

'It's the form, er, the *shape*,' floundered Ian, who used the term constantly and had no idea of what it meant.

'What are you on about?'

Farrow sounded breathless. This was either down to pure excitement or the onset of his hay fever. 'It means we can rework the idea. Make it a *landmark* series.'

'Will you talk English?'

'Instead of eight half-hours, we could go for fifty minutes' He paused, giving it time to sink in.

It didn't.

'You'll double your profit margin.' He added.

Delighted, Davey then went off to negotiate with his own personal BBC – a Big Bowl of Coke. He had been expecting ninety grand upfront once they agreed to the deal, but this? Even better. For a hundred and eighty grand, he might even go so far as to actually make the programmes.

The Vesbar was beginning to fill with tired office workers in need of a stiffener for the journey home. Outside, the traffic was chocker, murder, nightmare. A heat-haze shimmered off the road. What could have gone wrong?

'So what if there's someone new in charge?' he urged. 'The decision isn't only down to this bastard, is it? Can't be.'

Farrow threw down his double scotch. The capillaries around his nose and cheeks had grown pink and his hair was damp and curling up around his neck. 'You haven't been around for a while, have you?'

'What about the old controller? What'd he get the chop for?'

Farrow squinted at him and said significantly, 'Scott's on Gardening Leave.'

'What?'

'He's been moved aside, "*left*", if you get my drift . . . come on, Davey, you must know that the BBC doesn't ever actually sack anyone?'

'Don't they?'

'Not unless you *completely* cock things up.'

'Yeah, and then what?'

'You get booted upstairs.'

'What's he done, this bloke?'

'I reckon it's political. That or poor performance. Market share's been down lately. Lot of talk. The smart money's on him becoming Head of BBC Scotland.'

'Sounds all right to me.'

Ian broke into a peal of laughter. 'If you fancy Siberia

without the range of winter sports. Jesus, Davey, that's the absolute worst that can happen.'

Kayman gave him a long heavy-lidded stare, then said again, 'What about our project?'

'On hold. Everything's on hold. Virgil Chinnery was only appointed this morning so the details won't come out until next week.' He snorted derisively. 'Probably read about it before anyone deigns to tell us.'

'That's no good. This has got to go through now. I've got cash-flow problems.'

Farrow slumped in his uncomfortable chair, its curved wings digging into his armpits. 'There's nothing I can do. As a producer, you know the risks.'

'You should call the new bloke right now. Suss out where we stand.'

'Can't do that.'

'You do know him though.'

'We, er, don't see eye to eye.'

'In English.'

'He hates my guts.'

Davey rose and went to powder his nose. It was cool in the men's room and he found it easier to think in there. He made a brief couple of calls, ordered fresh drinks at the bar and pulled his chair close up to Farrow. The executive's shirt tail was exposed, his tie loose, lower lip pouting as he examined the bottom of his glass.

'How do I know this is all kosher?' Davey asked.

'Read it in *Broadcast*.'

'I'm not waiting till then. We were supposed to go through the proposal this weekend round yours. Do all that shape and landmark bollocks for your boss. Now you tell me it's off 'cos he's buggered off up north? On your say-so this means I'm down, what, nearly two hundred K here.' Davey leaned in, scowling furiously. 'If you was me, wouldn't you reckon this was a load of old dog's?'

Farrow peered through his lank fringe. 'Of course not.' There was clearly something wrong here, he realised. He'd met enough maverick Indy Prods in this business to weather their foibles and tantrums, but this guy had no *idea*.

'Bollocks. It's a wind-up. You tell the geezer with the brilliant idea "Oh sorry, don't need it now." Then what happens? Only turns up on telly in a couple of years with your name on it. Don't think I'm not wise to your game. Tell me I'm wrong, go on.'

Farrow pushed himself back in his seat. 'As a matter of fact you are. Firstly, each programme idea is recorded. Secondly, of course there's an outside chance that in the reshuffle your idea might slip through the net, but a Level One's a Level One. It'll just take more time, that's all.'

Davey formed a yapping mouth with his hand. 'Yeah, yeah.'

'You're still free to take it to the other channels.'

Davey remembered how he'd pissed on his chips at Carlton. Sure, he could try Four or the ITV regions, but this was meant to be a goer. They'd got his hopes up, the Beeb. And they were proper. Bit of history. Queen's Speech, Footie until they lost it. Cricket until they lost it. World Cup, Dad's Army, Eric and Ernie, Dr Who, Dimbleby and Attenborough and all the other toffs. They were decent, not your usual shysters. He scrutinised Farrow's face, searching for a tell. There was no way this prat was going to get the better of him. He was an old hand at this.

He bellowed, 'Show me the minutes of this meeting.'

Farrow rose to his feet. 'You know I can't do that. All the other Independent submissions are on that document.'

Davey grabbed his arm. 'I've had enough of you. You can't go from it's a goer on a Tuesday to forget it on the Friday. You're acting like some poxy teenage tart.'

'Welcome to telly.'

Davey's face boiled with rage. 'Right, that's *it*.'

*

Finsbury Cabs were now fully operational. The bullpen had been renovated with the cheapest materials available and the controller's hutch rebuilt with ply and MDF. Reece still hated the place but at least in summer you could drag the chairs outside and imagine you were in the Mediterranean. Not that he'd ever been there, but he'd seen the postcards sent back by the drivers who had. They depicted the same three scenes. In the first, a toothless crone sat on her doorstep, usually amended with a Biro'd-in arrow stating that this was Golf Tango Four's wife. The second was of a bronzed topless girl on a beach with a thong bikini bottom. This was Golf Tango Four's girlfriend – in his dreams. The third showed a clear turquoise pool in front of a high-rise hotel, always with the exact same couple in the water. Golf Tango Four never got a mention on this one, as it was sent back by the drivers with families.

There had been a hiatus after the events in April, but Reece was now back driving for Davey and paying him for the privilege. By his reckoning his gambling debt was now considerably reduced, even though Davey didn't keep a strict tally as the Petersons had. It was left to Reece to purchase a small Silvine notebook and keep a log of his payments. As ever, Davey never sweated the small stuff. He had for weeks been obsessing and fantasising over his big TV break, to the point at which Reece felt like decking him.

Nothing was heard from Simon Latimer after his arrest.

The Fraud Squad had made a valiant attempt to seize Finsbury Cabs as being part of his assets. However, he'd apparently thought forward enough to disconnect himself from the business once Davey became his partner. It continued to run but, like a headless chicken, everyone knew that it'd end up in the pot sooner or later. The drivers were making what they could and subbing the controllers for the work. Davey had lost interest in the place anyway, and made do with Reece's contribution.

The night Reece was contacted by Davey, he had immediately gone and told Rox. She'd said that she was busy at work and trying to forget about it all. Reece pushed her on it, wanting revenge as much as she did, but she steadfastly refused to hear any more. He guessed correctly that she wanted to bury the pain and dropped the subject. He saw her on and off, but Rox was bound up in work and often tired. He had the impression she was still angry with him. He adjusted his nights to fit in around Davey's erratic schedules and – on her behalf – kept note of his actions. To date they had remained legal, but he figured it was only a matter of time.

CHAPTER TWENTY-EIGHT

On his wife's insistence, Archie had lost the goatee and moustache, but he still retained his interest in the Fine Arts. After accepting him back into the family home in Nunhead, Shirley had laid down some ground rules: No more painting in the house; Archie's studio was to be relocated to their garden shed and there would be no more nude modelling, male or female, young or old. Archie felt like he was suffering the after-shocks of an affair even though he'd only ever shaken Rox's hand to thank her for the posing. He'd not even seen her since leaving her flat on the night Reece came round. Nevertheless, he promised Shirley faithfully that he'd stay away from her.

Bad news this art mullarky.

He'd not seen Reece either, having no need to visit Finsbury Cabs since they'd had the pull by the Old Bill and the Petersons ducked out of the deal. On that score, their brief had set up a series of obstructions, resulting in the court case being put back by another six months. He was still muddying the waters over the jurisdiction of the case and pitting the Met against the Airport Police. He'd also laid into Croydon Council, in whose patch they had been stashing the moody cars. This couldn't possibly be Taking Without the Owner's Consent (or TWOC-ing), as they had authorised Messrs Lamb and Peacock in a legally binding contract to clamp throughout the borough. To date,

Archie and Steve felt their counsel had treated them most cordially.

The call came at half seven on that Friday afternoon.

'You've been recommended. Said you might want a bit of business putting your way?'

In the shed, Archie was working on a still life on board. He put down his sable brush. 'Could be. Who's your contact?'

'Bill Peterson put me onto you.'

'Fairy snuff.'

'Can you look after someone this weekend?'

'Short notice.'

'Way it is.'

'What's involved?'

'Babysitting.'

'Can I bring a mate?'

Archie thought of Steve. Their wounds had healed, save for a long livid scar across the bridge of his nose where Steve had bent a lampstand over his face. Despite his exhortations, Steve Lamb had resolutely refused to reveal the whereabouts of the Rembrandt self-portrait, but at least he'd promised not to send any more pieces out and Archie half believed him.

There'd been nothing in the news about parts of stolen paintings showing up, but then the *Sun* didn't have a Fine Arts reporter, as far as Archie knew. Without any work from the Petersons, they saw less of one other and the bone of contention was buried for the moment. Truth be told, Arch was missing his mate, and now that there was work on offer, whom else to suggest but his old oppo.

'All right,' said the voice.

'The rate's a monkey a day, plus exes.'

There was an appreciative grumble at the other end of the line.

'Where's the job?'

'Down Epsom way,' came the reply. 'You got wheels?'

'Yeah' – thinking, Steve's got the Jag. 'We'll be in a scarlet Jag. E reg.'

'Can you swing by now?'

Archie focused on the daubing in front of him. Poxy fruit in a basket. It wasn't the same. 'Where are you?'

'Pick me up outside Telly Centre, Shepherd's Bush. I'll be with the mark.'

'Will do.'

Archie rang off and called Steve. 'Oy, wanker. Bit of work on.'

'Cant. Cant, caaaanttt.'

Vauxhall Cross and the car in front of the Jag had had the audacity to stop at the lights – not good enough for Steve Lamb, who rammed his palm on the horn, releasing a banshee wail like that of a disturbed toddler. Then he stuck his head out of the window.

'You could've got through them fucking lights EASY.'

Archie muttered something placatory, but he knew it would be fruitless. Here they were, stuck alongside every single other car that had been manufactured in the last ten years. Friday evening, going-home time. Solid, murders nightmare. Steve drilled his eyes into the neck of the man in the car in front as he continued his litany of curses. The driver was doing his best impersonation of a deaf man. Archie saw terrified eyes in the rear-view mirror.

'Wankers like that shouldn't be on the road.'

'Don't matter, Stevie. The Embankment's gonna be solid and all.'

'He could've jumped the lights like a *normal* person. Everyone knows amber means move it, move it, move it.'

Archie wondered what was it that made London drivers go mental once they were behind the wheel.

Steve shook his head, his voice becoming mournful and diminished. He spoke with a huge sigh, as if this were the last thing he wanted to do. 'It's no good. He's got to be taught. I'll get the tyre iron out the boot.'

Before Arch could say anything, Steve was half out of the car. Then the lights changed, so he ducked back in, over-revved the engine and chased the Ford over Vauxhall Bridge, keeping precisely two inches from the man's rear bumper. They then veered off left onto Grosvenor Road, Steve's *Sayonara* being another long wail on the horn. They sped another hundred yards before hitting another traffic-clot.

'Oh, dog's dicks,' spat Steve, reaching for his JPS.

For the next ten minutes, they barneyed on about whether they ought to continue along the Embankment or cut up through Sloane Square and risk trying Knightsbridge. Either way, they were going to be late.

'He'd better wait,' fumed Steve, smoke pouring from his nostrils. 'And he's got to front us the cash. I've been brassic for weeks.'

'He can't exactly do it on his own, can he?'

'You met the geezer?'

'No, but Bill's okayed him.'

This placated Steve for all of a minute. 'Shit. I had a pukka bit of gash lined up for tonight and all. I was gonna take her up the V & A – and I don't mean the museum.'

'Anyone I know out of the mortuary?'

Steve gave an ocular shrug, tapped his ash out on the tarmac. There was a sobbing in his cracked nicotine voice. 'Twenty-three, Arch. She's only bleeding twenty- three.'

'Leaving the Guide Dog at home, is she?'

'Tell you something, she's a right looker. Met her down the Deptford Spike.'

'Thought they closed that up?'

'Yeah, but the homeless still hang about there. We had a chat, couple of bevvies and Bob's your whatsit. Do anything for a couple of rocks, this one. Including a decent bunk-up round the back of the Albany. Good tits, tight little minge. Tell you what, I almost believe there's a God.'

'Don't you reckon shafting homeless crackheads is dropping your standards a bit then, Stevie-Boy?'

'Nah. You get used to the smell.'

'Thought that'd be more of a problem for her.'

'Would anyone, er, care for a drink?' asked Ian Farrow as they entered the spacious hall of his Tudorbethan mansion in Epsom.

'Cheers, yeah,' said Davey. 'Rum and coke if you got it. Beer if not.'

'Make that two beers,' said Steve. 'And whatever you're having.'

He and Archie gazed around in awe. This was the sort of place they'd only ever seen in the old black and white Boulting Brothers' films and dreamed of turning over but bottled out of when it came to it in favour of doing their own manor.

'Must've set you back a few pennies,' said Archie, craning his neck to study a portrait up in the galleried stairwell.

Farrow stopped in the doorway to the drawing room. 'Um, actually no. I inherited the old place.'

Steve raised his eyebrows Roger Moore style.

Davey followed Ian through. The room was oak panelled and there were plates up on the Delft rail. There was a Dorking red-brick fireplace with a gas log fire. Farrow went to a cabinet, poured another scotch into a tumbler and threw it back.

'Who *are* those two?' he whispered.

'Employees of mine,' said Davey.

The ride had been fraught. Having established that Farrow's wife and children were out of the country, Davey had ordered Ian to take him to his office in TV Centre. There, he bullied him into getting the documents from the recent Offers round and anything pertaining to his Documentary Idea. He had a look round the ICG area and even checked out the controllers' offices, but found them locked. The office of the Director of Television was the only one open: out of sheer malice Davey pissed in the man's pot plant.

When they emerged from the concrete doughnut, the Jag was waiting for them in Wood Lane. It contained two hot, volatile middle-aged men. One was built like a bullet with a horseshoe of stubble wrapped around his sweating pate; the other – the driver – had long lank hair, a caved-in smoker's face and a personal odour problem. As they fought their way towards Putney, he released a stream of abuse that surpassed even Davey for spleen and venom, losing points only on inventiveness and intelligibility. Steve had a trade-off with a woman in a shiny four-by-four in Putney High Street and Davey and Archie had had to intervene to stop him getting out and 'killing the rich bitch whore'.

Davey was impressed, and made a mental note to ensure he paid these two at least part of their fee.

He and Farrow sank silently in the back as they crawled through Roehampton and onto the A3. Kingston and the Tolworth Underpass were sheer murder, hell on earth. The traffic fumes made it hard to breathe and stung their eyes. If anything, it seemed to be even hotter now at eight-thirty at night. Finally, the traffic thinned out on the A2, and asphalt and metal was replaced by pine and grass.

'Got to get some ice,' announced Farrow. He wandered off down a corridor, throwing on lights as he went.

Davey motioned to Archie. 'Tell your mate to keep an eye on him.'

'Steve, keep an eye out.' Archie joined Davey in the drawing room. 'So what's the game?' he asked.

'Stick around here for the weekend. Make your presence felt. He's holding back on me and I want to know why.'

'Right you are.'

Davey pulled a plastic-covered ring-bound file out of Farrow's heavy briefcase. 'I'm going to take a butcher's through this.'

There was a yelp from the kitchen and the sound of breaking glass. Farrow hurried back through, nursing a bloodied nose.

'He hit me. He bloody hit me.'

Steve, appearing behind him said, 'He was going for a knife.'

'I was only going to cut the lemons for the drinks.'

Davey studied them, turning to Archie. 'Let's not have any communication problems here. He is BBC after all.'

Archie gazed levelly at him. 'You want to front me some of that cash?'

Saturday afternoon and Arch and Steve were watching the European match on Sky. Barcelona was one up against Bayern Munich and they had looted the fridge of beers. Steve balked at the guacamole dip, which Ian brought in on a tray along with the salsa sauce, hummus, cream cheese and tortilla chips.

'What is it?'

'It's avocado.'

Steve mimicked Ian's cultivated tone. 'It's Avo-cardo. It's crap, mate.'

Archie looked over from the winged armchair. 'We prefer a proletarian snack. Got any hot dogs?'

'I'll look in the freezer,' muttered Farrow.

Steve slurped his beer, slammed it on the polished table. 'Nah. Don't want to have to follow you about. Siddown.'

Through the leaded lights, a light breeze rustled the bushes.

'You could at least use a coaster,' Ian said, folding his arms.

The men emitted a high-pitched sarcastic tone, with Archie tweaking his T-shirt in the manner of a Victorian Lady attempting a curtsey.

Farrow had no idea of what to make of his houseguests. Born and brought up in the house, he'd been schooled at Winchester and Cambridge and begun his career as a researcher. After the treadmill years, he had made his name by producing a prize-winning documentary on street gangs in Bogota. Armed with a trusted guide and a flak jacket, he lost a cameraman in an ambush and would have been killed had he not used the dead man's body as a shield – his most notable act of bravery in a life that was no longer thrilling. On joining the Beeb, he worked for some years as an editor on a documentary strand, and then moved from production to his present role in commissioning.

Davey's departure heralded the cue for his keepers to party. Steve severed the phone lines, debilitated the drink cabinet and trawled the video collection for porn, finding none and settling for *Betty Blue*. The man reminded Ian of the pixellated abusers/grasses he saw on-screen in the editing rooms at work. Archie was a stranger fish. As vociferous as any London cabby, his specialist subject was painting, in which he seemed to be an expert. He had hoisted the lavish coffee-table books out from under their glass-topped tomb. The catalogue from the recent Pissarro exhibition at the Royal Academy caught his interest.

'Not bad, this geezer. Hardly your Premier Division like Monet though, eh?' He came to a colour plate. 'Hold up, that's Norwood,' he called out to Steve, who was channel surfing. 'Stevie, this guy painted round our way. Look, Norwood Junction.'

Steve didn't bother to look. Archie carried on studying the glossy images and Farrow inched towards the door.

'I wouldn't want to do that if I was you.'

Farrow looked at him inquisitively.

'Try and get away.'

'I wasn't . . .'

Farrow didn't bother finishing the sentence, as the remote had caromed off his temple. There were other 'accidents' that night; a broken newel-post when Steve tried sliding down the banisters, a smashed cut-glass decanter and some livid bruises on Farrow's torso when he tried to sneak out of his bedroom window and fell, with Steve's help.

Davey came by at five on Saturday afternoon.

'You realise this is kidnapping,' spat Ian.

'Says who?'

'The law.'

'Oh, them.' Davey made a derisory swatting motion. 'I've been going through these submissions. There isn't half some crap about. I mean, Customs officers at ferry terminals, superstores, gynaecologists? My idea's way out in front.'

'A lot of people say that,' bridled Ian.

'Come on. The viewers love crime. Specially your middle classes, they get a thrill out of it.' Davey tapped the folder. 'I don't see any reason why this new bloke shouldn't do it.'

'Told you. He'll want to start by re-structuring the commissioning process.'

'Do what?'

'He needs to make his presence felt, decimate a few departments, promote his pals, of which I am not one.'

Davey asked, 'You got his home number?'

Farrow shook his head.

'Then it'll have to wait till Monday. We'll give him a bell then.'

'You're leaving me here with these goons?'

'He fallen in de water,' mimicked Archie, in an approximation of Little Jim from the old Goon Show.

Davey asked, 'Where was it your wife's gone?'

'Provence. I'm supposed to join her and the children at the end of next week, once I've finished off the paperwork.'

Steve said, 'That's handy.'

'This is ridiculous,' spat Ian.

Davey pushed his face close up to Farrow's. His breath was rank from an all-night session and his tongue leathery from bad speed; the muscles around his jaw thrummed under the skin. 'Listen up, silly bollocks. I've had one bitch of a year and I've invested time and energy in this project, so don't you piss me about. The BBC owes me and we ain't letting it drop.'

'There's nothing I can do.'

Davey gave him a sardonic smile. 'We haven't even *started* on you yet.'

Archie sidled up to his employer. 'If we're staying on, I'd best see some folding.'

Davey plucked a wad of notes from the small pocket at the

top of his jeans. Easy come, easy go, he thought, handing over Reece's latest contribution.

'There's only a monkey here.'

'All I've got on me, lads. More tomorrow.'

'You can't keep me here,' keened Farrow.

'You prefer hospital then?' offered Steve, thinking of his baseball bat, which was out in the car.

'Hold up,' called out Archie. 'Don't hit him in the face. I've had an idea. Can you borrow us the Jag?'

CHAPTER TWENTY-NINE

A blazing Sunday afternoon and Soho churned and curdled with tourists. Old Compton Street swelled with slender Italians and Soho Square — lacking its blanket of office workers, despatch riders and drunks — was dotted with girls. The lower end of Berwick Street still smelled of cabbage and the back end of a Biffa lorry even though there was no market today. Further up, between the sun-baked pavements of Wardour and Dean Streets was a ginnel named St Anne's Court: halfway along it was Giuseppe's latest venture, a restaurant which, with breathtaking originality, he had named 'Salvatori's'.

In an area known for its extortionate business rates, he'd negotiated a short lease on the property, having realised that if he couldn't entice in the reviewers and trophy celebs in the first six months then it wasn't worth his while. It had previously been a failed eatery so it already had a decent kitchen, which was modernised to standards that satisfied the Health and Safety juntas. Following a lick of paint (beige, orange and teal — late Nineties urban ethnic), the purchase of job-lot artwork and a thorough re-think of the menu, they opened for business in mid-May: his new manageress, Rox Matheson.

She was perched on a stool by the door sipping lemonade. Bands of light bled through the wooden blinds, warming her forehead, cheek and neck. She kept her eyes in shadow. Her hair had grown out and was shoulder-length and dark, chestnut with a hint of henna. She'd often stick a clump of it in her mouth when concentrating and tie it back when at work. Rox wore a black T-shirt and Calvin Klein jeans, her day uniform. At night, she'd switch to pumps and a short shift dress, having found a couple of cheap designer numbers in a Notting Hill charity shop. She took the bookings, greeted and seated, supervised the kitchen and staff and mucked in when needed. She was determined to make the place work and was forging new friendships among the staff and regular customers.

At lunch the place filled with the Soho crowd from the casting and post-production studios, movie people, techie's from De Lane Lea and agents feeding their perma-desperate clients. In the evenings they catered for culinary tourists, theatregoers and couples. On Rox's persuasion, Giuseppe had poached a chef of the River Café School. Consequently, the food was excellent and the booking sheet nearly as long as an NHS waiting list. Giuseppe was overjoyed at Rox's organisational skills.

Rox was thinking about how she'd not had sex in six bloody months. It was an itch she couldn't scratch — worse, a mad longing which sometimes tempted her to grab someone off the street. Except that in these streets they were mostly gay. And beautiful, damn them. This was no longer a man-drought, this was a full-on *emergency*. Any more of this, she mused, then its communal showers and standpipes in the street and . . . hmm, communal showers. Her relationship with Ally had dwindled too. Hearing the ins and outs of her and Terry's life was no fun when she'd never even met the guy. Plus they'd now gone to Ibitha for the summer. Rox had received a postcard of an old crone on a doorstep, amended with an arrow with her name on it, Ha ha.

'All right there? What you dreaming about?'

'Shoes,' said Rox. 'Hi, Reece.'

'How're things?'

'Good.' She squinted as a sunbeam caught her in the eyes. She sensed there was something on his mind. 'What's up?'

Reece moved his weight to his other foot. He wore faded jeans and a white GAP shirt, open at the collar. Suited him. Nice to see him out of his suit too. She noticed he'd not caught the sun, whereas she spent her afternoons off catching rays in Soho Square.

'It's about Davey Kayman as it goes.'

Her face clouded over.

'I've been keeping an eye out. He's being a bit of a naughty bunny over in Epsom. I'm supposed to pick him up there in a while. Wondered if you wanted to tag along?'

'I thought we were going out?'

'This would be going out.'

'I see.'

They had planned to go to the cinema. A rare occurrence this, but a film had come up which they both liked the sound of. Rox had been thinking about her and Reece, going on a proper date. Their infrequent meetings still took place after work and he'd never once offered to do anything normal like take her for a candlelit meal or hunt through markets together or have rampant sex.

'Where's Epsom?' she asked.

'Surrey. Posh area. Come see how the other half live.'

She untangled her feet from the rungs of the stool. 'This is as near as I'm gonna get to a drive in the country, isn't it?'

'You get the fresh air and the chance to spy on a fugitive.'

'Who could resist?'

'You, for a start.'

'I suppose the film's out?'

'Your choice. Course I'd have to leave halfway through the movie to go pick Davey up.'

'Not much of a choice then.'

He put his shades on.

Rox considered it. She'd tried to block Davey and the events of winter and spring from her mind, especially spring. Now, here he was bringing it up again. Why? She supposed it was because he still wanted revenge as much as she did. And if she were honest, her hurt and bitterness hadn't gone at all. DS Strudwick, back at Shooters Hill, had been as gloomy in his predictions as anyone else: the case would remain open, but since there was no evidence that Davey was active, no one had been assigned to it. This annoyed her but she was doing her best. Had done her best. And now?

'What's the point?' she asked.

'Rox, it's up to you.'

'We've tried twice.'

'Okay then,' he crooked his arm so as she might put hers through it. 'Shall we go then? Pictures?'

'You're insufferable' she said, sliding down from her seat.

'Thank you, ta.'

'That's not a good thing, Reece. And you know damn well I can't resist having a go.'

He grinned cheesily.

'Hang on. If I go with you, then he's going to see me when we get there.'

'Thought of that,' he said, removing his shades.

'You leave me stranded there?'

'No.'

'What then? Am I supposed to hide in the boot?'

There was a pause.

'All set?' he offered weakly.

She gave a big sigh. 'So what's Davey up to this time?'

'You'll like this. Kidnapping?'

Reece wove through Piccadilly, round Trafalgar Square and crossed the river at Westminster. Rox gazed up at Big Ben, glowing golden against a denim sky. It still impressed her, as did central London, no matter how muggy or crowded or polluted it became. As they drove along the Albert Embankment, she was reminded of two things, first of the night she met Reece when they went that way to Battersea Park. Second, an afternoon a fortnight ago when out of the blue he told her to meet him on Vauxhall Bridge. Standing over the central stanchion, he had reached into her bag and pulled out her tattered *London A–Z.*

'You don't need this any more.'

'I do. North London's a wasteland to me. Look — it's got "there be dragons" on the map.'

'Why would you want to go up there anyway?'

'You got me there.'

'You know the centre, the south and the Tubes. That's good enough. Come on, Rox, stop being a tourist. Tear it up.'

She winced at the word. It meant stopping dead in the street, *Cats* and Angus Steakhouses, Carnaby Street and Camden Market tat. I-went-to-London-and-all-I-got-was-this-over-priced-shrinks-and-bleeds-in-the-wash-T-Shirts. Reading out the ads and the destinations in the Tube in funny voices. Failing to queue properly. Speaking to strangers. She hated them as much as everyone else now.

With a jolt she realised she was becoming a Londoner.

She had developed blinkers when passing *Big Issue* sellers (back in Manchester, she'd have bought a copy every time out of guilt). She planned her time around catching trains and grunted and rolled her eyes on Hither Green Station with every cancellation. She read the *Standard* and knew bars that stayed open late and clubs that were rip-offs. She praised London's plethora of cultural events and never had any time to go to any of them. She'd got lost in the Barbican. She had not, she mused regretfully, had sex in any of the parks. She longed to be out of the muggy heat and go to the country or seaside — but would never *dream* of moving there.

'Give it here,' she said.

Reece handed it to her and she broke the spine. Then, handing half back to him, they shredded the pages, laughing as they strewed the confetti of streets over a passing pleasure cruiser. She felt warm and giggly after that and Reece had put his arm around her as he led her back to his car.

She didn't even get lost for days.

He ploughed through Battersea, both of them blinded even in shades as a fierce sun flared up ahead. Reece told her of what he'd picked up from Davey about his latest plan.

'But he can't get a programme on telly just like that, can he?' Rox asked.

'He reckons it's a doddle, but it looks like he's run into difficulties. He's holding this BBC bloke in his house, using two lads as muscle. You know one of them.'

'Do I? Who?'

'You'll see. Old mucker of yours.'

They snaked around the Wandsworth one-way system and crawled up West Hill. Once up on the by-pass, the traffic cleared and Reece picked up speed. Sunlight dappled through the vaulted trees as they approached Epsom, which snoozed complacently in the evening heat. They found the house. It was large, at least eight bedrooms, set back from the road by a gravel drive and fronted by weathered wooden gates. Reece studied his watch.

'Davey's expecting me in half an hour. Thought we'd nip round the back so's you can have a shufti.'

'You're coming with me. I've learnt not to do this on my own.'

He drew past and parked further up the lane.

They found a public footpath running parallel to the house. Halfway down was a small electricity substation, and then it became overgrown by nettles and hollyhocks. Midges hung in the sweet-smelling air and shafts of sun exposed the translucency of the leaves, making them lime in the light. The chimneys of Farrow's house were visible through beech and fir. The path ran along the back of the garden, but there was a high slatted wooden fence. Rox counted fenceposts, noting that they petered out before the end of the property. Raising their arms, they waded through nettles until they came across two sections of chicken wire, against which a compost heap bulged pregnantly. Reece tore open a gap between the wire and the fence. There was blood on his hands, which he wiped on his shirt. He forced it open and they slipped through.

The garden was expansive, ninety metres or so in length with a gazebo; an aged Victorian greenhouse and a thriving rose garden. A well-tended lawn rushed towards the rear of the house, bisected by a snaking path that reminded Rox of the Yellow Brick Road. This led to a pair of French windows that were open. They squatted down out of sight of the house.

'That's him,' whispered Reece.

'He doesn't look like someone high up in the BBC.'

'They never do, apparently.'

Ian Farrow was slumped in a chair in the window. His hair was pasted to his scalp with perspiration and his face swollen and lined through lack of sleep. Davey was gesturing violently at him. Farrow made to move but Steve, stepping smartly up from behind, restrained him in a stranglehold.

'Steve Lamb,' Reece said. 'Nasty piece of work. Bermondsey boy with an eye for the ladies. Got a tattoo of a blank scroll on his shoulder. He fills in the name of each bird as and when.'

'Bird?' queried Rox.

Archie entered the frame. Reece said. 'Here's your friend now.'

Rox said, 'What's *he* doing here?'

'In case you didn't know, Archie's hired muscle. Him and Lamb come as a double act. Laurel and Hardy without the piano music. Next time you ought to check people out before you pose in the buff.'

'And how'm I supposed to do that?' she hissed. 'Give them a questionnaire? Are you a painter or a nutter? Do you draw with pencil or a big red crayon?'

'You know what I mean.'

'That got to you didn't it?'

'What?'

'Him painting me in the nude.'

'Not a problem,' he said, stone faced.

She inched closer. 'It is so true. And you keep up this big daddy protective thing towards me all the time, but you never tell me how you feel do you? You never say what's going on behind that mask. You're still being dishonest, Reece, in your own way.'

'Am I?' He seemed hurt.

'I never seem to know where I am with you,' she said.

He chewed the inside of his cheek.

She thought of their missed date tonight, and other times when they'd nearly got close. Why was it she only seemed to speak her mind when they were in danger? She hadn't time to finish the thought as Reece reached out a hand to the nape of her neck, drew her to him and kissed her. They keeled over, him on his back, her falling, scrambling on top of him, the smell of grass in their nostrils. He kept his hand on the back of her head, massaging her hair between his fingers, as their breathing grew more urgent. They matched their kisses, alternating tenderness with passion. It was languid, unforced. But as he rose under her, she felt the fear. Rox pulled away, wiping a dab of spittle from her mouth, eyes aglow.

'Can't get round me like that, Mister Reece.'

'Worth a try though.'

She wrinkled up her nose.

Then he stared so deeply into her eyes that she clamped herself to him, her hands reaching under his jacket to grip his torso.

Reece's mobile phone went.

'Where are you?' growled Davey.

There was a pause as he surfaced. Davey was pacing outside the windows.

'Not far.'

'Get me back to civilisation.'

'Right-o.'

He went inside and they scampered back to the bottom of the garden. Rox said, 'I hope you were kidding about me getting in the boot of your car?'

'Uh, no. It's comfy, honest.'

She stamped through the nettles, muttering something about men that Reece didn't catch as he hurried after her.

Reece nosed the car back towards London with Davey ranting on in the back, amplifying his plans for the telly series, saying he'd get it past the arseholes at the Beeb, do the jobs, film them and pocket the money both ways. He'd heard that documentary people didn't necessarily have to take their evidence to the Police and since he was the producer that was hardly on the cards. During a brief gap in the verbals, Reece suggested that kidnapping his potential employer might be a bit of a setback? It got a laugh.

'Nah, soon as we get the green light I'll tell Farrow that them two mongs in there are actors.' He adopted an archly innocent tone. 'No hard feelings mate – can't you take a joke?'

Reece hated practical jokes, knowing them to be sadism by another name. He dropped Davey in Harlesden, then drove on a hundred yards and sprung open the boot.

'I feel sick,' said Rox.

'Davey has that effect on people.'

'Car sick, from the motion.'

He helped her to clamber out and walked her up and down. It was growing dark and the plane trees bloomed high against a deep turquoise sky.

Rox said, 'I can't see him getting away with this, but if there's any way we can put a stick in his spokes, I'm willing to give it a go.'

He released a smile and then offered to take her home.

Reece had made up his mind too. He wanted Davey sorting and by whatever means. He was fed up with all the ranting and plots and schemes and feared that if they didn't do something soon then he might actually succeed. He'd seen lesser men grow to acceptance, get legitimised, become unassailable. Those who played the game well enough graduated to white collar crime, promotion through the ranks, a commission. From there it was a small step to being straight. On the books. Dodgy past buried.

They were awkward at the front door of Rox's place in Lee Green. Both were thinking of their nemesis. Too much time had elapsed since their last embrace. In the end, she didn't invite him up, but they locked eyes for way longer than was necessary.

CHAPTER THIRTY

The Farrow residence was quite the party zone. Empty beer and spirit bottles and food packaging were scattered everywhere, ornaments shattered and cigarette butts doused in cups, ground into carpets or left to smoulder on expensive surfaces. A lawn-mower was crashed drunkenly into a tree, a burnt frozen pizza sat under the grill and there was a cue ball shaped hole in the window of the snooker room. Out of the CD collection, Steve Lamb had purloined the Best of Rod Stewart, Simple Minds and Simply Red, in accordance with his motto of only owning blonde or simple things.

Ian Farrow endured the destruction in awed silence, the sole explanation for the mess coming from Archie, who told him that Steve didn't respect his *own* property, let alone anyone else's.

When Archie popped home to Nunhead, he'd told Shirley he'd be away for a couple of days, promising to keep his mobile charged up and to call often – a wise move as the fallout from their marital ruck still hung about them like the smoke from burnt toast.

On his return, Archie placed Farrow in a chair in the dining room and Steve secured him there with gaffer. He liked the sound of tearing tape.

'Oh God, what now?' moaned Ian, who in the interim had been allowed out into the garden while Steve took pot-shots at him with an air rifle.

Archie bent to his metal toolbox and snapped open the shutters. Farrow shied away.

'Look, I've told you all I know. There's a new controller. Virgil Chinnery's hot on change management and he'll want to get a new team on board ASAP.'

Archie offered him a blank stare, then removed a long wooden stick with padding at the end.

'Wh-what's that?' stuttered Farrow.

'Maulstick,' announced Arch, bringing out a ready-sized canvas. He began laying out his brushes on the varnished mahogany table.

Farrow spluttered. 'Painting?'

'Yers.'

'Fancies himself as a bit of a Leonardo,' slurred Steve who was half cut.

'I don't believe this,' said Farrow. 'The Bader-Meinhof gang didn't capture Patty Hearst just so's they could press *flowers* together.'

Archie waved a brush at Steve. 'Don't you go belting him in the face any more, right? I want to get the flesh tones right.'

Steve emitted a cancerous chuckle. 'I'll cut you a bit off if you want.'

'Excuse me?' enquired Ian.

Archie plonked tins of Windsor & Newton Oil paint on the mahogany table.

'Can't we do this somewhere else? That table's awfully expensive.'

Archie shook his head. 'No can do chief. Light's good in here.'

'Can't you put some paper down at least? Or some dustsheets? I think we have some in the garage.'

'Steve. You wanna go get the dustsheets?'

'Do I bollocks.'

*

Over the remainder of that clammy weekend, Ian Farrow tried to remember the survival skills he'd learned on his journalist's training week with the SAS. Unfortunately, he couldn't see how drinking his own urine or roasting a squirrel in a small pit was going to help. In escape terms he held out little hope; his wife and children were incommunicado and the neighbours rarely came by. His one chance would be when Mrs Reynolds arrived first thing on Monday morning.

Steve reached the door as she put the key in the lock. Mrs Reynolds came three times a week. She was short and plump and in her black tracksuit she resembled an underdone Christmas pudding.

'Who're you?' she asked.

Steve came back with 'Who are you?'

'I do for Mrs Farrow.'

'Do what?'

'Clean.'

'She's not here.'

'I know that.' Mrs Reynolds' eyebrows tipped towards a bulbous nose. There was a trace of a Dublin accent. 'Who are you?'

'Friend.'

She took a step closer. 'And Mr Farrow's left you here?'

'No, he's here . . . Long weekend.'

She peered through the crack. 'Looks like a hell of a mess.'

'Hold up.'

This was too much like hard thinking for Steve, who shut the door in her face and ran off upstairs to get Archie.

'Get rid of her.' Archie moaned from the bed. He'd not touched fortified wines in a while and a second bottle of Port was gnawing away at his liver.

'She's got a key. I dunno what to tell her.'

'Where's Farrow?'

'Cellar.'

Releasing a sigh, Archie swung off the bed and planted his feet on the floor. There was a squeak as his heel hit a child's toy. Caging his face in his hands, he drew his fingers down over heavy stubble, took a deep breath, then snapped open his eyes and stumbled off to look for a dressing gown.

When he descended from the gallery, Mrs Reynolds was stood in the hall, hands on hips, tutting at the damage.

'Mrs Farrow will go spare,' she announced.

Archie broke out a grin. 'Mr Farrow's in the bath. He says you're not to bother today. Come back Wednesday, all right?'

She ignored him. 'What's that smell?'

Archie flared his nostrils, getting day-old curry, burnt paper and turpentine.

'It's oils. I'm doing his portrait – for Mrs Farrow when she comes back.'

She squinted up at him. Rather than crow's feet, it looked like a murder of them had trampled her lined face. 'She's coming back then?'

Arch moved towards her. 'Look love, it's not down to me. You have a word with the guvnor come wens'day, right?' He steered her toward the door.

Despite her protests, she found herself firmly manoeuvred outside. When they refused to answer the doorbell, she went round to the side of the house. Through the kitchen window, she spotted Arch and Steve engaged in an animated discussion. She tapped on the pane with a coin. Archie put on a hundred-watt grin and met her at the back door.

'What is it?' he asked, cheerily.

She spoke with a self-important air, as if she shared the ownership of the property with her employees. 'If there's to be any changes, I'll need to speak to Mr Farrow.'

That wasn't likely, since he was trussed to a mangy settee in the cellar.

Archie knew her type and saw this battle of wills continuing for hours. Part of him was willing to unleash Steve on her just so that he could hunt about for a cuppa and get a fry-up on the go. Instead, he stepped out, wincing as the gravel pierced his bare feet. He took her by the elbow, oblivious to her protestations. Steve joined in, hurrying her back to the front of the house.

Reece drew up in the Mondeo. Davey emerged from the back seat.

'What's going on?' he asked through gritted teeth.

'Staffing problems,' announced Steve — glad that they were mob handed now. He couldn't handle old women, which was why he'd left his mum to die in her stinking flat on the Peabody four years ago.

Davey took one look, leaned into her face and said, bluntly, 'Sod off.'

Without a word, Mrs Reynolds walked past the gates and disappeared off down the road. Archie and Steve did an about-turn and headed back to the house. Reece stepped out of the car and began following Davey inside.

'Where you going, Reece?'

'Mind if I come in for a cuppa?'

Davey nodded, and they all went in.

She reeled out the BBC mantra. 'Sorry, he's still in the meeting.' Marley had been trying to get Virgil for Ian Farrow all morning.

'What about Gordon?' asked Farrow.

'He's in there too.'

'Have you had a word with the other PA's?'

'No one knows anything yet.'

'What's the word on Scott?'

'Scotland.'

'Scott's got Scotland? Shit, that bad.'

'Call you at home as soon as I know anything.'

'Actually, er, I'll be on my mobile.'

'I thought you were taking sick leave?'

'I am. But there's a problem with the phones down here,' said Farrow, eyeing the scar above the skirting board where Steve had hacked out the phone point. He switched off his cellular and turned to Davey. 'They're all still in the meeting. Jeff, Scott, Virgil, Gordon, Controller of Personnel, the lot.'

'Christ,' said Davey, 'how long can they have a meeting for?'

'The record's two and a half months,' replied Farrow with a dab of facetiousness. 'Something to do with reporting lines between managers. That or relative salaries.'

That earned him a nasty glare. Reece, who was sipping tea in the doorway, suppressed a smile.

'Keep trying,' said Davey.

Farrow did, calling on the half-hour, but there was no change in the change management team. At 2 p.m. – although Marley had been told that lunch was being brought in – it transpired that the BBC executives had all left for a meal at Orsino's in Holland Park.

'We ought to go up there and sort it with them,' snarled Davey.

'Yes,' agreed Farrow, 'and bring your henchmen to close the deal.'

'That's not a bad idea, as it goes.'

'Christ, do you know nothing of how we operate?'

Davey bared his canines. 'Tell me.'

Ian Farrow had had plenty of time to consider Davey's knowledge gap when it came to broadcasting.

'Look, Virgil Chinnery's not going to start any kind of regime yet, but what concerns me is your project. Sure, we've agreed a costing for the series, but I'm beginning to wonder if you know how it's going to be broken down at all?'

He had their attention.

'As soon as your programme's accepted, you'll need a highly detailed budget, which we'll then go over with the Programme Finance Managers. Trust me Davey, they're going to negotiate *every* item right down to the bloody teabags. Once we agree on that, there's the cash flow schedule. You're not going to get a hundred and eighty thousand pounds all in one go, you know. It's spent over the production period. And it's paid into a trust account from which *only expenses* are paid to the programme. You, as producer, will have to account to the channel for all spending.'

Davey glared murderously at him.

'And if you underspend we'll claw that money back. Everything has to be invoiced.' Farrow held up a hand to prevent any interruption. 'And don't even think about skimping on production costs and expect to pocket the difference. That's been done and we're onto it. Sure, you're guaranteed your production fee but, as I'm sure you know, that fee — your profit — is not paid until the programme is delivered *to our satisfaction*. It's all in the contract, Mister Hayes.'

That was a new one on Reece, who'd amassed Kayman, Kimmelmann, King, and sundry others.

Davey made no move. His jet-black pupils flooded his irises.

Archie's face was blank. Steve lit up a cigarette.

Farrow, wilting after his outpour, fidgeted with the loose gaffer on the arms of the chair.

Davey's cliff face was a scarp of rock, his trademark twitch throbbing under the pale skin, the sunlight forming a hot line over the long curve of his nose and gracing his cruel lips. Slowly, languidly, he blinked. Then in a second, he shot out a fist and punched Farrow full in the face. Farrow keeled over and took the chair down with him as he fell.

Archie let out a disgruntled sigh. This would mean reworking the painting.

Davey booted Farrow where he lay, kicking him hard in the thigh, spine and in his soft belly.

Farrow howled in pain.

Davey jabbed a finger at the cowering executive. 'Bollocks. There's no way I'm throttling this gig now. Sod you and your poncy friends. I'll get my way.'

Farrow had his arms clamped over his head.

Davey, face flushed, teeth bared, arms pumping the air, span round to face Steve and Archie. 'For a start we'll see what's worth having from this place. You two look around. Bound to be a Peter somewhere. I want cash, bonds, stocks, all that. Dig out what you can.'

Reece, watching Davey bark fresh orders, realised that the plan had come adrift. More importantly, he knew the signs and that Davey was losing it. He'd tell Rox about that.

Arch and Steve were scurrying about looking for anything of easily redeemable value. They found little, even on ransacking Farrow's desk and busting open the safe. There were some Post Office Bonds — useless unless you lived in Teesside or Teddington from where they selected the winners: also, some share certificates and the deeds to the house. His wife's dresser produced jewellery, but nothing to incite palpitations in Hatton Garden. As they trundled back down, Archie offered to appraise the paintings. Davey told him not to bother.

'How comes you got this house then?' he asked Farrow, who was nursing a bloodied nose with his hanky.

'It's inherited. It's all I have.'

'But you work in telly.'

'Not that good an earner, plus I have two kids and a wife who's about to take me to the cleaners.'

'Come again?'

'We're on a trial separation. That's why she hasn't tried to contact me.'

Steve leered at him. 'Someone playing away then?'

Farrow did not dignify this with an answer. And nor would have Marley, who was headstrong and coltish and the first person to give him decent oral relief since he gave up using Listerine.

Davey said, 'So you won't be missed, then?'

'I was supposed to speak with the family solicitor this week and look into selling the place.' He looked around. 'Sophia will get this.'

'And you'll get the bedsit what stinks of gas and cabbage,' said Steve, who knew rather too much about such things, having been the catalyst that had sent many husbands to that unhygienic hell.

Davey, striding around the large dining table, threw up his hands. 'You're telling me there's nothing here? You must have something tucked away.'

'Nothing.'

'And your wife won't pay to have you back?'

'I'm afraid I'll be of little value as a hostage, if that's what you're implying?'

'Bollocks,' Davey said.

CHAPTER THIRTY-ONE

Rox gave it some thought at home over a glass of wine. The windows were open and a cool breeze tickled the soles of her feet as she lay on the sofa clutching a cushion and watching the sky shade through the blues to indigo. Davey wants to become a documentary maker, but he's in trouble. Sure, it's a scam to leech money from the broadcasters, but was there more to it? He'd been mercurial these past months, faster than a lizard's tongue. Always one step ahead of the game. He's vain, arrogant and exhibits major sociopathic tendencies. What had Reece told her about the point of weakness? Find out what he values, if anything.

It came to her in a flash. Get *inside* his megalomania. Understand what he wants . . . it's not the money – that's his way in. It's what the money does for him. It's power and respect. And to impress whom? Maybe that didn't matter, but she knew now that the grinning shark was in the frame for fame. Fame or notoriety, he'd make no moral distinction. He wanted this badly, badly enough to kidnap a major executive. Rox smiled to herself as a plan began to form. She thought of the old Chinese proverb that said if you stood by a river long enough, you'd see your enemy float past.

Davey would be on a jet ski.

The next day, back at work, she started to quiz her regulars about their careers, remaining oblique as to her reasons, gathering information, squirrelling it away. The Soho location was perfect. She spoke with independent producers, techie's and cameramen. Exhaustingly, each of them appeared to be the master of their trade and the fount of all knowledge on the labyrinthine structures of broadcasting. There were sackfuls of axes to grind with directors coming off particularly badly; although high in the running were actors (ovine fantasists, perversely proud of their neuroses), contracts departments (wilfully pedantic bastards) and repeatedly, 'bean-counters' (she saw cackling Mexicans in a coffee warehouse). She wondered how an entire industry could operate on shifting blame and without any form of coherent management structure. Then she remembered about RailTrack.

She was also quite delighted by Reece's actions on Sunday, and spun the encounter in her mind, examining the moment, testing it, smelling it, owning it. Late, in the sticky heat of the evening, she lay on her bed, desiring him more than ever.

Since the spring, she felt they had grown closer – and not in a 'you're-like-a-brother-to-me-oh-ugly-man' way either. In their moments together, she'd made him open out. He'd confided in her, admitting he had only been abroad twice, once to Spain (liked it), once to France (didn't – and thought Britain should invade them for the hell of it). He told her he hated long fingernails on women as it lacked imagination, and that he disliked any vegetable that resembled a brain.

She in turn revealed she'd had nine sexual partners (the true number), that she'd once been caught paring the dead skin from her heels with a potato peeler and that it set her teeth on edge if she rubbed rough carpet or velvet against the weave. He looked at her weirdly after *that* one.

Reece had asked her what she thought of Londoners, now she was one. She pouted and said she wasn't. For a start, she said, she never measured distance in terms of aggravation: Bloody roadworks – forty-five minutes it was. Bloody train – an hour, an *hour*! How much more sparkling the evenings would be without this obligatory aria of complaint. Also, she told him that she thought the geographical turf wars were pointless, as it was a truly cosmopolitan city whose boundaries were defined by trade not class or location. And 'Londoners' could include anyone and everyone because it was a state of mind, and a particularly parochial one at that. Finally, that it seemed some London tribes liked to reinvent themselves often, like snakes shedding skins. And that a lot of them were up their own arses – but that was true of anyone in fashion.

'About the travel thing' . . . began Reece.

She'd silenced him by putting her fingers on his lips.

It was night in Steve's flat in Corbett's Wharf in Bermondsey and Ian Farrow was cowering on the leather sofa. Steve and Archie stood and suckled their bottles of Beck's like contented infants.

'Where we gonna tie him up for the night, then?'

'If you had some more furniture, we'd have a choice.'

Steve released an ornate burp. 'We're doing this Davey one hu*mung*ous favour.'

Farrow had been brought to South East London with his eyes taped over and when the gaffer was removed it tore off most of his eyebrows. If the pair had hoped to keep their location a secret, they had failed, as Farrow knew the Pool of London and could make out Tower Bridge through the thin curtains. Nevertheless, he adopted the strategy of not provoking them, although he was tempted to comment on the rancid stench, which was similar to a Parisian sewer after Bastille Day. Luckily, Archie noticed it as well.

'What *is* that stink?'

Steve sniffed the air, then went over to the kitchen bin. Recoiling, he grasped the overstuffed receptacle, pushed open the window and dumped it straight in the river. 'Summink's dead,' he muttered by way of explanation.

Archie said, 'Anyways, what we doing with him? I'm off home in a mo, so you're babysitting.'

Farrow felt his heart sink.

'We ain't taping him to the couch. My pride and joy that is.'

'What then?'

'I dunno.' There was irritation in Steve's tone as he fired up a JPS. 'Plus, Davey's not paid up.'

Archie scratched his chin. 'Yers. Well, he comes recommended.'

'Arch, if I don't see some folding tomorrow, I'm letting this tosspot go.'

Ian Farrow felt hope bob to the surface.

'No, you ain't.'

It sank once more.

Archie thrust his beer out at Steve. 'By the way, since we're talking about financial remuneration, you ought to know I still ain't forgotten about that Rembrandt.'

'Gallery never come back to me on the note.'

'What d'you expect them to do? Drop eight mill in the post?'

'No,' mumbled Steve, running a hand through his hair.

'What then?'

'They had the scraps off of the painting. Should've paid up.'

Archie drained his beer. 'Stick to twocking, mate. This is beyond you.'

Steve's face reddened and his greasy complexion took on the hue of raw meat. 'Leave it out. We're doing all right at this kidnapping lark.'

As they argued on, Farrow prayed that Mrs Reynolds would find the rescue message he had left for her. He had used the colourful plastic magnetic letters on his fridge at home to spell out the words: 'Help. Kidnapped. Call police.' Unfortunately, on her arrival, she was appalled at the mess and had decided on first making herself a cup of tea. After putting the milk back, she slammed the fridge door so ferociously that the letters clattered to the floor, leaving the phrase: 'pid nap all lice'. She read it twice, moving her lips as she did so. Then, deciding that it was the result of horseplay, she gathered up the fallen letters and re-alphabetised them.

Farrow, unaware of this, tuned back in to his captors' debate.

Steve said, 'I mean, least I'm trying to *do* something here, which is a lot better than your stupid painting. It's got no point, that.'

'Come again?'

'You heard.'

Archie's beer sailed past Steve's head and shattered against the wall. Farrow threw his arms over his head. Steve flew at his mate and they both went down. They fought pub style, giving it their all for twenty seconds of kicking, flailing, gouging and tugging uselessly at one another's clothes. In that time, Farrow inched along the sofa, cursing the squeaks emitting from the leather. He was halfway to the door when Steve floored him with a back-handed fist.

Archie called out, 'Don't damage the goods.'

Steve grabbed Farrow by the collar. 'What's he to you?'

'Five hundred a day plus exes, you twat.'

'Yeah, but we aren't getting paid, are we?'

Archie swung his foot into the back of Steve's knee. He concertina'd, then righted himself and threw Farrow against the wall.

'Pack it in, Stevie.'

'Why?'

'He's . . .' He struggled for something reasonable to say. 'He's . . . BBC.'

'Never watch it.' He thrust his face into Ian's. 'And I ain't got a licence.'

Archie grabbed Steve's other arm and thrust it up his back, releasing a sharp cry as the taller man dropped Farrow to the floor.

'He's valuable is what I mean.'

Steve gritted his teeth. 'How? Got the SP on that Sue Lawley story, has he?' Archie forced his arm higher.

'Arch?'

'Yeah?'

'You've gone soft in the head.'

Steve ducked down low, swung around and laid into Archie Peacock with all his might. He gave him solid lefts and rights, floored him and continued to kick until Archie was coughing up liquid on the floor. He booted him aside, pulled Farrow to his feet and, pausing only to grab the gaffer tape, threw open the lounge window and tossed him out onto the balcony. It was a twenty-foot drop to the choppy waters of the Thames. Farrow yelped but he was soon silenced, the only sounds coming from the water below and the harsh ripping of heavy-duty tape. When Steve came back in, he was calm and composed and had another fag on the go. He blew a big plume of smoke.

'There. Sorted.'

Archie lay on the floor, getting his colour back and testing his body for broken bones. He glared up at Steve, who stepped aside and lifted the curtain in a dainty manner. Farrow was cocooned in silver and lashed to the balcony railings. Archie said nothing, but climbed to his feet and left the apartment. Lamb, freed of his encumbrances for the night, popped into the bedroom for a swift hand shandy, then went off to the local for a jar or three.

Thursday was another blazing hot day. The sight of girls' legs bent back the van drivers' necks, shades were clamped on faces, shirts bright, steel and chrome shone, the streets bleached to ochre and khaki. Ian Farrow hung limply on the balcony with a seagull perched on his head.

Beneath him the river sparkled as another pleasure-boat

trowelled past heading for Westminster. He'd been awake since dawn, too weak to move and unable to cry out.

Steve slept in. He had been unable to locate his homeless girlfriend in the streets of Bermondsey or Deptford and had instead drowned his frustrations in beer, vodka and puff.

Davey Kayman left Charlie sleeping. She'd gone quiet on him of late and had taken to spending a lot of time with her other mates and girlfriends. He wasn't bothered about sex, as he'd upped his coke intake to three/four grams a day to help him think – and to get through this bother with the Beeb.

The two of them had taken a room off a friend of Simon Latimer's in Harlesden – a bit too near the Scrubs for his liking. Still, it was only temporary. He thought of the palace he'd be able to afford once the dosh came though. Might even get somewhere out in Essex. Time to start hassling those weasel estate agents.

Davey hoovered up a line and tapped his credit card forcefully on the mirror. Right, things to do. First, have Reece take him to get a paper, then deliver him to the new kidnap location in Bermondsey Wall East. Good idea that – to move the victim; he'd read it in some book about the Shiite fundamentalists.

On arrival, Steve's place looked a lot like Beirut, but without the cheery atmosphere. Reece, who was waved away at the door, was quietly surprised at the location. He'd known Steve lived in Bermondsey – but right here on the river? He'd tell Rox as soon as possible.

'All white mate?' muttered a befuddled Steve Lamb.

'Where is he?'

'Outside. Want me to fetch him?'

'What do you think?' scowled Davey.

Steve slid open the lounge doors to reveal Farrow in his silver carapace.

'What's this — *Alien II?*'

'Couldn't think of where to put him.'

'Cut him loose.'

Steve performed the operation with the skill of a Bolivian surgeon. Farrow, undernourished and unsteady on his feet, tried to rub life back into his limbs and keeled over on the couch. Davey tossed the new edition of *Broadcast* at him.

'Read that!'

'I haven't got my glasses,' he croaked.

Davey plucked them from the pocket of Farrow's shirt. 'Here.' He swivelled his gaze at Steve. 'You — go get us some coffees.'

Too hungover to argue, Steve stumbled off out. Farrow began to study the glossy industry tabloid. The front page concerned the appointment of Virgil Chinnery as Controller of BBC1 and outlined his strategy for the station. There were glowing reports concerning his achievements and his suitability for the post. The Head of Broadcast and the Governors were solidly behind the decision and all mention of his predecessor had been omitted in a Stalinist purge.

Farrow said, 'Okay, yeah, we know this.'

'Try page five. Sidebar,' snapped Davey.

He had never had so much bother as in the last two days getting Farrow to try reaching Chinnery. The earliest his PA thought Ian might be able to see him was after the Edinburgh TV Festival. The meetings had blossomed as virulently as cold, or flu, or the Ebola virus. His diary had no windows, no slots or chinks or cracks or any other method of entry. You could not burgle this calendar, sneak your way in and have it away with September. Virgil Chinnery was impregnable, the man with the Fortress Diary. Had Farrow known his home address, Davey would have had him kidnapped as well. Take the lot of them. They'd give him a bastard meeting then.

Also, each time Ian spoke with Marley, her tone became more concerned. Was he all right? He sounded ill. Could she see him? No, she absolutely *had* to see him. Anyway, Sophia was gone so there was absolutely no reason why he shouldn't let her come round – unless he had *someone else* there. Farrow waved the cellular helplessly at his captors: male exasperation leaping between them like sparks off a Van de Graf generator. Davey nixed her coming down and decided on the Bermondsey move to curtail such nosiness.

Farrow cracked through the pages of *Broadcast*.

'Congratulations,' said Davey, flatly.

A paragraph under 'Shorts' informed Ian Farrow that he was to become the new Acting Head of Special Projects (Factual). He groaned.

'What's the problem?'

'They're shunting me aside. It's a placebo job, a moron's post. Like working in marketing.'

Davey tossed his mobile at Farrow. 'Phone.'

'Marley, hi. I read the news in *Broadcast*.'

'Oh, did nobody tell you?'

Farrow took a long breath. Another BBC mantra, this being one they should carve above the portico of Broadcasting House in place of all that educate, inform and entertain crap.

'No. What's going on?'

'Not a lot. They're all away.'

'Who is?'

'Jeff and Scott took off for Tuscany this morning. Head of Broadcast's off from tomorrow, it's like a ghost town here actually.'

Farrow put his hand over the receiver. 'They've gone on holiday.'

'WHAT?'

'What about Chinnery?' he asked of Marley.

'He's taking time off to prepare his speech for Edinburgh.'

'You could've told me this.'

'I didn't know till I came in today.'

'Marley, it's your bloody *job* to know.'

There was hurt in her voice. 'Ian, you won't let me see you — what am I supposed to do? There's even a rumour that the reason you're not in is you're going for the Channel Four post.'

'What Channel Four post?'

Embarrassment fringed her tone. 'Ohm umm, Factual commissioning? Head of Dept's gone for it. They're boarding tomorrow.'

Farrow ground his teeth. 'Jesus.'

Steve entered the flat with a cardboard tray on which were three polystyrene cups of coffee and one full of sugar that looked like something out of a gritting lorry.

Davey whisked the mobile from Farrow's hands and killed it.

Farrow cradled his drink. 'Like I told you, I've been left behind in the reshuffle. This lot makes Caligula look generous.'

Steve asked, 'Caligula?'

'Roman Emperor. Tortured and murdered his relatives, elected a horse as consul, declared himself a god.'

'Pukka.'

'Don't get ideas,' snorted Ian.

Davey rose and went to stare at the river. There was silence save for coffee slurping. The buzzer went and Steve admitted Archie. He'd shaved and wore a clean T-shirt, which almost girdled his flabby stomach. It had Rembrandt's face on it. He had several fresh bruises from his encounter with Steve. He strode over to Davey and poked a chubby finger in his back.

'Oy, I've had a word about you. The Petersons say they're none too happy about you using their names as references. Plus, you owe them big-time.'

Davey made his face like a cliff. 'What's it to you? You'll get paid.'

Steve added, 'We've only seen a monkey since Sunday.'

'I'll sort this,' snapped Arch.

Davey looked from one to the other. 'You want cash? I'll go over the Cab office and clean out what's not gone down the bank. Be about a kilo and a half each.'

'Sounds about right,' said Steve.

'Then you can piss off.'

Archie, sensing there was more, cocked his head to one side. 'Or?'

Davey's facial muscle twitched. 'Or you let me run with this for a couple of days and I'll double your wedge.'

'Take the money,' said Farrow, not unexpectedly.

They glared at him.

'I'll take it,' Steve said.

'How much if we stick around?' asked Archie.

Davey said, 'You both get five grand apiece. Easy money.'

Although he was a good foot shorter than Davey, Arch still managed to thrust his bullet head right up close to his face. 'You're in deep shit if this don't come off.'

Davey cast him a supercilious smile, then crouched in front of Farrow. He spoke carefully, weighing his words.

'Right. You ain't any good to us, silly bollocks, but what do we know about this new controller?'

'Chinnery?'

'Yeah. What you got on him?'

'You're asking me how you can blackmail him?'

'Spot on.'

'Bit extreme, isn't it? Just for a commission?'

Davey shrugged. 'Is he a woofter?'

'If you mean homosexual, then yes, as a matter of fact he—'

'Backs against the wall,' blurted out Steve. 'Sausage jockey alert.'

'I'll call this prick myself,' Davey announced. 'Give me his PA's number.'

Farrow reeled it out and Davey pressed buttons. He did a fair imitation of a harried middle class, middle-aged man.

'Hello, Natascha? David here. I'm on my way over to Virgil's but I've lost his number. Could you? Thanks.'

He rolled his tongue under his lower lip and pulled a face, directing it at Farrow. He punched more buttons. 'Virgil Chinnery?' A crocodile grin spread across his face. 'You don't know me, but I know a lot about you.'

'Do you?' The voice was flat with disinterest.

'I know all about what you get up to. Nonce.'

'That's nice. Frank – that's Frank, isn't it?'

'Who's Frank?' Davey asked. 'One of your under-age chickens?'

'This is a stunt.'

'Far from it, mate. You're a right Michael so I've heard. Now—'

Chinnery cut in. 'What's a Michael?'

'George, Barrymore, Jackson.'

'This is a joke. If you call again, I'll have the number traced.' And with that he hung up.

'Sod!' said Davey, tossing the mobile aside.

'Thing is,' deadpanned Ian, 'in our business, you'd stand a better chance of blackmailing him if he were *hetero*sexual.' He slapped his palms on his knees and struggled to his feet. 'Right, you won't be needing me any more, so . . .'

Steve pushed him back down. Davey Kayman remined still, his eyes black and cold. Dust danced in the sunbeams and smoke fragmented lazily off Steve's latest JPS. He sneered at Davey, 'Looks like you're buggered, son.'

Davey was about to reply to this when the buzzer went. Without thinking, Steve released it. Seconds later there was a knock at the door. He opened up and Rox Matheson walked straight in.

'Aya,' she said. 'Remember me?'

CHAPTER THIRTY-TWO

Two of the men recognised her and two of them didn't. Rox was carrying a black canvas bag and wearing grey trousers and a jacket over a pink T-shirt.

Steve Lamb gave her a slow, appreciative once over. 'All white, darlin'?' he purred, then, out of the side of his mouth, 'I'd use her shit for toothpaste.'

Archie glowered at him, turned to Rox. 'Hello love.'

'What do you want, slag?' scowled Davey.

'Well-mannered to a fault. That's our Mister Kimmelmann.'

A vein thudded in Davey's temple at hearing his birth name spoken with such confidence. One of the things Reece had done of late was to visit Sam King in Buckhurst Hill and get some background on his son.

Davey said, 'Who?'

'Though it's not that now. It was King, like your dad, then several others for all your "business" projects. Kayman's the one you prefer. Private joke, is it? Making your name like "Cayman" as in "Islands", as in offshore banking?'

Farrow stared at Rox.

'She's gotta be filth,' grumbled Steve.

'Model,' said Arch.

Steve flattened his paunch. 'Bet she takes it up the C & A.'

Rox ignored him. 'The thing is, Davey, we've been watching you for a very long time, me and the team.'

'She *is* Old Bill,' bellowed Davey. 'I knew it.' He strode towards her but Archie blocked him and forced his arms down by his sides.

Rox stood her ground. 'You don't want to do anything you might regret. This is all on film.'

Davey lasered his gaze around the room. It fell on Farrow, still crouched on the sofa. 'You wired up?'

'Not him,' Rox said.

He stared at Archie. 'You come in last. Grass.'

Archie slapped him. 'Don't play silly buggers.'

Davey put a hand to his smarting cheek. 'Him then. That wanker.'

Steve tried, but the last time he had summoned a convincing innocent expression was when he was four.

'Steve,' warned Arch. 'You ain't . . .?'

'It's the bird.' Stepping forward, Steve tore the bag from Rox's shoulder, tipping out a digital handicam, which fell to the floor.

'That's you bollocksed then,' said Davey.

Rox raised a hand and extended her middle finger at him, then, revolving the digit, she pointed out of the window. 'You don't think I'd be stupid enough to come in here without backup, do you? There's a DV camera positioned right over there.'

Across the hundred-metre stretch of the Pool of London was the dirty sugar cube of the police boatyard building, St John's Wharf and then, in one of the windows in Orient Wharf, a cameraman waving his acknowledgement of her signal. The apartment was one of a series of eighty flats built by a housing association for the local residents.

Of which Reece was one.

On dropping Davey off Reece had realised that he and Steve were neighbours, separated only by the Thames. That afternoon, in great excitement, he had taken Rox to his home, led her to the window and pointed out Cherry Gardens Pier, Chambers' Cold Store and Steve's place in Corbett's Wharf.

'Brilliant,' she said, adding. 'So, finally I get to see the Inner Sanctum.'

'Is it what you expected?'

'Yeah, what a dump,' she grinned. It was the opposite, obsessively tidy and well furnished. There was a cream sofa with a throw, Russian carpets on bare, polished wood and a low coffee table. An urn sprouted tall dried pampas grasses. A bowl was filled with smooth pebbles: a beech sideboard graced one magnolia wall, on it the chrome midi unit seemed out of place with the natural fabrics and colours.

'It's dead tasteful,' she added. 'Do all this yourself?'

'Kind of.'

Rox stood close, too close, this being her latest plan to get inside his pants. She'd noticed there were no framed photographs, nothing that made it his, as if he'd wiped every bit of personality from the place. Surely he'd not done that on her behalf?

'It's simple. This was the original show-flat when they built the apartments. When I moved in, I paid extra for the furniture and fittings. Cuppa?'

She nodded and he went off to the galley kitchen. Much as she'd like to think it was ingenious of him to buy up the show home, it simply added to the sense that he was this nowhere man, one who left no imprint on the world. And to live in a showroom? Weird. But then he'd never laid claims on being original. And what did her idea of flair come down to anyway? Wacky wall colours and scarves draped over lampshades. Hardly the Design Council was it?

When he came back with the teas, she was squinting through the window at the shimmering Thames.

'You reckon they've got that bloke in there?'

'Certain of it.'

He handed her a cup. 'What we going to do about Davey, then?'

She took a sip. 'Okay, here it is.'

'He's got a zoom lens over there,' said Rox. 'I've seen the footage and it's brilliant. Great sound as well.' She folded back the lapel of her jacket to reveal the Mic. Steve immediately tore it off her, then spun her round and pulled the transmitter from her back pocket. His other hand gripped her arse. She forced it away. Steve carried the transmitter to the balcony, tossed it in the river and drew the curtains. The room was suffused in orange light.

'I thought one of you might do that,' she said, drily. 'Which is why I have my sound recordist using the directional parabolic Mic as backup. He's over there and all.'

'Sound recordist?' asked Davey, the frequency of his jaw-twitches coming closer together.

She focused on him, making up in intensity for what she lacked in size. 'It's ironic, Davey, because while you've been cobbling together the biggest load of bollocks that telly's never going to see, I've had the commission all along, and it's going to be prime-time viewing.'

Davey pursed his lips – rather prissily, she thought.

'Because I've been making a documentary about *you* and your kind for months. The expensive wine scam, the thefts of computer equipment from hospitals, selling them on to primary schools. I've been watching – and taping you for a very long time. Why did you think I kept showing up? And how did you think you got away with it that night when you nearly *raped* me? Eh?'

The room cooled at her shouting the word. The air became charged, volatile, as if the syrupy summer heat were about to resign itself to thunder and rain.

'Yeah, forgotten about that, hadn't you? But then, I'm nothing to you, aren't I? Hey – well *that's* about to change.'

Davey was genuinely taken aback. 'Do what?'

She grew more effusive. 'I mean, you should have twigged it when I came for you after the acting class rip-off back up in Manchester. I was naïve enough back then, weren't I?'

He looked blank. For him this was several skins ago.

'Remember? Michael Caine?'

'You're a big man, but you're out of shape,' joked Steve, more Daffy Duck than Michael Caine.

Rox said, 'Ever heard of Chorlton Films, Davey?'

He hadn't.

'He has though, hasn't he?'

Farrow, shocked and amazed at the turn of events, knew enough to agree with her. At this point, he'd have said anything to get away. 'Sure, they're an independent programme supplier.'

'You *know* her?'fumed Davey.

'Not personally, no. But I know their work.' He gave Rox a slender smile. 'You never tried to put this idea through us, then?'

'Bit difficult in the circumstances,' replied Rox. 'Since the BBC was about to commission *him*. By the way, Ian, we'll do our best to keep your involvement in this out of the papers.'

He nodded grimly.

'And I believe the Head of Granada's going to have a word with Virgil.' She had picked up the name Virgil from Reece, who had heard it enough times as Davey ranted on in his cab.

Farrow said, 'So this is for Granada then, is it?'

'That's right.'

Davey barked at her. 'All right. Enough of the shop-talk. What's your angle?'

Rox formed a pleasant smile. 'Right now, nothing. I'm here to tell you that we're all done and the police are outside.' She lowered her voice a notch. 'Don't you reckon kidnapping a BBC executive was a bit much? Christ, what were you hoping for? A date with Philippa Forester?'

For once, he was dumbfounded.

'They're expendable, Davey, executives.'

'Too true,' said Farrow, who had decided that if he ever got out of this alive then he'd go into consultancy work, where he could tell other people they were shit and get paid for it.

Rox announced, 'Ta-ra, Davey Kimmelmann. Thanks.'

'Get her,' he said.

Archie hesitated, but Steve moved in on Rox, paying unnecessary attention to her breasts as he clasped her from behind.

'Leave it, Steve,' growled Archie. 'If the filth are on their way, this only makes it worse.'

Davey showed his teeth. 'Only got her word for that.'

Steve held fast. She was repulsed by his odour of stale sweat, semen and fags.

'They're outside,' she said, struggling. 'If you look in my bag, you'll see there's a mobile. We arranged that if I don't call in five minutes then they bust in. Either way you lose.'

They held their positions.

'You've got about two minutes left.'

Archie and Steve were both thinking of their escape, considering a leap off the balcony and a swim to the nearest barge, provided that the pollution didn't kill them first.

Ian Farrow looked from one captor to the next.

Archie faced Davey, pulled back his fist. 'You ain't paid us neither.'

'Wait,' barked Davey. 'If she'd told the filth, they'd be all over us by now. None of this five minutes bollocks.'

Rox said, 'One minute.'

Archie gripped Davey by the neck. 'Why should we believe you, Toe-rag? You lied to us *and* the Petersons.'

Davey gurgled, colour draining from his face.

Steve paused in his attempt to force a scaly hand down the front of Rox's trousers. 'Arch?'

'Yers?'

'Thought you said she was a model?'

Archie said, 'That's true. Why'd you pose for me, then?'

'You're connected to Finsbury Cabs and the Petersons. You were research.'

'Like to research her,' chimed in Steve. No one found that amusing, so he twisted Rox's arm until she yelped in pain.

'If you know the Petersons,' demanded Archie, what are their first names?'

'Terry and Bill.'

Again, she had got this off Reece.

'Let her go, Steve.'

Steve did so, then began surreptitiously smelling his fingers.

She reached for her mobile and bag. 'See you all downstairs then.' Rox tucked away the cellular and the video camera and went for the door, opening it halfway before Steve kicked it shut.

'Wait. If we hold onto her, we can get to the motor.'

Archie rolled his eyes. 'Yeah, that works with the Bermondsey cozzers, who'd *never* beat the crap out of us.' Archie dropped Davey, fought with the curtains, drew apart the lounge windows and began clambering out onto the balcony. Wrinkled water slapped the brickwork below.

'Get back in here,' boomed Davey, regaining his voice. He tapped his watch and bared his teeth at Rox. 'Right, they aren't coming, so what's the problem?'

'No problem.'

'Something's gone wrong, otherwise you'd be gone. No, scratch that. You wouldn't have even come here in the first place.'

Her shoulders slumped as she flopped down next to Farrow.

'All right, there is a problem. We've got the footage and it's brilliant, even the hand-held and night vision stuff. Some of the sound's a bit duff in places but we'll smooth that over by using v/o. We've got interviews with the schools you did over, and with Simon Latimer – who's out on bail in case you'd like to know.'

Davey Kayman registered no emotion.

'We won the commission back in late February, about the time you and I were going to do that supposed drug deal? Well we're due to deliver at the end of next month. Got most of it synched and edited. The transmission date's late autumn.'

'And?'

She turned to Ian Farrow. 'Only the boss sold the company three months ago and it's all gone to pot. Turns out there was nothing left in the kitty. We've been running a ghost ship since then.'

'Haven't you got other work?' asked Farrow, quietly. She shook her head.

Davey said, 'Hold up. If you got this commission then you're flush. You've got all the dosh from the broadcaster.'

'If I might jog your memory,' began Farrow. 'The trust account is apportioned as and when. Also, it's illegal to use the funds for anything other than the programme. Perhaps the finance managers queried the costings or there's been an underspend?'

'What's he on about?' asked Steve, who had been lost for ages.

'Both,' said Rox. 'Basically, we can't afford to finish the programme. The editing facility wants paying and they've got all the tapes. I'm not letting this go. It's my project and I'm not going to be held to ransom.'

'What kind of shysters are you lot?' keened Davey.

'Same as you, but better educated?' offered Farrow.

Everyone wondered who would hit him first.

Davey sneered, 'You must have access to funding?'

'We're a small company. I'm told the banks have been tried, and private investors, but I reckon the Directors are going to declare insolvency, which will mean the end of it.'

Farrow opened his mouth to speak, but closed it again.

Davey asked, 'Why're you here then?'

She looked at him fiercely. ' 'Cos I want to finish this programme.'

'And?'

'And I need someone to tide over the costs.'

'You mean *me*?'

She looked at Steve. 'No, him. Whuhh.'

Davey laughed. It was a long scattergun report that died as instantly as it'd started. Steve tried to join in, but he'd never mastered a henchman's chuckle and was soon wheezing and coughing. Archie watched in silence.

'That is priceless,' said Davey.

'You'll get something in return.'

'Obviously.'

'Your Get-out-of-jail-free card. You know it's my choice as to whether I hand over the evidence to the police or not. Now, you help me out and I'll give you the nearest thing to immunity, which is time. You release Farrow and pay what I ask and we'll let the Fraud Squad fight us in court for it. Gives you plenty of time to set up your defence or flee the country or commit Hari-Kari or whatever.'

'And what else?'

'You get to be the star,' she said, bluntly. 'I'll interview you in blackout. You can defend your actions. It'll make for a cracking show. I mean, what's the point in being a criminal — you might as well be a master criminal?'

Davey thought about it. There was the chug and wash of a pleasure cruiser as it mowed past. Steve lit another cigarette from his last. The curtains billowed and sunlight played about the room, making golden ropes on the ceiling. Davey's face, pale, obsidian-eyed, was a mask. The tense movements of his jaw had calmed, a motor idling. He seemed poised, in control.

'How much?' he asked, finally.

'Twenty-five thousand.'

Steve took care of the whistling.

'Cash,' Rox said.

'Yeah, right.'

'Like I'd accept a cheque off you? I'd need a banker's draft at the very least.'

'I ain't got twenty-five grand,' he spat.

'Haven't you?'

Davey reddened. First time Rox had seen that. Archie and Steve looked none too happy about it.

'Nah – this is all bollocks,' said Davey Kayman.

Rox, skating on thin ice from the moment she had walked in, prayed she was going to get away with it. Apart from the gen Reece had given her, what she'd said so far she had gleaned from her contacts at the restaurant. The learning curve had been a steep one and she'd thought her brain was going to snap with information overload. Davey had overstepped the mark, she was sure of that, but how much control had he lost? Could she use his paranoia against him? Would he tumble that she was connected to Reece? Would Archie blow the whistle on it? She had pondered that problem with Reece, who told her that the Petersons were Arch's bosses and he'd not dare cross them. The logic was in place – pay me and you get a break – and she looked the business with the borrowed equipment. Now it was time for the big one. The proof.

'Is it?' she asked sweetly.

He scowled. 'Yeah, it's all flannel.'

She bent to her bag, removed several sheets of rolled-up fax paper and handed them over to Davey. He leafed through them.

'This is a copy of the main schedule of the contract with Granada. It states the nature of Chorlton Films commission with them and some of the details. More than that, I can't give you.'

Davey scanned the pages.

Rox observed him calmly. Inside, she was a maelstrom. She had, last night, made a long, begging phone call to Ally's new flatmate, a researcher at Granada TV. Once she'd convinced her, Dawn had stolen the blank contract; completed it to her specifications and faxed it down. It was Rox's ace card.

His eyes ran down the pages. He fanned them out and passed them to Farrow, who glanced at them and immediately spoke up.

'That is absolutely a genuine contract. We'd have screwed you on the number of repeats though.'

Davey seemed to fold.

Rox scoped Archie and Steve's faces. They looked weary and grey, as if anticipating their prison pallor. She held out her mobile to Davey.

'You want to call Charlie and discuss it?'

'Nah.'

'You'd best make your decision as my crew's getting tetchy over there. Twenty-five grand and I'll keep it all from the Fraud Squad.'

Davey Kayman gave an almost imperceptible nod, his facial muscles slackening as resignation took the helm.

Rox paced to the window and signalled across the river. She felt a small glow inside, but she wasn't there yet – not by a long way.

'When do you need it?' he asked.

She spun round and said brightly, 'How about tomorrow?'

'Yeah and how about never? Never would be good.'

'Tomorrow. Used notes, in small denominations. That's how you work.'

'See what I can do.'

'I'll tell the editing facility right away, so they'll release the footage.'

Davey went off to the bathroom. Inside, he stood sniffing hard and staring at the cracked paint on the ceiling. Shit, he thought, he'd had the feeling of late that he was being watched and had put it down to the coke, that or the Met. But this proved it. Yeah, all those times when he'd had this niggling sense in his peripheral vision that there was *someone* there. People talking about him. Sidling away as he barged past. He almost laughed. It wasn't paranoid if you really were being watched, filmed, made the star of your own movie. He felt warm, then cold again. Consequences. He snorted the last of the gram and tossed the wrap in the bowl. Flushed it.

Right then.

Davey strode back into the living room and paced around her, his tone becoming more obtrusive and demanding as his confidence returned.

'Nah, nah, come on now, silly bollocks. Tit for tat. If we're gonna do this, then you gotta give me value for money. First off, I wanna see what you've got so's I know where I stand with the law. I want to see this programme of yours.'

Rox was ready. 'No problem. If you get the money together by lunchtime, I'll book a slot in the screening room. We'll run what we have for you tomorrow afternoon.'

'Second, I can't do twenty-five K. Ten at the most.'

'No deal. You and your junkie slut girlfriend might be trying to snort the entire national product of Bolivia, but I know you've got plenty salted away. You could try your Dad if you want,' she added, smiling.

Davey's cheek fluttered wildly.

'Plus, of course, you never pay *anyone*, Davey, we all know that.'

Steve glared murderously at his current employer.

'Twenty-five K or I go straight back to the police,' she said.

Davey raised a hand in acceptance, looked away out the window. Was that camera still filming him? He stepped away out of sight.

'You'll need another ten big ones now,' threatened Archie.

'Do what?'

'We want paying and all.'

Rox beckoned to Farrow. 'Come on. Let's go.'

'He stays here until we're done,' growled Davey.

Rox thought about it. 'Okay — but we're going to carry on shooting. Keep him in view of the window at all times. Move him and I blow the whistle.'

'Oh God,' sighed Farrow. 'Another day with the Neanderthals.'

'Less of that,' said Arch, hoofing him in the shin.

Steve, struggling to keep up, asked, 'What happens to us?'

Rox said, 'I think you've confused me with someone who gives a shit.'

CHAPTER THIRTY-THREE

Rox sat cross-legged on Reece's sofa with a large glass of wine. Since leaving Bermondsey, she'd spent the day making numerous calls and visits, one of importance to Salvatori's where she rearranged her shifts to free up her time. After a sweltering, fraught day, the shadows were lengthening and Rox had stopped trembling at last. She took a deep swig, murmuring appreciatively as the Chardonnay cooled her throat. Reece had wanted to go to his local, the Town of Ramsgate on the corner, but she'd persuaded him to get in some food and two bottles of wine at the Wapping Safeway's.

'Still there?' she asked.

Reece kept his eye on the telescope. 'Don't know what you told them, but they're being good as gold.'

'For starters, they think you're spying on them with a camera, not standing there with a telescope.'

Across the water, Farrow sat rigid on a stool as Archie sketched him. Steve was slumped along the length of his couch in a beer-stained T-shirt and sweatpants. He kicked Archie in the calf with one of his ugly bare feet.

'What's the point of doing that now?'

'Practice.'

'We're bollocksed, you know that.' There were empty beer cans all around him.

'Davey is,' said Arch, rubbing out Farrow's mouth for the umpteenth time.

'And me – it's my gaff. Hassle enough we've got the case coming up, but with this . . .'

'She's only after his money.'

'You're telling me she won't call in the Old Bill as soon as she gets it?'

He used a stick of charcoal to carve Farrow's lip-line once more. 'All I know is they got their eye on us.'

As if to confirm his opinion, the phone rang. Archie grabbed it off the side, turned to the window, gave a thumbs up and erased the shading on Farrow's nose.

'She giving you drawing lessons on the blower?'

'Yers,' Archie said.

Rox giggled and put down the phone. She'd taken Steve's number back in the flat and, whenever they looked like they might be getting antsy, she called to remind them of the continued surveillance. Reece formed a smile.

'You've got more front than Selfridge's. Davey was doing his nut all day, had me bombing all over the place doing pick-ups. Even asked me to clear my slate, pay him upfront what was owing.'

'Hope you told him to get stuffed?'

'He got nothing out of me.'

She brightened. 'That's it? You're clear?'

Reece looked at his feet.

'Come on. You can't go on paying him now. He's history.'

'The debt remains. Can't ignore that.'

'That's stupid.'

He looked away. 'Fine. I'm stupid.'

'Ooh, end of conversation,' she replied, mocking.

Reece carried on staring out of the window. Rox drank her wine, then rested her head back on the sofa and gazed at the ceiling. Aside from calling in favours, she had, that afternoon, booked some time in a screening room in D'Arblay Street through a girlfriend. It was flexible for tomorrow, but still relied fifty-fifty on luck and Davey not twigging.

'When d'you reckon I should go in and get Farrow out?' Reece asked.

'We'll have to wait until Davey gets the money.'

'Okay.' He turned towards her. 'But I'm not watching those two all night.'

'Come over here then.'

Reece came over and kissed her. Their bodies met and he moved on top of her, then slid off onto the sofa and pulled her up onto his lap. Rox responded, spreading her legs round his waist and digging her toes into the deep cushion. Reece was good, she'd give him that: unhurried, and content to replicate his passion from Sunday and not try fumbling at her clothes.

Unlike the way she was feeling.

She gripped him tight, smelling his scent, enjoying the tongue-thrust and the velvet sensation of skin on skin. She began to move her pelvis rhythmically, her heartbeat gaining speed. She struggled to gain entry into his shirt. His arms enfolded her, stroking her back, hair, cupping the nape of her neck. There was a wide gap between the back of her T-shirt and trousers. He exploited it, jogging a digit down the tiny hillocks of her vertebrae, then roving his palm a hair's breadth above her lower back. She felt the downy hairs rise — attracted to him by static.

He was hard down there. Here on the sofa? It'd be all right, wouldn't it? They surveyed each other's territory, mapping the information with fingers and thumbs. She thought about the next move. Would he scoop her up and carry her to the bedroom? (She'd peeked in an earlier toilet break. It appeared as nondescript as the rest of the flat: no time to snoop properly.) Or take her here, rolling off onto the floor and pushing aside the stocky furniture. Or? It was driving her insane; she wanted it so much, but? But? There was a natural pause. They gazed at one another, unspoken requests welling up in expanded eyes. It now occurred to her why all those crappy paintings of puppies and young girls had such giant irises. It was love or lust, chemical either way. She chose his left eye to focus on.

'Have you got anything?' she asked.

He lowered his eyelids in acknowledgement, kissed her briefly, then lifted her up and carried her through.

'Traditional, huh?' she said, as her ankle bashed the light switch.

He laid her on the bed and began to unbutton his shirt.

'No, not yet,' she said. 'I've been waiting months for this present and I get to unwrap it.'

He clambered onto the bed, lifted her arms and pulled her pink T-shirt over her head. She felt exposed in her bra, odd when she'd been comfortable in her nakedness for Archie. Where did that one come from? He kissed her shoulders, working efficiently around them, up to her neck, onto her arms. She hoped he wouldn't see the small clusters of moles on her back. Or if he did, point and laugh or liken them to the constellation of the Great Bear as one previous salivating oaf had done. He lay her on her back, planting a moist row of kisses from her throat to her cleavage, then up and over the swell of her breasts. He changed position, landing his mouth on her stomach. As he chewed away, she prayed he wouldn't blow hard, making those farty noises as Mark had so liked to do.

She shook her head. Concentrate! He nuzzled down further, lapping at the shore where her skin met her pale blue knickers (new jeans in white wash. Big mistake). Also, she'd had no time today to get home, change into skimpy black ones. Or even her little black dress; not even her favourite fuck me shoes, which hadn't had an outing in months.

She pushed away the hand that had undone her trouser button and was working on the zip.

'Reece, hold up.'

He stopped: waiting, she knew, for an explanation.

'Look, um, I want to do this, but right now it seems . . . I dunno.' She gazed at him, beaming her thoughts telepathically across the hot air.

'Okay.'

His tone was even, not giving it away if he was disappointed. He stayed there, reaching out a hand to stroke her hair, her small chin.

'Okay?' she asked, a note of pleading entering her voice.

'Okay.'

'No really, Reece? Is that okay?'

He smiled. 'Another time, all right.'

'Yeah, but, you know.'

'I know.'

He sounded brisk, wanting to move away from the car crash of embarrassment. 'You're nervous now that it's finally happening. So am I, as it goes.'

She opened her eyes wide and squeaked. 'You have read that in a *book*!'

He feigned mock outrage. 'Me? Read? Only women read.'

'It's *bleed*.'

'And read. Thought I'd say what was on my mind.'

'Truthfully?'

He lay down beside her. 'Big day tomorrow. How about we take a break and go get some grub?'

She kissed him delightedly. Reece rose from the bed and she followed him through to the kitchen and stood behind him as he pulled groceries out of the fridge.

'By the way, Reece. I expect a damn good screw after this is over.'

'Now you're teasing.'

'No, I'm not.'

Davey and Charlie's world was not rosy. Although the sash window looked out over a neat row of gardens, the inside of their room was in disarray. The ticking on the large mattress was torn and the stuffing spewing out of it. It was stained too, and the duvet was dumped carelessly on it—like a crimped cotton turd. Charlie's clothes were everywhere, in bin bags or piled up in the tall wardrobe. The headboard and other pieces of the bed rested against the wall as neither of them had bothered to put it together.

In the epicentre sat Charlie, lighter and silver foil in hand as she sucked crack into the clouded, crystalline barrel of a Bic ball point. Her eyes were encrusted with mascara, the lids raw. There was scarlet around her nostrils from where she'd had a summer cold. Her piercings remained, but she'd sawn off her Rasta hair extensions near the root, having become fed up with their continual itchiness and the smell when she accidentally set light to them. She wore combats and a scalloped neck T-shirt. There was dried semen on her thighs. Lately, she had started letting Latimer's friend fuck her in the afternoons in lieu of rent. Davey knew all about this, but let her get on with it as she was getting to be such a pain. They hadn't screwed in a while, not straight sex anyway. Privately he had become disappointed by the standard of her recent blow-jobs and was about ready to upgrade her. Right now, he was stacking irregular piles of notes on top of an old battered briefcase. Charlie was whinging.

'Why don't we do a runner? Sod off out the country?'

' 'Cos they're watching the house. Reece said he saw the tail and couldn't shake it. Plus, if that cow gets wind, she'll have the Old Bill on us.'

'You're scared of *her*?'

'I'm not scared of nothing. I don't like looking at serious time, all right?' Davey sniffed, and then sniffed hard again. He'd had an extra two grams of toot that day. Problems. This Rox girl knew every stroke he'd pulled in the last months. She had the contract and equipment and Farrow had backed her up. He'd belled Toby Lomax earlier in the day to check the legal side of the relationship between the filth and the broadcasters and found that what she'd said was kosher. It was entirely down to her whether she released the footage or not. First, he had to see it and *then* he'd decide how incriminating it was. Might all be circumstantial bollocks for all he knew.

'I got to know what she's got on us.'

Charlie said, 'You, you mean.'

'Your bank accounts, love. Your dodgy kites.'

'I did that for *you*.'

He resumed counting, ignoring the venom that spewed out of her. It wasn't until Charlie started to hit him that he punched her. She smacked into the wall with such force that the windowpane rattled. A plane went over, drowning her snuffles. She lay slumped, her head caged in her hands.

'Fuck you, Davey. I'm gonna go back home.'

'Yeah, you do that.' He tossed her a twenty. 'Here's the train fare. Piss off back to Buckinghamshire or wherever it is you come from.'

Davey did his maths. He'd drained all the money he could from the cab office, the club at Gant's Hill and his major stash here under the floor. Other money-bricks were dotted round North London, sealed in water tanks, under lagging, in pipes, in false ceilings — squirrelled away for this, the career nuclear winter. There would be no time to fake the notes although he could do the usual: hand her a wedge topped and tailed with real money, newspaper inside the bundle. Nah, knowing this bitch, she'd check every tenner and want a receipt.

He continued to till his options, leeching the loam soil of his thoughts as the evening died and the bulb above them produced a milky glow through its paper corona. As the house creaked and moaned around her, Charlie, rocking slightly, dabbed the floor for crumbs with her chewed-up fingers, her crack radar on full.

CHAPTER THIRTY-FOUR

The temperature had risen and Soho was on fire. Golden Square sizzled, Berwick boiled, Wardour wilted; even Kingly Street in the shade of Liberty's was a soup of rancid heat and the tang of Dumpster was everywhere. Black cabs bucked and jerked, clutches screaming as they paused for trade, cars beached themselves on meters and only the buses bobbed sedately in the fumes, adept in the roiling heat.

The screening rooms in D'Arblay Street were a short dogleg up from Salvatori's, where Rox had been since ten awaiting Davey's call. She felt detached, like a balloon tethered to the world by a ribbon in the hand of a child. Giuseppe wasn't in this morning and she was meant to be running the show. It was past midday when Reece rang to let her know that Davey and Charlie were on the move and that he had the money in a battered black briefcase. Rox immediately broke into a sweat. She'd been coping poorly all morning and had forbidden herself to handle any glassware. Yesterday's activities were audacious enough, but words were words and twenty-five grand was a lot of money. Trembling, she phoned her friends.

No gym-bag or carrier. Briefcase. Black. Battered. Bring one.

She'd spent the night at Reece's on his sofa, drunk with fatigue and a good bottle and a half of wine. They kept alternate watch on Archie, Steve and Farrow but the threesome remained confined to quarters. Reece had gone out at midnight and driven through the Rotherhithe Tunnel to Bermondsey to check on them himself. Satisfied, he then went over to Harlesden, inventing a pretext to drop in on Davey.

There, he took a half-hour of his ranting on about that bitch Rox and bastard broadcasters before he grew restless. Charlie, he noted, was well gone. He left, speeding down to the A40 then up onto the Westway, massaging its gentle curves and rises and dips in the smooth amber light. He came off at Baker Street, dropped down to patrol the centre of town, feeling more at ease, comfortable with the windows open, tanned by neon.

She met Davey and Charlie outside the screening rooms.

'Have you got it?'

Davey held up the case. Rox gazed at Charlie, impassive behind her impenetrable shades.

'Let's go in then.'

They entered the air-conditioned reception area, where Rox greeted the receptionist as if she had known her all her life, rather than the five nights and one drunken late lunch in Salvatori's.

Veronica said, 'If you'd like to go through?' demonstrating with a manicured hand a pair of chrome-plated double-doors.

'It's all set up,' assured Rox.

A tall, bespectacled, suited man emerged and greeted Rox effusively, taking and shaking her hand in both of his. 'Miss Matheson, I wanted to say how pleased we all are with the way the series is going. You must have taken quite a few risks.'

Rox, blushing, said, 'Thanks, Graham. Good to have your support.'

'Can't stop. Lunch at Soho House again. *Bloody* talent.' His eyes loomed heavenwards as he bundled past them out of the door.

He was carrying a black briefcase.

'Graham Bishop, one of the top bods at Granada,' explained Rox.

Or, Ally's brother Graham, who had taken a couple of hours off to be there.

Rox took another pace forwards, but Veronica interrupted her with a call. She took it at the desk and Davey and Charlie were forced to move aside, gaze at the pot plant, the framed certificates, the old projector mounted in a Perspex case. Rox wound up her call and turned to her guests.

'That was my crew over in Bermondsey. Checking that Mr Farrow's all right.'

'Course he is,' snapped Davey. He was keen to see the last months of his life on screen, his anxiety and anticipation as ever, chemically enhanced.

Rox said, 'You'll call soon, as we're finished here. Okay?' Davey nodded.

A blond-haired young man in an Iron Maiden T-shirt came through the doors. 'Five minutes?' he queried.

Aussie Pete had always fancied doing a bit of acting. Rox and Graham had banned him from improvising.

Nonetheless, he cast a connoisseur's eye at Charlie's breastage before he disappeared back behind the doors.

They went through to the small screening room and Davey headed for front row centre. The projection booth was illuminated, but the screen was dark. Charlie sat the other side of him, shades still welded to her face.

Rox said, 'I'd better see the money now.'

Davey hoisted the briefcase onto his lap and spun the combination dials. The catches opened with a satisfying dual snap. Twenty-five thousand pounds did not look as impressive as she'd hoped, and these were not the neat, packed blocks you saw in the films. These were soiled and crumpled, grubby, fanned at either end, pinched together with elastic bands, Barnardo's bundles.

'I'll count it first, if that's all right?'

He slid the briefcase across to her and Rox gingerly fished

out the first stack. She was used to handling money, cash less so in these plastic days, and found it hard thumbing through the leaves, sometimes miscounting, trying to keep the edge on her nerves and the tally in her head. Nearing the lower third of the last pack, she began to relax. It was all there, more or less.

'You're a few quid short.'

He shrugged. 'So sue me.'

'Think we can bear the loss,' she said, placing the money back on the quilted floor of the case.

Davey shuttered the money, spun the locks and placed the case on the floor between him and Charlie. 'Let's see what you've got then?' He folded his arms regally.

Rox turned and gave a signal to the projection booth. 'Be a minute.'

Charlie took out a joint.

'You can't smoke in here.'

The doors swung open and a mixed group of people entered the screening room. They wore Soho blacks and greys; all Prada'd up or virile in Versace, Kleined. They nosed their way to the front with barks and snorts, costing this and demographic *that*.

They all carried briefcases.

Davey tried to stare them out. His turf now. His show. He even shushed them. They ostentatiously blocked the screen. One self-important-looking man gave a flourish to the projectionist's window.

'Excuse me?' demanded Rox.

An impatient 'Yes?'

'We're running a documentary in here.'

'No can do. One thirty-five. Tango Brief. Running the new cinema ads in a mo. Clients here in two shakes. Sort it out with Reception.'

'I've booked the room for two hours, one till three.'

As they continued to argue, Davey and Charlie were left sunk in their chairs like unwanted relatives.

The advertising people put down their cases, almost as one.

Rox and the Adman argued with strained *politesse*. Then the lights went down. There was total darkness for perhaps five seconds, then the screen filled with white. Light played on the bewildered advertising people's faces. Someone called to stop the film. Rox found that it was her – and that she was shouting in the face of the man.

'I don't give a toss if you're Tango or Tonka or whoever. I've got my clients *right* here and they're expecting a *major* Landmark Documentary. Now, I suggest we go *immediately* and sort out the bookings.'

Her ferocity surprised her. As she moved to the door, she was pleased to see that the advertising executive was now following. The doors swung shut behind them, leaving Davey and Charlie and the suits. Davey checked the briefcase between his knees.

'Fuckin' playtime this, innit?' he said to no one in particular.

The suits looked from one to another. Davey glared at them.

The door flew open again.

'Okay,' said Rox. 'Be a minute.'

There was murmuring in the ranks. Slowly, the other advertising account people paraded to the exit, figuring their chief had lost the toss. The door bumped shut as the last one crept out.

Davey and Charlie faced front. A minute passed.

After two minutes, when nothing had happened and no one had returned to the room, Davey felt the steel of fear.

He broke open the case with his bare hands. Someone with a sense of humour had placed a wrinkled piece of cardboard inside: written on it, in pen, was the motto. 'Will lie, cheat or steal for food.'

The suits were nowhere to be seen, nor was the projectionist, and nor was Rox. At the desk, Veronica explained that Rox had been called away on an errand and, no, she had no contact number. Davey bellowed at her about his money, threatening reprisals. Frostily, Veronica offered to summon the police. At that, Davey tore open the door and he and Charlie stumbled out into the blazing street.

'Bitch!' he yelled, hauling out his mobile. 'Bitch bitch bitch!'

'It's Reece,' he said, buzzing the buzzer.

'Come on up.'

He sprang up the short flight of stairs and rapped smartly on Steve's door. Inside it was Dresden, Nagasaki, Chernobyl. At some point in the evening, someone's patience had snapped and the easel lay in pieces with its spine broken. Beer cans and cigarettes were scattered randomly about and a photo of a spread-eagled model lay beached, its frame smashed to shards. Farrow was curled foetally on the couch, days of greying stubble on his cheeks, his eyes hope-gutted. Archie, who had a black eye and ferocious scar on his neck, was making tea.

' 'Bout time someone showed up. We been doing our nut over here.'

'I'd never have guessed,' Reece said.

Steve was behind him, unhooking his filthy denim jacket from a peg.

'I'm going out for fags.'

Reece allowed him past. Never liked the guy.

Steve headed out, slamming the door. Good, one less problem.

'Artistic disagreement?' Reece asked, noting a fractured painting stick. One end was smeared in dried blood. Come to think of it, Steve's nose was a bit torn on one side.

'Yeah,' muttered Archie, bringing out the teabag on a spoon. 'Want one?'

'If it's going.'

Archie hunted for milk. Found none. 'Have to be black.'

'Sugar?'

'None of that either.'

'Forget it.' Reece indicated Farrow with a thumb. 'I've come for this one. Davey wants him elsewhere.'

'He gets sod all till we get paid.'

'He belled me a minute ago. Says it's all square.'

Archie winced as he sipped the hot liquid. 'With Rox, you mean?'

'Yeah.' Even as he answered, he knew it had tumbled in Archie's mind. Rox had rung five minutes ago to say she was back at the restaurant with the money.

He shook Ian Farrow by the shoulder. 'Come on. We're off.'

'No, you're not.' Archie was near now, eyes on him. 'Come on, I weren't born yes'day. You and her set this up.'

Was it worth the denial? He knew Archie of old.

'What d'you want? A cut?'

'Not a bad idea.'

'It's not down to me. She's the brains.'

'And the looks.'

'And the looks,' agreed Reece.

They looked sorrowfully at one another.

Reece said, 'I'd say she'd go for a third. Want me to bell her?'

'No, you're all right.'

Reece got Farrow to his feet and bundled him towards the exit.

Archie said, 'Hold up. Best whop me one for Steve's benefit.'

Reece obliged, whacking Archie with his open hand. Archie flew to the floor. 'Sorry mate,' he murmured.

He opened the door, supporting Farrow's weight. Lamb loomed into view in the corridor.

'Forgot me wallet, I . . .'

His expression assumed murderous intent as he glimpsed Reece about to release their prisoner. Charging into him, he punched and pounded Reece who, encumbered by Farrow's weight, collapsed. Steve then aimed a barrage of ferocious kicks at his torso and ribcage, arms pumping the air and spittle flying from the exertion. But, even as he felt his ribs snap,

Reece was back on his feet and rounding on Steve with his bare fists.

Blood and mucus rained from Lamb's damaged nose as the first punch connected. He began to work out, landing hooks and jabs and roundhouse punches as he systematically took Steve Lamb apart. The leathery skin seemed to suck in the blows, flowering into scarlet welts, the sap oozing out of him. Reece bust two fingers in the process, but continued to hammer at the man until he was backed up against the wall.

Reece felt a tugging behind him. Archie, recovered now, barracking, trying to pull him off by clinging to his belt. Reece swung round and instinctively raised a fist. Archie punched him hard in the stomach. Winded, Reece doubled over, gasping for breath. He never saw Steve tear down the curtain rail. As the metal pole slammed on his neck, Reece saw silver stars.

Archie snapped.

He paced back and ran at Steve, butting him in the face and sending them both flying onto the sofa, which tipped over and tossed them into the corner. Steve grabbed a long sliver of broken glass and slashed Archie across his upper arm. The flesh fell away, revealing a long meaty gash. Archie clamped a hand over the cut. Blood spilled through his fingers. 'Right then,' he said.

Reaching behind him, Archie fished out his staple gun from his metal toolbox. First, he belted Steve in the face with it, which laid him out cold. Ordinarily, the machine was employed to secure his canvases to the wooden frames, but it came in useful for stapling Steve to the floor. Farrow looked on in horror as the machine thunked and grunted, stapling denim to skin and skin to wood. Once the job was complete, Archie stood and wiped the sweat from his roiling, heaving brow.

Reece heard muffled moans, saw dim colour, felt like he was floating in a deep dark chamber.

Archie Peacock hadn't finished. He stamped through to the bedroom and, throwing open the cupboards, tossed out stacks of porn videos, jazz mags and a deflated, perma-surprised blow-up doll, mouth whitely encrusted as if she'd had a fit. He found a suitable weapon. One of Steve's souvenirs of Amsterdam. The cock pump. It was a hollow plastic cylinder with a rubber suction device attached to one end. He unravelled the tubing and, panting from his exertions, laid it out on the bed.

Suddenly Steve was on him, bloodied, punctured, insane with rage. He gripped Archie's head from behind and gouged his fingers into his eyes. Archie grabbed a drawer from the unit and whacked him in the shins with it. Steve howled as the bone snapped and hundreds of tiny spherical objects rolled about on the ground in all directions.

Archie tried to focus. Pills of some kind. Steve was clutching at his broken shin, his face a mask of blood and viscera. Grabbing him by the hair, he slammed Steve's face on the floor with all his remaining strength. The poppers exploded under him and amyl nitrate filled Lamb's mouth and nasal passages. His heart went into massive overdrive.

Archie found the cock pump and jammed it over his mouth, fitting the rim over Steve's lips and the exposed cartilage and bleeding mush of his nose. Archie's arm gushed blood but he held firm as with his good hand he operated the pump and siphoned the oxygen from out of Steve's lungs. Lamb flailed madly as Archie sweated and heaved, but soon the asphyxiation was complete. Steve bucked and fell as his heart failed him.

Tears prickled his eyes as Archie clambered painfully to his feet. He felt faint as he noticed his one red arm. Satin sheets. He tore a wide strip from them and made a makeshift tourniquet. He went back through and wasn't particularly surprised to find Reece and Farrow gone.

CHAPTER THIRTY-FIVE

Reece took Ian Farrow to a café in Waterloo where he fed him a late breakfast and some inside information.

'You'll have guessed me and Rox are in on this.'

Farrow nodded, took a mouthful of egg. He gazed at his matted hair and the beginnings of a beard in the mirrored wall opposite. He wondered how he could look so good when he felt so terrible.

'Good you never let on,' added Reece.

'She was very convincing, but I knew something was up when she asked Hayes . . . *Kayman,* to tide her over on the programme costs. It doesn't work like that.'

'No?'

'If there were financial problems then the broadcaster has the budget to cover it. And if her company had become insolvent, then Granada would have taken over the completion of the programmes.'

'Played a blinder though, didn't she?' he said, with pride.

'Did it work?'

Reece explained how Rox's contacts had equipped her with the hidden camera and Mic. Then later, how she had arranged the screening room and persuaded Graham, Aussie Pete and the waiters and waitresses at Salvatori's to pose as media types. How in that five seconds of darkness, they swapped the briefcases and waltzed off with Davey's twenty-five large.

All down to her.

Farrow said, 'Well, *you* did all right back there.'

Reece shrugged, still feeling the pain in his head and in his broken fingers.

'Where is she now?' Farrow asked.

'Not far.'

'Will she be all right?'

'I'll see that she is.'

'Thank her for me, will you? In fact . . .' he reached into his pocket and pulled out a crumpled business card. There was a spot of blood on one corner. 'See she gets this, could you? Tell her to give me a call.'

Reece walleted it.

'And what happens to Davey? Tell me about him?'

'He's an Argonaut, a con artist. All those scams he was going to stick in the programme – he was doing them all himself. He was after getting you to pay him to rip people off.'

Farrow's mouth hung open. 'Good God. If he'd won the commission, then the Beeb would've actually been *funding* his crimes?'

'Don't worry about it. You keep Jim Davidson in work, don't you?'

Farrow let that one go. 'And now?'

Reece sipped his coke. 'He'll be after us – only he's got no backup and no way of funding any.'

'You realise I'll have to report this. Davey can't expect to get away with kidnapping.'

Reece raised his undamaged hand. 'Actually mate, that's where you want to be a bit clever. Call in the Old Bill and you connect yourself to him. It'll all come out in the papers and won't do you any good.'

'Yes, but look what he did to me and my home?'

Reece leaned in, lowered his voice to a gravel-like tone. 'Right now you're in at the shallow end. Best you write it off. I'm sure your people at the BBC don't want the aggro and you'd much rather come the hero, wouldn't you?'

Farrow lowered his eyes in agreement.

Reece went on, 'I'll handle it from here on. Davey's got to think he's up shit creek and that the Old Bill are everywhere. Get himself worked up. I'm going to help that along, but what I need from you is a favour.' Reece pursed his lips, struggling with some inner quandary. 'I want you to grass up his girlfriend. She won't see it now but it'll be helping her out.'

Farrow placed his knife and fork together and asked for directions to the nearest public phone box.

At five that afternoon, acting on information received, the police raided the Harlesden address and found Charlie Ribbons trying to flush several grams of coke down the toilet. She was arrested for possession of a controlled substance and taken to the local nick, where she was charged and released.

Charlie emerged from Westbourne Green Police Station onto a fume-filled street near the Westway. Inside, in the cool cell and then in the recycled air of the interview room, she'd wanted to scream and shout. To fling every profanity she could think of at the stupid plods – just like she'd done when she was nicked for shoplifting and drugs in her teens. But somehow she'd not got the energy for it. It was always so boring, the waiting, the scorn, the warnings, the lectures. She'd sat there on the plastic seat, uncomfortable in her clothes, willing them to get on with it so she could get out and go score again. But it irked her, the way they treated her. Not interested. Only doing their job. She'd wanted to say, 'Look, I'm not street trash. I'm not like the others. I'm more than them. I like a bit of coke and crack now and again, that's all. Where's the harm in that?

Aw, fuck them, thought Charlie, as she walked to the nearest Tube.

The Hammersmith and City Line took her eastbound. It followed the Westway and sank down, passing defaced pillars, cement bays and empty lots. She'd change at Baker Street, head for Euston and see if her mates were in. Charlie stuck her feet up on the seat, daring anyone to tell her to move them. Idiots, can't they see I'm different? Special? The song came to her. Chrissie Hynde and the Pretenders. She'd loved their stuff. Wanted to be like her once. What had happened to that?

Baker Street was crammed with sweating commuters and she was buffeted in the wash as she changed trains. That song was still on her mind. She wanted to hear it, *had* to hear it, only her CD's were back home. She tramped along the tunnels, hot, tired, wanting a drink. She realised she hadn't any money left. Davey had taken it all. Ten minutes later she was on a Westbound Metropolitan train. The illuminated sign on the front read 'Amersham'.

Davey Kayman was slumped in the dim recesses of the Wheatsheaf pub in Rathbone Place. He'd been doing his sums. Enraged at being unable to reach Archie, he'd guessed that it had all gone pear-shaped. His reaction? Sod 'em. At least they won't need paying. And Farrow? That little venture had never paid out dividends and it was time to cut losses there. He'd figured out Rox was scamming him from the moment she walked into the place over at Bermondsey. Clever bitch. Would have been admirable if she'd done it to someone else, but right now he wanted to maim, torture and kill her. Slowly. She'd get hers, he decided, soon as he was back up on his feet.

But it was gonna get worse before it would get better.

Reece had called to say that the Old Bill was swarming round Bermondsey.

Davey told him to get over to Harlesden, check it out. Minutes later, Charlie belled to say the filth were outside. Davey hung up; decided he'd better stay put, out of the sun, which was still streaming in off the street. He looked at a couple of tourists up at the bar. Might be a watch there worth lifting? Plus that Handicam. Easy to fence up Holloway. God, it would be like starting all over. He drained his sticky glass, bought another rum and coke, sat back under the stained-glass windows. His mobile went off.

'Where are you?' Reece asked.

'Pub.'

A beat. 'You want taking anywhere, only I'm going to work soon.'

Christ, thought Davey Kayman. The world goes on. 'I don't think so,' he said, sarkily.

Reece hesitated. 'Wondered if we could have a word, face to face?'

'What about?'

'Remember you asked about my slate? I want to clear it now.'

'Oh yes?'

Here was a ray of sunshine: this prat with his stupid old-fashioned sense of loyalty and responsibility. Eight grand he'd had off him and never paid the Petersons more than the original stake of ten. And for that he'd secured the Cab office, which turned over a tidy profit when it wasn't being razed to the ground.

'Reece? You been up the city yet?'

'Not yet.'

'Call you back.'

Reece waited while Davey phoned the controller. He was back in five.

'I'd of thought the filth would be there by now.'

'That girl?'

'Yeah. Right, pick me up. I'm in the Wheatsheaf.'

Reece arrived fast. Said he was in the West End anyway.

'What's happened to you?' Davey asked, eyeing the cuts and bruises.

'The wife's down to her fighting weight,' he lied.

Davey kicked out a chair for him. The tourists had left and the pub was empty save for three postmen from the Sorting Office across the road.

'So?' Davey asked.

Reece went and bought a coke, then delved with difficulty into the pocket of his black jeans. With a wince, he pulled out his battered exercise book. 'We're down to fourteen K on the debt, round-about.'

'Are we?'

The usual trick. Question the amount. Reece showed him his neat writing. There were columns detailing each donation he had made to Davey's criminal activities. It had been quite a bit in these last months and the tally was an odd age-reverse as it sank from terrifying twenties to temperate teens.

'Thirteen, nine. I took the liberty of taking off extras on the unpaid work. Waiting time and petrol comes to nigh on four grand over three months.'

A sunbeam lasered in through the doorway. Davey felt tired. He couldn't be doing with more ructions, not today.

'So,' continued Reece, 'that brings it down to under ten.'

'Call it ten, then,' Davey said. He didn't like being handed the bill.

'Ten it is.'

Reece raked his eyes around the small wooden room. 'Davey? Know how bad things always seem to happen on Friday afternoons? How anyone with shit to shovel does it then – specially to screw up your weekend?'

'Tell me about it.'

'It was me and Rox turned you over. How'd you think she knew all about you?'

To his credit, Davey kept his poker face for a nanosecond. However, the instant he leapt at Reece, he found himself being bundled out of the pub and into the car. Reece was driving a borrowed Beamer.

'Where we going?' he croaked, recovering from the punch in the larynx Reece had administered to silence him.

'For starters, the cab office.

Davey reached for the door handle.

'Central locking.'

They cruised along Theobald's Road, dipping down at Farringdon then up into Clerkenwell. It was a perfect summer's evening, the buildings golden, the trees verdant green, the sky swimming-pool blue. Even the lights were with them.

Davey said nothing as Reece marched him into the office and up the stairs, snipping off the controller's response to a POB in mid-sentence. A Nigerian driver followed their hurried footsteps as they rose up and across the cracked, fire-stained ceiling. Reece took Davey to the big blue-grey safe under the desk and told him to get it open. He was halfway into his excuse before Reece was mashing his head on the computer keyboard. Davey did as he was told after that, spinning the combination locks and levering open the handle.

'Your passport's in there, right?'

Davey dug it out.

'Thought so. Off we go, then.'

He had him back in the Beamer and halfway along the Gray's Inn Road before Davey found his voice.

'What's the deal then?'

Reece stuck on his shades. 'Your freedom in exchange for mine. You let me off the debt; I'll see you get to the airport. I've got some bunce on me for the fare. Europe, America. You choose, only you don't come back to London, not for a long time. And if you do I'll hear about it.'

'Sheriff of Dodge, are you?'

'I'd advise you to take my offer.'

'Why should I listen to someone who's gone and ripped off every penny I got? And since this is all down to you it means you're lying about the filth coming after me.'

'Correct.'

The Beamer nosed out into the fast lane on the Euston Road, and sped under the underpass.

Reece went on, 'Think about who your enemies are? Here's a clue. Torching the cab office, sticking an ambulance in your Shoreditch gaff?'

'Oh, them.'

'The Petersons are not known for their coping skills.'

'Think I care about their piss-ant operation?'

They came in sight of the Westway. Above it, the sun was a huge red ball suspended in orange fire.

'Reckon you ought to start, as they're none too pleased with you. Apart from anything else, Archie's their employee of the month. Your using him and Steve without their proper say-so is – he searched for the words – against *protocol*. They don't like being fucked around over debts.'

'So?'

'So they've had a word with me and all.'

Davey went cold. Reece held up his mobile so Davey could see.

'I haven't said where you are, but they can reach me on this anytime. You'd better pray they don't call between here and the airport.'

Davey stared at the cellular, so often his method of business; now a possible instrument of – what? Torture? Death?

Reece asked, 'We're square then?'

The sun blinded them both up on the Westway.

'Right?'

'Yes,' agreed Davey.

Reece buzzed down his window and tossed the account book out onto the road. 'Load off my mind,' he said, cheerily.

After that they fell to silence as Davey sank back in the soft leather. As they dropped down via the Bush to join up with the Talgarth Road he got to thinking that it had been a good run. He had been in there with the Beeb, even if they had scuppered him with the bureaucracy in the end. What he needed was someplace he could get his teeth in; somewhere with a plentiful supply of mooches and marks. A place where he wouldn't have to learn a language: one that respected a man of his abilities.

By the time they were up on the Chiswick flyover, he'd wrung it down to New York or LA.

Junction Four took them off towards Heathrow where the planes crowded the muggy summer sky. They were within sight of the roundabout at the entrance when Reece's mobile chirruped. Hoisting it to his ear, he listened and shook it as the signal evaporated in the long amber tunnel.

'Well?' asked Davey, as they emerged.

Reece said nothing.

Davey tried to clamber over the seat, but Reece pushed him back with his good hand. Davey tried again, shrieking and clawing, but Reece delivered another blow to his larynx.

'Tell them you never got the call,' coughed Davey.

'Can't do that.'

'Tell them the signal was bad. You never heard properly. Come on, what's it to you? You can let me get a plane and no one's any the wiser.'

Reece circumnavigated the Terminal Building and headed back under the runway tunnel.

'Davey?'

With a hint of hope. 'Yeah?'

'I dunno if you believe in reincarnation – but if you do you might want to start thinking about what you want to come back as. My money's on a wasp.'

Davey scrabbled to get out, kicking furiously against the door panels and trying to smash the window, until Reece slowed up, reached over and laid him out with a single deft punch.

When he came to, he was face down on a wide apron of asphalt. Some kind of hangar or industrial unit. Muffled voices coming from his left side. He tried to move his head but it hurt too much from the blow. With maximum effort, he twisted his torso around. The Beamer sat squat in the heat haze. Reece was talking to two men, but they were right in the sun and he couldn't make them out. Reece getting into the car now. The exhaust coughed.

Bollocks. Right, he's off, so I'm gonna have to deal with these fuckers. Stay calm. More Peterson mugs – easily bought. Tell them . . . tell them Reece had it away with my money. Him and the girl are flush. I'll lead you to them and we'll split the take three ways. Oh yeah, look, we're talking, what twenty? No, make it fifty, a hundred grand. You boys tell your bosses you did the job and I'll use my wedge to disappear. Change my name. Start somewhere else. Davey Kayman, the Comeback Kid, that's me.

The men approached. David Kimmelmann howled inside as he recognised the brothers.

Reece heard what sounded like a sharp handclap as he turned the corner and headed back into town.

Archie knew he wouldn't be able to dispose of Steve's body until it was dark. He phoned Shirley, re-dressed his wounded arm and gathered up all the painting gear that hadn't been broken, trodden on or otherwise pulverised. He went to the Famous Angel for lunch and a pint, then hung around King Stairs Gardens, wondering when or whether the Old Bill would show up. When they didn't, he went back inside and mopped up and wiped away all traces of the blood and the fighting. He worked efficiently, building up a sweat, and when he had finished he threw the cleaning equipment in a nearby wheelie bin.

At five forty-five, he received a call from Tel Peterson, who had spoken to Reece. His orders were to take care of Steve and the brothers would reimburse him for his trouble over Davey.

Archie went off home for a kip, returning at dusk with a set of dustsheets and some durable nylon yachting rope. He was amazed at how quickly the place had begun to smell, but then remembered it always smelled like that.

Steve was glassy-eyed and inert.

Arch wrapped the body in the sheet, bound Steve securely with the rope and heaved him into the Thames. Steve bobbed, half sank and floated maddeningly back in his direction. Archie used the curtain pole to push him away and watched as the body sailed out into the current. He prayed he would make it to Limehouse or Greenwich, maybe even Woolwich.

Steve had liked a drink in Woolwich.

There was still some staining where Steve's corpse had lain. Archie looked for a rag in the kitchen but recalled he'd dumped everything out earlier in the day. He had an idea. Airing cupboard. Tear up a blanket. There was one in there but, as he gazed at the boiler, he realised that something was out of place. The lagging was too thick, looked like an orange Puffa jacket. He tugged away at it like a terrier, ripping the down and fibre until he revealed the tank. He broke out in an expansive grin as he saw, wrapped around it, the blistered canvas of his favourite Rembrandt.

CHAPTER THIRTY-SIX

Rox lay on her bed exhausted, feeling the muscles in her arms, thighs and bottom shiver and contract. Her body felt as though it had been put through an emotional car wash: wetted, washed, shampooed, brushed and tickled from every angle until she emerged shiny showroom clean, the crud from her troubles washed away. She was basking in a post-coital perfection that she only ever felt when she'd done it for the first time with someone new.

Okay, so technically it was three times, and it had gotten better with each round. Reece (comfortable naked, she was pleased to note; also, an absence of embarrassing briefs or socks) had gone to make a brew. She smiled to herself, gazing out at the afternoon sun winking through the leaves of the trees. It seemed complicit in their lovemaking.

Three days had passed without repercussions and there had been only one vaguely relevant story, which had appeared in the *Telegraph* under the headline, 'Double Dutch'.

Late Sunday morning, a caretaker at the Dulwich Picture Gallery had found a sealed cardboard tube lying on the top step of the gallery entrance. Popping the lid, he found inside not one, but two, Rembrandt self-portraits. The original, it transpired, had a long oblong section missing from the lower section of the canvas. The copy was good, but the experts weren't fooled. They praised the quality of the brushwork, but were critical of the drawing, with one art connoisseur stating that 'The lips weren't right'. A gallery statement confirmed that the original had been stolen almost a year ago and that they were 'surprised and grateful' that it had been returned. The copy was being examined for prints, but it looked as though the artist had wiped it clean, thus preserving his anonymity. As to its future, the Serious Fraud Squad opined it would most likely be exhibited in the Police Museum.

A further development had the West Midlands police announcing that a museum in Droitwich had the missing parts of the painting, which had come wrongly addressed to them some months ago. There was also a note, but the cheap glue had failed to hold the cut-out letters in place and they had been unable to make head or tail of it.

Reece entered with two mugs, placed them on the bedside table and began to kiss her again, first on the shoulder, then a trail up her neck, making her giggle, then hard onto her love-softened lips. She responded, wrapping her legs around his thighs and squeezing.

'God, I love it the first time,' she said.

'All downhill from now on, then?'

She raised a superior eyebrow and he pecked her on it. She slid her hands over his bruises, which were indigo and raw scarlet at their epicentres, bleeding outwards to greeny-yellow, a spectrum of pain. 'Doesn't that hurt?' she asked, poking his side.

'Yes, it does.'

She clambered on top of him, rubbing against his pubic bone. He cupped her breasts, and she leaned forwards, allowing the weight of them to rest in his hands.

'You never said how it went today?' he asked.

'Oh, all right. He's offered me a job.'

'What?' Reece sat up. 'Tell me.'

Earlier, she had been for lunch with Ian Farrow in a brasserie in Heddon Street. Reece had pestered her to call him and when she capitulated Farrow absolutely *insisted* that he take her out. Monday being her next half-day, she offered that up, hoping he'd refuse and that the idea would dissipate. To her surprise and annoyance, he accepted immediately.

Clean-shaven and in his work suit and tie, Farrow was far more impressive than he'd seemed on the floor of Steve's flat. Intimidating even. Nonetheless, he wore a boyish grin as he explained that as a result of his PA's spin on the events, he'd become an office hero. He'd sworn Marley to secrecy of course, which meant that the tale had spread around TV Centre quicker than poor ratings or stories of deviancy in the Cabinet. Adversity had benefited him, and his diary was now so full that it was haemorrhaging meetings. Even the security guards regarded him with less than their customary loathing.

They sat, ordered drinks and unfurled sails of white linen. For the first five minutes, Farrow's mobile chirruped until he switched it off. He explained that the story – as filtered through to the apparatchiks in their Oxford dachas – had been deemed highly sensitive and was to be kept from the press at all costs. The last thing anyone needed within the BBC was another faked documentary saga. It was deemed praiseworthy that Farrow had had the sense to keep the lid on it all and he was due to meet with Virgil Chinnery later on that afternoon. He suspected that some kind of compromise would be reached and that a job with a meaningless name would be created especially for him – commensurate with a hike in salary.

They ordered seared tuna and the *carpaccio* of beef and Rox told him a little of her life to date; that she'd run a bar in Chorlton, come down on a whim, that she was happy in her work. Farrow tried to wheedle ambition out of her and simply could not accept that she was not interested in 'working in telly'. He explained that the Factual Department had produced all those fabulous DocuSoaps and that realism was the way forward.

Rox, benefiting from two glasses of wine, told him that the idea of titillation in the name of investigative journalism did not appeal. At that he threw in the towel, handed her his business card and told her that if she ever changed her mind, he'd do his best to find her something.

'Oh, you pillock,' said Reece.

'Thanks, ta,' she said.

They were lying side by side now, sipping their tea, her leg over his.

'Why did you turn him down?'

She leaned up on her elbows. 'I've always hated all that cushy jobs-for-your-mates stuff. It's what I thought it'd be like when I came down here.'

'Yeah, and we're all soft southern *bas*tards,' he replied, elongating the first syllable to mock her. 'Look, you helped him out. He's offering to help you. That's the way the world works.'

'Mister Cliché.'

'Got to be based on truth or they wouldn't become clichés.'

She cupped her hands around her mouth. Made a loudhailer. 'Coming in thick and fast now. Red leader, red leader. Alert.'

He folded his arms behind his head.

'Look,' she said, 'I like it where I am. I meet people, I'm in charge.'

'You're worked off your feet.'

'I don't mind.'

'So you'll stay there for ever?'

Having no answer, she reached for the sheet to pull it up, but it was down on the floor and tangled round the legs of the bed.

'Rox, you're smart. These opportunities aren't going to come along all the time. I'm not saying you've got to join the BBC, but keep in touch, he might find you something you never knew you wanted. Stop fighting everybody.'

'Oh, right – *now* I get the long speech.'

She formed a scowl. Rox swung off the bed and was about to rise, when Reece pulled her back, folded his arms around her. His matted forearms were dark against her pale skin. Two of his fingers were splinted and taped together.

'Your trouble is you like your act too much. Little Miss Hard-done-by-northerner.'

His touch soothed her.

'Give it a thought is all I'm asking.'

'I'll think about it.'

He kissed her then, and the softness of it grew to hard, deep meshing of their mouths. They fell back, entwined, savouring the feel of flesh and the taste of each other. Reece pulled her to him and he slipped inside her.

'God, that's good,' she said. 'I love the feel of your cock inside me.'

'Block bookings, reduced rates,' he offered.

He was driving her up to town for her evening shift, easily nego-tiating Lewisham and the Old Kent Road as they rode against the grain.

'What are you going to do with your part of the money?' asked Rox.

'No idea. You?'

'Shopping, holiday, frippery.'

'Yeah?'

'No. I'll stick it in the bank for now.'

'Good move.'

Reece had told her about how he squared his debt with Davey, but not about Davey's demise, telling her instead that he'd put him on a plane to America. She seemed content with that and he felt it unnecessary to elucidate further. He'd also explained about Archie, and she'd agreed he could have a third of the money.

Bill and Tel Peterson didn't require any of the take. Reece had asked them. Privately, he suspected they were embarrassed that the Davey situation had been allowed to continue unchecked for so long, which was why their solution was so radical. They rarely did their own dirty work and this sent out a warning to others. The brothers also waived any further claim on Reece and insisted that he stop for a drink to seal the agreement. That took care of Saturday night and most of Sunday, as you didn't turn down a drink with them, even if you were teetotal.

'When do I see you next?' asked Rox.

The sun was behind them, illuminating her chestnut hair.

'Soon.'

'When?'

'Bit of a prob, us both being on nights. I'll have to drop by the restaurant sometime.'

She turned to him, bridling. 'Could you be *less* specific?'

He whispered something very nice in her ear. She grinned, showing all her teeth.

'We have one *weird* relationship,' announced Rox.

They sailed over Waterloo Bridge, fishtailing around a dawdling bus. Rox stared out of the window at her new adoptive town. An idea came to her.

'Reece? How much have you got in your float?'

He tapped the cigar box full of change. 'I dunno, why?'

'Have a look.'

He did so. 'Bit low. I'll get a sub off the controller.'

She waved fifty pounds in tenners. 'Here, pay me back when you can.'

'You sure?'

'Sure.'

'I don't like owing money.'

'You coped well enough before.'

'Fair enough. I'll drop it by sometime.'

Pulling up in Dean Street, Reece gave her a long, lingering kiss, although she had to stand on tiptoes on the kerb while he stood in the gutter. They hugged close, not wanting it to end, consoled in that they had the smells and the memory of each other to tide them over their shifts. She, for one, wasn't planning on washing again.

406

He watched her go, then hung beside his beached motor. After a few minutes he strode along the passage after her. He came in view of the restaurant and slunk into the shadows.

Rox was carrying an armful of serviettes. She'd changed clothes for the evening into a skirt, top and pumps. He saw how at ease she was, how capable, how beautiful. She must have sensed his presence, because she turned and looked in his direction. Reece darted away, back to his car. The radio was bleating. He'd gone by the time she reached the corner.

She smiled and went back to work.

Eros was gummed up with tourists; the dam of them breached at the crossing, flooding along Coventry Street towards the brash buildings and sad acts of Leicester Square. Reece surfed down Haymarket and took a right into Pall Mall. Monopoly London. Reaching under his seat, he patted his own little windfall. He'd taped it there for safekeeping. He easily negotiated the traffic and swam back up to Piccadilly where the car became suffused by golden sunlight.

Reece took in the torrent, the buses and bikes, the cars and the cabs, and then, as they poured and frothed and gurgled into the underpass together, he grinned: glad, so glad, to be a part of the heart and the beat of it all.